Copyright © 2025 by NL Amore

All rights reserved.

No part of this publication may be reproduced, distributed, or transmitted in any form or by any means, including photocopying, recording, or other electronic or mechanical methods, without the prior written permission of the publisher, except as permitted by U.K. copyright law. For permission requests, contact NL Amore.

The story, all names, characters, and incidents portrayed in this production are fictitious. No identification with actual persons (living or deceased), places, buildings, and products is intended or should be inferred.

Discreet book cover design by Temptation Creations. Model cover design by Coffin Print Design.

Copy and line edit by Sarah @ The Word Emporium.

Proofreading by Jo @ Line by line.

Formatting by Meghan Hollie using Atticus.

Published through KDP Publishing Amazon.

1st edition 2025.

Foreword

Content Warnings

This story does have a happily ever after, but please be aware it contains some very sensitive topics that some readers may find upsetting. It's important to look after your own mental health and be aware of what you are reading.

Desired By You can be read as a standalone, however, it is advised you read Loved By You and Tamed By You before as there will be some spoilers and dual timelines within all three books.

Love isn't always easy, it can be messy, a little toxic and complicated at times. Sometimes things aren't always as they seem and it takes time for the truth to surface.

If you would like to read this story without any potential spoilers and feel comfortable enough to read without seeing the trigger warnings, please skip the next page.

If you would like to check them, please make sure you are comfortable with the content warnings on the next page before reading.

Content Warnings

This story mentions, Sexual Assault, Rape, Therapy, Violence, Cheating PTSD, alcohol abuse, drug use, drug overdose, alcohol as a coping mechanism, domestic violence, child abuse, suicide, death of a parent, Prison, murder, childhood trauma, absent parent, loosing a loved one in the line of duty, harassment, emotional, physical, phycological, and financial abuse. Theft. Coercion.

Playlist

Prologue
What was I made for? – Billie Eilish
Chapter One
More To Life – Stacie Orrico
Chapter Two
Naughty Girl - Beyonce
Chapter Three
Mount Everest - Labrinth
Jealous – Nick Jonas
Chapter Four
Ugly Heart – G.R.L
Chapter Five
Show Me How You Burlesque – Christina Aguilera
Chapter Six
Desire – Olly Alexander
Roc Ya Body – M.V.P

Chapter Seven
Waking Up In Vegas – Katy Perry
Chapter Eight
Blurred Lines – Robin Thicke
Chapter Nine
River – Bishop Briggs
Chapter Ten
Till The Dawn – Drew Sidora
Finesse – Remix – Bruno Mars
Chapter Eleven
Turn Heads – Dem Franchize
Bad Girl - Usher
Chapter Twelve
She's Like a Star – Taio Cruz
I don't Want To Miss A Thing – Sonny Tennent
Chapter Thirteen
Who You Are – Jessie J
Edge of Glory _ Lady Gaga
Chapter Fourteen
Too Sweet - Hozier
Devil In A Dress – Teddy Swims
Dress – Taylor Swift
Hotel – Montell Fish
Chapter Fifteen
Circus – Britney Spears
Lady Marmalade- Christina, Lil Kim, Pink, Mya
Dirty Diana – Michael Jackson
Chapter Sixteen
Open Up – Gallant
Haunted – Beyonce
Chapter Seventeen

I Wanna Know - Joe
Permission – Ro James

Chapter Eighteen
Closer – Neyo
Too Close – JP Cooper

Chapter Nineteen
Often – The Weekend
Just a Lil Bit – 50 cent

Chapter Twenty
Last Night's Mascara – Stripped Back Version – Griff

Chapter Twenty One
Bitter Sweet Love – James Arthur
Earned It – The Weekend
Loose Control – Teddy Swims

Chapter Twenty Two
Colors - Halsey

Chapter Twenty Three
ADHD – James Arthur

Chapter Twenty Four
Lonely Together – Avicii, Rita Ora

Chapter Twenty Five
Taste – Coco Jones
Candy – Doja Cat
Drunk and Incapable – Krishane

Chapter Twenty Six
Or Nah – The Weekend

Chapter Twenty Seven
Trouble – Ray LaMontagne
Turn Around – Conor Maynard, Neyo

Chapter Twenty Eight
Just Like Magic – Ariana Grande

Dance For You - Beyonce

Chapter Twenty Nine

Restless Mind – Sam Barer, Avery Anna

POV – Ariana Grande

Versace On The Floor – Bruno Mars

Chapter Thirty

Love Me Like You Do – Ellie Goulding

Chapter Thirty One

Goodbyes – Post Malone

Happier Than Ever – Billie Eilish

Chapter Thirty Two

Bloodline – Alex Warren

Chapter Thirty Three

Just Give Me a Reason – Pink

Only Love Can Hurt Like This – Paloma Faith, Teddy Swims

Chapter Thirty Four

Coal – Dylan Gossett

Chapter Thirty Five

When the party's over – Billie Eillish

Chapter Thirty Six

Power Over Me – Dermot Kennedy

Fortnight – Taylor Swift, Post Malone

My All – Mariah Carey

Chapter Thirty Seven

This Love – Camila Cabello

Thinking Of You – Katy Perry

Chapter Thirty Eight

Secret Love Song – Little Mix, Jason Derulo

Residual – Chris Brown

Chapter Thirty Nine

Secret Love Song Part 2 – Little Mix

Kissing Strangers – Usher

Chapter Forty

Never Let Me Go – Florence and The Machine
One Last Time – Ariana Grande
Nights Like This – The Kid

Chapter Forty One

Back To Friends - Sombr

Chapter Forty Two

War of hearts – Ruelle

Chapter Forty Three

Breathe Me– Sia

Chapter Forty Four

It Will Rain - Mars

Chapter Forty Five

Help Me - Usher
Silver Springs – Fleetwood Mac
I love you I'm sorry – Gracie Abrams

Chapter Forty Six

Call your Mom – Noah Kahan

Chapter Forty Seven

Brother – Kodaline

Chapter Forty Eight

APT – ROSE, Bruno Mars

Chapter Forty Nine

Sorry – Justin Bieber
Freakum Dress – Beyonce

Chapter Fifty

Get Me Bodied – Beyonce
Breakin My Heart – Mint Condition
Queen of The Night – Whitney Houston
I See Red- Everybody loves an outlaw

Unchained Melody – Sonny Melody
Chapter Fifty One
Save Me – Nicki Minaj
Look After You – The Fray
Chapter Fifty Two
Trading Places - Usher
Chapter Fifty-Three
Family Affair – Mary J Blige
Chapter Fifty Four
Friends – Ella Henderson
Chapter Fifty Five
Because Of You – Neyo
The First Time – Damiano David
Chapter Fifty Six
Run Through Walls – The Script
Chapter Fifty Seven
Labour – Paris Paloma
Chapter Fifty Eight
I see Fire – Ed Sheeran
Venom - Eminem
Chapter Fifty Nine
Always Remember Us This Way – Lady GaGa
Chapter Sixty
The Night We Met – Lord Huran
I don't wanna miss a thing – Aerosmith
Chapter Sixty One
Daddy I Love Him- Taylor Swift
You Don't Own Me - Saygrace
Chapter Sixty Two
Landslide – Fleetwood Mac
Chapter Sixty Three

Stand By Me – Florence and The Machine
Give You My Name - Mclean
Epilogue
It Isn't Perfect But It Might Be – Olivia Dean

Dedication

To the girl reading this who has spent her whole life never feeling good enough, who's been made to feel like she needs to hide her true self to please others. I hope this story makes you see that there is someone out there who will love you, and want you just as you are, because you are more than enough.

Prologue

Gabby Fifteen years old

I've always been the good girl. The do as she's told girl. Never puts a foot wrong girl. I know when to voice my thoughts and when to be quiet, when to smile and when not to, when to be gracious and demure. To remember my manners and to know my place, and my place was to be a wallflower. To never cause a fuss, to blend in, and never be a nuisance. Until one night, something happened that rocked my family's world, turned it upside down and inside out, all because I forgot my place, and now, we are all paying the price.

The plan was always to move to New York so I could attend Juilliard, my dream, or rather my mother's dream. Becoming a prima ballerina was always what I was raised to be. It was the only time in my life I took center stage in anything; when, just for a moment, all eyes were on me and my talent, and I felt seen. But now I'm not sure Juilliard is on the cards. My father suggested it might be best if I do something a little more *sensible* with my life. Something that would not only benefit my family but also a potential husband and his career. Because that was another expectation. I'd marry well, play the dutiful wife, and produce children. What I wanted didn't really matter. It was just what was expected from the world I was raised in.

"Gabriella, we'll drop you off, and Albert will collect you after your meeting and bring you to the new house." My mother's voice snaps me from my thoughts.

"You're not going to stay with me?" I ask hesitantly.

My mother turns in the front passenger seat, her eyes hidden by her large Chanel sunglasses. Despite the aircon being on full blast and blowing in her direction, not a hair on her perfectly styled brunette bob moves. My mother will never look anything less than perfect.

"No, darling, we have to meet the removal company. I spoke with Suzanne on the phone. She's expecting you."

I nod in acceptance, anxiously chewing on my bottom lip.

"Gabriella, stop that. What have I told you about doing that to your lip?" my mother scolds.

"Sorry," I mumble, looking down at my lap and intertwining my fingers, needing to distract myself from the nausea brewing in my stomach.

"We're here," my dad says with little emotion in his tone. He's barely spoken to me, let alone looked at me, since everything happened. I know he's disappointed in me. They both are. My actions could have ruined his career and caused quite the scandal, and even though they say what happened wasn't completely my fault, their actions suggests otherwise. So, when they suggested I go to a therapy group, I agreed without protest. Do I want to be here? No. Do I want to share with strangers what I did? what I let happen to me? Absolutely not. But I need to make things up to my parents, learn from my mistakes, and move on. I want, no, I need them to be proud of me again.

I hesitantly step out of the car, brushing a nervous hand down my light blue summer dress and hooking the strap of my Louis Vuitton purse over my shoulder. I shut the door of my father's Range Rover, taking in a deep breath and giving my parents a small wave. I don't miss the way my mother waves back, but my father's gaze remains head on, and it hurts to not have him acknowledge my departure.

I wonder if there will ever be a day where my dad can look me in the eye again.

I turn to face the run down looking building, gripping the strap of my purse so tightly: like it's the very thing holding me up right now. I head towards the door, heart thumping in my chest.

You can do this, Gabriella. just one foot in front of the other.

I push through the glass door and I'm instantly met by a woman with gray hair, glasses, and a wide, welcoming smile from behind a glass screen.

"Hey there, sweetie, are you here for the TeenHood meet?"

I nod, biting down on my lip anxiously. She gives me a sympathetic smile and steps closer toward the glass panel that separates us.

"It's the second door on the left. Ask for Suzanne when you get in there. Don't worry, they're a nice bunch."

"Th-thank you," I manage to get out.

I walk down the narrow hallway, the sound of my Prada sandals tapping on the hardwood floor echoes around me. I note the sign on the brown door, stuck on with Scotch tape that says *TeenHood*.

Closing my eyes for the briefest of moments, I take in a deep breath before pulling open the door. Stepping inside, the room falls silent, and all eyes are on me. I stand frozen in the doorway, eyes wide, as I scan the room and the faces staring back at me. The room is full of girls, maybe twenty, at a guess. Most around my age or a little older, all scattered around the room, sitting on a couch, at tables, drinking mugs of something, or playing card games.

I startle when a hand is placed on my shoulder, and I let out a little squeak, completely caught off guard.

"Oh, my goodness, honey, I'm so sorry. I'm Suzanne, you must be Gabriella?"

I take a second to register her words and focus on her. Red hair, black thick-rimmed glasses, clutching a clipboard, and wearing a white t-shirt with a badge that says Suzanne, TeenHood Counselor.

"Uh yeah, yeah, I'm Gabriella," I say, my mouth feeling dry.

"It's lovely to meet you. I'll introduce you to a few of the girls, then once you've settled, me and you can have a little chat. Does that sound okay?"

Remembering my manners, I straighten my spine and give her the smile I spent years perfecting. "Sure, that would be great. Thank you so much for having me here today, Suzanne."

"Follow me." She gestures, and I do. Walking behind her, I feel myself shrink under the weight of the stares. I follow Suzanne over to what looks like a canteen hatch. The sound of laughter floats through the air and it makes me smile.

'Girls, Gabriella has arrived. Can you help get her settled?"

"Sure thing," a female voice yells back.

"They'll look after you," Suzanne says reassuringly, giving my shoulder a squeeze before walking off.

I stand there, like a lost lamb, wringing my hands and then pinging the elastic I have on my left wrist, looking round the room, waiting for whoever just replied to appear. The sound of laughter grows closer and I turn my head to see a blonde and a brunette step through the door from what looks to be a kitchen.

They chat amongst themselves until they both stop in their tracks and eye me up and down. With them both dressed in black leggings and oversized sweatshirts, I feel so out of place in my designer summer dress my mother insisted I wear. Determined to try and appear confident when I felt like a shrinking violet, I clear my throat, offering my hand with a smile. 'Hi, I'm Gabriella. It's lovely to meet you," I say, my voice a little shaky.

They take it in turns to shake my hand, eyeing me suspiciously.

"Hey, I'm Ali. This is Ria," the blonde with the most stunning blue eyes I have ever seen says.

"Hey," Ria says with a big smile. She's just as beautiful as Ali, and I suddenly feel so inadequate standing in front of them. At a guess, I'd say they were a few years older than me.

"So, if you are anything like us, you might be thinking this place sucks. You don't wanna be here, and it's a load of shit," Ali starts.

"Ali, language. We've just met her," Ria scolds.

"You good with cuss words, Little G?"

Little G?

A weird little zap of excitement at her giving me a nickname hits me.

I giggle. "Yeah, I'm good."

"Good. So, as I was saying, you may think this is all bullshit—that's how I felt when I came here and so did Ria but, this place is epic. Suzanne is the best and even though we are eighteen and nineteen now, we still come because, well, it's a place where we aren't judged and can just be us."

Sounding exactly what I need, I sigh in relief, my shoulders relaxing.

"It's great here. I love it here more than home." Ria smiles. I smile back, already feeling at ease around them.

"Just a heads up. The only girl you need to watch out for is Nancy over there. She likes to think she's better than all of us, and FYI, she'll swipe those Prada's straight off your feet, so keep your feet rooted to the floor at all times." Ali points over to a blonde in the corner who has her head buried in a magazine.

Ria rolls her eyes. "She's not that bad."

Ali furrows her brows. "Not that bad? Remember when Hannah got that new jacket, and it mysteriously went missing?" she says making air quotes with her fingers. "Then a week later Nancy happened to have got one for her birthday. Yeah, my ass she did."

I snort a very un-lady-like laugh. God, I love them already.

"Noted," I say.

"So, where are you from?" Ria asks, gesturing for me to follow her. We head over to a large sectional couch and sit down. They both relax on the couch, tucking their legs under their butts. I, on the other hand sit, ramrod straight on the end, legs together, still clutching the strap of my purse.

"Ugh, we just moved to New York," is all I say.

"What made you move?" Ali asks.

An awkward silence falls between us as I lower my head, searching my mind for something to say. Do I just blurt out and tell them? I go to speak, but Ali beats me to it.

"You know what? That was a dumb question to ask, and you don't have to answer. There's a mutual understanding here. We all know to an extent why we are here. Just know that when you are ready to talk about it, we are here to listen, okay? Whatever it is, you can tell us. We won't judge. We all have a story here."

I nod, appreciating her kindness and understanding as a feeling of relief washes over me. I've never had a safe space to talk about how I really feel. I've always said what I thought my parents wanted to hear. My lip trembles at the thought, and I try to stop it, biting down so hard I taste copper.

Don't cry. Don't cry.

"You look like you need a hug. Can I hug you?" Ria asks, already crawling across the large corner couch to sit beside me before I can answer.

She wraps her arms around me, and her sweet vanilla scent surrounds me. I expect to clam up, to feel on edge and uncomfortable, but I don't. I've never felt so relaxed and comfortable around people I've just met. There's just something about these girls.

I lean into her hug, not realizing how badly I need this. My parents aren't affectionate people. Sure, I know they love me, but they are not the type of parents to show love in the form of hugs or physical touch.

Tears roll down my cheeks and I quickly swipe them away. Feeling so vulnerable in this moment, but strangely, feeling safe to be.

"Okay, okay, I'm going to need in on the hug," Ali announces, getting up from her spot on the couch and sitting the other side of me, wrapping her arms around me.

We sit like that for what feels like hours. They let me cry my silent tears and just sit with me. No words needed, no questions asked.

Wiping my eyes, I exhale a long breath.

"Wow, what a great first impression, huh?" I laugh nervously.

"You're fine, babe. We would never judge you. We've been where you are. Coming here is scary. It's the unknown. But trust me, we've got you, okay? Stick with us, Gabs, and you'll be fine," Ali says, brushing my tears away with the pad of her thumb.

Even though I've only just met these girls, and I've not shared a word of my story, I've never felt more accepted, more supported, or more seen than I do right now. Like maybe I am enough. I have a feeling with them by my side I may be able to navigate my way through this nightmare I'm currently living in.

Chapter One

Gabriella

"... not sure what time I'll be back, but I'll text you. It's chaos here. Diana is ready to rip someone a new one." Ali's exasperated voice booms through my car's Bluetooth as I drive.

I chuckle. "No worries. God only knows how long this dinner with my parents at the country club will take. Apparently, they have a surprise for me." My tone is mocking.

"Let's hope it's not like the last surprise when they tried to set you up with that dud, Adam." I shiver at the memory. Adam was, without a doubt, the most boring man I'd ever met. My big toe holds more charisma than he has in his entire body. He just sat there, talking about his retirement plans and the problem with today's society—that we are all about living for the here and now and don't plan for our futures. Riveting date conversation. I felt bad as my parents really believed he was a great match, so I said it was a mutual thing and we just didn't vibe.

"Oh, God, don't remind me." I sigh.

"Babe, I better go. Diana is on the warpath. Have fun, love you, bye."

"Love you, bye," I repeat before hitting the call end button on the screen of my Lexus. A gift from my parents. A gift, like all gifts, came with strings. I was to meet for weekly, sometimes twice weekly, meals. They were less than thrilled when I moved in with Ali, aged eighteen, when I attended Juilliard. My parents wanted me to remain at home where they could *keep me safe,* which was actually code for, control my life. So, for the past six years, I have done the hour drive to see them for dinner. In my mind, it's been a small price to pay for the freedom I have gained since living with Ali and truthfully, it helps ease the guilt I feel over what happened when I was a teen.

I pull into the country club entrance, glancing out the window at the golf course that surrounds the club, that familiar burn of anxiety hitting the back of my throat at the idea of seeing my parents. I won't see them for a while as we are away next week for Ria's bachelorette weekend. So, all I need to do is smile and nod and make it through the next few hours. Parking up, I exit my car, taking my purse, and handing my keys to the valet guy. I smile sweetly and make my way through the large automatic door, heading straight for the ladies' bathroom to freshen up before meeting my parents.

The bathroom is white with gold accents and the smell of lilies fills the air as I scurry into the stall before anyone can see me. Sitting on the closed lid of the toilet, I take off my tennis shoes and swap them for the black pumps I keep in my purse. My mother despises my casual look, as she calls it, so I make sure to wear my best clothes and heels whenever I see her.

Making my way out of the stall and to the basin, I take out my favorite nude lipstick from my purse, coating my lips before puckering them. I've never been big on makeup. I've always had naturally long lashes, thick dark hair, and olive skin, thanks to my dad's Spanish roots. I smooth a hand over my head, making sure not a hair is out of place in my sleek ponytail. I take a few seconds to look at my reflection, analyzing if there is anything my mother or father could disapprove of. I've paired a simple white blouse with a beige tweed skirt, a skirt I hate, but it's Catherine Monroe approved.

As I wash my hands, that familiar thump-thump of my heart returns. Seeing my parents always stirs up a level of anxiety that I find difficult to control. With shaky hands, I take a towel and dry them so vigorously my skin begins to sting. I toss the towel in the hamper, and with all the strength I can muster, I head out towards the members' lounge.

The minute I enter the vast room, I spot my mother, and a lead weight drops into the pit of stomach when I notice it's not just her and my dad. With every step I take, my heart rate picks up and the urge to flee intensifies. Just before I can even think of a swift getaway plan, my mother waves me down with an enthusiastic arm.

"Gabriella, darling, over here," she practically purrs.

I head for my mother, leaning down to kiss her cheek, her Coco Chanel perfume invading my nostrils, making me feel a little queasy. It should be a comforting smell as it's all my mother has worn since I can remember, but that scent drags up feelings of failure, disappointment, and inadequacy.

"Mom, lovely to see you." My dad rises to his feet, buttoning up his suit jacket to greet me, making me feel like I'm a business associate, an acquaintance, not his daughter. He gives me a half-hearted hug and a kiss to the cheek, then follows up with pulling out my chair next to my mother, and I dutifully take my seat, my eyes widening when I settle on the three unfamiliar faces sitting across from us.

"Hello," I say hesitantly.

"Darling, do you remember me telling you about Janet and Carl?"

No

"Oh yes," I reply in a way my parents would expect me to.

"and this is their wonderful son, Patrick." My eyes turn and lock on the tall blond guy who's sitting next to his dad. He looks like he belongs on the cover of a magazine. He has the whole prep school vibe going on. Big blue eyes, dirty blond hair, and a smile that looks like it cost a fortune. Just like every other guy my mother has tried to set me up with.

Here we go again.

He leans up out of his seat and extends an arm across the table, and, like I've been brought up to do, I return the gesture.

"Pleasure to meet you." I smile as I shake his hand.

"The pleasure's all mine," he says, with a hint of flirtation in his voice.

"Janet and I thought you and Patrick would really hit it off. He's living in New York, working at Braxton Law Firm. Isn't that wonderful, Gabriella?"

"Wow, that is wonderful," I say, matching her tone. "That must be a demanding job. I can't imagine there's much time for a social life," I reply, hoping someone might get the hint.

I feel my father's glare on me without even having to move my head. My father has this incredible talent for being able to convey exactly what he thinks without uttering a word, and I know he doesn't appreciate my underlying comment.

"It is, but I make time for those who are important to me," Patrick replies, obviously not getting my tone. I want to roll my eyes, but I refrain. Instead, I reach for my glass of water and take a sip.

"Gabriella, your mother tells us you are working as an accountant. That must keep you busy," Janet says. She's mid-fifties, at a guess, with short, light brown hair that's graying around her temples, pulled back from her head with a ghastly-looking headband, and like my mother, she wears a set of delicate pearls around her neck and a brown tweed jacket.

That's not what I do anymore, I internally scream. But instead, I reply saying,

"Yes, very busy, but I enjoy it, so it doesn't feel like work. What's the saying? Find something you love and you'll never work a day in your life." The table falls into polite laughter and I glance over at my parents, who are beaming with pride, so I know I've done my part. I've played the role of the dutiful, hardworking, charismatic daughter; someone worthy of parading about like a new purse.

The next two hours feel like five. I sit and listen to Carl drone on about his golf score, the latest case he was working on, and then, when Patrick chimes in to share his thoughts on the current stock market, I want to stab myself in the ear with my dessert fork.

Get me out of here.

Sure, there is nothing wrong with Patrick. He is good looking and polite. He just doesn't have much about him. He is as bland as the salad we had for our starter.

I check my watch, noticing the time, and use that as my window to get the heck out of here before Janet starts talking about her book club again. Don't get me wrong, I love a good book, but something tells me Janet doesn't read what I read.

"Mom, Dad, I'm so sorry, I better head out. I don't want to be driving back to the city too late."

"Of course, darling," my mother says, glass of red wine in hand. "You get going, your dad will walk you out to the valet." Before my dad can answer, Patrick stands.

"I'll walk her out to her car, Mrs. Monroe." The smile on my mother's face makes me want to roll my eyes and dry heave. She really thinks she's picked a good one here. My mother loves nothing more than to play matchmaker.

"Well, isn't that sweet of you, Patrick. Thank you. Gabriella would love that."

Gabriella can speak for herself.

I want to say no, but I have the good sense to agree and say my goodbyes before walking side by side with Patrick to the valet area.

"I'm sorry if you felt ambushed tonight. I didn't realize myself till you walked in that it was clearly a setup," Patrick says shyly, which catches me off guard. He seemed so confident and self-assured at the table and I wonder if he feels the need to act a certain way in his parents' presence the same way I do.

"It's fine. I had a lovely evening," I lie, but it's not his fault. If his parents are like mine, I feel sorry for the guy.

I hand over my ticket to the valet. I turn to face Patrick. Most women would go weak at the knees for his white teeth and dazzling blue eyes, but he just doesn't do it for me. I'm not sure if it's the defiant girl within me who's decided she hates Patrick just to piss off her parents, or if he just isn't my type. But I wouldn't know, because I've never allowed myself to do what I want. I am forever trying to please my parents, to make up for my mistakes.

I almost sag in relief when my car pulls up. "Well, this is me. Thanks for walking me out."

Patrick scratches the back of his head awkwardly, worrying his bottom lip with his top teeth. "It's no trouble. So, do you think I could get your number and take you out to dinner sometime soon?"

I still, a little caught off guard that he wants to keep up this charade. "I am, erm, I'm away next week."

"How about before you go?" he suggests.

Like the good girl I am, I reply, "Yeah sure, that would be great."

He hands me his phone and I type in my number before handing it back. Our fingers gently brush and I feel nothing, not a thing. Maybe I'm broken, or maybe it's nerves, maybe it's been this whole night, and how cornered I felt, but I'm not attracted to this man. But will I tell my parents that? Like hell I will. I'll lie and say I had a great time, that Patrick was the perfect gentleman, and he's taking me out to dinner.

Taking my keys from the valet, I thank him before I round my car. Patrick follows, opening my car door. I sit inside, pressing the button and lowering the window as he closes my door.

"I'll call you," he says will another mega-watt smile.

"Great, I-I look forward to it," I manage to get out.

"Drive safely."

I smile and nod as he steps away, and then I pull away from the curb, not giving Patrick a second glance in my mirror.

Sagging in relief, I drive further away from the country club, wondering what the heck that was. My mother has hit a new low tonight. She's suggested I date many of her friends' sons over the years, but she never has ambushed me like that.

A mixture of anger and frustration courses through me, and I know I need to rid this feeling from my body. I glance at the clock and do the math: I'll just make it if I floor it back to the city. Yes, that's exactly what I need—my go to way to unwind and release tension. I crank the stereo, music blasting through the speakers, and I press my foot firmer on the pedal. The anxiety that filled my body slowly dissipates the closer I get to the city, to my secret place, where I feel authentically and unapologetically myself.

Chapter Two

Gabriella

Beads of sweat roll between my breasts, chest heaving, heart thumping almost painfully against my ribcage and, with every thump, the last of today's adrenaline leaves my body.

"Okay, quick water break, and we'll go again," Kaz, our dance instructor, yells over the music. I walk over to my gym bag, reach for my water bottle, and drain half its contents.

"Is it me or does tonight's routine feel intense?" Luna asks through panted breaths.

"Yeah, for sure," I reply, my words just as breathless. Luna is my friend from dance class. I saw a flyer for a late-night heels class at my local gym, and on a whim, after an intense dinner with my parents, I swung by the class to trial it and I loved it. It's been two years since I started, and I sneak away every Thursday night to dance.

It's my little secret. I'm not ashamed of it, but I like having something just for me; a place none of my everyday friends know about; a hobby my parents can't judge because hell, Cathrine Monroe would have a lot to say about her only daughter parading around in skimpy dance shorts and heels. It's a far cry from my Julliard attire. I loved my time at Julliard, but after landing a jump awkwardly, my knee was never quite the same. Sure, by most people's standards, my knee was fine, and it didn't impact my day to day life, but for the life of a ballerina, it was a deal breaker.

So, I decided to train as a Pilates instructor, and I teach eight classes a week and do some accountancy work freelance when I want the extra cash. I love it, but for my parents' sake, they think I do that full time, and my Pilates classes is my side job.

"Okay, so this time I am going to have you come up and perform the routine in small groups. First up, Luna, Aria, Summer, and Gabriella."

Tossing my water bottle in my bag, I reach up and pull my scrunchie to tighten my long, thick ponytail and make my way to the center of the studio, facing the back wall of mirrors.

I take my starting position alongside the other girls. We spread out, giving each other enough space. Arms raised, and crossed at the wrist, we wait for the music to start. Kaz lowers the studio lights and the sultry beat of a *Beyonce* track hums from the speakers. I rotate my hips, bending my knees, and bring my arms down. I instantly feel the adrenaline pumping around my body as I smooth my hands over my hips, spinning on the balls of my feet and landing on my knees.

"Yes, ladies," Kaz praises loudly over the music.

I lower my body to the floor, arching my back, thrusting my hips into the floor, and the room erupts into whooping and cheering. It's so empowering being in a room full of women supporting one another, no shame in embracing their sexuality and femininity. It gives me a buzz.

Lifting my chest, I roll my body so I'm up on my knees and repeat the body roll until I am in a standing position. I continue the routine, spinning and moving my hips seductively. We end the routine on our knees, slightly parted, arms outstretched, and head down. Chest heaving, I inhale trying to regulate my breathing. The routine was intense tonight, but it was exactly what I needed.

The room erupts with more cheers and claps. I take a seat in the corner, back against the mirror, and watch as the next group takes their positions and begins. I watch in awe as women of all shapes and sizes, from all different walks of life perform the same routine and move their bodies so freely.

It's not that I don't think Ria or Ali wouldn't understand, they absolutely would. But I like having this little piece of my week just for me. Something no one knows about. Before I know it, the class has come to an end, and my favorite part of my week is over. Hooking the strap of my black gym bag over my shoulder, I hold my wallet in my hand, knowing I'll grab a smoothie from the juice bar on my way out.

"You were on fire tonight," Luna says as we head out of the studio and down the stairs.

"Thanks, so were you," I say, my words still a little breathless.

"You looked super tense when you first walked in. Everything okay?"

I think about giving my usual 'I'm fine' answer but I'm still reeling a little from the meal with my parents and knowing Ali will be out till the early hours at work and Ria is busy wedding prepping and getting the girls to bed, I don't have anyone to vent too, so I offload a little.

"Ugh, yeah, just family stuff." I huff.

"Want to talk about it?" Luna asks.

"Yeah, that'd be nice," I say as we approach the juice bar, and I look up at the menu that hangs above the cashier. We both order a green juice, and once we have our drinks, we walk outside, heading towards Central Park.

"My parents, they can be pretty overbearing, and my mom ambushed me today at lunch and tried setting me up with her friend's son."

"Oh, God, no, she didn't," Luna gasps, clutching my arm.

"Oh, she did, and he's just like all the others, and he was sweet, but just not what I'm looking for, you know?"

She scrunches up her freckled covered nose and nods in understanding, taking a sip of her juice, tucking a strand of her strawberry blonde hair behind her ear.

"She makes me so mad, so I use class as my release," I continue.

"I hear you. My classes and the pressure from my dad to come top is kicking my ass, so this class and my job at the club are the only thing getting me through the week." Luna sighs. She's a couple of years younger than me and studying to be a nurse at the local college.

"Amen to that," I say, tapping my smoothie cup with hers. We do a little lap of the park and then head back to our cars in the parking lot at the studio.

"See you Saturday," I say as I get in my car, feeling a hundred times lighter for taking this little piece for me. Away from expectations and judgment. I just wish I was brave enough to share it with my everyday world.

Chapter Three

Brad

Routine keeps me in check. It's the only thing that does. Some people might call it obsessive, but for me, it's survival.

Most of my days begin and end the same. I wake, I shower, I eat, I go to the gym, I go to work, I call my sister, I come home, shower, bed, and repeat. I may squeeze in a random hook up and trips to the bars in between, but if I don't follow those order of events every day and tick them off my mental to do list, then it all goes to hell.

When you have an addictive personality, you need to choose your addictions carefully.

The military helped with that. It kept my head straight and my hands busy. But when I got out, old habits came knocking, and it took everything to keep me from slipping. Now I stick to what works.

Hot water runs down my back as I drag a hand through my hair, forcing myself to focus.

Today is a break in routine, and I hate that. I'm moving out of my apartment once we get back from Jack's bachelor weekend, and so I've had to push some meetings to the evenings. Not ideal.

I shut off the shower, step out, and wrap a towel around my waist. Breathe. Adapt. Get through the day.

I enter my now empty closet—only a few items of clothing remain on hangers, just enough to see me through till we head to Vegas. I slip on a pair of black jeans, black military style boots, and a black t-shirt. Like everything in my life, I keep my wardrobe easy, basic, and organized.

My phone buzzes on top of my dresser. I look and see a text from the group chat I have with Jack and Harry, my best friends and business partners.

Jack

> Brad, you still on for the investor meeting at Diamonds?

Harry

> I've heard 'great' things about Diamonds.

Brad

> Yep, you put it in our diary.

Harry

> What, you guys have a diary? I wanna be in the diary.

Jack

> The shared diary is for grown-ups, Harry.

Harry

middle finger emoji

Jack

Brad, you still okay to drop my Amex off to Ali for the bachelorette weekend?

Harry

I'll drop your Amex off. I bet Ali Cat would love to see me.

Jack

I don't trust you with my Amex, and I think Ali would rather walk on broken glass than have you go to her apartment.

Harry

middle finger emoji

Brad

On my way now.

I put the phone down on my dresser next to the chain. Picking it up, I run my thumb over the familiar numbers etched on the silver tag.

I exhale, the ache still lingering, but I push on, fastening the chain around my neck. I grab my keys and phone, already mentally running through the night ahead. Stop by Ali and Gabriella's. Stop by the club, then my meeting. Keep moving. Stick to the plan.

I park up outside their apartment building, punch in the security code, and head up to their floor. I knock twice on the white wooden door, and a few moments later, I'm greeted by Ali, blonde hair piled up on her head, and wearing a pink yoga set.

"Hey, you," she greets warmly, a lot warmer than she greets Harry. They are forever going at each other. Personally, I think there's something there between them, but I'll let them figure that out.

"Hey," I respond, stepping inside their apartment as she opens the door wider for me. I've been here a few times. I've dropped them home after a night out because I am always the designated driver. It's what I would call a typical girl apartment. Everything is pink, white, clean, and smells of something sweet.

I pass her the Amex card, and she brings it to her chest. "Ah, thank you. What a man Jack is. Can you believe he's giving us a credit card for the weekend?"

"Love will make you do stupid things," I say dryly as I follow her towards the kitchen.

She turns to face me and rolls her eyes. "Can I get you a drink?"

"Just a water, please." She reaches inside the fridge and slides a bottle of water across the countertop towards me. Undoing the cap, I look around. "Is Gabriella here?"

She nods, taking a sip of her own bottle of water. "She's getting ready for her date."

I'm caught a little off guard and my stomach dips. "A date with who?" I ask curiously as she doesn't often date. Gabriella is younger than all of us, and I'll admit, I have a soft spot for her and feel protective of her in a different way than I do for Ali or Ria.

"Some guy her parents set her up with. She doesn't seem very excited about it," Ali says.

"So why is she going?"

"God only knows. You know what she's like. She can't say no."

"Have you met him? What's he like?" I ask a little more sternly than I intended.

"Chill, Papa Bear. She's a big girl. She'll be okay. Besides, if her parents set them up, I have every faith he will be dull and boring and she will be home by 9 pm." I feel my jaw tensing, and I toss the bottle of water between my hands.

"I better head out. I'll go say hi to her before I go."

"Sure, I have a date with Channing Tatum anyway." She grins, waving a bag of chips at me. Knowing she means a movie, I roll my eyes in a playful way and head towards Gabriella's bedroom.

I hear a frustrated huff coming from there. The door is open, and I tap it with my knuckles. "Knock knock," I say, scanning the room, but I can't see her. Her large white wooden bed takes center stage in the space. A mound of clothing is piled up on her bed. Her walls are a crisp white with framed photographs of our friends, some artwork of ballerinas, and her days as a dancer. A desk with a lamp that's lit sits in front of her picture window, and a light streams from the bathroom door where I can hear her rattling around.

"Hello," I call.

She walks from her bathroom wearing a white bathrobe, her long silky black hair hanging in loose waves around her face. She startles, clutching her hands to her chest. "Oh my god, Brad, I didn't hear you."

I let out a low chuckle. "Sorry, I just wanted to say hi before I left. I hear you have a date?" I tease.

"Uh, yeah," she says, chewing on her bottom lip.

"You don't sound very excited about it?"

"No, I am. I just don't know what to wear, and he's going to be here soon, and he texted me earlier saying he booked that new seafood restaurant near Times Square, and I said sounds great, and now I wanna throw up."

I press my lips together. Gabriella rambling will never not be funny. She does it when she's nervous, and I find it endearing.

"Why did you say that? You hate seafood," I state.

"Because I clearly lack the ability to say no to people," she says, rummaging through the pile of clothes, pulling out a black dress, holding it up, then tossing it behind her.

"You really need to work on that people pleasing thing you do," I say flatly.

"Yeah, I know. I'll get right on that after this date, so pray that I can swallow and keep the fish down." I almost choke at the idea of her swallowing.

She holds up a simple black dress with long sleeves and a high neckline, and length that falls just below her knee. "Does this dress say, I'm not really into this, so can we just be friends?" she asks, holding it against herself.

I eye the dress. "What shoes are you wearing?"

She bends down and picks up two different shoes. "Well, if I liked him, I'd wear my YSL heels." She holds up a strappy sandal with a high stiletto. "But I'm thinking my Karen Millen pumps." She holds up a black, flat ballet slipper shoe.

"Yeah, YSL screams 'take me home and fuck me', Karen Millen says 'thanks for dinner, let's be friends, I'll see you Sunday at church'," I say playfully.

She snaps her fingers and points at me, "Perfect, just the message I want. Karen Millen, it is." I laugh, shaking my head as she goes into her bathroom, taking the dress with her.

I take a seat on the end of her bed, watching the shadows of her silhouette on the bedroom wall that shines through the bathroom door as she changes.

"So, what's his name? What does he do?" I call."

"Patrick. He works at a law firm or finance, I can't remember. Likes to play golf," she yells back.

"Hmmm, he sounds fun," I say sarcastically.

"Doesn't he?" she says, matching my tone as she reenters the room. The black dress she's now wearing is loose but still tight enough that you can make out her insane curves. She's my friend, but I can appreciate how beautiful she is, and she takes care of her body. Much like me, she loves her fitness, and it shows.

Her long hair is now styled back in her staple high ponytail, and it's only now I see the light dusting of make-up she has on. She has these insane eyes. Brown with flecks of amber that catch the light. I remember the first time I laid eyes on her in that club. I was so enamored by her and how she carried herself. She was stunning. The more I talked to her and got to know her, I knew I had to keep my distance and build that friendship wall quickly. She was too good, too pure, too innocent for someone like me. She was the type of woman you made your forever. But I can't do forever. I'd tarnish her. And I can't do that to her because she's one of life's good ones. Gabriella was a breath of cool air in the middle of the desert. Rare and hard to come by, but when you do, you soak up every second of it because you know it's fleeting. I know she could never be mine, I'd never allow it, because she was destined for things that I could never give her, so I embrace the parts I do get to have, because I'd rather have pieces of her than nothing at all.

"So, does this look okay?" She spins and puts her hands on her hips.

I look her up and down and nod. "Beautiful. If he's a prick or you get in trouble, you call me, okay?"

"I will," she says, walking towards me, pressing a feather-light kiss to my cheek. "Thank you for the help."

I rise to my feet, towering over her, and wrap my arms around her. I'm not really a hugger, but with her, it feels like the most natural thing in the world to do.

"Gabs, your date is here," Ali yells from the other room.

Gabriella visibly stiffens before she steps out of my hold, smooths her hands down her dress, and heads out of her bedroom. I follow, wanting to meet this man.

He smiles when he looks at Gabriella and then his face drops, and his eyes darken when he looks at me. I appreciate it didn't look very good watching her leave her bedroom with me trialing behind, but it is what it is. I'm her friend, and I'm not going anywhere.

"Hey," Gabriella says shyly, and Patrick hands her a bunch of red roses.

"Thank you. I'll pop them in some water." She turns to walk away, but quickly turns back.

"Sorry, Patrick, this is my friend Brad. Brad, Patrick."

Patrick holds out his hand, and I reluctantly shake it, only doing it for Gabriella's sake. He's dressed like a typical rich preppy boy. Blue eyes, blond hair, and hands so soft it tells me he's never done an honest hard day's work in his life.

"Good to meet you," Patrick says, never breaking eye contact. I say nothing.

"I better head out. Have fun." I wave to Gabriella and Ali, ignoring Patrick, and walk right by him. There is a little niggle in my chest. It's irritating and uncomfortable, but I can't figure out why it's there, so instead of trying to work it out, I ignore it, lock it away, and move my thoughts to my evening routine because letting myself feel never ends well.

Chapter Four

Gabriella

"... and Larry reckons if I continue, I could make partner in the next two years," Patrick mumbles around forkfuls of food.

All I can do is nod and smile. "Wow, that's incredible," I say, trying my best to sound interested.

"It's rare for someone of my age to reach..." His words fade as my brain zones out. I've been on this date for nearly two hours, and all this man has done is talk about himself, his job, his high school, lacrosse career, and I am pretty sure he's checked out his reflection in his spoon on a few occasions. God, he really is a self-absorbed prick and so different from how he was with me at the country club. Why, why would my mother think he would be a good fit? I don't think he has asked me one single question.

"Gabriella, are you okay?" I shake my head and blink rapidly.

"Yeah, sorry, that's... that's really an incredible achievement, Patrick. You should be so proud."

He straightens his spine, his pearly white teeth on full display as he smiles arrogantly.

I want to roll my eyes, but refrain, and instead stab my fork at the seabass on my plate, which thankfully has been over-seasoned and therefore slightly palatable. But seriously, who takes someone out for fish of all things for a first date? I've had to fight to not dry heave the entire evening. It'll take me at least three washes to get the smell out of my hair.

"So, what is it you do?" he asks before taking another forkful of food and shoving it in his mouth.

Wow, finally, he asks me a question.

"I teach Pilates at a studio near Central Park. I love it, it's–" I don't get to finish because Motor Mouth Mike uses it as his golden opportunity to talk about himself again.

"Ah, the Serenity studio. I've heard of that. I go to the gym round the corner. I've been going for a few years now. My trainer says if I continue I could…" And, I'm back to drowning him out. I reach for my glass of wine, draining its contents as I continue to smile and nod.

Get me out of here.

It's 9.30 pm and we are thankfully heading out of the restaurant from what I can safely say is one of the most boring dates I have ever been on, and that's saying something after Adam. At least he asked me questions. I honestly think Patrick would have had a better time alone with a mirror.

"So can I take you for a drink, or we can head back to mine for a nightcap?" Patrick suggests as he slides his hand in mine, as he walks me towards my car. I flinch, pulling back my hand.

I'm sorry, were we just on the same date? What part of it gave him the impression I wanted to go anywhere else with him? I think I uttered maybe six words. The rest was him just talking about himself.

"Oh, I'd love to, but I have an early morning class and I need my beauty sleep," I say apologetically.

"Fair enough," he replies, not sounding overly bothered, and I can't decipher if that pisses me off or makes me feel relieved.

We reach my car and I get my keys out of my purse, turning to Patrick, and that lead weight in my stomach appears. I hate ending a date, especially when it's been a real dud.

"Thank you for a lovely evening," I say, trying to avoid eye contact. He closes the space between us, and I recoil.

Oh God, please don't kiss me.

"I had a great time," he drawls, his tone low.

"Yeah, m-me too," I lie.

He leans in and I move my head to the left, praying he'll land on my cheek, but then he moves the same way, so I move the other and then it happens again and we are in this awkward exchange of head bobbing.

Oh, hell on a cracker, make it stop.

Finally, I admit defeat, and because I am too damn polite for my own good, I stand there and await his mouth on mine. I wrinkle my nose as he kisses me like a 6th grader. Closed mouth, lasting seconds, and then he pulls away, looking mighty pleased with himself. I fight the urge to wipe my mouth, and instead, I smile back and say, "Thank you."

Thank you? Yeah, good one, Gabriella.

Chapter Five

Brad

Saturday nights, like most clubs in New York City are the busiest nights and The Boardroom is no exception. We are at full capacity, and security has started turning people away.

I'm behind the VIP bar helping Kate, our bar manager, as her team prepare for opening, before I head to my meeting. I know they will have things running smoothly, which is exactly what we need now that Jack's nights are spent at home with his fiancée, Ria, and Harry is still in London.

"Kate, I'll drop by before closing," I yell over the music and point toward the back door to stress my point.

'No problem. Catch you later. Have fun," she shouts back with a wave. Pushing through the staff entrance door, I pull my phone and clock the time: 7.30 pm... right on time. I scroll my contacts and hit Facetime on the same name I do every night without fail.

The ringing tone echoes through the hall as I make my way towards my office. Just as I reach the door, a little voice filters through the speaker on my iPhone.

"Hey, Uncle Marco." I smile at my five-year-old nephew and instantly feel a little more at ease. He is one of the few people who call me by my real name. A name that is attached to parts of my life I'd like to bury and forget, but Luca is one of the only good things that's attached to that name.

"Hey, bud, how's your day been?" I say, opening the door to my office and stepping inside. "Good. Mommy took me to the park and for ice cream, and then she got me the Legos I wanted." He beams through the phone.

"She did, huh?" I say with excitement in my voice.

"Yeah, wanna see?"

"Sure." He disappears from the screen and I relax back into my leather office chair and balance my phone on the stand I keep on my desk.

He returns holding a box almost as big as him.

"Look, see, see, it's the one with the plane."

"I see. You are very lucky, bud. Did you thank your mom?"

"Uh huh," he mutters, still looking at his box, his big brown eyes wide and excited, and his mop of dark hair framing his angelic face, looking every bit the Italian boy he is. When my sister told me she was pregnant at eighteen and the father was less than interested, I stepped in as much as I could. Luca needed a male figure in his life, and my sister needed support. With our dad and older brother, Matteo, in prison, and my younger brother, Dario, in the military, it left me and our mom to help Alessia. Luca is a good kid, and my sister is someone who just got a little lost in life. When our dad and brother went down for a drug exchange gone wrong, she was barely a teen, then I left for the Marines and her life spiraled. I hold a lot of guilt for leaving, but it was the military or end up the same way as my dad and brother. The least I can do for Alessia is step up and be some kind of male figure in Luca's life and help guide him so he doesn't end up like any of us Russo kids.

"So, now you've got the plane, what am I gonna get you for your birthday, bud?" I ask.

"Uh, I don't know. Maybe the rocket, or the truck, or the boat."

I chuckle. "How about you write a birthday wish list and you can send it to me?"

He nods excitedly. "Are you ready for bed? You brushed your teeth and listened to your mom?" I ask, knowing he's been playing my sister up. I missed a lot of his first year as I was still in the military, so I try and see him as much as I can, and I video call him every night without fail to say goodnight and check in on my sister.

"Can I speak to your mom?"

"Mom, Uncle Marco wants to talk to you." He hollers so loudly, I'm pretty sure they heard him upstairs in the club.

My sister comes into view. Jet black hair just like mine, and the same whiskey-colored eyes.

"Hey, you good?" my sister asks as she looks into the camera, and it's then I notice how red her eyes look and the paleness of her skin.

"Yeah, I'm good, are you? You look tired, sis."

She yawns. "Yeah, I'm okay. Luca has been up since 5 am, and it's just been a busy day. Once he's in bed, I'm on the couch curled up with a glass of wine and *Sex and the City*."

Most twenty-four-year-olds would be out partying or seeing friends. My sister is tucking in her son and spending another lonely night in her apartment, and it hurts my heart a little that she had to grow up far too quickly. But I'm so damn proud of her. She's an amazing mom, and everything she does is for Luca.

"I'll come, see you when I get back from Vegas, okay?" I say, reassuring her. "I'll take Luca for the day, and you can go do something for you," I suggest.

"Sounds good to me," she answers, her voice sounding a little lighter.

I look at the time on my phone and know I need to end the call.

"Sorry, sis, I gotta go. I have a meeting I need to get to," I say, taking the phone from the stand and picking up my keys.

"Sure thing, Luca..." she calls, "come say night to Uncle Marco." Luca appears on screen and waves.

"Bye, Uncle Marco."

"Bye, bud, talk tomorrow." And then the screen goes blank, and my chest feels a little lighter. Talking to my nephew and my sister has become part of my evening routine. No matter where I am in the world, I've never missed a call with them, and it's the one part of my day where the world stops and nothing else matters but them.

Before leaving, I change into a black dress shirt, suit pants, and black shoes, then head out of my office toward the back exit to the parking lot, dreading this evening's meeting, but they are big investors and could mean the difference between another club opening or not. I unlock my car, settle into the leather seat, turn on the engine, and spin out onto the busy New York street, cranking up the stereo and tapping my fingers against the steering wheel to distract the heaviness in my chest. Tonight, I feel off balance, and I can't pinpoint why.

"... we think this is the future and we would like The Boardroom franchise to be a part of it," Tanner says, sliding a brown folder over to me. Tanner is around my age, light brown hair, and has that boy next door look about him. It's clear from watching their dynamic that Oscar is the brains of the company and Tanner is the charm.

I eye the folder, the noise and bustle of the club making it a little hard to focus. Being in the club industry, I'm no stranger to a business meeting in a bar, although it would never be my first choice. I pick up the folder and flick through, noting the figures on the back page. It's a heck of a lot of money they are willing to invest.

"I'll have to discuss this with Jack and Harry, of course, but it's a great offer," I say, nodding as I turn each page. What they are offering is great, but what they don't know is that we have other offers to expand. Until I see the other offers, I'm keeping my cards close to my chest.

"The entire business proposal is there. Look over it, take a few weeks, and then we can get together and plan our future relationship together," Oscar says, running a hand through his salt and pepper hair. He's about ten years older than me, and a little arrogant.

I smirk. "You are making it sound like a marriage proposal," I say.

He lets out a deep belly laugh. "I like to think of my business arrangements like a marriage. Just like my wife, you'll need to sign on the dotted line to get any cash from me." He grins, flexing his jaw that looks like it's been carved by surgeons.

Wow, what an ass.

"We'll look it over and get back to you," I say, looking at my phone and noticing it's nearly midnight and so is a great time to make my excuse to leave.

"I need to head back to The Boardroom. It's been a pleasure, gents. I—" I go to continue, but Oscar interrupts.

"Oh, you can't go yet. You're about to see the reason we brought you here."

I eye him curiously and look around at the small, intimate club with a lounge vibe. Brown leather chairs and dark wood tables fill the room. I saw there was a main room below when we entered, but we were shown to what I assumed was a VIP area. There is a wide stage next to our table, which, until now, I hadn't paid any attention to. The opposite end of the room is a mirrored bar that stretches across the room and all the staff are women in tight black dresses, and I've been curious about this place since Oscar suggested we meet here. It's not your usual club, it's a cigar lounge meets a burlesque show.

"You're going to want to stay for this, trust me," Oscar says, his facial expression matching Tanner's. As if right on cue, the lights dims, and the room erupts into loud cheering. A sultry beat flows through the room, and a singular light appears in the middle of the stage, focused on a woman, dressed in a black skin-tight bodysuit, black heeled pumps, and her long dark hair hanging down her back as she sits in a hoop hanging from the ceiling. She clicks her fingers in time to the beat of the music, and when the tempo changes, the hoop spins to face the audience, causing the men to whistle and clap enthusiastically. She leans back, dropping the top half of her body so she hangs from the base of the hoop. My eyes drift from her long, toned legs and up her body till it lands on her face, which, to my surprise, is covered with a masquerade-style mask.

She continues to maneuver and twist her body through the hoop. Holding on with one hand and widening her legs as the hoop rotates above the stage. I glance round the room and watch as the men in the room look on in awe. She moves effortlessly, commanding everyone's attention. The lights flash, snatching my attention once again, where more women appear in similar outfits and masks, taking positions at the poles that have appeared. I sense it's about to get a little wild when some of the girls enter the crowd and meander around the tables.

Oscar twists in his seat and grins. "I told you; you didn't want to miss this." I nod in acknowledgment, and then my eyes are back, focused on the women on stage. A redhead appears behind Tanner, trailing her index finger across his jawline before disappearing.

I lift my whiskey—my one drink for the evening—and as the cool liquid trickles between my lips, I'm stopped in my tracks. My eyes zone in on the woman who was in the hoop as she now moves front and center. She has curves that would drive a man wild, and when she drops to her knees, throwing her head back and smoothing the palm of her hand from her throat down her body to in between her legs, my dick strains against the fabric of my briefs.

Fuck, who is that girl?

She stands out for many reasons—her hair that shimmers like silk with every movement. The stage lights make her red mask dazzle, catching my eye. My jaw tenses as I watch in fascination. She moves like she's gliding on water. Smooth and effortless, and when she turns and contorts her body in a way that has her ass up and hips tilting, it's then I notice how perfectly heart-shaped her ass is, and fuck, if she's not the hottest woman on that stage.

I lean over towards Tanner. "Do you know any of their names?" I ask, pointing to the stage.

"Nobody knows. They aren't allowed to give out the girls' names. They give out fake ones. It's all secret to protect their identity. Believe me, I've tried finding out a few," he yells over the music. "But you can request a private dance. That's the only way to get real close to them."

I sit back in my chair, my gaze never leaving her. I'm not often caught off guard by a woman. It takes a lot to hold my attention. I've never been short of a female companion, but there's something about her. I'm drawn to her, I want her, and as I watch her dance, I decide that I need to find out who the girl in the red mask is.

Chapter Six

Brad

It's our first night in Vegas for Jack's bachelor weekend, and I haven't been able to get the girl in the mask out of my head. All my usual tricks to get my mind focused have failed. She's been running through my head like a movie on repeat, and I can't shake the feeling that I'm meant to find her.

Harry arranged a VIP booth in the Omnia Club in Casaers Palace, where we are staying. Jack let it slip that Ria and the girls were heading there for her bachelorette tonight, and suddenly our plans for the casino changed. I bet every dollar in my bank account Harry and Ali will be fucking before the weekend is over. Her reception towards him was frosty, but you can taste the sexual tension between them.

"Well, that took a turn, didn't it? I thought you two were going to end up fucking right there on that couch," I say to Harry as Ali walks away and heads towards the booth the girls have. The girls had a set of bachelorette dare cards and Harry, never one to not get involved, pulled a card to give someone a lap dance, and Ali was his victim. "Yeah, well, the night is still young," Harry says, but his focus isn't on me, it's on Ali. I have a lot of time for Ali. She's a lot like me. She's guarded, puts on a front, and keeps her cards close to her chest, and I'm grateful for her friendship.

A hand wraps around my forearm, and I know who it is without turning my head. Her delicate hand smooths up my inked skin, and I turn to embrace her.

"Hey, baby girl." Gabriella's big doe eyes look up at me. She's tiny. I tower over her at 6ft 4, but her slight frame fits into mine as she wobbles on her heels and giggles.

"I'm drunk." She hiccups and then giggles again.

"I can see that."

"I wanna dance. Dance with me." She begins to pull at my black dress shirt and lead me towards the dance floor. She's in a black dress that sparkles when it catches the club lights. It has long sleeves and barely covers her ass, and it's not something she would usually wear, but paired with the YSL heels, fuck, she looks hot as hell.

She's your friend.

If someone asked me how I felt about Gabriella, I fear it would be an essay answer. It's not as simple as 'she's my friend'. It is more. I don't see her like a sister, and I think of her as more than a friend, but I have no desire to make it more than what we are. Because I don't have it in me to be something to someone, least of all her. So, I settle for keeping her in the special spot in my heart that will only ever be reserved for Gabriella Monroe.

"I don't dance, baby girl. You know that," I say as she continues to pull me towards the dance floor where Ali, Kate, and Harley, who work at our club, are dancing with our old friends, from the marines, Mason and Brett.

"Fine." She huffs in defeat. "Then you can watch me dance."

"Happy to." I grin, giving her a wink. She smiles back, waving, stumbling slightly, and I give it thirty minutes before I'm carrying her up to her room and putting her to bed like I've done many times before. The girl can't handle her liquor. A few drinks, and she's three sheets to the wind. I don't actively encourage drinking, but for Gabriella, it allows her to come out of her shell a little and it's a beautiful thing to witness.

I sip on the whiskey I've been nursing. Not even in Vegas will I stray from my one whiskey rule. Drinking excessively has got me into trouble in the past. I relied on it to help me cope with stress, which isn't ideal, so I can't risk falling back into old patterns. It got me out of bed, it got me through the day, and it got me to sleep. One drink allows me a little pleasure, but never enough to fully lose control.

"Damn, she can move. Is she a dancer?" Brett asks, coming up beside me, his eyes fixated on Gabriella. I love Brett, but first he was sniffing round Ali when we first met up with the girls this weekend and now Gabriella. He can fuck off.

"Yeah, she went to Julliard, I think," I mumble.

"Shit, she's good." I follow his line of sight and watch Gabriella dance between Kate and Ali. Sure, they can all dance, but there's something about the way Gabriella moves. Her hips rotate, and she backs up against Ali and smooths her hands down her body; it reminds me of the girl in the red mask. I shake my head to rid my mind of her and focus on the girls. I observe a guy try to wedge his way between her and Ali, and my body tenses.

Ali turns away and dances with Kate, and I watch with burning jealousy as the guy snakes his arms around Gabriella's waist and moves in sync with her. I drain my drink, ice included, and crunch it so vigorously I'm surprised I don't crack a tooth. I unashamedly stare as she dances with this man for three songs. Wrapping her arms around his shoulders as he nuzzles into her neck. On the one hand, I'm happy for her. She must like him if she's dancing with him, and I know she doesn't give herself freely to men, so this is a big deal for her, and the other, I want to storm over there and tear him off her.

Not able to watch this display a second longer, I turn to Brett and say through gritted teeth. "I think I'm going to head up to the suite."

He nods in understanding, and I go to leave when I hear him say, "You might want to wait a minute."

I turn my head to see where he's looking, and I see an exchange between Gabby and the guy. They are no longer on the dance floor, but standing to the side, and he has her by the hand. She shakes her head as if she's telling him no, and she tries to pull her hand free. The prick doesn't seem to be getting the message and pulls her back towards him by the waist. She holds her hands up to his chest and tries to push him away.

Oh, fuck no.

Without hesitation, I stride over to them, clamping a firm hand down on his shoulder. "I believe she told you no," I say sternly.

They both glance up at me, and relief flashes over Gabriella's face. It makes my heart pound harder in my chest, knowing she needs me.

"Fuck off. We were just talking. Mind ya business. The guy yells back, moving Gabriella closer towards him. If I wasn't annoyed before, now I'm fucking raging. I gently move Gabriella to the side and square up to this Zac Efron look-alike.

"I said she told you no. Now get your hands off her before I break them."

He lets go of her hand and holds his up in surrender. I'm well aware of my appearance and the demeanor I give off. Being tall and covered in tattoos has its advantages at times.

"Good boy. Now run along," I mock, and he scurries away without giving Gabriella a second glance. I turn to face Gabriella, pulling her into me. She nestles her face into my chest, and warmth spreads throughout my chest as I press a soft kiss to the top of her head.

"Are you okay? Did he hurt you?" She shakes her head and then looks up at me, her eyes heavy and bloodshot.

Oh, she's had way too much to drink.

"No, I'm fine. He wanted to go up to his room, and I said no. He told me to not be a tease and then…"

"Hey, you are not a tease. You can dance with him, and then if he offers more and you say no, it's fucking no, okay?" I bite, angry that he didn't take no for an answer. She nods in understanding, and I hold her tighter and press a kiss to the top of her head.

"I want my bed," she mumbles into my chest. I let out a low chuckle.

"Let's get you upstairs."

Without thinking, I scoop Gabriella up like a bride and carry her.

"My hero." She giggles. "My feet are killing me."

"I got you, baby girl," I whisper, pressing another kiss to the top of her head as she begins to drift off in my arms as I carry her through the hotel.

We reach our floor, where our suite is opposite the girls. Gabriella stirs in my arms and mumbles, "I think I'm gonna be sick."

I contort my face and wince. "Oh, God, please don't." I can't be dealing with her throwing up over me.

"Quick, get her in the bathroom." Kate says. She's followed us back and panicked voice echoes in the hallway as she swipes her key card at the door and opens it. I rush through.

"Where?" I yell, feeling myself panic that she's about to vomit all over me.

"This way," Kate yells, kicking off her heels and attempting to run, but she's just as drunk and falls against the wall and begins giggling.

Jesus Christ.

She opens a door, flicks the light on, and bursts into laughter.

"Whoops, wrong room." She's opened the door to a closet and looks at me and laughs. "It's a closet. I thought it was the bathroom." She slaps her forehead with the palm of her hand. "Silly Kate."

I look at her deadpan. "Kate?" I say, looking down at Gabriella, who is now beginning to dry heave.

"Oh yeah, this way." Thankfully, the next door is the bathroom. I settle Gabriella down on the floor next to the toilet, crouch down beside her, and hold back her ponytail in time just as she empties the contents of her stomach into the toilet bowl, trying to ignore the god-awful smell of the alcohol that she's spewing up.

"That's it, get it all out," I encourage, rubbing small circles on her back.

"I'm sorry," she manages to say in between throwing up. "You should know, I only throw up in front of people I like and feel comfortable around."

"I'm honored," I say, my tone laced with sarcasm.

"Oh God, I think I'm going to be sick," Kate slurs, covering her mouth.

"What?" I all but shriek, as she starts pacing the room, fanning her face with her hands.

"Yeah, if I hear people puke, it makes me puke. I have really sensitive gag reflex," she mumbles behind her hand.

"Aren't you training to be a nurse?" I question, furrowing my brow in confusion.

"Yeah, yeah, I am. I need to work on the gagging thing," she mutters.

"Might be a good idea," I say flatly.

As I finish my sentence, Gabriella makes a loud gagging sound, and more vomit is expelled from her body.

Seriously, how much did she drink?

"Oh God, it's..." Kate groans, and I can see she's about to spew.

"Oh, fuck no..." I shout, petrified she's about to spew all over the bathroom floor.

I dart my eyes around the room, grab the trash can that's next to the toilet, and hand it to her. She falls to her knees next to me, clutching the trash can, and begins to vomit.

Fuck my life. Now there are two of them.

I have one hand rubbing small circles on Gabriella's back and the other now holding a trash can for Kate as they throw up in tandem.

How did I end up here?

Kate finally stops vomiting, wiping her mouth with the back of her hand, her mascara running down her cheeks. She looks like she's been through the ringer. She collapses back against the wall, still clutching the trash can, and groans. "Oh God, I'm so sorry. Please don't fire me."

I chuckle. "You're good, Kate."

"This is why my boyfriend broke up with me. I know it. I have no gag reflex. It was a real issue for him." she mutters to herself.

I can't deal with drunk women, yet somehow, I am always the one holding the sick bucket.

Not knowing what to say to her, I turn my attention back to Gabriella, smoothing my hand in circles on her back as she seems to have settled down and stopped vomiting. Christ, I'm sweating from the stress. I'm feeling the need to strip off my shirt before I pass out or start vomiting too.

"What the hell's going on in here?" My head spins to see Ali standing in the doorway, her eyes scanning the room, taking in the scene.

"Apparently, everyone has a weak gag reflex and can't handle their liquor," I reply dryly.

"Sounds about right," Ali agrees, bending down to help Kate up. "Come on, girl, let's get you and your weak gag reflex to bed."

"I'm sorry, I just can't handle it." She begins to cry, wrapping an arm around Ali. Christ! Vomiting, drunk girls are one thing, drunk girls crying is another thing altogether.

"I know. Just don't go deep throating anyone this weekend, okay?" Ali jokes.

"Okay?" Kate whines, leaning on Ali.

They leave the room as Gabriella sits up and falls into my body.

"Ugh." She groans. "Am I a mess?"

"Only a little." I chuckle.

I help her stand and take her to the basin. I take what I hope is her toothbrush, put some paste on it, and hand it to her. She manages to brush her teeth with her eyes shut, swaying side to side. I place my hands on her hips to steady her, stepping in a little closer, and despite her intoxicated state and the vomiting, she still smells sweet like cherries. I can't help but inhale and nuzzle my nose into her hair; her scent does something to me. There's a weird flutter in my belly. I need to get a fucking hold of myself here.

"Right, let's get you to bed," I suggest, needing to distract myself from my wandering mind. I lift her, knowing she won't make it to the bed on her own. I follow the sound of Ali's voice talking to Kate and carry her into a large cream-colored room with a huge bed in the center that faces the wall full of windows overlooking the Vegas strip.

"Here, put her in bed with me. They can both sleep with me." Ali gestures to the bed. "If these two hadn't let the team down, we could have given you the night of your life, prison break." Ali teases, and I can't help but chuckle a little at the use of the nickname Ali uses for me.

"Minus the vomit and the unconscious state, this would be any man's fantasy," I say, shaking my head as I lay Gabriella next to Kate, who is face down on the mattress snoring.

"I think she needs this dress off," I call to Ali.

"I can sort her. Thanks for carrying her in. Usually, I have to do it. Poor girl can't hold her liquor."

"She really can't," I agree, looking down at an already sleeping Gabriella curled up on her side. "Keep her on her side or her front, and give her some water, and call me if you need anything."

"Yes, Dad," she mocks. "This isn't my first rodeo with drunk Gabby. I got her. I'm just going to grab some water."

I nod, and without thinking, I lean down and press a chaste kiss to her forehead.

"People have you all wrong, you know." I startle, lifting my head to see Ali hasn't left the room, and she's watching me from the doorway.

I furrow my brows, unsure of what she means.

"You have this whole big, bad Brad thing going on." She waves her hand around. "The stern face, the tattoos, the 'I don't give a fuck' attitude. You're single, in Vegas, could be off doing whatever you want, yet you are here, looking after a drunk girl holding her hair back, and putting her to bed. There needs to be more men like you," she says softly.

I'm taken aback by her words. She's right, but I wouldn't do this for just anyone.

I clear my throat, unsure of what to say. "Yeah, well, I have a sister, so I would hope someone would look after her in this state." It's not a lie, but it's not why I am here. She smiles in understanding, tapping the door frame with her fingers before leaving.

My eyes fall to Gabriella, sleeping soundly, curled up on the edge of the bed. I crouch down so my face is close to hers and press another light kiss to her forehead while I whisper, "Night, *Mia Cara*. Sweet dreams."

Chapter Seven

Gabriella

Regrets. I have many of them, and last night is up there with them. I got myself in a state and vomited in front of Brad. Lord, just take me now. It's all over for me. I can't look him in the eye today. I only drink around people I feel safe with, and I feel safe with him. Far safer than I probably should. I shouldn't have put that on him. I'm a grown ass woman, and yet I drink like a fifteen-year-old at prom. I stare back at my pale complexion and my messed-up ponytail in the bathroom mirror and rub a hand down my face, wiping last night's mascara away with my fingertips.

I splash cold water on my face and brush my teeth twice, the stale taste of alcohol and vomit still very much in my mouth, and I decide a trip to the gym will sort me out. Needing to wash the regret away, I hop in the shower and scrub myself clean. Does showering before the gym make sense? Not really. But I need to feel clean. Fitness is my life. Dancing, running, or Pilates have been my escape. For those minutes, I am free. I don't hear or feel anything other than the burn in my body. It's the only time my mind feels empty. I just let myself be and get lost in it. I exit the shower, drying myself off with the softest cotton towel I have ever used. I leave the bathroom and I tiptoe past Ali's bedroom, careful not to wake her and Kate, but I hear my name.

"Gabs... are you alive?" Ali's voice echoes. I chuckle to myself and turn to enter her bedroom. Ali is sat up in bed, hair all over the place, trying to focus her gaze on me through one squinted eye. Kate lies beside her, face down, making a noise that sounds like a wounded animal.

"I'm alive... are you two?" I giggle, pointing between them.

"I'm okay. I think Kate might need an IV." Ali yawns.

Kate rolls onto her back, covering her face with her hands while she groans. "Uggghhh, everything hurts. Please tell me that vomiting in a trash can in front of Brad was a horrible dream."

"No can-do, honey," Ali says. "You also told him you had a weak gag reflex."

"Oh god." Kate groans in despair, covering her head with a pillow.

"Where's Ria and Harley?" I ask, clutching my towel.

"The guy's suite, rattling headboards, no doubt," Ali says with a sour expression on her face.

"Who's Harley with?" I ask hesitantly. My stomach forms a little knot at the idea of Harley hooking up with Brad. I don't have time to question why that would bother me, so I silently plead that someone responds quickly to cure my worrying mind.

"I reckon Mason. They were very cozy," Ali says, wiggling her eyebrows.

The door to our suite opens, and steps echo through to the bedroom.

"Ria, Harley, is that you?" I call. A flash of auburn hair followed by a rosy-cheeked Harley who peaks through the doorway, and Ali whistles.

"I need a shower," Harley says shyly and then leaves.

"Yes, girl," Ali yells. "We'll have the full debrief later."

"I'm going to head to the gym. Does anyone want to join me?" I ask.

Ali and Kate both look at me like I've grown a second head. "No." They both say in unison. I let out a little laugh when the sound of more footsteps approach us. I clutch hold of my towel tighter in case it's one of the guys, but in walks Ria with a wide grin on her face and just fucked hair.

"Good morning." She smiles, her voice light and airy.

"I slept in the wrong suite last night it sounds like a wild time over there." Ali huffs.

"It was." Ria winks and slips into the bed beside Ali, the grin still spread across her beautiful face. Her big blue eyes sparkle with glee, and it makes me happy to see her like this. Ria has been through so much. She deserves this happiness.

"I need a nap." Ria yawns, snuggling in beside Ali.

"You've got two hours, ladies, before we need to be at the pool," Ali says.

I use that as my warning to get going.

"I'll be back in an hour," I say as I rush out of the room before they can keep me talking. I need to burn off this feeling. I feel... off.

Needing to get to the gym to silence my thoughts I quicken my steps to my room. I didn't have time to unpack my suitcase yesterday, so I rummage through and find my yoga pants and matching crop top.

I hunt for something appropriate to cover me in the gym, but all I find are dresses. I packed in such a rush that I forgot my tee I usually wear.

"Damn it," I hiss. I never go to the gym in just a crop top. My self-esteem or my mother's words would never allow it. The only time I do, is in my heels class.

"When you dress like that, Gabriella, you are asking for attention."
"Don't wear that. You are giving men the wrong impression."
"What did you expect when you drink and dress like that?"

Phrases I have heard on repeat since I was a teen echo through my mind, and I close my eyes as if that will make them magically vanish. I've always been told attention is a bad thing, well, attention that comes to you because of how you look. I had to wear my hair a certain way, my make up a certain way, my clothes a certain way. Enough to look pretty and put together, but never enough to draw attention. Just enough to blend in and not take center stage. That awful swell of anxiety begins in the pit of my stomach, and it makes me want to just stay in my room and do a workout in here.

No, fight this, Gabby. You deserve to be seen.

My feet pound against the treadmill while beads of sweat trickle down my back and chest, alerting me that I have pushed my body to the fullest. This feels good. This is what I needed; to sweat out the toxins and let my mind rest for just a minute. Music blasts through my headphones and nothing exist. I was thankful that the hotel gym was empty when I arrived. I mean, who is working out in Vegas?

Probably not many. I managed to buy a t-shirt from the hotel gift store that says I love Vegas in big letters. Not my usual style, but it covered up everything I needed it to. I slow my pace to walking and take a sip of water, welcoming the cold liquid as it soothes my burning throat. Knowing I need to stretch, or I will ache like a mother trucker later, I make my way over to the mats.

I place my water bottle down and quickly scan the still-empty gym. The sweat-soaked t-shirt clings to my body, and I need to get rid of it. I reach the hem of my shirt and pull it up over my head and discard it next to my water bottle. I capture a glimpse of myself in the full length mirror. My skin is glowing from my workout and my abs look more defined. I work hard to have the definition I have, but I can't ever bring myself to let anyone see it.

I reach above my head, stretching my arms and bending my spine slightly. I inhale and then fold forward, exhaling as I get into the downward dog position, feeling the stretch in my back and legs. I repeat the movement, the music still blasting through my wireless headphones. My hips begin to move to the beat on instinct, and as I bring my hands to the floor, I widen my hips and legs and reach between my legs, pushing the stretch. I close my eyes, really leaning into the burn pulsing through my body. I love the feeling of stretching after an intense run.

I bring my body back to a standing position, raising my arms above my head for one final stretch. Opening my eyes, I let out a startled scream when I see the familiar silhouette of a man standing a few steps behind. But when I rip off my headphones and spin to face him, my breathing a little ragged, I instantly relax when I take in the glorious sight of his bare, toned, tattooed skin dripping in sweat. He gives me a small smirk; one so quick I might have missed it had I not been staring at his features.

"Need a hand stretching out, baby girl?"

Chapter Eight

Brad

When I walked into the gym after my early morning run, I did not expect to stumble upon Gabriella, bent over, panting, sweating, and stretching her insane body. The woman is fire. Every inch of her toned and defined, and it's doing things to me and evidentially my dick, if the tent forming in my running shorts is anything to go by.

Stand down, soldier, your services are not required at this time.

But, fuck, I wish they were. This little soft spot, crush, whatever the hell you wanna call it, that I have for her, is becoming increasingly difficult to manage. I have control of every aspect of my life, but I worry this may be something I can't. *Blurred Lines* by Robin Thicke blasts through the gym speakers, and I step a little closer to where she stands, unmoving and silent.

"You okay?" I ask, concern in my voice that I've startled her.

I watch her throat bob as she swallows, and suddenly an image of Gabriella on her knees in front of me, opening up her pouty lips, flits through my mind, and I have to clear my own throat to stop a groan escaping.

She's your friend, she's your friend.

I couldn't tell you when this shift happened. When I suddenly started looking at her differently. I think it's always been there, but the feelings are intensifying, and add in that there is something about her that reminds me of the girl in the red mask at the club. Maybe it's the curves of her body, the way she moves, the thought of bending her over, claiming her, making her mine. It has been my every thought, and I think it's the reason I can't seem to look at Gabriella as just my friend anymore.

"Gabriella," I say slowly. "I'm sorry. I didn't mean to make you jump."

Her wide eyes look at me, and it's as if she fixes a mask back in place, and the sweet smile that always graces her face appears as she says, "No, I'm fine. Sorry, I had my headphones on. I didn't hear you come in. Did… did you go for a run?" she asks, her words hurried as she bends down to pick up a white t-shirt and fumbles to place it over her head. The fabric falls over her body, drowning her, hiding her.

I furrow my brows. "What the hell are you wearing?"

"I, erm, didn't have anything appropriate to wear in the gym, so I had to go to the hotel gift shop. This was all they had. I heart Vegas, yay." Her voice has a nervous edge to it.

"What's wrong with what you were just wearing?" I question. She was wearing a matching yoga set that clung to her in all the right places. She looked incredible in an outfit most women wear in the gym.

"It, erm… was a little too erm… revealing. I needed something to cover up here," she says quietly, gesturing to her stomach and chest.

Sympathy, anger, I don't know what simmers in my body. *Who's made her feel this way?*

I close the space between us. "Hey," I say, lifting her chin with forefinger and thumb. "You don't need to hide or cover up. Do you hear me? You're beautiful and don't need to hide." Her eyes widen at my words, and I worry I've overstepped.

I've noticed how she always hides in the background, how she never wears or says or acts in a way that would draw attention to herself. The only time she does is when she lets her hair down and has a few drinks, but again, she only does that when she's around her friends, around people she feels safe with. It's with that thought that I realize that maybe I make her feel safe, and that thought has my body tingling in an unfamiliar way. I've done a lot of wrong in my life, let people down, made mistakes, and hurt people. I didn't think I was capable of making anyone feel safe, but I want to. I want to make her feel safe.

She reaches for the hand that still grips her chin and gives it a little squeeze. "Thank you," she says softly.

"So lose the shirt, quit hiding, and anyway, I can't be seen with you wearing a I heart Vegas t-shirt."

She lets out a small laugh; it's light and airy and makes me smile. "Yeah, it's giving Joey in London vibes, right? Could I be any more of a tourist?"

The look of confusion on my face must show because she clamps a hand over her mouth and sighs. "Friends, you've seen the show *Friends,* right?" she asks.

I shake my head. I've never had the time to watch TV. I've seen the odd movie, but that's it.

"No, not really my thing," I say.

"I'll make a deal. You promise to watch one season of Friends with me, and I'll take off the shirt. No deal and the shirt stays on," she challenges as she folds her arms across her body.

I mull over her words and smile. We've hung out together, but it's usually as a group with the others. I like the idea of hanging out with her, so before I talk myself out of it, I say. "Deal. Lose the shirt."

She grips the hem, and I think she will whip it off quickly, but to my surprise, she peels it off slowly, teasing me, revealing an inch at a time of her golden skin. Her toned stomach muscles flex with the movement. She pulls it a little further, revealing her perked breasts, pushed together by the black sports bra she's wearing, creating a killer cleavage. One I'd very much like to swipe my tongue through.

The last of the shirt goes over her head, and she tosses it to the side.

"Is that better?" she asks, giving me a challenging stare, hands on her hips.

I don't know if she's meaning to, but it's as if she's flirting with me and I grin, giving her body a once over with my heated stare, and say, "Good girl. Much better."

An obvious tremor pulses through her body, and her cheeks pinken at my words. It brings me more joy than it should, knowing I may be affecting her in the same way she's affecting me.

"I'm, erm, going to finish my stretches," she stammers, before turning and walking back to the spot she was working out in.

'I'll be over here," I say, pointing to the pull up bar.

I need to get my head together. Distract my wandering mind, I reach up to hold on to the bar above me.

I count to ten in my head, enjoying the burn in my arms and upper back as I pull my body up until the pull I'm holding reaches my chest. I fall into a steady rhythm, and new beads of sweat roll down my chest and back as my breathing grows heavier. I make the mistake of glancing in the mirror where the reflection of Gabriella, twisting and bending like an elegant goddess, takes over my brain, and my movements falter. My arms give out and my feet hit the mat below as I let out a frustrated growl.

"Are you okay?" Her sweet voice filled with concern rings from behind me. I turn to face her, my breathing ragged.

"Yeah," I huff.

She walks toward me, sipping on her water, and my eyes focus on the way her throat bobs as she swallows and my dick begins to rise again.

Fuck's sake, not again.

"I don't know how you do those," she says, gesturing to the pull up bar. "I have the upper body strength of a kitten." I smirk at her comment, and because I am clearly in the business of torturing myself, I offer to help.

"I could teach you."

"Teach me what?" she says just loud enough for me to hear over the music. Oh, there are many things I'd like to teach, Gabriella. But for now, I'll settle with this. The thought takes me by surprise.

"Pull ups," I say, taking the water bottle from her hand and taking a small sip before handing it back to her. I run my tongue along my bottom lip, savoring the taste of her cherry flavored chap.

"Erm, sure," she agrees hesitantly. I point to the spot where I need her to stand. She is a tiny 5ft 2, so I know I'll need to lift her so she can reach the bar.

"Do you trust me?" I ask her in a serious tone, but with a little wink to keep the moment lighter.

She nods and I take that as my permission to move closer. I place my hands on her slim waist She lets out a little gasp at the contact, and heat floods my chest at the feel of her warm skin beneath my calloused hands.

"I'm going to lift you on three and you are going to reach up and hold on to the bar. Got it?"

She nods again.

"One... two... three..." I lift her. She's as light as a feather, so delicate and small in my hands. "Have you got a tight hold of the bar?" I ask.

"Uh huh." Her body tenses under my hold, and truthfully, I feel wound as tight as she is. I don't know why I am doing this, but I can't stop now.

I release her from my hold, and ump up to hold on to the bar as well, getting myself in a comfortable position so we are face to face.

"I don't think I can hold on," she says hurriedly, a little panic in her tone as she looks up at her hands hanging from the bar above us.

"Swing your legs and wrap them around my waist, and I'll guide you," I say gruffly.

She looks at me with wide eyes.

I repeat the words. "Wrap your legs around my waist and rest your weight on me." In a controlled way that only an experienced gymnast or dancer would do, she lifts her toned legs and hooks them around my waist; her crotch now pressed just above where my hardening dick sits. Our chests pressed together so we are almost nose to nose.

I swallow, clearing my throat, needing a moment to focus before we move.

"When I move, you move with me and mirror me, okay?" I instruct.

"Okay."

"Good girl," I tease, earning a small smile from her and then I pull my body up, taking hers with me. She does as I said and mirrors my movements. I watch in fascination as the small muscles in her sculpted arms flex as she pulls her body up and down. We make it to five pull ups before the friction of her body against the head of my dick becomes unbearable.

Her eyes flutter shut.

"Hey, eyes on me, Gabriella. You can't close your eyes when you're with me."

She opens her eyes, her amber irises fixed on me as if she were trying to understand what I meant by that comment. I'm unsure myself. We continue to move and the usual burn I would feel in my body is overshadowed by the sight of her moving up and down in front of me. The placement of her hands above her head forces her breasts together. Visions of her bouncing up and down on my hard cock while I pin her hands behind her runs through my mind and a groan works its way up my throat. The noise startles us both, her eyes widen once again, and I grind my teeth together, angry for letting my thoughts get the better of me.

We reach fifteen pull ups and before I explode in my running shorts or lift her down and bend her over, I decide now is a good time to end this torture.

"Unhook your legs," I say quietly. As soon as she does, I instantly miss the warmth her body gave me.

I jump down and then place my hands back on her waist to lift her down.

"See, you're a natural," I say through panted breaths, stepping away from her, needing to create some distance.

She gives me a weak smile and shit, I need her to speak. To say something. Anything.

"I... I better get going," she stammers, walking over to where her t-shirt and headphones lie. "We have a reservation at one of the pool cabanas, and Ali will kick my ass if we're late."

She nervously stumbles around the mats, gathering her things. It's clear something has affected her. Is it me? Is she imagining riding me the way I was picturing her.

"Thanks for your help. Catch you later," she yells as she pulls open the door, and then she's gone.

I need to get a grip on this before she becomes my new addiction.

Chapter Nine

Gabriella

"... tuck that pelvis in ladies... good... hold for three," I call out as I walk round the studio. It's my last class of the day, and I am ready to collapse in a heap when I get home. I've been so busy since we got back from Vegas last week, and honestly, I'm grateful I have. It's kept my brain busy and given me no time to think about Brad and the weird shift in our friendship. I've always found him attractive, but there are so many reasons I'd never even try to entertain the idea. He's older than me, more experienced than me, why would he want me? But the way his eyes danced over my body at me in the gym, the way his hands brushed my bare skin, and the way he made me feel safe in a way that only he seems to be able to do, gives me hope that maybe I could have someone like him fall for me.

"Okay, ladies, get comfortable, and we will do five minutes of meditation before we finish." I change the track on my iPod, and the calm music hums through the speakers. I settle on my mat at the front of the glass and look on at the fifteen women.

It's 6.55 pm and my heels class starts at 8pm across town. I need it. My mom has been messaging me all day, asking if I will be at dinner on Sunday. I haven't seen her since before Vegas, and I know she's getting twitchy to see me, or rather, quiz me about my date with Patrick. I haven't heard from him, so it's clear the feeling was mutual. Thank God.

After the class ends, I rush past reception and make my way to my car. A Beyonce track starts pumping through the speakers as I pull into traffic, and I relax into the seat, knowing I am done with my classes for the week and I have the weekend free before I fully devote myself to my friends' wedding.

I pull into the dance studio's car park, and as I gather my things, my phone chimes with a text message. I swipe the screen and my brows furrow when Patrick's name flashes up.

Patrick

> Hey Gabby, your mom tells me you are back from Vegas. I'd love to take you out on another date. I think we were both a little nervous, and I'd really like to try again. Call me. Patrick x

Not having the time to even consider his offer, I toss my phone in my bag and head into the studio. As soon as I walk in, Luna waves me over to where she sits, putting on her heels. I drop my bag and settle beside her. 'Hey," I say, a little breathless.

'You look tired," she says. "Long day?"

"Try long week." I huff, taking my heels and knee pads out of my bag and taking off my tennis shoes.

"Well, make sure you get some rest because Saturday's my birthday. You're coming, right? We're going to go to that new club, Havanas."

"Of course. I wouldn't miss it." I smile as I lace up my heels and slide the pads on.

"Yes, can't wait. Come on, Kaz wants us up front in class."

I take my spot in line with Luna, a few steps behind Kaz. When the R`n`B track begins playing my heart begins to thrum erratically. It's the same track that played at the pool party in Vegas. I almost miss my cue, my mind too busy drifting back to our weekend there. The song stirs up memories of Brad's front pressed to back, a protective hand resting on my hip as we all gathered in the water listening to the celebrity DJ.

I spin on the balls of my feet, raising my arms above my head. The memory of holding the pull up bar, my legs wrapped around Brad's waist flickers through my mind, and how good it felt to have him between my legs. I twirl and his toned, tattooed chest, glistening with sweat, hits me. I try to ignore it, but when I squat down rotating my hips, an image of him beneath me as I grind down on him flickers through my mind, causing tingles to work their way up my spine at the thought. My steps falter slightly, but I recover quickly, ready to take three steps forward and repeat the sequence. Beads of sweat roll between my breasts and I suck in a greedy breath as I shake my head to clear the images and prepare to go again.

Holy crap, where did that come from and why did I like it so much?

Chapter Ten

Brad

Havana's is buzzing; the music is so loud it vibrates beneath my feet. The flashing lights cast over the sea of bodies swaying to the music. This place wouldn't be my usual vibe, but it's where Chris, one of our investors at The Boardroom insisted we meet. With Jack a week away from his wedding, and Harry getting things in order before he leaves for London for the next six months, it was left to me to have this meeting. If you could call it that. It was a group of men talking business, smoking cigars, and drinking high end liquor. I've met Chris's business associates, Elijah and Henry, and truthfully, I thought they were entitled pricks, but I wasn't about to tell them that. They have money, and lots of it, and are very keen on helping us expand The Boardrooms, so, I play my part and entertain their shit talk and hang off their every word to seal the deal.

"So, Brad, Chris tells us you used to be in the military," Elijah asks, puffing on his cigar and leaning forward, his round belly hanging over the waistband of his pants.

"That's right." I nod. "Twelve years of service."

"Impressive. I bet you saw some things."

"Sure did," I mumble.

More than you could ever imagine

I suddenly feel the weight of the tags resting on my chest.

"So, what made you leave?" Henry, the younger one, asks.

Not wanting to divulge my life story to these men, I simply say, "It was time to leave. I served my country, and it was time to start a new venture." They both nod, seemingly happy with my response. We all notice a group of women on the dance floor. My eyes instantly zone in on one. She has her back to me, her dark hair trailing down her back like silk. Leather pants cling to her round ass, an ass that no doubt was built in the gym. The way she moves her hips seductively to the beat of the music has me hooked. I can't tear my eyes off her. I am thankful when her hair falls over one shoulder, and I am teased with a glimpse of her toned back. Something about the girl on the dance floor feels oddly familiar.

I decide I want to know who she is. I take a sip of my whiskey, savoring the bitter taste as I watch her move her body in a way that should be considered illegal.

A low whistle escapes Elijah's mouth. "Damn, who's the girl in the leather pants? I'd like to take her home."

Chris lets out a low chuckle. "What do you think your wife would say about that?"

"She'll be in bed with a headache. She'll never know." He grins in a way that makes me want to knock his teeth out.

What a prick.

My focus goes back to the dancefloor. The woman turns, and my eyes bug out when the familiar doll-like features of Gabriella Monroe come into view, and suddenly it feels difficult to swallow.

Fuck, I'm in trouble here.

"Fuck me, she's even better from the front." Elijah groans.

Yeah, you can fuck right off, dick face. No way is he going near her. I rise to my feet the minute I notice her leave the dance floor and head over to the bar.

"Fancy seeing you here," I shout over the music. Her head whips round, her long dark locks swinging over her shoulder as she gasps.

"Oh, my god. W-What are you doing here?" she stammers. Usually she would greet me with a hug, so her reaction tells me she's a little uncomfortable with my being here.

"Business. What are you doing here? Who are you here with?" I question, wondering what's got her acting so strange around me.

"Erm, my friends, from, umm, my gym. It's my friend Luna's birthday." She points to the group of girls.

"What can I get you?" the barman asks.

"A water for me, and she'll have a..." I say, directing my words to Gabriella.

"A cosmo, please."

The barman begins making our drinks, and I take a step closer to her, her sweet cherry scent invading my senses. Everything about Gabriella Monroe is so sweet, and the idea of how sweet she would taste enters my head, and I instinctively run my tongue along my lower lip.

She's your friend, your younger friend.

"Thank you. You didn't need to buy me a drink," she yells over the music, folding her arms across her body, her arms now covering her exposed stomach. She looks nervous, uncomfortable, and the idea doesn't sit well with me.

"You look different, you look—"

She interrupts me before I can finish. "Ridiculous right? I told Luna this wasn't very me."

"Hot. I was going to say you look hot, Gabriella." Her eyes widen as she looks up at me. She stands at a tiny 5ft 2 next to my 6ft 4 frame, and she has to crane her neck to look up at me.

"You think I look hot?" Her tone is surprised.

Has she seen herself?

"Yes, and just about every man in this club has eyes on you, so don't shy away. You have nothing to worry about." I worry I've taken my comment too far, but when her face softens and a small smile forms I relax.

I reach out and tuck a strand behind her ear, and she flinches in surprise. You'd have to be blind not to think Gabriella Monroe was anything but beautiful. With big brown doe-like eyes, olive skin, full lips, and a slight roundness to her cheeks, she is a natural beauty. She's not usually one for make-up but tonight she looks different, and I like what I see. I go to speak, but the barman places our drinks on the bar, and I hand Gabriella hers before taking my bottle of water.

"Water?" she asks, her brows furrowing.

"Yeah, I'm driving. I can take you home when you're ready," I offer.

Taking a small sip of her cosmo, she shakes her head. "No, I'm good. A few of us are going to get the subway back. There's a stop right by my apartment."

Like hell she is.

"No, I'll take you home," I say, my tone firmer this time.

"Brad, I'm fine, you don't need—"

I close the space between us, coming so close my teeth almost graze her ear, lowering my tone I say, "I'm not asking, Gabriella. I wouldn't be your friend if I let you leave here alone, when every man in this place is looking at you like they want to take you home and devour you. You are leaving with me."

Her body stiffens as she takes in my words. I straighten up and look at her.

"Okay," she says softly.

I give her a terse nod, happy she didn't fight me.

"I, erm, better get back to my friends." She gestures with her thumb over her shoulder, directing it toward the large group of women huddled together on the dance floor.

"Just let me know when you're ready to go," I say as she turns on her heel, heads back to her friends, and leaves me standing there watching her perky ass sway as I try to figure out where that came from. Sure, I want to make sure my friend gets home safe, but there was something else inside me that took over then, something that felt a lot like jealousy and possessiveness that crept into my soul. She's slowly looking like more than just a friend to me now.

Chapter Eleven

Gabriella

"... you're leaving with me."

Brad's words echo in my ears. They sent a shiver down my spine. It was unexpected, but a weird part of me liked it. I maneuver through the sea of bodies and find Luna and the other girls. I find Luna, her mouth a gape. "Who's the tattooed hottie that's looking at you like he wants to eat you for dinner?"

I turn my head and sure enough, Brad is still standing where I left him, leaning against the bar and watching... me?

"Oh, that's my friend, Brad. He's not looking at me like that," I shout back, hoping she can hear me over the thumping beat.

"Is he single?" Luna asks, her eyes dazzling in mischief, and a weird feeling in my belly stirs. The idea of Luna and Brad makes me feel weird.

"Uh, I think so," I say hesitantly.

"Oh, my god, put in a good word for me, will you? He looks like he would ruin you, in the best way." She winks, and there's that feeling in my belly again. What is it? Nausea? Jealously?

I give her a half smile. "Sure, I'll speak to him."

"You're the best." She squeals, grabbing a hold of my hand and pulling me further into the crowd, and Brad slips from my view. A thousand thoughts rush through my mind as I sway to the music. He said I looked hot. No man has ever told me I look hot. Sure, I get called pretty, but hot? Those kinds of compliments have always been reserved for others. Me, I'm the pretty one, the cute one, the sweet one. But here tonight, with eyes on me, I feel alive. I feel desired, but tell me why right now, I only want to be desired by the one man I shouldn't want to want me.

Three hours and two more cocktails later, I am ready for my bed. I'm used to dancing in heels, but even my feet have a limit. Brad has had a watchful eye on me all evening, and I've been grateful for it. There's been some real sleaze bags in here, but I've managed to avoid their advances. I say goodbye to the girls. They want to head to another club, but I am done.

I make my way over to where Brad has been perched for the past hour, talking to our mutual friend Chris. We all attended his wedding to Nancy, my friend from Teenhood last year.

"Hey, Gabby, great to see you again," Chris says, giving me a friendly peck on the cheek.

'Hey," I say sweetly, suddenly feeling really uncomfortable with what I'm wearing. This is far from my usual attire.

"Did you have a jacket with you?" he asks.

I shake my head, regretting not bringing one, but Luna told me it would ruin my outfit. Brad must sense my discomfort as he slides off his black suit jacket and hands it to me. I mutter a small thanks as I put it on. It drowns me so I roll up the sleeves and fold my arms around my chest to keep it together. It smells of him—spice and cedarwood—making my belly flutter. It's the most intoxicating, masculine scent. Very Brad.

We say our goodbyes to Chris and I follow Brad out the club and out to the busy New York sidewalk. Crowds of people gather, waiting for yellow cabs or chatting amongst themselves. Just as we approach the end of the sidewalk to cross the road, Brad reaches out his left hand out toward me wiggling his fingers as if gesturing for me to hold his hand.

I don't hesitate. I slide my hand into his and lace our fingers. It's warm and comforting and sends a little tingle up my arm. I know it's a friendly gesture, but I like how it feels.

We cross the street, never breaking our contact and when he sees my little legs are struggling to keep up with his wide strides, he slows his pace, which my feet in 4-inch heels are grateful for. He leads me towards his Porsche Panamera GTS, and I expect him to release my hand and round the car to the driver's side, but instead, he unlocks the car, opens the passenger door and gestures for me to get inside.

The cosmos have clearly given me some sort of courage because in a teasing tone, I say, "Such a gentleman."

A small smirk forms on his lips. "When I wanna be."

Those words do something to me, and suddenly I feel hot, and the desire to flee hits me. I can't be trapped in a car with him when I clearly can't control my thoughts, let alone my mouth. I fear I am about to make a fool of myself... again, in front of him. But like the obedient girl I am, I slide into the passenger seat. He closes the door climbs in the driver's side.

With us enclosed in his car, his proximity feels too much, and when he turns the engine on, I fumble for the window.

"You're not going to vomit again, are you?" he asks, concern in his voice.

"No, no, just wanted some air," I mumble.

Music blasts through the speakers. It's a song I've never heard before, but it feels very him. The dancer in me can't resist a good beat, but I resist, sinking into the soft leather of the seat.

We zoom through the streets of New York in silence. Brad is never much of a talker, but there is something about his silence I find comforting and safe. I can just be myself when I am around him. I don't have to pretend, and I like that about him. My eyes grow heavy, the sound of the engine and the music relaxing me, but the car begins to slow as we approach flashing lights that filter into the car.

"What the hell?" Brad mutters under his breath. I sit up straight and take in the sea of ambulances, police cars, and three cars crashed together, being blocked off by an officer placing road blockers out.

"Stay here," Brad says, exiting the car and walking up to the officer, where they exchange words before Brad walks back towards the car and gets back inside.

"What's going on?" I ask, worry in my voice.

"They are closing the road, potentially all night. Major accident."

A wave of panic washes through me. "H-how will I get home? This is the only way to my apartment other than the subway."

"You'll stay at mine." He says as if it's no big deal as he reverses the car, turning his head to look over his right shoulder, gripping the back of my headrest and spinning the wheel with the palm of his hand. That shouldn't be as attractive as I've just found it, but holy hell.

"I can't. I... I-I need to get home." I begin to sweat, shrugging off his jacket and tossing it into the back seat, instantly regretting it when my bare skin meets the cool leather.

I don't miss how his head turns slightly and his eyes scan my body till they meet mine. I swallow hard.

"I'll take you home in the morning, but you're not taking the subway."

Accepting my fate, I twiddle my fingers and say, "Okay, thank you."

I spend the rest of the journey mentally preparing to spend the night at his apartment. After my inappropriate thoughts in class a few days ago, that now seem to be a daily thing, I'm not sure how I am supposed to keep cool calm and collected when I'm inside his apartment, with him, alone. We pull into an underground parking lot, and he swings into a space effortlessly.

I follow him into the elevator and I bite down on my lip nervously, looking up at the ceiling.

The elevator dings and we step out to a dimly lit hallway, and I note his door is the only one on the floor.

"You'll have to excuse all the boxes. I only moved in a few days ago, and I'm waiting for the rest of my stuff to be delivered," he says, turning the lock and opening the door, ushering me in.

"That's okay, I don't mi—"

My words are cut off when he flicks the lights on. Small towers of boxes litter the open space. The dark kitchen cabinets catch my eye, and the large wooden island takes center stage in the area. The apartment has an industrial feel to it. I walk towards the middle of the room, taking in the exposed brickwork and high ceilings. A large window covers the far wall, giving a view of the Brooklyn Bridge. It's beautiful; it's dark, edgy, moody, it's so... him.

"It's amazing, that view," I say in awe, reaching the window and pressing my hand to the cold windowpane, watching the flickers of light speed across the bridge.

"Thanks. That view is what sold it to me," he says, heading toward the refrigerator. "Do you want a drink?"

I nod. "Water, please." When he hands me a bottle, I immediately twist open the cap and guzzle it down, desperately needing to ease this dryness in my throat I've had since I got in his car.

"I'm gonna take a shower. I'll find something you can sleep in," he says.

I swallow the last drop of my water, wiping my mouth with my fingertips. "No, no, that's fine. I can just sleep on the couch in this," I say, gesturing to my clothes.

"Gabriella, you can't sleep in leather pants and my new couch hasn't arrived yet." I look round the room and notice that there isn't a couch.

Oh Shit.

"My guest room isn't ready yet either. I only have my bed." An awkward silence falls between us as I stand wide eyed.

I can't share a bed with him.

My expression must say it all because, on his next breath, he says. "You can take my bed and I'll sleep on the floor."

The words are out of my mouth before I can think about them. "N-No, you can sleep with me."

"I, uh ha-ha." I nervously chuckle. "I mean, you can sleep in the bed with me. It doesn't have to be weird. I won't let you sleep on the floor, or I can sleep on the floor or a box, yeah, a box. I'm small enough, right, ha ha." And there's that awkward, goofy laugh I do when I'm nervous.

Dear God, Gabriella, stop talking.

A small laugh leaves his lips. It's deep and stirs something up inside of me.

"Gabriella, I'm not going to let you sleep in a box. We can share the bed."

"Great, looking forward to it. Do you want to be the big spoon or the little spoon?" I blurt out. Clamping my mouth shut I mentally chastise myself.

Seriously, stop talking.

He smirks and gestures for me to follow him. Before I do, I take off my heels, hook them on my fingertips, and follow him up a spiral metal staircase to what I presume is his bedroom. The industrial theme continues in his bedroom, with dark furniture and a large bed, and the same amazing view fills the wall of windows.

"You can sleep that side." He points to the side of the bed that's closest to the window and I'm thankful because that's the side I like to sleep on. He steps behind me and his hot breath dances across my neck. "But for the record, I'm always the big spoon." A small gasp escapes my lips, my heart racing at the idea of cuddling in bed with Brad.

"Let me find you something to wear," he says, turning to walk through a door that I assume is his closet. He's gone for a moment, just enough time for me to catch my breath, and he returns holding a black t-shirt.

"Thanks," I say, taking it from his outstretched hand.

"Do you want to use the bathroom first? My guest bathroom hasn't been set up yet."

"No, I can wait. You go first. I'm going to text Luna. Let her know the road is closed."

He nods and disappears to the bathroom.

I let out a long breath and flop down on the bed, staring up at the exposed brickwork and the dark wooden beams that run along the ceiling, telling myself to get it together. This is no big deal. It's Brad, your friend Brad. Your hot, older, tattooed, carved from stone friend, and you are going to share a bed with him.

The sound of running water echoes from the bathroom and I take that as my sign to get changed. I unzip my leather pants, sliding them down my legs and wince when cool air hits my bare ass.

You had to wear a thong tonight of all nights.

I fold the pants neatly and then whip my crop top over my head, covering my exposed breasts with one arm, just in case he appears. I don't want to make this any weirder than it is. I put on the t-shirt, thankful it falls to my mid-thigh and my ass isn't on full display. I take my phone out to text Ali that I won't be back tonight, so she won't worry.

I take a second to scan the room again, noting the dark bedding and the soft glow of the wall lights that illuminate the large room. Not only is it industrial, but there is something artistic about the space. A large painting hangs above his bed, all fine lines and brushwork in a mixture of grays and blacks. I couldn't tell you what it is, but I could stare at it for hours. As my eyes travel the wall, they land on the bathroom door.

He didn't close it.

The sound of the running water hitting the tile grows louder with every step I take. Before I know it, I am practically pressing my nose against the door and taking in the heavenly sight before me. Steam fogs up parts of the shower glass, but what I can make out. *Holy shit.*

The muscles on his tattooed back flex as his arm moves in rhythmic movements. A low groan echoes around the space. It only takes me a second to realize what he's doing. A small gasp escapes me. A growing ache forms between my legs, and I squeeze my thighs together to suppress it. His movements quicken, the steam filling the glass, making it harder for me to see. My own breathing quickens as my nipples harden against the fabric of his t-shirt.

What am I doing? I'm watching my friend 'self-care', as my friend Clara from dance school used to call it, in his shower like a creeper. But I can't tear my eyes away. His groans get a little louder, and with it, my heart rate. It's almost deafening, and the ache in my core gets heavier. I need some sort of release before I lose my mind.

He throws his head back and a deep growl erupts. I gasp at the sight, and it must be louder than I intend because his head whips round. Startled, I drop my phone, and it lands on my foot, ripping a cry from my lips. It must have bounced because I see the shimmer of the pink case under the chair. I bend down and crawl to reach it, the fabric of the t-shirt rising up my back, exposing my bare ass. When I look up, I'm greeted with a dripping wet Brad, a white towel wrapped around his glorious waist.

"Enjoy the show, Gabriella?" He looks amused.

Oh God, kill me now.

I spring to my feet, phone in hand, and I wave it at him. "No, I just dropped my phone," I say, sounding more breathless than should be considered acceptable at this very moment.

"What were you doing with your phone near my bathroom door?" he asks, folding his large arms across his chest, the grin never leaving his lips.

I do my best to think on my feet. "I was trying to get cell reception to call Ali. She's at home preparing for her work trip. She might be going to Europe, you know?"

"Is she?"

"Yeah, did you know some parts of Europe are like six hours ahead of New York?"

"I didn't," he replies.

"Yeah, well, it is, so I wanted to try and speak to her to get used to the time difference." I realize I am making absolutely no sense here.

"Interesting," he mumbles.

"I, erm, need to pee... on the toilet... in your bathroom... if that's okay?"

Why, why am I so awkward around him? Oh, maybe it's because you keep having thoughts of him naked and riding him, Gabby.

He stifles a laugh. "Sure, wouldn't want you to make a mess on my bedroom floor, now would we?"

I inhale a sharp breath, his words swirling between us. Words that imply something other than my need to pee, I fear.

"Thank you," I say hurriedly, rushing past him. I slam the bathroom door shut, pressing my back against it.

Well, shit... I don't think I could have made that any weirder if I tried.

Chapter Twelve

Brad

I shouldn't smile. I shouldn't have just enjoyed the way she squirmed when I caught her watching me. Shouldn't have gotten off in the shower when she was just meters away. But I couldn't help myself. There was no way I could share a bed with her and hold on to my restraint without giving myself a release.

I may be able to exercise self-restraint and create boundaries in most areas of my life, but I know my limits. I never expected her to know what I was doing, let alone watch, but a sick and twisted part of me loved that she did, and from her flushed cheeks and uneven breathing, I think she enjoyed it too.

I dry off and opt for a pair of black boxer briefs. Usually, I would sleep naked, but I'm not a complete ass. I don't want to make her feel uncomfortable, and truthfully, if she wants me to sleep on the floor of my guest room, I will. She exits the bathroom, looking sheepish, unable to give me eye contact, and that's not what I want.

I walk towards her, where she stands awkwardly, phone still clutched in her hand.

"Hey, are you okay? I didn't mean to make you uncomfortable," I say, keeping my tone soft.

She sighs in relief, and her shoulders sag. "Oh god, no, I'm sorry. I was the one who invaded your privacy. I hope I didn't make you feel uncomfortable. I'm so—" I cut off her words by tugging her toward me, and she falls into my chest. I wrap my arms around her like I've done so many times before. I know she's three words away from going into full blown Gabriella rambling mode; something she does when she's nervous, and that's the last thing I want her to feel because before anything else, she's my friend.

She relaxes in my hold, and we stand like that for a little while. It's been a really weird evening. I cup her face and angle her to look up at me. "We good?" I say, eyeing her curiously. A wide smile presses across her face.

"Yeah, we're good."

"Good," I say, pressing a kiss to her forehead and releasing the hold I have on her, needing to create a little distance because my brain is fried after tonight, and now isn't the time to make sense of it. I look at the clock and it's just gone 2 am. Knowing I'll be up in less than six hours, I walk towards my side of the bed and pull back the covers. She places her phone on the nightstand, and I flick off the lights, leaving only the glow of the Brooklyn Bridge filling the room.

"Do you want me to close the blinds?" I ask her as we slide into bed.

'No, I like the lights," she says softly, her words followed by a yawn. She wriggles around and moves so far over that she's practically hanging off the bed.

"Gabriella, I'm not going to pounce on you; there's no need to cling to the edge of the bed like a koala hanging from a tree."

A little laugh falls from her lips, and she buries her face in the pillow.

"I know that. I just wanted to give you your space. You know, kind of like I should have earlier."

I run my tongue along my bottom lip, grinning to myself.

God, this girl.

I reach over, hooking my arm around her waist, and tug her towards me, leaving a safe distance between our bodies for obvious reasons. She squeals in surprise, and I nuzzle my face into her silk hair. She smells of cherries and of something I shouldn't want. I should move my arm, I should give her the space a friend would, but when I feel her hand grip my arm and she wriggles a little closer, I leave my arm exactly where it is and let myself drift off holding on to the girl who is looking less like my friend and a lot like someone I desire.

Just before sleep steals me I whisper, "Night, Mia cara."

Warmth blankets my body and a bright light makes it difficult for my eyes to adjust. It takes a few moments for my vision to focus. The morning sun streams through the windows, filling the room with an orange glow. I turn to look at my alarm clock: 8.54 am.

What the hell? I never sleep this late.

I attempt to move my left arm, but something stops me. My eyes drift down to where my body is tangled with another.

Gabriella.

Her head rests against my chest, and her arm lies across my bare torso. Her leg hooks over mine, and my hand is resting against her bare hip. Her dark hair splayed out behind, and the morning sun gives her skin a glow. She looks like an angel, sleeping so peacefully in my arms that I don't want to move.

Usually, I would be panicked, thrown off kilter that my entire morning is now out of whack. I've missed my early morning run, and usually by now, even though it's a Saturday, I'd be heading to the club or doing something work related. But with Gabriella in my arms, the need to complete those tasks seems insignificant. A calmness I'm not used to washes over me, and I tighten my grip, not wanting to let her go. I've never been the dating kind, never really spent the night sleeping in the same bed as a woman, especially one where nothing happened, but I think I could get used to this feeling and this view.

My thoughts are interrupted when Gabriella stirs and stretches out beside me. I tilt my head to watch her as her eyes flutter open. She looks up at me through long, thick lashes, a bemused expression on her face.

"Good Morning, Gabriella," I say softly. It takes her a few seconds to register, and then she leaps up and grips the covers to her chest.

"Oh, my god," she shrieks.

Okay, not the response I was hoping for.

"Good morning to you, too," I say, my tone laced in sarcasm. I stretch my arms and twist my body slightly, releasing the tension in my back.

"Did we..." she says, and it's barely a whisper.

"No, Gabriella," I say dryly. "There was an accident, and the road was closed, remember?"

Realization dawns on her face. "I remember, sorry. I'm so used to sleeping with Ali, and I like to cuddle. I shouldn't have been lying on you like that. God, I really need to learn boundaries, I—"

I stop her rambling by tugging her by the arm and pulling her back down, flipping us both on our sides so we are chest to chest as I wrap my arms around her. She squeals and giggles and I let out my own laugh. I think I've laughed more around her in the last few weeks than I have in the last five years. Everything feels a little lighter when she's around.

"You don't need to have boundaries with me, okay? You want to stay in my bed and cuddle, you can. If I didn't want you here, I wouldn't have brought you over," I say, a slight sternness in my tone, needing to stress to her I don't do things I don't want to do. Life is too damn short to spend it pleasing other people. When you have experienced a lot of loss in life like I have, you learn that fact pretty quickly. Losing Scotty and losing family members at a young age will do that to you. Loss doesn't always mean death, another hard fact I've learned.

She stills in my hold, her big brown eyes looking into mine, and gives me a rewarding smile, and it's then I realize what I said. I offered her to stay in my bed whenever she wants.

"Do you want some breakfast?" I ask.

"Please," she says softly. I begrudgingly let go of her and drag myself out of bed. When I stand, I notice my morning wood.

Fuck.

Not wanting her to see, I head straight for the bathroom, making sure I shut and lock the door, knowing I'll need to deal with my situation before facing her again. I hit the shower button and turn the dial to cold. I take off my boxer briefs and step inside, my body stiffening as the cold jets of water hit my inked skin. It takes only a minute for my body to adjust to the temperature, and it's thankfully dealt with my throbbing dick.

Deciding I've tortured myself enough, I turn off the shower, stepping out, and wrapping a towel around my waist. I quickly brush my teeth and then leave the bathroom, searching for Gabriella, but she's nowhere. Assuming she's gone in search of my guest bathroom, I head for my walk in closet and stop in my tracks when I am met with Gabriella's bare ass bent over as she attempts to put on her leather pants.

"Well, this is becoming a regular thing, isn't it?" I tease. I know I've startled her when she yelps and loses her balance, nearly falling into my neatly hung shirts. On instinct, I reach for her, gripping her tiny waist and hauling her body into mine.

"Oh my god, you scared me." She gasps.

I look down at the ground and let out a low chuckle when I see her pants are stuck round her ankles.

"What were you doing?" I ask, amusement in my tone.

"I figured you'd be awhile in the shower, so I came in here to get dressed and put back your t-shirt."

Feeling the desire to tease her a little, I lower my mouth to graze the shell of her ear. "And why did you figure I'd be in the shower awhile, huh?"

She audibly swallows, and her spine stiffens. "Erm, you know, to get clean and stuff."

"If you wanted to see a morning show, baby girl, all you had to do was ask." She turns on her heel. Her cheeks flushing a crimson shade and I wonder if the bare skin of her ass cheeks would turn the same under my touch. The image of Gabriella bent over as I drive into her from behind comes to the forefront of my mind. I need to get a handle of these intrusive thoughts.

I step away from her, opening the top drawer of my closet and pulling free a pair of black sweatpants and turn and leave, putting space between us because if I didn't, I fear I'd do something I'd regret and something she doesn't want, because men like me don't end up with a woman like Gabriella.

Chapter Thirteen

Gabriella

I watch in fascination through the reflection of the mirror in the bridal suite of the Plaza Hotel at my friends. How beautiful and confident they are. I've admired Ria and Ali since the very first day I met them. The way they carried themselves, the way they fought through their trauma, and have become the women they are today.

I often wonder what it would feel like to feel comfortable in your own skin. To have this innate confidence that allows you to do and to be who you want. My parents struggled to have me. I was their miracle child. After countless miscarriages and attempts at IVF, my mom found out she was pregnant just when she was ready to accept that children weren't on the cards for her. My mom and dad poured everything into me, but with that came expectations. There was a way my parents expected me to behave, to talk, to dress, and to conduct myself, and when I didn't meet those expectations, I was made aware of their disappointment, and so it became easier to fall in line. To do as they asked and never question it. Some messed up part of me felt like I owed them. They tried so hard to have me. I should at least try my hardest to be what they hoped for, but whatever I did, no matter how hard I tried, it never felt enough.

So when I was fifteen, I rebelled. I got so tired of trying to be perfect that I let a friend convince me to sneak out and go to a party. It was a night that changed the entire trajectory of my life, and I have been trying to make up for it ever since. Doing everything I can to stay in my parents' good graces, even if it's at a detriment to my own happiness.

"... ready?" Ali's voice tears me away from my wandering thoughts.

I give my head a little shake, bringing myself back to the present. "Sorry, what did you say?"

"I asked if you were ready. Theodore wants Lexi and Elle to practice walking down the aisle one more time. He's convinced they will go rogue and do their own thing. Could you take them down? I'm still doing my makeup," Ali asks, pressing powder onto her cheeks. Theodore is the overbearing wedding planner, and he's fussed all morning about making sure Ria's daughters walk correctly down the aisle and don't mess up his vision.

"Sure, come on, girls," I call, zipping up my makeup bag. I give myself another quick look in the mirror. My lips are painted a crimson red, not my usual color, but the makeup artist insisted it would make my brown eyes pop, and compliment my dark hair and the olive green satin bridesmaid dress I'm wearing, and she's right. I don't hate what I see in the mirror. But maybe, just for today, I can lean in to being who I want to be. Take a little risk, be comfortable in my skin, and not worry about trying to be someone I'm not.

The wedding ceremony went off without a hitch. Lexi and Elle walked down the aisle like little angels, Jack and Ria declared their love for one another in front of their loved ones and now listening to Jack speak about his wife and watching the way he looks at her hasn't left a dry eye in the house.

"To Mr. and Mrs. Lawson," Harry yells. It's been filled with cream roses and candles, and it feels whimsical and romantic. As one, we repeat his words and raise our glasses to Mr. and Mrs. Lawson. I take a sip of my champagne, the bubbles tickling the back of my throat as I drain my glass.

"Woah, careful. I was hoping you'd make it to 10 pm before I had to carry you up to bed," Brad's voice teases beside me. I choke and reach for my napkin, covering my mouth to prevent spraying the table. Brad looks devilishly handsome in his black tux. He's undone his bow tie, and it hangs loosely around his neck, the top two buttons of his shirt open just enough to get a peek of the dark tattoos that I know decorate his entire body. His beard is a little thicker these days and his dark hair falls perfectly.

My mind drifts back to last weekend when I woke up in his bed, his body tangled with mine; how good it felt to be held by him, like the most natural thing in the world. My body heats at the memory, and I reach for my glass of water. I've always been physically affectionate with my friends, but men? That's a different story. But Brad has always been the exception. I know there isn't an expectation from him. I feel comfortable in his presence. He has a protective aura around him. He's a walking contradiction. He looks like he would kill you and keep you safe all in the same breath.

"Hey, that was one time in Vegas," I protest, needing to pull back the focus to his comment and not my burning desire to mount him.

"Actually, I've carried you up to bed four times now." He holds up his hand, signaling with his fingers. "Chris and Nancy's wedding shower, their wedding, Jack's birthday, and Vegas... but who's counting?" His tone is playful as he gives me a wink that could melt your panties off.

"I..." Lost for words, I bite the inside of my cheek, thinking of something to say.

"Aww, Gabs, he's your hero." Ali giggles behind her champagne. I glare at her through the table centerpiece and she holds her hand up in surrender.

The champagne must be working its way through my system because a confidence I don't usually possess falls from me. "I can handle my drink just fine, thank you very much. I don't need a hero, not tonight."

It turns out I absolutely do need a hero. I reached my limit about four drinks ago. I hug the toilet bowl, willing my body to either expel the alcohol from my body or let me live.

Nothing comes, so I stand on unsteady feet and make my way to the basin, washing my hands and then making my way back to the main ballroom. I focus on putting one foot in front of the other, my steps faltering, and I hit the wall. Giggles burst from me as I'm scooped up by strong hands.

"You okay there, Gabs?" a male voice asks. I turn to see who my savior is.

"Noah," I slur as I look at Ria's brother through glazed eyes. He looks like Ria, but his jaw is more defined and his hair short in a military-style buzz cut.

"Yes, that's me," he says playfully. "Do you want some help walking back?"

"I don't need a hero." My words sound even more slurred this time.

Jesus, Gabby, get it together.

"I know you don't, but I'm going to help you anyway, okay?" Noah snickers and walks us toward the ballroom.

"Okay, but don't tell the others, okay? Between you and me, I've had too many drinks," I whisper and then proceed to hiccup.

"You would never know. You're hiding it well," he teases.

"Thanks," I say, a little louder than required, and hiccup again.

Noah pushes us through the double doors. The sound of loud chatter and faint music fill my ears and the scent of liquor has my stomach rolling.

"I need to sit down," I declare, unwrapping myself from Noah's hold.

"I'll get you some water," he says, before he heads over towards the bar, where I can just about make out the back of Ali and Brad. I stumble toward some chairs, and the need to lay down takes over. I drag two chairs together and lay across them.

This feels nice. I'm just resting my eyes till Noah gets back.

My eyes flutter close and just as I drift into a peaceful slumber, cedarwood surrounds me and a voice I'd be able to pick from the noise in a crowded room says, "Come on, Mia cara, let's get you to bed."

Chapter Fourteen

Brad

Once again, I'm the one left carrying a drunk Gabriella to bed. I walk the long corridor towards Gabriella's room she was meant to be sharing with Ali but since she's off bumping uglies with Harry, and I'm the only one who knows after catching Ali leaving Harry's office earlier this week after they had a lunchtime hook up, I'm left looking after Gabriella, which normally I wouldn't mind, but after our unexpected sleepover last week my mind's fucked.

She's all I think about, well, her and the girl from the club. They intertwine in my head and plague my thoughts. I rag Jack and Harry for simping over their women, and yet here I am, about to board the simp train and join them. It concerns me how freely Gabriella wanders in and out of my mind, and I seem powerless to stop it.

We reach the bedroom door, and Gabriella stirs in my arms.

"Ugh, where am I?" she mumbles, her head slumped against my chest.

"I'm taking you to bed," I say, swiping the keycard in the door and pushing the door open with my foot. I hurry in before the door has a chance to swing back and hit us, and hit the light panel with my elbow, lighting the large room with a yellow glow.

I walk over to the edge of the large oak bed and carefully lay Gabriella down. As soon as her back hits the sheets, her drunk eyes try to focus on me, and I can't help but smirk.

"Ughh, Brad... the room... it's spinning... make it stop." She groans, covering her face with her hands.

"I'm a man of many talents, but even I can't do that," I say as I take a few steps back, sliding off my jacket and placing it over the back of the chair that sits next to a small round table and then sitting down, taking my phone and wallet out my pocket and dumping them on the table.

I roll the sleeves up on my shirt and undo another button. Gabriella sits up and swings her legs off the bed, sitting up and crossing her legs, drawing my attention to her shoes.

I'm not big on fashion, but there is something about the heels Gabriella wears when she's out—sexy and feminine—and I wonder what she would look like in just those white satin heels that have bows on the ankle. She stands and starts unhooking the thin straps of her dress, unzipping the side, and letting the fabric fall from her body to the ground.

My eyes widen in surprise. Fuck, she is wasted. She wouldn't get undressed in front of me if she wasn't.

"I'm hot," she declares, kicking her dress to the side. My greedy eyes rake up her body. Years of being a dancer and working as a Pilates instructor have crafted her legs into the sexiest legs I have ever seen. It's when I reach her waist and take note of her tiny white lace panties that tie at the sides and the matching strapless bra that a surprised groan escapes my lips and my dick twitches.

Fuck. Me

She pulls pins from her hair, placing them on the nightstand as if I'm not in the room, as if she isn't just standing there looking like every man's desire wrapped up in a white lace bow.

I clear my throat. "Do you need a hand?" My tone is heated and low.

What the fuck am I saying?

She pulls the last pin from her hair and slumps down on the bed. "No, I'm good," she says, bringing her foot up as she attempts to unbuckle her strap. Her foot falls twice, and I'm up and out of my seat and on my knees in front of her before she can make a third attempt.

I clutch her ankle in my firm grip and say, "Let me help." Her heavy eyes look at me and she nods slowly.

I begin unbuckling the dainty strap, slide her foot out, and place it on the ground. I reach the other foot, but she lifts it, pressing the heel into my chest as she lets out a giggle.

"You're like Prince Charming with the glass slipper."

I smirk as my hand strokes up the back of her calf, making her inhale sharply. "There's nothing prince-like or charming about me, baby girl."

"No?" she questions, an eyebrow raising in curiosity. "What are you then?"

"I'm more like the villain." I watch in fascination as a grin sweeps across her red lips. "I quite like the villains. I think they are often misunderstood."

"Is that so?" I say, sliding her foot out of her shoe.

"Uh huh."

I watch her abs flex as her breathing becomes heavier. Her bronzed skin makes the white of her underwear pop, and I try not to think about how easy it would be to tug at those ribbons on her panties and bury my face between her legs while I devour her.

"I like your hands," she says, her tone a little flirtatious, and I like it more than I should.

"Do you?" I say, my tone matching hers.

She nods slowly. "Yeah. I don't know anyone with tattoos except you. It's hot."

I don't say anything. Instead, for some unknown reason, I begin massaging her foot. She moans, and it spurs me on. She lets out a squeal when I reach a sensitive spot on the arch of her foot, but it's quickly replaced with another moan that has my dick throbbing painfully.

"I knew you'd be good with your hands," she says suggestively. I don't know where this newfound confidence of hers has come from, but it's edging me toward a very dangerous line that I might cross if I don't regain a little control here. I release her foot and stand over her, needing to stop this from going too far. She isn't a random hook up, it's Gabriella. A drunk Gabriella.

"Do you have something to wear to bed?" I ask looking round here room for an overnight bag.

"Uh, yeah. In the closet. Sorry, am I making you uncomfortable?" she asks, attempting to stand. She wobbles slightly as she folds her arms over her bare waist.

Needing to reassure her I say, "No, you're just making it really fucking hard to remain your friend and gentleman when you are looking like that."

Mentally slapping myself for saying that, I walk over to the closet, find her case and begin searching through it.

The first thing I'm met with is an ugly-looking baby pink jacket that I've never seen her wear. I lift it and hold it up. "What the fuck is this?"

She rolls her eyes and huffs. "Ugh, my outfit for my mother's lunch tomorrow."

"It's... tweed," I say, furrowing my brows.

"Oh, I know, and there's a matching skirt. My mother loves it. She owns an insane amount of tweed. Tweed jackets, hats, pants, skirts...news flash, Catherine," she says, animatedly holding up her hands. "Other materials are available for purchase."

I purse my lips together and hunt for something to cover her before I explode in my pants like a horny teenage boy.

"If you don't like it, why don't you wear something else?" I ask as I pull out various bags until I finally find a pair of silk pink pajama shorts and a matching top. It's still sexy as hell, but it will be more bearable than what she's currently wearing.

I pass them to her and she slips them on as she says, "Oh, dear God, no, my mother would clutch her pearls if I turned up looking less than perfect." She's clutching her neck with her hand, and suddenly the vision of my own hand wrapped around her neck as I thrust into her comes into view.

Fuck, I need to stop this.

"If you don't want to go, why don't you just say no?" She holds on to the bedframe for support and laughs like I've suggested the most ridiculous thing.

"Yeah, good one. You don't know my mom, or my dad... or me," she says the last part so quietly I almost miss it. I want to ask her what she means, but she continues. "Maybe I could just fake my own death, so I don't have to go."

"Seems dramatic," I say dryly, refolding her clothes in her suitcase, letting my OCD urges take over.

"Look, if you met my mother, you'd understand." She reaches round her back and, in a Houdini move, pulls free her strapless bra from beneath her top and then throws it in front of me in her open suitcase.

"Do you know what I'd love to do? Just once?"

I shake my head.

"Just once, I'd love to tell them to just... fuck off."

I laugh. "Do it."

"Whoops," she says, clamping her hand over her mouth and then releasing it. "And now I said a cuss word. My mom would spank my butt if she heard me say that... well, actually, she'd get the nanny to do it. She'd be scared of chipping a nail."

What the fuck.

I'm confused, concerned, and turned on all at the same time.

I don't know much about Gabriella's past or her parents, but from the little parts I've heard, or she's shared in the past, they are very strict, overbearing and put an insane amount of pressure on Gabriella, and for some messed up reason, she acts like she owes them something.

"I just want to say, no, Mom, I don't want to come to your pretentious lunch with your pretentious food with your pretentious friends," she says in a mocking tone.

"Do it. You're an adult. You can do what the fuck you want," I say and she looks at me, brows furrowed as if I have just suggested the most ridiculous thing.

"Catherine Monroe would never accept no. It's just easier if I go, trust me."

I don't say anything. Her phone pings with a message, and she roots around in her purse for it as I pack everything back into her suitcase.

I watch on as she attempts to type a message on her phone and walk, but she stumbles and drops the phone. She drops it for a second time, and that has me walking over and ushering her towards the bed.

"I think you need some sleep. It's been a long day."

"You take me to bed a lot," she says on yawn, lowering herself down on the bed.

"I do," I say in agreement. Unbuttoning my dress shirt.

"Why?" she asks, head twisted slightly, and her eyes track my movements as I shrug off my shirt and lay it over my jacket.

"Because you're my friend and I want to make sure you're safe. Besides, everyone else is occupied, so it was left to me."

Her face falls and I feel like an ass. I didn't mean for it to sound like that. Before I can reassure her, she interrupts my thinking.

"Is Ali hooking up with somebody?" she says, eyeing me curiously.

"I don't know, she just asked if I could look after you till, she got back."

She seems to accept my answer as she doesn't press me further. Instead, she stares up at the ceiling, hands linked and cradling over her stomach.

"I wish I could do that." She sighs.

"Do what?" I ask taking a step closer so I'm at the foot of the bed.

"Just hook up with someone." She says, waving a hand in the air.

"Why can't you?" I ask as I unhook my belt, pulling it free and dropping it to the floor.

She sits up, like the girl from the exorcist, and I flinch in surprise. She stares at me deadpan. "You've met me right."

"I believe so, yes," I agree, amusement in my tone.

"I don't do hook ups because one…" She holds up a finger to stress her point.

"I am awkward as hell, two, men don't go for girls like me, and three…" She pauses, looking down at the floor.

"I'd be a disappointment," she says quietly.

"I don't believe that for a minute."

"It's true, I haven't had sex in so long, I think I've forgotten what to do," she says, looking back at me.

My eyes widen at the revelation.

"How long has it been?" I ask not really wanting to know the answer. The idea of Gabriella having sex with someone makes my stomach recoil.

Why the fuck am I asking?

"Erm, about five years maybe... do we have any water in here?" she says nonchalantly as she gets up and proceeds towards the dresser, opening the cupboard door to the mini fridge.

"Sorry, what, five years?"

She takes out a bottle of water, unscrews the cap, and guzzles down half the bottle before she lets out a satisfied gasp but doesn't say anything.

"Gabriella, what do you mean, five years?" I say, my tone frustrated.

How has she gone that long without sex?

"Yeah. It was with my last boyfriend, Kyle, but he dumped me after I asked him to... umm... do something, and he said it was gross and then he ended it."

"He what?" I practically spit. "What did you ask him to do?"

She continues to drink her water, avoiding answering my question, but then she says,

"He never wanted to have sex, and when we did, it was so... so boring. I once made a joke about having sex outside. I read in a magazine that it heightens everything, you know, the thrill of being caught, and he said only animals have sex outside. Then I suggested he... go down on me. One of my friends from dance said her boyfriend did it and it felt amazing, so I asked him and he said it was disgusting and then dumped me the next day, so I've been too scared, I guess, to be with anyone else since."

She takes another sip of water and a strange feeling works its way through me. Anger maybe? The idea of someone treating her like that and denying her pleasure, and making her feel that way. I'm starting to see a side of Gabriella she doesn't show, or rather hasn't been allowed to show. A part of her that is fighting to come out, to be seen and wanted, and she just hasn't found the right person to share that with; the idea of that makes my chest feel heavy.

"I think your boyfriend may have liked cock instead." I say, in hopes of making her feel a little better.

She splutters, spraying water everywhere, and coughs. I rush over to her, taking the bottle from her hand and place it on the dresser.

Her head falls back and hysterical laughter erupts from her as she wipes her mouth with her fingertips, smudging her crimson lips ever so slightly as she does. She stumbles over her own feet and falls into my chest. I wrap an arm around her petite frame to keep her upright.

"Sorry... that... made me laugh," she says quietly.

"Good. I like seeing you laugh," I say, my eyes searching her face, taking in every delicate feature. I take in her big brown eyes, her flawless skin and the small beauty spot that sits just above the left side of her mouth. My attention is captured by her lips and the smear of lipstick. Without thinking I dust my thumb over the corner of her mouth and wipe away the lipstick. A small gasp falls from her lips and her hand flies up to cover mine as I cup her jaw. I should move my hand. But I don't. Instead, I bring my face closer to hers, inhaling her cherry and floral scent that's fast becoming my favorite smell. "But I'm serious. A woman's asking you to eat her out and you say no, then you need your head fucking testing," I say with a little more bite to my tone. "And for the record, you are absolutely the type of woman men go for. You're perfect, Gabriella, and I'm sorry some prick made you feel less than."

She smiles, flashing her perfectly white teeth. "He was a prick." She sniggers, and I laugh right along with her.

"Any man who would deny you what you wanted, Gabriella, isn't worth your time."

She bites down on her full lip, making my heart race and my blood pump harder around my body.

"You always call me Gabriella, never Gabby... why?"

"Because you have a beautiful name. Why would I want to shorten it?"

I watch her throat bob as she swallows hard, making my now aching bulge strain against the fabric of my suit pants.

Her suggestive eyes have me weak, and I know I could cave at any second. Tonight we are pushing limits, and I don't know how much longer I can resist. I could so easily bring my mouth to hers and taste how sweet I fear she is. But once I do there would be no going back. It would ruin our friendship because, ultimately, I know she doesn't want me like that. She doesn't see me like that, and I think her rejection would hurt more than battling with my feelings for her. That thought is sobering, and I grit my teeth and release her from my hold and step back, running a frustrated hand through my dark hair and turn away from her, exhaling.

Fuck.

"I'm going to get ready for bed."

She says nothing, just nodding as I walk past her to the bathroom, slamming the door and storming over to the counter in search of a toothbrush and paste.

I brush my teeth so vigorously my gums bleed, but I welcome the pain, and the sting when I rinse with mouthwash.

I consider taking a cold shower, but a small knock echoes from the door. I open the door to find Gabriella clutching her stomach.

I close my eyes, accepting my fate. I open the door wide, gesturing for her to enter. She rushes over to the toilet bowl and gets on her knees, expelling the contents of her stomach into the bowl. I walk over to her and crouch down beside her, gathering her hair in my hands and begin my routine of smoothing my palm over the center of her back in circles in an attempt to bring her some comfort and reassurance as she hurls into the toilet bowl.

I wait until she's done and pass her some toilet paper to wipe her mouth, and she collapses back against me. I hold her, waiting for her to catch her breath as she curls into my bare chest so perfectly as if she was made to fit in my arms. I wish things were different between us, I wish I could tell her how I feel, and act on my feelings and be with her the way I am desperate to be, but we aren't meant to be, I know she's meant for someone else, someone better, someone who deserves her in all the ways that I don't. I've done too many wrong things in my life to be worthy of a woman like her. Being friends with Gabriella may be the toughest test of my restraint, and it's becoming harder with every passing day to handle, but, if this is the only way I can have her, then I'll take it, because a life without Gabriella in it doesn't feel like one I want to exist in.

Chapter Fifteen

Gabriella

I am painfully hungover. I got an Uber here because putting one foot in front of the other was a challenge. I woke up alone with a text from Brad saying he had to sort something at the club. I don't understand what he needed to do at 9 am on a Saturday that was so important, so I am going to take a wild guess that it was to avoid me.

I made a complete ass of myself last night, and sitting here at my mother's WA lunch at the country club is my punishment.

".... and so I told Amanda that if she wanted to avoid the penalty charge, she needed to clear up her front lawn. Honestly, it's a disgrace," my mother whines.

I take another sip of water and then tear a chunk off my bread roll with my teeth, praying it eases the nausea while I internally roll my eyes at my mother's conversation with her friends. I shuffle in my seat, the tweed material of the skirt itching the backs of my thighs, making me want to rip it off.

My mom leans into me and hisses through gritted teeth. "Don't eat your bread like that, Gabriella, and will you say something?"

I chew my bread and don't say a word. Lifting my spoon, I scoop it away from me into the soup and bring it to my lips. It's something green and pale that looks a lot like what I was hurling up last night. I wince as the sickly taste hits my tongue and I swallow it down like it's the best thing I've ever tasted.

"Mmm, isn't this soup delicious?" I say with a toothy smile. My mother's friends all nod in synchronization like a pack of nodding dogs.

I turn to glance at my mother as she gives me a look that lets me know that she approves.

"It's so lovely you could join us, Gabriella. Your mother tells us how busy you are with city life in New York. You young ones, living life. I was married and on my second baby by your age. Is there anyone special in your life?" my mother's friend, Vanessa, asks with far too much interest for being casual. I'm all too familiar with that curiously disapproving tone, thanks to my mother.

Before I can speak, my mother places her hand over mine, letting me know she will take the lead here. "Gabriella has been seeing Janet's son, Patrick, and I must say they look great together."

Seeing is a bit of a stretch. I've had one date with him, and I've been avoiding his text messages.

"Speaking of... Patrick... over here," my mother calls, waving. I follow her line of sight to where Patrick and a group of people, all wearing tennis attire, stand around the bar.

Oh, kill me now. The universe hates me today.

Patrick grins before making his way over to our table, and I want to shrink and hide.

"Hello, Mrs. Monroe," he says, making my mother beam. "Good afternoon, ladies." His eyes fall to me. "Gabriella."

I give a weak smile. "Hello."

"Oh, Patrick, please, call me Catharine," my mother coos, and I nearly bring my bread roll and soup back up.

"Okay, Catharine. Gabriella, can I steal you for just for a minute?"

My mother takes my hand to haul me up out of my seat. "Of course. Take all the time you need."

Gabriella can speak for herself.

I glare at my mom, and she glares back at me with a look I know means 'behave and do as you're told'.

Pressing my lips together, I smile and follow Patrick toward the bar.

"Did you get my texts? I'm starting to think you're avoiding me." His tone is a little whiney and desperate and not at all appealing.

I let out a nervous laugh. God, I'm no good at this. "No, no, I've just been super busy. I was away, I've been working, and my friends got married yesterday so it's been busy busy. I was going to text you," I say, beginning to sweat.

"Well, good, because I was hoping to take you out again."

An awkward silence falls between us. My gut tells me to say no, to stand up for myself, but I feel my mother's eyes on my back, and with the pleading look Patrick gives me, I find myself caving. "Sure. When were you thinking?"

"Next week sometime? It's Henry's bachelor party tonight. We're heading to New York."

"Sounds good. You should try Aurora's. They do great cocktails."

Why did I say that? He doesn't strike me as a cocktail man.

He does his familiar toothy smile and says, "I'll check it out. So, I'll call you later in the week and we can fix a date?"

I nod. "Sure." Then, to my shock, he leans in and presses a kiss to my cheek. It's quick, and yet I didn't recoil. Hmm, maybe I judged him too quickly last time. Maybe I am the problem. I write men off too quickly, and maybe I am being a little stubborn because it's someone my mom set me up with. I may not have recoiled in disgust when he just kissed my cheek, but I know I didn't feel the way I did when Brad held me last night, and for a fleeting moment, I thought he might kiss me. It's all I've thought about this morning. The memory makes my stomach contract and flutter. I don't have the time to wallow and think about my messed-up feelings towards my friend. I turn on my heel and head back to the table of waiting women. I take my seat and shuffle my chair in as I place my napkin over my lap, noticing all eyes on me.

"Is everyone okay?" I ask, confusion in my tone.

"Yes, darling. Just you and Patrick look so good together. What did he want?" my mother asks.

"Oh, he asked to take me out next week." The table erupts into a chorus of pleased sounds.

"How lovely." My purse hanging off the back of my chair begins to vibrate. My mom huffs. "Will you answer that. It keeps ringing. You should have turned it off, Gabriella. It's very rude."

I hurry to pull the phone free from my purse and see Luna's name flash across the screen. "Sorry, it's a work client. I need to take this," I say, excusing myself. As I exit through the doors, I swipe my phone and bring it to my ear.

"Hello."

"Finally, girl, I've been calling you all day," Luna's voice wails through the phone.

"Sorry, I'm at lunch with my mom. What's up?"

"Just checking you'll be there tonight. I'm heading early today."

"Oh crap, I forgot." I rub my forehead feeling a headache coming on.

"Please, Gabs."

"Yes, yes, I'll be there."

"Yessss. Thank you, thank you," Luna yells so loudly that I have to pull the phone away from my ear as I chuckle.

"Okay, see you later. Bring your best moves. It's going to be a busy night."

I wait in anticipation for my cue to start spinning in the hoop. My skin tingles with nervous energy.

Every time I do this, I remind myself they can see me, but I can't see them. I always open the nights I work. I never venture off the stage. I never give private dances. It's been my little secret for two years. Luna started here for some extra cash. She hates living off her parents, and she asked me along. I did one night and I've worked one to two nights a week for the past two years. I don't do it for the money. No, I do it for the buzz, for the thrill of being wanted, desired, to have all eyes on me, but with no expectations, no judgment. I feel powerful, in control, things I have lacked all my life, and it makes it all the more enjoyable knowing no one knows it's me hidden behind my mask.

The men cheer as the hoop spins, and I contort my body.

The beat changes, and that's my cue, along with four other girls, to enter through the curtain. The heat of the stage lights and the smell of liquor hit me as soon as I release the hoop, and it disappears up into the air. The roar of men's voices booms over the music, and my blood starts pumping.

I make my way over to my usual spot, swaying my hips as I saunter to the opposite side of the stage. I reach up and grip the pole and slowly walk around it, lifting my other hand and wrap it around the cool steel, then pressing my back and butt against it, sliding down and then working my way back up. Whistles and cheers filter through the air, and I continue with my routine and with every passing beat and each turn and sway of my body, I grow more comfortable and thrive off the atmosphere.

The track changes. It's slower and sultrier, and this is when most girls descend the stage and make their way through the audience, tempting men and encouraging them to request a private dance. A moment of bravery flickers through me, and my feet carry me down the steps in front of me, and I walk around the tables next to my side of the stage. I run a hand along the back of a man with light brown hair wearing a dark blue shirt.

"Yess, baby, you can come over here and sit on my lap..." one man from the group calls. I ignore his advances and move to the next table, where a large group of men sit. I spy Luna's auburn hair flash under the lights, and I make my way over to her, swaying my hips seductively.

"Yes, honey... bring that sweet ass over here," another man calls. It should repulse me, and in any other setting, it would, but here, I feel safe. A thrill zaps through me, and I lean into Luna, who's wearing an emerald green leotard and a gold mask. We move our bodies as one, earning more attention from the men at the table, and I feel high from the thrill of it.

The song starts to fade out, and Luna takes my hand and guides us both back up on stage to end. Two girls spin in hoops that hang above us. They look so elegant and ethereal and for just a second,

I am so caught up watching them, that I forget I need to find my position on stage.

Spinning and dragging hands up and down my body, I turn and grip the pole, leaning my head back, my long, dark hair sweeping the floor as I arch my back. I rotate my body so I am against the pole just as the song ends, the lights fade and cheers and whistles fill the room. My breathing is ragged, my body on fire from exertion, but the feeling pulsing through me is euphoric.

We make our way backstage, everyone cheering and high fiving the successful performance. Only a few girls are due to go back out for another routine before the private dances go ahead in the side rooms.

Jessica, the stage manager, hands out bottles of water, and I take one gratefully. I press the bottle to my burning forehead and welcome the chill and cooling effects it offers.

Luna pushes her way through the crowd of girls and throws her arms around me. "Aaaah, Gabs, you were hot out there."

I wrap my arms around her. "Thanks. I actually had fun out there in the crowd."

"Well, that's good to hear because you have been requested for a private dance."

I almost choke on my own saliva. "Sorry, what?" I spit out.

"Someone has requested to have you in one of the rooms."

I freeze, my eyes widening to saucers behind my mask. "I... I... I can't do that. No, Luna, no."

"Yes, you can."

"No, I can't," I protest.

"Yes, you can, and you are. Come on, Gabs. We've been doing this for a couple of years together. Just dance for a few minutes and then leave."

Fear floods my body, and my heart rate picks up, alerting me to danger. No, I can't do this. Dancing on stage is one thing, but privately, that's another.

"Luna, please, I can't be alone in there. What if he tries something, or…"

"Hey," she says, gripping my shoulders and staring me dead in the eyes, "there are cameras in the room. The clients know the rules—no touching unless you initiate it. Besides, if you feel uncomfortable and want to end the dance, hold two fingers up to the camera above the door or hit the button on the wall, and security will be in, okay?"

I mull over her words and nod slowly. Yes, I can do this. I promised myself I'd come out of my comfort zone, which is why I walked into the crowd in the first place. I'm safe, and I don't even need to go near him. Yes, I can do this.

"Okay, show me the room."

Luna walks me to a room with a gold number seven in the center of the black door, turns the handle and opens it. I step inside and with each step I take, my heels clatter against the shimmery, hard floor.

A singular chair sits at one end of the space and at the other end of the room is a pole like the ones on stage.

"So, how does this work?" I say, clawing my wrist with my nails, making my skin sting.

God, I am nervous.

"You'll be in here waiting. You can face away to start with if that will make you feel more comfortable. That's what I do. He will take a seat, the lights will go down, and the music will start. You dance, and it's up to you if you want to go closer to him and give more of a lap dance or stay near the pole."

I nod.

Luna takes my hands and gives them a squeeze. "You are in control here. You have all the power in this room, not him."

"Okay…" I say, my words barely a whisper.

"Relax and enjoy. I'm going to be next door. I'll see you after." She wraps her arms around me and squeezes me till it's hard to breathe.

"Good luck. You've got a few minutes before they let him in," she says, releasing me before she heads out of the room.

My legs feel like jelly as I make my way over to the pole and grip it with a shaky hand, turning around so my back is to the waiting chair.

I tap my nails against the pole, counting to ten in my head to calm my erratic breathing. The click of a door opening makes me flinch, and footsteps enter the room.

He's here.

My natural instincts is to turn around and get a look at him, to say hello or try and get a sense of what he might like or ask him why he chose me. But I remain in position, hand gripping the pole and one leg slightly bent, ready to twirl around the pole.

The chair creaks as he takes his seat and then silence. My heart beats so loudly I'm sure he must hear it, and my breathing is no quieter. I close my mouth, releasing a slow, calming breath and as I do, the lights turn down to a low silver hue, casting a shadow of myself on the wall in front of me.

The song *Dirty Diana* blasts from the speakers, taking me by surprise, and my mouth quirks up in a smile. I know Luna had something to do with my song choice. Diana is my club name, and it seems pretty fitting.

I take hold and walk round the pole, keeping my gaze fixed on the floor. When I do a full rotation, I lift my head slightly, letting me catch sight of his black boots and dark jeans. For just a second, I question if I recognize the boots.

Thousands of men have these boots, Gabriella.

Luna's earlier words about me having all the power ring in my ears and it gives me the confidence to move away from the pole and glide over toward the waiting man in the shadows.

Feeling brave, I rotate my neck, flicking my hair as I do, then placing my hands over my pubic bone and slowly smooth them up my body, all the way up my neck, pushing my hands into my hair. Adrenaline pumps through my body and I know I could get addicted to this high. I take two steps forward and just as more of him comes into view and I'm almost in front of him I turn away from him, leaving my ass in full view, my leotard having ridden right into the crack of my cheeks.

Deciding to embrace it, I move back till I feel my heels hit the front of his boots and rotate and grind my ass down into his lap, hovering just enough to make contact, but not so I am fully seated. A low growl sound comes from him and it spurs me on. I once again repeat the movement, but this time I brace my hands on his thighs. They are thick and hard and my hands tingle. My alter ego takes over and I widen my stance so I am straddling his lap, but still I have my back to him.

My eyes widen when I feel his growing erection between my ass cheeks. I don't know if this is pushing the boundaries of what's acceptable in here. I should stop, I should step away, but it gives me a twisted thrill knowing I am making this man feel this way. That me, and only me, is having this effect on him.

I continue my torture, and my body freezes when large hands grip my waist. That should be my limit. But it isn't. His strong hands sear into my skin, and I decide I want a glimpse of my mystery man. I rise to my feet. He must sense what I'm about to do because he lifts me from his lap and spins me so I face him. A little squeal escapes my lips, and my feet falter. I close my eyes, reaching out to grip the man's shoulders to steady myself. On an exhale, my eyes spring open and meet dark, whiskey eyes I'd recognize anywhere.

Chapter Sixteen

Brad

"Gabriella," I manage to say on a struggling breath.

Gabriella, she's here. She's the girl in the red mask. The girl I haven't been able to stop thinking about since I laid eyes on her. I came here in hopes of getting rid of my thoughts of Gabriella. She's plagued my every waking and sleeping moment, and it's messing with my head. I thought finding this mystery masked girl and having a moment alone with her would alter my brain, help me forget, and move on. Give me a new focus and obsession, but now I know the two are the same woman, I am absolutely fucked.

"W-What are you doing here?" she says, just loud enough for me to hear her over the music.

"What am I doing here?" I hiss in annoyance. "What the fuck are you doing here?" I don't mean for it to come out as harshly as it does, but a mixture of emotions is invading my brain, and I don't know what to think or feel.

Gabriella. It was her all along.

I have so many questions. I step closer to close the strained space between us, but she steps back and rushes to the door.

"Wait," I yell, and I'm hot on her heels. She runs down the corridor towards the exit sign, her heels clicking against the hard floor.

"Hey. What's going on?" a man's voice bellows down the corridor, but I ignore him. Gabriella disappears into the darkness of the open door, and I pick up my pace to reach her. She clambers down the steel fire escape, and I take the steps two at a time, my chest burning with a mixture of exertion, fear, and utter confusion.

"Hey." The voice from earlier is now behind me. A security guard, I assume, rushes down behind me, but I continue.

"Gabby, wait," I holler as she disappears behind a wall. I never call her that, but I need her to stop and listen to me. I round the wall and find her just as she tears off her mask and tosses it to the ground. Before I can speak, the guy who was chasing us appears, gasping for breath.

"Are you okay? Do you need me to throw this asshole out?" he says, pointing at me.

I don't give her a chance to answer. "This asshole is her boyfriend, so fuck off." I don't know why I said it. I just need him to go so I can talk to her.

"No, I'm fine. He can stay. I'll be back in soon." She tilts her head just enough for me to see her broken expression.

The man nods, giving me a suspicious look, and I glare right back.

Once he leaves, I take a few steps towards her and she backs away, holding her hands up in surrender.

"Brad, please, just... just go and pretend this never happened," she begs, her voice cracking.

"I can't do that. I want to know what you are doing working here."

"It's none of your business," she bites back, her tone full of anger.

Annoyance swells in my gut. "Well, you made it my fucking business when you gave me a lap dance, Gabriella, so start talking." Her body flinches as if my words have physically struck her.

"I didn't know it was you," she hisses. "If I knew it was you, I wouldn't have agreed to do it." Her words cut like a knife, deep and painful.

Any anger I held towards her dissipates as I watch a tear roll down her cheek.

I close the space between us, tugging her into my chest and gripping the back of her head as I press a kiss to her temple. Sobs wrack her body and I hug her.

When her cries begin to settle, she lifts her head to look at me. "I'm sorry. I didn't mean it to sound like that. I just meant, no one knows I work here." She sniffs.

"No one?" I question, furrowing my brows. She shakes her head. "Ali and Ria don't know?" I question.

"No, and you can't tell them, please." Her tone is pleading as she steps away from me, creating some distance, which I hate.

"I won't, but you need to help me understand. Are you doing it for the money? Are you in some sort of trouble, because I can help, you can always come to me and—"

She cuts me off. "No, no, it's nothing like that. It doesn't matter," she says, trying to end this conversation, but I'm not budging.

"It does matter," I say sternly.

"No, it doesn't. You wouldn't understand," she says as she frees herself from my hold and steps away.

"Try me," I say in a challenging tone, crossing my arms over my chest.

Her eyes flare with anger under the glow of the street lamp, and I've never seen them like that, and it hurts, knowing she's kept such a big part of her life a secret from me.

"I wanted to feel something, somewhere that no one knew me. A place where no one would judge me, a place where I would feel seen."

My brows furrow, not understanding what she means. "How long?" I ask.

"Two years," she whispers, and hangs her head as if she were ashamed.

"Fuck, Gabriella, are you serious?" I spit. Anger flaring in my chest. Thinking of how many men she may have danced for, how many have looked at her the same way I have been doing. I clench my fists and take a deep breath before speaking again.

"You're right, I don't understand. Why would you need to work here to feel like that?"

"Because," she bellows, wiping her cheek with her hand, sniffing before continuing, "all my life I've been told what to do, how to act, what to wear. Men have either wanted me in a way I wasn't ready for or made me feel like I was the problem, like I wasn't enough. I'm twenty-five years old and I am terrified of intimacy and letting a man into my life because I am scared I won't be good enough." She pauses, looking up at the dark night sky. "I don't know if you've noticed, but it takes me a while to feel comfortable around people."

Yes, I had noticed. I notice more about her than she realizes.

"I want to date. I want to find someone to settle down with, but I can't get past a first date because I shut down and cut them off because I know what the next part will be. They will want intimacy and I freak out and run scared."

"Gabriella, if a man isn't willing to wait until you feel comfortable being with them, then they aren't the man for you," I say, jealousy burning in my core.

"I know that, but I'm scared I'll never be ready, so a friend asked if I would be interested in dancing here, and I took it. I thought it might make me feel more confident, more comfortable in my own skin so that I can feel ready to open myself up, maybe find someone to..."

"To fuck. You want to fuck one of these men?" The words fall out, leaving a bitter taste in my mouth.

She physically flinches at my words again, and I feel like the biggest asshole.

"No, I didn't come here so I could fuck someone," she spits back.

"I didn't mean that, I..." I stop, at a loss for words because truthfully, I don't know what to think or feel. My mind is a jumbled mess.

A silence falls between us, the tension and awkwardness getting too much. I reach into my back pocket for my cigarettes and lighter. I pull one from the box, placing it between my lips and flick the lighter. A small flame glows and I suck on the tip of the cigarette till it ignites. I stuff the packet and lighter back in my pocket. Taking a long drag, bringing my thumb and pointer finger to grasp the cigarette, tilting back my head, I puff the smoke into the night sky and let my shoulder sag, my body relaxing just a little as I exhale.

I'm not a big smoker, not now anyway. I only allow myself one a day and some days I don't feel the need, but right now I could chain smoke this entire pack with how high my stress levels are.

"I'm sorry," I say quietly. "I don't mean to be an ass."

She folds her arms across her waist protectively. "I know."

"You could have come to me. I would have helped."

I take another drag of my cigarette and puff the smoke into the air. Mocking laughter falls from her.. "Yeah, okay."

"What's so fucking funny?" I hiss. Shit, I am pissed. I need to rein it in. It's Gabriella.

"You, saying I should have come to you. Don't you think that would be a bit weird? H*ey Brad*, I know you don't see me like that, but do you think you could fuck me because you seem to be the only man I feel comfortable around and then I can get over this issue with intimacy and sex so that I can find myself a boyfriend and potential husband. Yeah... that wouldn't have been weird at all." She falls back against the wall, running her hands through her hair.

I stand there, stunned, replaying her words. She feels comfortable around me. She wants to find someone to settle down with. Too many thoughts and emotions swim in my head. I take one last drag of my cigarette and toss it to the side. Blowing out the smoke as I step towards her.

"You think I don't see you like that?"

She shakes her head.

A hiss escapes my lips, and I run my hand through my hair, shaking my head. "I'll do it." The words leave my mouth without really thinking about the gravity of what I'm offering, but all I know is I want to help her. I want to be that person for her, I can't bear the thought of someone else being with her right now, helping her with this, and it's with that thought that I realize, I'd do just about anything for her.

She backs up, her brows furrowed as if she were processing my words.

"You're insane. You can't do that."

"Why?" I ask, taking a step closer.

"Because it would make things weird, and you don't..." I press my index fingers to her lips to stop her talking, sensing she's about to ramble. I lower my head so I am painfully close to her lips.

"If you need me, use me. If being with me helps you, then I'm all yours, Gabriella. For as long as you need."

I remove my finger from her lips, and to stress my point further, I cup her face, running the pad of my thumb over her bottom lip, causing her eyes to flutter closed.

"And to be clear. I do see you like that." My voice is low and gravelly, full of heat and want for this woman, and then I do something I never let myself do. I give in to my urges and I press my lips to hers. It soft and gentle, it's everything I'm not, but for her, I want to be, because Gabriella doesn't deserve the fractured and tortured parts of me.

Her body melts into mine as her hands fist my top. I tap my boot against her feet, signaling for her to widen her legs, and she does, allowing me to push my knee between her thighs. To my surprise, she grinds her center against my thigh and lets out a whimper as I push my tongue inside her mouth. She welcomes it, and our tongues intertwine, creating the most intoxicating and consuming kiss I've ever experienced. I'm not a big kisser, never understood the need for it. It felt too intimate, but Gabriella is the type of woman I sense craves that level of intimacy, but she's also someone I want to show it to, and that scares me. I don't have a chance to let my thoughts wander anymore.

Cheers and whistles ring out. We break the kiss and turn to see a crowd of drunk men gathered at the end of the car park, attempting to get into waiting cabs.

When we turn back to each other, our eyes lock, and I swallow the lump in my throat that's making it feel impossible to breathe. The reality of what I have just offered her weighs heavy in the pit of my stomach. We've already crossed the line of friendship and entered new territory with that kiss. I know I am playing with fire, I'll worry about all the "what if's" later, but for now I need to know what she wants.

"So, what will it be, Gabriella? Do you want my help?"

Chapter Seventeen

Gabriella

The last part of my heels class went by in a blur. I drove back to my apartment on autopilot, not remembering any of the journey. As I turn the key in my front door, my phone vibrates in my gym bag. I pull it free and see a couple of new texts.

Brad
> Gabriella, please call me. We need to talk.

I don't reply—I've been ignoring him since he made his offer three nights ago—and open up Ali's message.

Ali
> Hey G, I don't think I'll be home until early hours. Don't wait up. Love you.

I walk into the apartment and head to my room, tossing my gym bag on the floor and make my way to my bathroom. My body feels hot and sticky from class and I am desperate to wash the day off.

I step under the strong jets of hot water and instantly feel my body relax. Closing my eyes, I wipe away the day's make up. Flashbacks of Brad brushing my cheek and pressing his lips to mine almost has me reaching between my legs. I've never been kissed the way he kissed me. It was tender, and slow, and far more intimate than I think it was meant to be. I've always fancied Brad, but quietly. I'd never act on it or ever imagine us being together because it just wouldn't ever happen. I was his friend. His younger, quiet, and slightly awkward friend. I may be inexperienced and naïve, but I am switched on enough to know that friends don't kiss friends that way. I reach for my favorite cherry-scented shampoo, lather up my hair, and massage my scalp. Everything aches: my head, my shoulders, my back. I don't know if it's from my shift at the club, the endless punishing workouts I've put my body through the past two days, or the weight of guilt for treating Brad the way I did.

I mull over my words to him as I exit the shower and begin drying my hair. I put on my underwear, pink silk PJs and matching silk robe, and decide a night rotting on the couch is needed.

I feel too churned up to eat, so I decide on a fruit smoothie and settle down to watch my favorite TV show. I'm about halfway through an episode when a knock sounds at the door.

I pause the TV. A muffled voice comes through the door and nerves twist in my stomach. "Gabriella, I know you're in there. Please open the door."

I hesitantly make my way over to the door and open it. There he stands, head to toe in black, leaning against the doorframe. "Can I come in?" he asks.

Unable to speak, I nod and gesture for him to come inside. Folding my arms across my front protectively, I suddenly feel so small and awkward. I can't look him in the eye after the other night.

"Do you want a drink?" I ask as I turn to head towards the kitchen.

"Water, please." he says, making his way over to the couch where he sits down. "Is Ali home?" he asks, looking round the room as if he were looking for evidence of her being here.

"No, she's out for the night." I take two bottles of water from the fridge and make my way over to him, sitting back in my spot on the couch, still avoiding looking at him as I pick at the label on my water bottle.

"Is this the famous *Friends* show you love?" His question surprises me. My head springs up to look at him, and I'm met with a grin that would have any woman opening up their legs for this man. My body heats and my cheeks flush at the idea, and I swallow hard, so hard I know he notices when his gaze drifts to my throat.

"It is," I say so quietly I am unsure if he heard. An awkward silence falls between us, and I'm close to jumping out the window to get away from him.

We sit through an entire episode of Friends without saying a word.

"Okay, so tell me if I got this right. They don't know that they know," Brad murmurs, looking at my TV with a perplexed expression.

I chuckle under my breath, loving that he was actually paying attention.

"Yes, they didn't know that they knew, but now they know, so they don't know that they know, you know?" I say to him.

"No," he says flatly, rubbing his forehead as if a headache were forming.

I cover my face with a cushion to hide my amusement. The credits roll and he shuffles around on the couch next to me. "We need to talk about the other night," he says firmly, and I drop the cushion to look at him.

"Do we though? I'm good with pretending it never happened." I laugh awkwardly and I want to slap myself.

"Yes, Gabriella, we do and to do this, I'm going to need you to look at me." His tone is firm.

I try to look at him, but I can't. My body won't move. He rises from where he sits and kneels in front of me, taking the water bottle I'm fiddling with and places it on the coffee table.

He reaches for my face and tilts my chin with his forefinger and thumb. "You have nothing to be ashamed or embarrassed about. I am here to help you if you still want." His words sink in, and his calm and collected demeanor helps all my fears and anxiety over this whole situation dissipate. I know Brad. If he doesn't want to do something, he simply won't do it. His being here solidifies that he meant what he said.

"Okay," I whisper. A mixture of anxiety and excitement swirls inside me. I'm really going to do this with him?

He releases my chin and sinks back into the couch next to me. "So, let's talk about it. What do you need from me?" He says it so calmly as if he were asking me for my takeout order.

My eyes widen to saucers. *Well, that's a loaded question.*

"I don't really know. I've never done anything like this. I don't know what you want me to say."

"Just say what's on your mind."

"I'll need a drink for that," I joke. As soon as the words leave my lips, he's up off the couch and heading towards the kitchen.

"What are you doing?" I ask, a slight tremor in my voice. He opens the fridge and pulls out a bottle of rosé wine. He opens a couple of drawers until he finds a bottle opener.

"Loosening you up," he states as he pulls the cork out.

"Where are your glasses?" he asks, and I point to the cupboard behind him.

He fills a glass halfway and brings it back over to me.

"Are you not having one?" I ask, confusion in my tone.

He shakes his head.

I bring the glass to my lips and swallow down the sweet crisp wine. I'm not a big wine drinker, but right now I could drain the bottle.

"Woah, easy, you're just taking the edge off here, not drinking yourself into oblivion. I need you coherent for what I have planned for you." His words have me choking. He rubs circles on my back as I catch my breath.

"What you have planned for me?" I splutter.

"We'll call it lesson one," he says with a slight smirk.

"And what's that?" I ask, not sure I really want to know, but wanting to know all at the same time.

"If this is going to work, I need to know what your limits are, what you are willing and not willing to do. What you want to do. What you like and what you don't like."

He reels off his words and I have a wave of bravery because I freely say, "Well, I'm up for anything because I have very little experience. You might as well call me Veronica the virgin, haha." *Oh God, Gabby, shut up.*

The smirk never leaves his face as he says. "But you've had sex, right?"

"Yeah, well, if you can count lying there while your boyfriend lies on top of you like a stiff board and keeps his socks on and only gets himself off, then yeah, sure, I've had loads of sex."

"You can't be serious?" he asks, shock in his tone.

"Deadly," I say, taking another sip of my wine.

He scratches at his temple, and I continue to sip on my wine. God, I'm gonna need another glass in a second.

"Okay, so what got you off? What did you like?"

"I wouldn't know. I never did," I admit quietly, my cheeks warming with embarrassment.

"Never what?"

"Finished, reached the finish line, got the grand finale."

"Are you telling me you've never had an orgasm?" he says, eyes wide, as if I am saying the most unhinged thing.

'No, well yes, I think so. I have alone, I think, but..." I stumble over my words. This feels so weird to talk to him about in such a casual way. I don't want him thinking of me as some inexperienced juvenile, but that's how I feel. His hands land on my thigh, and the contact has me flinching. Not with fear, but with an unexpected surge of desire for this man. I want to do this with him, but I'm scared he doesn't want me in the same way, and he's only doing this out of obligation to help a friend out. I place my wine glass on the coffee table in front of me and I begin snapping the elastic on my wrist as the awkward silence falls between us. He reaches for my wrist, and I stop. My band snapping is replaced with the pad of his thumb, rubbing soothing circles over the red flesh, and with every stroke, I feel myself relax a little.

"Gabriella, you would know if you had one or not. It's a yes or no answer," he says softly.

"Yes, yes, I have," I say quickly, trying to appear more confident than I really feel.

He stands up, and I'm convinced this is it, he's regretting what he offered and he's leaving. But he begins removing his jacket, unhooking the cuffs on his dress shirt, and rolling up his sleeves, revealing the intricate artwork on his forearms.

"W-what are you doing?" I lift the wine glass and go to take another sip of my wine, but he plucks it from my hand, draining the glass and placing it back down on the coffee table. He kneels down in front of me and my breath catches in my throat.

"Giving you an orgasm, one that won't have you questioning if it is one or not." He says it so casually, as if he's offering me coffee and a bagel.

"R-right now?" I stutter.

"Right now," he repeats. "If that's what you want?" I sit there, too stunned to speak.

"Gabriella, if this is going to work, I need you to use your words. I'm not pressuring you. If you don't want this, just say, and we'll stop."

My hand moves to cover his that's placed on my knee, and I give it a squeeze. Brad makes me feel safe. Maybe this is what I need to do to get over this fear I have. I know he would never want more than whatever this is, and as long as I keep that in mind, this could work. It's just a friend helping out another friend. I can get a grip on my feelings towards him.

"I want this," I say, my throat feeling drier than a Graham cracker.

He gives me a nod in understanding, places his other hand on my other knee, and widens my legs. He moves in a little closer, bringing his mouth to my ear, and whispers, "I'm about to make you feel so good, Mia Cara." His words have my insides quivering. I love when he calls me that. Holy hell, I'm not going to last here.

His mouth presses against my neck and moves to a sensitive spot on my collarbone I didn't know was there, I flinch and giggle, and he moves back to look at me.

"Sorry," I say shyly. "It tickles."

He moves back to where he was and presses his mouth to the same spot, and I giggle again.

"I'm sorry, I'm sorry I'm just nervous. You're you, and I'm me, and this is…"

"I know, you just need to get out of your head, baby girl. Relax." His use of 'baby girl' has heat flooding to my core.

"I know, I know, I'm sorry. I am in my head. The brain is such a powerful thing. Did you know that when we die, the brain still lives for like seven minutes and replays all your best moments?"

"Fascinating," he says, amusement in his tone and a slight grin on his face.

"Isn't it? It plays them like a movie, all your favorite moments, the people you love, all the important moments and people in your life as you cross over. The best parts of your life literally flash before your eyes. Isn't that amazing? And—"

My rambling is cut off by his index finger pressing against my lips. "Baby girl, I'm trying to get you off here, and you're rambling."

"Sorry," I mouth.

"Do you trust me?" He removes his finger. "Of course, I wouldn't be doing this with you if I didn't."

"Good, let me try something." He reaches for my robe and gently tugs and loosens the knot. It falls open, revealing my hardened nipples that strain against the silk fabric of my camisole. Slowly, he pulls the cord of my robe and gathers it in his hands.

"Close your eyes," he whispers, putting me at ease.

I do as I'm told, and the silk fabric presses against my eyes as he ties it together at the back of my head.

"Now, all you need to do is focus on my touch and my voice."

I swallow anxiously and nod as his hot breath dances across my collarbone once again, but this time, it doesn't tickle. He presses open mouth kisses up my neck, each one searing into me, sending bolts of pleasure right to my core. His lips press to mine. It's fleeting and not nearly enough. My breathing changes to small pants of anticipation of his next move. Strong hands grip my hips and tug me closer to the edge of the couch, and the tips of his fingers hook into the waistband of my shorts, and I lift my hips on instinct as he takes them.

I go to move my hands to cover my underwear, but his hands catch my wrists.

"Don't you dare hide from me, Gabriella." It's almost a growl, and it sends another bolt of pleasure in between my legs. He releases me, and I do my best to relax my body. "Do you know how sexy you look like this? Blindfolded, wrapped in silk and lace, and all mine." A whimper escapes my lips as his hands graze the sides of my breasts, and his thumbs dust over my nipples.

He's barely touched me, and yet I'm already close to the edge.

His hands skim under my cami that's ridden up, touching the bare skin of stomach. My body is on fire, and his touch seems to be the fuel that ignites it, and I want more. I rotate my hips slowly, desperate for some friction, and I gasp when his thumb strokes over the lace fabric of my panties, just near my clit and I internally beg for him to do it again.

My silent prayers are answered when his hand slides inside my panties and he swipes his fingers through my folds.

"So wet for me already, baby girl." He groans, and holy crap, I am, embarrassingly so, and yet, I don't care. "Please..." I whimper. I don't know what I'm asking, but I just know I need him to do more. There's a desperate ache building that I needed him to soothe.

"Is this you begging, Gabriella, because I could get on board with that?" he says with a slight hint of amusement in his tone as he rubs his finger in small circles over my clit and it pulls another moan from me.

"Yesss..." I hiss as he continues. I bite down on my lower lip to stifle the moan that wants to rip from me. Suddenly, he removes his hand, and I go to protest, but he's dragging my panties down my legs.

My body hums in anticipation of his next move. When I feel his palms slide up my inner thighs, tiny tremors run all over my skin. I try to close my legs on instinct, but he clamps his hands down on my thighs.

"Relax, Gabriella, let me in." His tone is firm but reassuring at the same time. I take a centering breath, reminding myself of why I'm letting him do this, and that thought allows my body to soften and my legs to widen.

"Good Girl."

He repeats the movement, smoothing his calloused palms up my soft thighs, and I melt into the couch cushions when his hot mouth presses a kiss so close to my sex I think I stop breathing.

"Breathe, Mia cara," he croons, wrapping his strong hands around my thighs and tugging me a little closer and then pinning them to the couch. He maneuvers me with confidence and ease so I am putty in his hands.

I take a moment to catch my breath, but it's stolen the minute he slowly pushes a finger inside me.

"Fuccckkk," he groans out.

"Oh, my..." I gasp in a mixture of shock and pleasure. The stretch, the slight burn, and the building pressure feel too much. It's been so long since I had a man touch me like this, but for someone so strong and guarded, he's surprisingly gentle with his movements. I may be opening up for him, but with every touch of my skin and kiss he plants on my body, I feel like I am experiencing an entirely hidden side of Brad Russo.

"Is this all for me? Is this what my touch does to you?" He adds another finger and begins working them at a pace that has my eyes rolling and my hips grinding down on his fingers.

I moan in pleasure. When his thumb starts rubbing my clit and he begins to work his fingers a little faster, my core tightens, a pressure so intense building that I have to grip the comforter that's beneath me for something to hold on to before I fall over the edge.

My breathing has turned to deep, breathless gasps. The sounds of my arousal fill the apartment and something unfamiliar works its way through my body. It feels like an impending wave, one that's about to crash its way through me and break me apart. I grip Brad's arms. "Brad... please... I..." My words are lost when he brings his mouth to mine and presses a bruising kiss there as he curls his fingers inside me, hitting a spot that has me seeing stars.

His lips leave mine and his hot breath fans my neck.

"Does that feel good, baby girl? Does this greedy pussy of yours like riding my fingers?" I swallow, fighting desperately to find a word that would accurately depict how I'm feeling right now, but I'm at a loss. I feel myself tighten around his fingers, a shudder fluttering through my body as I grip the back of his head to stabilize and steady myself as I ride this wave of ecstasy.

"So fucking beautiful."

This is nothing like I've felt before, and in this moment, I think I'd give, do, say anything he wanted. It's all consuming. I don't want it to end, and I surprise myself when I plead with him.

"More." It falls from my lips on a breathless whisper.

"More?" He repeats and there is a hint of something in his voice that tells me he's enjoying this, maybe just as much as I am.

"Yes." I pant.

When his fingers curl inside me and he moves them faster, hitting a spot, it has me frantically searching for something to hold on to. My hands meet his exposed forearm, and with every pump of his fingers, I feel the tight ridges of his muscle flex. My inability to see heightens the feel of his skilled fingers moving in and out of me, the scent of his cedarwood cologne, a fragrance that will now be embedded in my skin.

My legs start shaking, a deep, hot pressure builds, and I think about begging him to stop because it all feels like it's too much to handle. I release the grip on his arm when I feel him his body move closer, his hot breath fanning my neck as his wet tongue glides up my exposed neck, then planting a kiss to my pulse point, that has my back arching in a bid to get closer to him.

"Good girl. Come for me, Gabriella, let go. I've got you." His raw voice coaxes into my ear and that's all I need to let myself go and give something to him that I've never given to another man.

My body convulses as I ride my high, pleasure unlike anything I've experienced before crashing through my veins, floods my body, and all I can do is ride the wave and let it take me. The palm of my hand glides up my neck and applies pressure to my throat, needing more, but not quite brave enough to ask. His movements slow as my body goes slack, and it takes a few moments for my breathing to even out. I wince a little when he removes his fingers, hating the empty feeling.

My eyes blink rapidly when he removes the makeshift blindfold, and I look down at my half naked body, open and sprawled out on the couch before him. I'm too spent to think about covering up, and weirdly, I don't want to. I look up and my mouth falls open when he brings his fingers to his mouth and sucks them clean. "Mmm, so fucking sweet. Next time, I'm having a proper taste of you, Mia cara."

I'm still processing what just happened, but I know one thing for certain: I want to do that again. With him.

Chapter Eighteen

Brad

"It's just not adding up." Harry huffs in frustration and tosses the papers on the desk. He's right, it's not. Over the last year, thousands and thousands of dollars have gone missing. Not enough to flag anything on a day to day basis, but when our accountant said our accounts didn't balance, we took it upon ourselves to investigate, convinced he was wrong. He wasn't.

"Do you think it could be a staff member?" Jack suggests, taking another look at the stack of files on my desk.

"I don't know. We can rule Kate and Harley out," Harry states, and Jack and I nod in agreement.

"I'll ask Kate to keep an eye on her next shift, and I'll look at the cashier logs to see if anyone has used their key cards at odd hours."

"Good plan," Harry confirms. "I'm sorry I'm leaving you with this shit show."

"Yeah, me too. We'll be in Florida and then back for a few days and then on to our honeymoon," Jack adds.

"Yeah, don't worry. You both go get your dick wet and I'll man the fort," I tease. Harry glares at me, and I realize what I've said.

"Who are you fucking?" Jack directs his question at Harry. "Is this the mystery girl you told us about at the wedding?"

"Err, yeah, she might come and visit me in London," he says nervously, scratching the back of his head.

I don't know how long they think they can keep this up without getting caught, and that idea makes my mind divert back to Gabriella and what happened between us the other night. The way she opened up to me, both physically and emotionally, has only intensified my desire for her. If she wasn't already running through my head daily, now I know she's the girl behind the mask and I've watched her come undone, I fear I am well and truly fucked. I doubled my workout efforts this morning in a bid to quieten my mind, and it did nothing.

"Well, when I get back, I want a name," Jack says, standing and tapping his knuckles against the desk. "Got it?" He points at Harry. "We don't do secrets."

Harry salutes playfully. "Sir, yes, sir."

"What time are we meeting at the restaurant?" I ask, trying to steer the conversation away from Harry and his secret girl.

Jack loads the coffee machine on the bar at the back of the office and the sound of it brewing along with the rich scent floats through the air.

"I booked it for eight o'clock. Anne and Carl are coming to collect the girls around four, so I'll head out soon so I can see them before they go."

I look at my watch: 3.23 pm.

"You get going. Harry and I will finish up here. I'll call Kate and brief her," I say.

Jack walks over, placing two steaming mugs of black coffee on my desk.

"You sure?" he asks, eyeing me. "Oscar called. He may have some new units ready to view out in LA in the next few weeks. One of us needs to go out there and check them out. He needs calling—"

I cut him off. "Yes, yes, I got it. I'll handle it. Get outta here. Go see your girls." A small smile forms on his face at the mention of his step-daughters, and he looks like the happiest man to walk the earth.

"Thanks. See you later. Don't be late," he says, pointing at Harry.

Harry waves him off dismissively, not looking at Jack as he types something on his phone. "I won't."

I wait for the door to close before asking, "So, Ali's going to London with you?"

He looks up from his phone, grinning, showing his perfectly straight white teeth. "She sure is."

"How did you convince her to do that?" I ask, picking up my mug of coffee.

"I fuck like a god, and she knew she couldn't go too long without my cock." I almost choke.

I shake my head. "I don't know what she sees in you some days," I tease.

"Like I said. I fuck like a god." He grins and winks, and I roll my eyes.

"Are you planning on spending the night with Ali tonight?"

His brows furrow. "Erm, I guess so. Why? If this is you asking to join us, I'm gonna have to say no. I love you, but that would be fucking weird and besides, I'd have to break your hand if you touched her."

"Oh, fuck off. I don't wanna join, and I'd never touch Ali. I just wanna know if I need to cover your ass later with Gabriella so she doesn't suspect anything. I'll give her a ride home or something."

"Uh, yeah, probably. Good thinking." A thrill runs through me that I will be able to get Gabriella alone tonight and maybe move on to our next lesson. I pick up my phone and send a text to her.

> **Brad:** Hey, I need to see you before dinner. What time will you be home?

The message shows as read instantly, and the three dots appear.

> **Gabriella:** Why? Everything okay? I'm home now.

> **Brad:** I have a gift for you. Are you alone?

> **Gabriella:** A gift? What kind of gift? Yes, Ali won't be back till after six.

> **Brad:** Good, I'm on my way.

Less than an hour later, I'm outside Gabriella's door clutching a pink gift bag. She opens the door, and steals my breath, wearing a red dress that hugs every curve and makes her tanned skin glow.

"Hey," she says a little breathlessly, as if she ran to answer.

"Hey. You look..."

"It's too much, isn't it? I'm not wearing it. Ali left it out for me, but I decided against it."

"Hot, Gabriella, you look insane. Red is your color." Her cheeks flush the same shade as her dress, and she nervously tucks her long, wavy hair behind her ear.

"Come in." She gestures, and I step inside.

"I'm just trying to get ready for tonight. What's this gift you have for me?" She walks down the corridor and I follow like a dog on a leash, fixated on her round ass cheeks as the material moves with every step she takes.

She spins to face me. "Brad, did you hear me?"

I look up and swallow, my mouth suddenly dry, and I'm in need of something to quench this sudden thirst I have.

Her, I need her.

"No," I say, barely getting my word out.

"I asked if you could help me out of this dress. I think the zipper is stuck."

"Absolutely." I place the gift bag on her bed and gather her hair in my hands, moving it to one side.

My fingers tug at the zipper, and it glides down effortlessly, exposing her back. I can't help but stroke the backs of my knuckles against her bare skin. Goosebumps scatter as my fingers drift down to the bottom of her spine. Without thinking, I place my hands on her hips, press a kiss to her bare shoulder, and her head falls slightly to the side, exposing her neck even more to me. I press another kiss to her neck, and a small moan of appreciation falls from her lips. I want to continue. Push her down on her bed, tear this dress from her body, and devour her, but we need to take this slow.

So, I do the sensible thing and stop. "All done." Her body sags at the loss of the contact, and she turns to face me.

"Thanks," she says quietly. "I'll go in there and get changed." She gestures to her closet. "Don't go in there on my account. I've seen what's under the dress, baby girl." I wink, needing to bring some playfulness back between us.

She presses her lips together and her cheeks pinken once again. She turns her back to me and lets the dress fall to the ground. Pink lace panties cover her peachy ass and the sight has my balls tightening. She grabs a pink t-shirt and gray sweatpants off her bed and slips them on before she turns to face me. She takes a hair tie from her wrist and gathers her hair into a ponytail as she looks at the gift bag I've placed on the bed. I'm mesmerized just watching her doing everyday things.

"Is that my gift?"

I nod. "Yeah. Open it."

She picks up the gift bag, and I take a seat in the chair at her desk, in her window.

She pulls out the matching pink tissue paper and sticks her hand inside the bag. "You know, it's not my birthday for another few months, right? Why are you..." Her words stop when she pulls the small white box free and sees the picture on the front. "Is this a..."

"Vibrator, yes," I declare.

"W-What's it for?"

"Well, most people use them to get off."

She looks at me deadpan, and I can't help but chuckle.

"I know that, but why have you got me one, and why is it this weird shape? It looks like a shrimp."

I throw my head back and a deep belly laugh leaves my body, the kind that makes your body tingle and your face ache. She laughs along with me, and watching Gabriella's face light up when she laughs is one of the most beautiful sights.

"I can assure you, it's not a shrimp. This..." I say, standing and taking the box from her hand. "Is a special kind of vibrator. Remember how you said you wanted to have sex outside?"

Her eyes widen. "I told you that?"

"Yes. Among other things."

Lowering my voice, I move, closing any space between us. "As much as I'd love to fuck you out in the open, I think we need to work up to that and get you more comfortable first."

"W-work up to that?" she stutters, and I smirk. "Yeah."

"Okay, so how does this help with that?" she asks, tapping the box.

"You're going to wear it at dinner."

Her mouth falls open and I press my lips together to stifle a laugh. She looks so animated. "You want me to wear that to dinner?"

"Yes."

"At dinner with our friends?"

"Yes," I reiterate.

"You don't have to, if this is too much too soon." I don't want to pressure her, but I sense there is something inside Gabriella that is begging to come out, and I'm here to guide it out of her.

"No, no, I want to, but why?" she asks, narrowing her eyes.

"Just trust me, it'll be worth it," I say, dragging my thumb over her bottom lip. I want to kiss her, but I realize from our last two encounters I am getting entirely too comfortable with kissing her so freely and I need to set some boundaries here. Touching her is one thing, kissing is another.

"So, baby girl, you up for it?" I ask, giving her a challenging stare.

She stares at the box in her hand and chews at her bottom lip. I think she will refuse, but to my surprise she stands a little taller, matching my stare she confidentially says, "Yes, bring it on."

Chapter Nineteen

Gabriella

I must have lost my damn mind, left my senses and my panties apparently at home. When Brad proposed that I wear this thing to dinner, at first, I thought he was joking. But when I realized he was serious, I had two thoughts. I can do what I always do, run scared and say no, or take a risk and do it. After all, this is why I am doing this with him. I need to get out of my comfort zone, push the limits and boundaries, and open myself up to new experiences, grow in confidence, and I won't do that if I stay within the lines I've drawn for myself. Sometimes we need to color outside of the lines, and today is one of those days. I've taken on the energy and confidence I have when I'm dancing at the club. The only difference here is that I don't have the shield of my red mask. But that's what I want. To merge my two worlds into one, but when you have been made to feel that who you really want to be is wrong, that's a hard mountain to climb and get over, but I have Brad now to help me, and it starts tonight. Maybe this is the push I need to break out of my shell.

But you can do this, Gabby.

After Brad left, I got ready and then opened up the box fully. I followed the instructions and clicked the on button before I slipped it inside me, making sure the tail part covered my clit as the step by step guide stated. I won't lie, I was very grateful for the illustrations. I was expecting it to buzz, or do something, but nothing, and there wasn't time to figure it out. Ali came bursting through my door, and I had to throw the packaging under my comforter.

"Are you okay?" Ali asks, sitting beside me in the back of the cab. "You keep fidgeting."

"Yeah, I'm good. It's these pants. Just a little tight," I say, adjusting the waistband of the leather pants I wore out a few weeks ago. I thought pants were a safer choice. I was worried the thing was going to fall out of me when I walked.

We arrive outside to find Jack, Ria, Harry, and Brad all standing outside the double doors that lead to the Italian restaurant.

We greet our friends and walk through the doors where the hostess welcomes us. I follow our friends, but a large hand wraps around my arm and pulls me back. I turn, and it's Brad.

"Over here," he mutters. He leads me towards a corridor where a sign for the bathrooms is.

"What's up?" I ask. He looks around and then zones in on me.

"Are you wearing it?"

"Yeah," I say, holding my purse in front of me as if it is concealing what's underneath my pants.

He gives me a pleased grin. "Good girl. How do you feel?"

"Full," I say dryly. "I don't know if I did it right."

He leans his forearm against the wall and covers his mouth with his hands, but the way his eyes light up, I know he's fighting to keep a laugh inside.

"Did you turn it on?" he asks. I look around to make sure no one is listening in.

"Yes, but it didn't do anything," I whisper.

"It will." He takes my hands and guides me back, but we break hands as soon as we enter the main dining room and see Jack waving us down.

"Where did you go?" Ria asks as I take my seat.

"Oh, I needed the bathroom." The lie slips off my tongue with ease, and I lift my menu to cover my face in case anyone detects it.

"What's everyone having?" Ria asks. "Now the wedding is over and I don't have a dress to fit into, I'm having pasta and a dessert, oooh and the bruschetta and..."

"Girl, just order one of everything." Ali laughs.

"Have whatever you want, sweetheart. I don't know why you insisted on being carb-free before the wedding. You're perfect as you are," Jack says, staring at his wife.

Ria blushes and leans over the table to meet Jack halfway and kisses him.

"Oh, please, I haven't eaten yet and I'm ready to throw up my dinner. We get it. You're in love. But save it for the honeymoon, yeah?" Harry pleads.

"Don't be a sourpuss, H. Maybe if you treated a woman and complimented her the way Jack does, you might find a woman who can stand to be around you long enough to fall in love with you," Ali says.

"You weren't complaining last night when I, aaaahh, the fuck?" Harry yells, his face contorting in pain.

"Sorry, my heel must have caught your leg," she says innocently. I want to ask what he was trying to say but I think better of it and decide the situation needs defusing before it escalates.

"Ri, are the girls excited for Disney World?" I ask, scanning the menu.

"So excited, Lexi has been watching the parade videos on YouTube and planning all the merchandise she wants to buy, and Elle just keeps asking if Minnie Mouse will be there." Her face glows as she talks about her girls. "It will be nice to spend some family time before we head on honeymoon. Jack's been in Disney Dad training mode." She giggles.

"Have you seen the place? There are like fifty-eight parks and so many apps, it's like planning a military operation," Jack explains, a flicker of fear alight in his eyes.

Harry slaps Jack on the back. "Good job you've got lots of experience with that, then." We all chuckle, and as I scan the wine list, something vibrates inside me and I let out a small yelp of surprise.

"Are you okay?" Ali asks. Everyone's eyes are on mine, confusion on their faces, all of them except Brad, who looks very pleased with himself.

"Yeah, yeah, I just thought I saw a bug, but it wasn't." I laugh, embarrassed by the sound I just made.

Ali eyes me curiously and turns back to her menu, to place her drink order with the waiter who comes up behind her.

The vibrating happens again, but this time it lasts longer, and it feels good. Too good. Like something I should not be experiencing at the table with my friends. The part that's covering my clit begins to move and I close my eyes, trying my best to ignore the feeling. Why has it started buzzing now? Did I knock a button when I sat down?

The feeling intensifies, and I fear a moan will escape. A waiter appears beside me, and panic swirls inside my gut.

"What can I get you to drink?" As he finishes his sentence, it stops. I breathe a sigh of relief.

"A glass of rosé, please." He leaves, and everyone falls into a comfortable chatter. Ali starts talking about her upcoming work trip and how she's still uncertain of where they are sending her, but it will be for a couple of weeks. I go to add to the conversation when the vibrating starts again, but this time the vibrations feel quick, like little pulses of pleasure shooting through my core.

"Is someone's phone vibrating?" Ria asks, and I freeze. *Holy hell, can they hear what's going on inside of me?* Everyone checks their phones.

Brad quirks his lips and stares at me, dead in the eyes as he says, "Is your phone vibrating, Gabriella?" I don't get a chance to reply. The buzzing continues and this time it's consistent. I squeeze my thighs together in a bid to fan the flames of the fire that's igniting within me, but it only intensifies.

I decide I need to focus on something, a singular spot to distract the building pressure that makes me want to roll my eyes and rub myself against this seat. Seriously, I'm a mess. The waiter places my glass of wine in front of me and I reach for it, draining it in one go.

"Woah Gabs, we haven't even ordered." Harry chuckles.

"Sorry, I'm thirsty. Could I get another, please?" I ask the waiter holding up my empty glass as he begins to walk off. I hand him the glass, and as he leaves, the vibrations intensify. It's then I notice Brad on his phone, tapping his thumb on the screen at exactly the same time as the pulses of vibration go through me. I narrow my eyes at him.

Is he...?

My fingers hook the edge of my seat as a whimper falls from my lips, and all eyes focus on me again. "Are you okay?" Ali asks, pressing the back of her fingers to my forehead as if she were checking my temperature.

"Yes," I breathe out. "I'm good. It's just a little warm in here."

"Are you sure? You look like you are in pain or about to burst. Do you want to go home?"

I let out a laugh. It's pained and I shuffle in my seat. "No, I'm fine." I cross my legs over, making sure I give Brad a swift kick under the table.

"Ow," he yelps.

The vibrations stop, and I grin. "I'm great."

"Did you just kick me?" Brad hisses.

"Whoops, sorry, my heel must have caught your leg too." I narrow my eyes at him.

I've caught on to your game, Bradley Russo.

A different waiter appears ready to take everyone's order. When he works his way down towards me, the vibrations begin again and I want to scream. This is the biggest mix of pain and pleasure. Brad casually orders his food, all the while tapping at his phone under the table.

From the corner of my eye, I see Ria root through her purse. "I'm telling you, someone's phone is vibrating, Jack, check your phone. It could be Anne about the girls," Ria says, pulling her own phone out.

Ground, open up and swallow me whole, please.

Jack holds up his phone. "Sweetheart, nothing. It's not vibrating."

The vibration stops and I let out a sigh of relief. I need to get to the bathroom and get this thing out of me, but I fear the evidence of my arousal is going to be left on my seat. I know I have to burn this underwear. They are ruined.

I kick my leg to catch Brad's, but Harry yelps. "Ah, what the fuck, Ali?"

"I didn't do anything."

"Sorry, that was me," I say weakly as I look over at Brad, who continues to smirk but thankfully pauses my torture.

"... and for you, Miss, what can I get you to eat?"

"Hi, can I get the bruschetta to start, and the tomato paaaaaaa..." I cry out, my pitch reaching a level only well-trained dogs could hear.

My legs begin to tremble.

"Are you okay, Gabs?" Harry chuckles.

I let out a slow breath when the vibration stops.

"Sorry, can I get the tomato pasta with the buffalo mozzarella?" I pant.

"Are we singing out orders now?" Ali Chuckles and everyone around the table laughs.

My cheeks burn in embarrassment. "No, I'm so excited about this pasta. Yay, carbs," I say, waving my menu in the air, my voice verging on another whimper.

"I'll take your..." he reaches for my menu and I grip a hold of it.

"No, please, don't." My tone is pleading and desperate, as if he were stealing something of value. I fan my face with it. I glare at Brad and he winks. He winks. I'm wound so tightly right now, I don't know if I want to punch him in his rugged face or beg him to bend me over this table and finish me off.

The waiter nods and informs us he will put our orders through and I breathe a sigh of relief when the buzzing stops and continue to fan my face with the menu. I turn to look at Ali and Ria, both looking at me with confused expressions.

"Are you well?" Ali asks bluntly.

"I'm fine. Just, it's so hot in here. I think I need some air." I attempt to rise from my seat, but Brad starts tapping his fork against his glass.

"Gabriella, before you do, I'd just like to say a few words."

I stare at him, deadpan. Really? Right now? The man of very few words suddenly wants to make a speech at the dinner table after tormenting me for the past thirty minutes.

"I'm not one for words, but I just wanted to wish Jack and Ria a happy holiday with your beautiful family. I hope it's the trip you have been wishing for. Harry, I'm gonna miss your shit banter, so don't stay in London too long." Everyone laughs and suddenly my heart swells. I truly believe he means every word he's saying.

"And, Ali, I'll miss your sharp tongue while you're away, and don't worry, I'll keep a close eye on our Gabby girl. I'll take good care of her." Ali wraps her arm around me and pulls me towards her.

"You better. We've never left her this long," she says, making a sad face.

"Hey, I'm gonna be fine," I assure her.

"I know, but let Brad take care of you, okay. If you need him, you call him," she says sternly.

"I will," I agree, with a slight roll of my eyes.

"Okay, no more, or I'll start crying, and so will Harry and Jack," Ali jokes, fanning her face with her hands. Jack and Harry give her a disgruntled looks and she blows them both a kiss.

I think my torture is over when it's been a solid five minutes without any vibrations and I'm left with a heavy ache in my core, one so uncomfortable I need to do something about it before I burst.

I think about leaving, but the waiter appears with my wine, and as I go to thank him, a strong vibration zaps through me that has me up and out of my seat.

"I need to pee," I declare, louder than needed, my words falling out on a strangled moan.

"Okay, Gabs, are you sure you're okay?" Jack asks, eyeing me suspiciously.

"I'm great, chat among yourselves, I'm gonna go, erm, pee, and you chat. Yes. You chat, I'll pee," I say, pointing to them and then myself. I don't wait for any of them to comment on my ramblings. I hurry to the bathroom on shaky legs, the vibrations continuing, making the walk difficult.

I burst through the bathroom door, not taking in any of the décor, and hurry into a bathroom stall. The vibrator, now stuck on what I presume is high, continues to buzz and the part that's over my clit is pulsing. I think about leaving it in, ride this wave, and falling apart in this bathroom stall, but I refuse to have an orgasm here. Not like this.

I yank down my leather pants, pushing my hand in between my legs, hooking my finger and thumb around the tail of the vibrator, my fingers are instantly coated with my hot arousal and I wince. Dear God, I am a mess.

I pull it free, relief instantly flooding me, but the vibrator falls between my fingers, hitting the floor and sliding under the bathroom stall. My eyes widen in horror and I crouch down, sticking my hands underneath, but I can't find it. Panic floods my body.

"Oh, shit." I pull up my pants at lightning speed, open the door and frantically search the floor of the ladies' bathroom for my pink shrimp-shaped vibrator. My eye catches something next to the trash can under the sink.

Come on universe, throw me a bone.

I do something that would send my germophobic mother into a spin. I get down my hands and knees and lean to reach the vibrator.

I'm so close to touching it, but the sound of my name startles me and I hit my head on the cabinet.

"Ouch," I yelp.

"What are you doing?" I back up, still on my hands and knees, and look up at Ria and Ali above me, foreheads furrowed, mouths agape.

Well, Gabriella, this may be rock bottom. You're on all fours, in a restaurant bathroom, reaching for a vibrator. How are you going to explain this one?

"Ha Ha, I'm fine. I dropped my phone." I clutch the sink and heave myself up, catching a glimpse of my flushed face and disheveled hair.

"Seriously, are you okay? You don't seem yourself tonight," Ria asks, concern in her voice.

"Yes, I'm fine. I, uh, got my period. I just have some cramps," I say, turning on the faucet and scrubbing my hands like a surgeon preparing for surgery.

"You got your period?" Ali questions.

"Yes," I reply.

"But we have the same cycles, and we just finished our period last week."

Oh shit, she's right. I turn off the faucet and reach for a fancy hand towel from the basket beside the sink to dry them.

"I'm having another one," I declare, praying they will believe my lie.

"Another one?" Ali asks, folding her arms and eyeing me curiously. Not believing any of my bullshit.

"Yeah, that happens sometimes," I state.

"I don't think it does, Gabs. Maybe you should see a doctor," Ria suggests.

"I will, I'll call tomorrow." I begin to breathe a little easier, hoping they believe my lie when the vibrator begins buzzing. Ria looks around and my eyes widen as I pray the damn thing doesn't buzz its way out from under the countertop.

"There's that buzzing again. Seriously, can no one else hear it? Am I going mad?" Ria asks.

"I think that is my phone. Silly me. I've left it in the stall. You two go back and I'll be right out."

I walk back into the stall and close the door. "I'll be out in a minute." I wait for them to leave and sag against the wall. I hate lying to them. It's not that I don't think they will understand or be supportive, of course they would. I just don't really know what this even is. I need to figure this all out before I invite anyone else into this mess and make sense of it. The walls of the bathroom suddenly feel like they are closing in on me. I need some air. I need to get out of here. The burning ache in my core, the weight of my lies, is all becoming too much. I need space to breathe and to think. I open the bathroom stall, forgetting all about the rogue vibrator that lies on the floor, and leave the bathroom. I double step to the side exit and walk on shaky legs into the alley beside the restaurant.

Jesus, I'm a mess.

I need to get home and deal with it immediately before I do something I will regret in the morning. I'll make an excuse, continue with my cramp story, and get a cab. Yes, great idea.

Just as I reach into my pocket for my phone, the door swings open and out steps Brad, undressing me with his eyes as he stalks toward me. A big, fat grin spreads across his insanely hot face.

"You doing okay out here, Gabriella... need a hand?" he says with a wink, making me squeeze my legs together to suppress the pressure that's building. I press my hands to his hard chest and try to step past him as I say, "No, thank you. I think you've done quite enough for one evening, I'm going..." My words are cut short when he pushes my hips to the wall with one hand, and captures my hands in his other hand, pinning them above my head.

"Oh, I've not even started yet, baby girl."

A woosh of air escapes my lungs, leaving me breathless as he presses his hot mouth to my neck. A whimper escapes me. "I need to get home," I pant.

"No, you're going to finish yourself off, and I'm going to watch." His tone is low and heated.

My eyes widen, and my heart thumps erratically.

"W-what, out here?" I stammer.

"Yes," he drawls.

"But, but someone might see."

"I'll cover you. No one will see but me."

My body vibrates at his words and the idea of doing this. Can I do this? No, I can't do this. But this is what I wanted. I'm done being scared, little Gabby.

I swallow what feels like a large cotton ball and nod my head slowly. He releases my hands and steps back just enough to watch me reach for the button on my pants. I pop it open and then slowly pull down the zipper. My eyes follow his tattooed covered hands as they reach into his pocket and retrieve a packet of cigarettes and a lighter. A flame lights the space between us and I watch in fascination as he brings the cigarette to his mouth, wishing his mouth was on me instead.

My eyes flicker up to his. They are full of heat and desire and it's the only encouragement I need to slip my hand inside, and as I do, he exhales a long, slow breath, the smoke feels as if it were cloaking us like a blanket, making us invisible to the rest of the world, and that image gives me the courage to begin moving my fingers towards the waistband of my trousers and move down.

"Good girl," he says on a raspy breath. My own breath catches in my throat when my fingers meet my clit and I begin to move them.

I am so close already; this won't take long. He's been edging me all evening. I close my eyes as the pressure from earlier returns, and with every movement, it intensifies, and my thighs quiver.

He braces his arm above me, shielding me from anyone passing.

"Does this turn you on, naughty girl? Getting yourself off, knowing anyone could catch you?"

I gasp, my back arching away from the wall when his thumb brushes my painfully hard nipple through the fabric of my top.

"Please, I... I need you to do I, I beg, my fingers slowing their assault on my swollen nub.

He takes another drag of his cigarette, leaning his head back as he blows out the smoke.

"You can beg all you want, Mia cara, but I'm not letting you go until you make yourself come, and you know, they'll come looking for us soon, so I'd move those fingers a little quicker if I were you. Unless..." He covers his hand with mine, guiding my fingers up and down over my clit.

"You like an audience when you come. In which case, take your time. I've got all night."

Oh my god, Brad is hot, but dirty talking, looking at me like he wants to devour me Brad is sinful and it spurs me on. I quicken my pace, locking my eyes with his dark, whiskey ones, until my core tightens and a singular word has me gripping his jacket as I free fall.

"Come."

My head falls back against the brick wall and my desperate pants echo around us. My chest heaves and I think I could come again from the way he's looking at me with his hooded eyes.

"Sei cosi bella cosi, amore mio," he purrs, brushing the tip of his nose with mine. I know enough Italian to know what he just said, and it sends my heart racing.

"You look so beautiful like this, my love."

Chapter Twenty

Gabriella

"And don't forget to lock the doors and eat. Make sure you eat, okay?" Ali says, zipping her suitcase. She's been fussing all morning. She's heading to Paris for work with the fashion magazine she works for. It's her dream to go to Paris, but I'll admit, with Ria in Florida on holiday and Ali gone, I'm going to feel a little lost. Since I met them, I've never spent more than a week away from at least one of them.

"Yes, Mom, I will," I say teasingly.

She wheels her case to the front door, and I follow behind, pulling her carry on.

"Okay, you call me, anytime and Brad. You call him if you need anything and he's going to check in on you." I roll my eyes at the idea of him checking in on me as if I were a little child, but a flutter in my belly stirs at the thought of seeing him.

"I will. You need to get going. You don't want to miss your flight," I say, pinging the hair elastic that's on my left wrist.

Her hand covers mine to stop me from continuing with my nervous habit.

"Gabs," Ali says softly. I look up at her, her tear-filled eyes softening when a tear of my own rolls down my cheek.

"Come here," she says, throwing her arms around me and pulling me into a tight hug.

I owe so much to Ali. She offered me a home when I was running from mine. She's helped me through my darkest times and pulls me out of my shell when I need it. I know we won't live together forever, and this time on my own will be good for me. But, God, am I going to feel a little lost without her.

"I'm going to miss you." I sniff.

"Not as much as I'm going to miss you, Little G." I chuckle, the tears falling harder now at the use of my nickname she gave me back in our therapy group.

We break the hug and both wipe our tears.

"Okay, you get going and if you fall in love with a French man, I need to meet him before you marry him, okay?"

She laughs, shaking her head. "You'll be the first to know." I open the door, and she blows me a kiss. "Love you."

"Love you, Ali." I close the door softly and turn, and slump against the door.

It's just you, little G.

"Great job, ladies. See you next week," I say to my class as they head out of the studio.

Not quite ready to leave, I decide I'm going to dance. I used all of my upper body strength teaching back to back classes today, but I have a buzz of nervous energy that has been there since Ali left yesterday, and I need to get rid of it.

I root in my bag for my heels but stop when I feel the familiar satin ribbon of my ballet slippers. I don't often practice ballet anymore. It fills me with mixed emotions. It ties me to a time in my life when I was constantly scrutinized by my parents, my mother in particular, and my knee injury. But I loved it. Not wanting to go back to an empty apartment just yet, I pull out my pointe shoes and sit on the ground. I slide my feet inside the slippers with ease; the fabric molded to fit and take my time crossing over the satin ribbon around my ankle and up my calf. I reach for my phone, connecting it to the speakers, and hit play on my playlist.

I stand up, taking slow steps towards the mirrored wall and the bar that lines it. I briefly look at myself in the mirror: my hair in a high bun, my cheeks still flushed from class, and my back sports bra and yoga shorts cling to my small frame. I've always had issues with my body. No matter what I looked like it never seemed to be good enough. Growing up, just about anyone deemed it acceptable to comment on my body—my mother, my friends, dance teachers, men. Everyone had something to say.

I rest my hand on the bar and lift my other one in the air while I stand in first position. I wait for the beat of the music to change and begin a variation from my dance school days.

I move away from the bar, doing a piqué passé into a plié, into a sous-sus fifth, a pirouette. I move around the studio, losing myself in the song, feeling lighter than I have in months. I miss this. I miss this version of me. When I could block everything out so it was just me and the music. Life has felt a lot lately, and this is what I needed.

I end with a fouetté. Turning on pointe, never managing the full fouetté required to complete the Swan Lake variation, but the burn in my legs and the sting in my chest alert me that I've pushed my body to the max, which satisfies me, and I stop my spins. The sound of applause from a singular pair of hands echoes round the studio when the music fades, and my body freezes. When his cedarwood scent wraps around me, I instantly lower my shoulders and relax my frame. I haven't seen Brad since the night at the restaurant a few nights ago.

I turn to face him, my heart skipping a beat when he looks at me and smiles at me like I'm the best part of his day. No one has ever looked at me the way he does.

"What are you doing here? Shouldn't you be heading to the club?" I say breathlessly.

"Yeah, I should, but I wanted to check in on you now Ali has gone and..." He stops, his expression tense as he mulls over his words.

"And what?" I ask hesitantly, a knot in my stomach forming.

I have this deep feeling that he's going to stop this, whatever this is. That some part of him regrets offering to help me with my intimacy issue, so I square my shoulders, preparing for him to say that we should go back to just being friends, but instead he says, "See you. I just wanted to see you, Gabriella." His eyes search mine as if he were looking for something, but I'm not sure what.

I can't help but smile so wide it makes my cheeks ache. "Well, now you've seen me," I say softly.

"Yeah, I see you." His gravelly tone takes my breath away. And then he steps closer and cups my face, pressing his forehead to mine. "You are a beautiful dancer."

"Thank you," I manage to say on a shaky breath, gripping the lapels of his jacket to steady myself. We stand like that, saying nothing, just being. He breaks our embrace and steps back, running a hand through his hair as he exhales.

"So are you doing okay since Ali has gone?" A little confused at his change of tone, I clear my throat. "Yeah, I'm okay. It's a little weird and quiet, but I'm keeping busy."

"Do you want to grab some food before you head home?"

I look down at my outfit and back up at him. "I'm a little sweaty and this is all I have."

"Okay, we'll get takeout and you can come back to mine."

"Yes, but I don't have a change of clothes," I remind him, gesturing to my body. He grins, his eyes raking over my body.

"You don't need clothes on at my apartment, Gabriella."

Chapter Twenty-One

Brad

I've barely touched Gabriella, and already she's worked her way into my mind so much so that I am changing my routine. I should be at the club right now, preparing for opening. Checking the books, briefing the staff before the night ahead, but instead I offered Kate double time if she could cover and I ended up at Gabriella's Pilates studio, slipping inside when she was dancing and fuck, is she incredible.

She's so light on her feet, twirling and leaping with such grace that she made it look as easy as breathing. I still don't fully understand why she hides so many parts of herself. Why she walks around with the weight of so many pressures and not have the confidence to tell people what she wants. I wish she could see what I see when I look at her.

After convincing her to leave her car at the studio and come back to mine for some takeout, we took the short drive to my apartment.

She took a shower while I kept myself busy plating up our dinner and fighting every urge to barge in there and claim her in the shower.

No, I know that isn't what she wants. She just wants me to help her feel more comfortable in her own body, and build her confidence, ready for the next guy. The guy who will get to keep her, and the realization of that is like a dagger to the heart. If this is going to work, I have to remember she isn't going to be mine at the end of this, and as painful as that outcome may be, it's for the best. I can't give her what she wants and what she deserves.

The dining table I've had custom-built hasn't arrive yet, so I set places at my large kitchen island and pour Gabriella some wine and myself my whiskey, neat.

I take my seat on the stool and Gabriella walks in, her long hair tied in a ponytail, hanging over one shoulder, wearing one of my black t-shirts. It hangs mid-thigh, her bronzed toned legs on full display and fuck me, I want to lift her on this counter and have her for dinner instead of this rice dish.

"Mmm, this smells so good." She moans, sending a direct wake up call to my dick. She takes the seat beside me, the shirt riding up, exposing more of her toned thigh, and I have to clear my throat and look away.

"I've put your clothes in the washer. They shouldn't take long, and then I'll dry them."

She picks up her chopsticks and begins digging into her food. "You're so domesticated, it's hot. I don't think my dad knows how to fold a shirt, or my mother, for that matter. They couldn't understand why I turned down their offer of paying for a housekeeper."

"What, they wanted to get you a housekeeper? What the hell do your parents do for work? Your dad does something in law, right?"

"Yeah, crazy, right? He's a judge, and my mom does nothing but lunch. They met at law school so she has her degree, but they married and she never worked. Even when she had me, I always had a nanny. My mom was always with my dad at dinners or functions."

"I'm sorry," I say quietly. It seems pointless, but what else could I say?

"It's fine. They grew up the same way, but when I have a family, I want to be there, you know?"

I nod. "So, you want kids?" I think I knew this, but hearing it just solidifies another reason why we would never work.

"I think so. I see Ria with Lexi and Elle, and I think I'd like that one day. I think I'd like at least one, but I don't want a child growing up lonely like me, so I don't know. What about you? Don't you have like five siblings, right? I bet that was fun growing up."

I wouldn't call it fun; the words torturous, abusive, and a nightmare come to mind.

"I'm one of four. My mum had me and my two brothers, one after the other, so she had three under three, and then she had Alessia when my youngest brother was ten," I say before shoveling more food into my mouth. I hate talking about my family unless it's about my sister.

"Wow, your mom is a queen," she says in surprise.

"I don't really see my family. It's complicated. I just talk to my sister and my nephew, really."

"What do your brothers do?"

I still at her words. I want to open up to her, but she doesn't need to be tainted by the troubles of my family. So I keep it light. "My brother, Dario, is in the Marines. He's deployed at the moment, has been for the last eighteen months. He's younger than me, and then my older brother, Matteo, he's in prison."

A silence falls between us. I expect her to press for more details, but I'm grateful when she changes the subject, hopefully sensing this is hard for me to talk about. It's like she knows what I need without me having to say it.

"Would you like kids one day? You are so good with Lexi and Elle, and I bet your nephew loves you," she says, looking at me with affection in her eyes.

I shake my head, reaching for my whiskey and taking a sip. "No, that life isn't for me," I say bluntly, and something in her eyes dims at my words.

Another awkward silence falls between us as we continue to eat. It's stifling, and I need to clear the air. "It's, erm, my nephew's birthday party tomorrow. Just a few people at my mom's house. Would you like to come with me? I think he'd really like you."

The light that I just dimmed flickers back into her eyes, and she smiles, covering her hand with mine. "I'd love to."

A conversation alone with a woman, sharing a meal, is a foreign thing to me. But with her, it feels like the most natural thing. She seems more comfortable here this time, moving around my kitchen as if she's always been here.

I clear the plates, washing them, drying them, putting them away, and she sits sipping her wine.

"You're very tidy," she comments, looking around my kitchen as she stands and moves around the island towards me.

"It's how I like it, keeps me out of trouble," I say, looking her up and down. I reach for the bottle of wine and hold it up, offering her another glass.

She worries her lower lip. "I won't be able to drive if I have another."

"You could always stay here," I suggest, my tone low. I watch as her throat bobs when she swallows.

"Do you want me to stay?"

"Do you *want* to stay?" I reply, wanting her to have the choice.

She nods slowly, and my heart thumps wildly against my chest at the idea of having her all to myself. All night.

I begin pouring the wine, stopping when it's almost at the top, then, stepping closer, pressing our bodies together. "Then I want you to stay," I say, running the backs of my fingers against her soft cheek.

She leans into my touch, and I press a kiss to her head.

To my surprise, she asks, "What else do you want?" I can't help the grin that spreads across my face at her question. A question I know she wouldn't have had the courage to ask me a month ago.

I pluck the glass from her hand, taking a sip of the fruity wine before I place it on the island. I grip her hips and lift her, placing her on the marble counter and standing in between her legs, nuzzling my nose into her hair.

"You."

She swallows so hard it's almost audible.

I reach for the elastic in her hair and tug it free, letting her hair fall like waves of dark satin around her shoulders.

"I love your hair like this," I say, tugging gently at the strands. A blush creeps across her make up free cheeks. Her dark lashes framing her amber eyes that are so hypnotic I could get lost in them, and I know I'd be grateful when I was unable to find my way back, because I think losing myself in Gabriella could be my new vice.

"Lie down," I whisper as I guide her back onto the counter. She does without hesitation, and her willingness to do as I ask only makes me desire her more.

I smooth my hands down the inside of her thighs, parting them till her knees meet the counter. It's then the scrap of material she calls underwear comes into view. The signature bows on the hips make it so easy to unwrap her. I let out a groan of approval, making her close her legs, but I clamp my hands down on her thighs.

"Keep them open," I demand, and her chest rises and falls rapidly. I push up my shirt that hangs on her like a dress, revealing her toned stomach, and I lean down to press a kiss to her hot skin.

She jolts at the contact, and I repeat the movement, pushing the shirt up higher, exposing her breasts, and sweep my hands over them, her nipples puckering as a gasp escapes her lips. Her breasts fit in my hands perfectly and I roll my thumb over her now hard nipples, earning a moan that makes my dick twitch. I lean down further, taking one in my mouth, and suck as her back arches off the countertop and a hand clamps down on the back of my head.

"Yesss," she hisses as I continue. She writhes beneath me, so responsive to my touch. I run my tongue between her breasts, down her body, and as I meet the lace of her panties, I begin untying the bows as if she were a gift and stand up, pulling the tiny piece of pink fabric away from her skin, exposing her glistening pussy.

I groan in appreciation. "So wet already, baby girl." I pick up the glass of wine, taking another sip as my gaze meets Gabriella's hooded eyes. "Do you know how long I've waited to taste you?" I lower down and swipe my tongue through her wet heat, and she sits up at lightning speed.

"Nooo," she gasps, her breathing ragged.

"No? You don't want me taste you?" I eye her curiously.

"No, yes, I ummm, don't want you to feel like you have to, I..." Her words from the wedding come flooding back. How she asked her ex-boyfriend to go down on her and denied her, telling her it was gross and that thought only spurs me on, determined to show how much I want her.

"Mia cara, I have been craving your taste since I met you. Don't deny me out of fear. I want to do this," I reassure her, cupping her face.

"Are you sure?" she asks hesitantly, chewing on her bottom lip the way she does when she's nervous, and I notice she's pinging the band around her wrist. I cover her wrist with my hand and run my thumb along her lower lip.

"I want you, Gabriella. Every part of you that you are willing to let me have. You are in charge here."

She lies back slowly, letting me know she wants this. I wait till she's comfortable and nudge her thighs apart again. I take a second to take her in, half dressed, her bare pussy exposed, and waiting, for me. The first time I touched her was all about her, her comfort, her needs, helping to break down that wall of vulnerability she hides behind daily that I didn't get a chance to savior a moment for it to sink in that I am finally seeing her in a way she's felt too nervous to share with anyone in a long time, in a way I've wanted to see her for so long if I were being honest with myself.

After allowing myself just a second for the tremor of adrenaline to pulse through me, I waste no time burying my face into her wet pussy and I eat. I lick and suck on her clit, and she's just as sweet as I'd imagined. I devour her, my movements pulling a moan from her that hangs in the air, encouraging me to continue.

Her legs begin to shudder and I wrap an arm around her thigh, tugging her a little closer and then push a finger inside her just a little, circling her entrance lightly, teasing, giving her just a taste of what she is craving. I glance up, watching her chest rise and fall between as her moans fade into desperate whimpers.

"More. Please."

Her words let me know I've pushed through her walls of insecurity, and she wants this just as much as I want to give it to her.

"Mmm, so fucking tight and wet." I push my finger all the way in. She feels warm and soft as silk. I add another finger inside her, pumping my fingers slowly while I continue sucking her clit and she starts to rock her hips against my mouth.

"Yes, that's it, baby. Ride my face," I growl against her hot skin.

"Oh, shit..." I can't help but grin at the words that fall from her lips. My dick strains painfully against the fabric of my briefs and it's taking all my power to not take her right here in my kitchen. But this moment is all about her.

I continue pumping my fingers, her arousal coating them and the sound echoing around the space. She tries to squeeze her thighs shut and I hold them apart with my forearm, flattening my hand on her stomach to keep her in place.

Her walls tighten, her manicured nails scratching along the surface of the counter.

I release her clit from my mouth. "Hold on to your legs and pull them back," I demand in more of a growl. I'm just as turned on as she is. I want, no need, her to come undone for me.

She does as she's told. "Good girl."

The move has now opened her up even more, showcasing her glistening thighs, coated in her arousal.

I continue pumping my fingers, curling my fingers until I hit that sweet spot that has her back arching off the counter. Her hooded eyes are full of heat and seeing her like this is enough to make me come without her even touching me.

"Please, don't stop," she says on a strangled breath. She doesn't need to ask me twice. Gabriella pleading for my touch may be my new weakness. I don't think I could deny her anything.

Her walls begin to spasm and I circle my tongue over her swollen clit one final time, sucking hard as her orgasm rips through her. I look up and watch in awe as her body succumbs to the pleasure. Her body shudders, and I don't stop my fingers moving until she releases her legs and lets them fall against the counter.

I rise, looking down as she's spread out, utterly spent. I bring my fingers to her mouth, and she opens without hesitation.

"Suck," I command, and she does, moaning around my fingers. Swirling her tongue over the tips of my fingers and I groan, imagining how good it would feel on my cock. I remove my fingers from her mouth, knowing I probably shouldn't kiss her, because kissing means intimacy and this isn't meant to be anything more than a friend helping out a friend yet, I go against what my head is telling me and go with what my heart and apparently what my dick wants. I pull her up and crash my lips down on hers, pushing my fingers into her hair and kissing her with a sense of urgency, as if she may disappear if I don't hold on to her.

Her hands find the hem of my shirt, and we break the kiss for just a second as she lifts my shirt over my head and tosses it, and my lips are back on hers, our tongues intertwining, and I feel myself getting lost in her. I pull back, stroking the pad of my thumb over her jaw, pressing my forehead to hers, and in a moment of weakness or utter madness, I confess. "I think I could get addicted to you."

She mirrors my actions, and her next words have me feral.

"I want to touch you," she whispers and then kisses me with a want that no woman has ever expressed toward me.

Not wanting to deny her, I lift her off the counter, my hands cupping her bare ass, never breaking our kiss. I carry her up to my bedroom, pinning her to the wall when we enter my room. I can feel myself falling and getting so lost in her, I can't think clearly. I'm losing my head, but there's this invisible string that pulls me to her, and I don't think I have the strength to fight against it. But I know if I have all of her, I'll never recover when she leaves me. But I can give her what she wants without having all of her.

"If this is too much, and you wanna stop, you tell me, okay?"

She nods. "Use your words, Gabriella. I need to hear you say it."

"Okay, I will tell you if it gets too much," she confirms, her voice breathless and labored, but it's what I needed to hear. I take a step back, reaching for the buckle on my belt.

"Have you sucked a cock before, Gabriella?"

Her eyes widen, and she shakes her head.

"Words, use your words," I demand again, pulling the belt free.

"No, no, I haven't." She scans my body with her heated eyes.

"Well, you're about to learn." There's a primal tone to my voice as I drop the belt to the floor and work on unbuttoning my suit pants.

"Get on your knees," I demand, and like a natural submissive, she lowers herself to the ground, looking up at me through her thick lashes, and fuck, if it's not the hottest sight.

I give her a wolfish grin, pulling my pants and underwear off, my hard length springing free as she inhales sharply.

"You're..." She swallows hard. "Pierced."

"You can take it," I tell her reassuringly.

Placing one hand on my thigh, she wraps her hand at the base of my cock, and I hiss at the contact. My cock, now leaking with precum, is just inches from her mouth.

"Move your hand up and down." She strokes my hard length, rolling her thumb over the silver ring of my piercing on the head of my cock, and it pulls a deep moan from my chest. My body ignites when she repeats the movement a few more times, becoming more confident with every stroke.

I watch in fascination as she leans in and then moves back, hesitant, to take me in her mouth. She looks up at me and then back down at my throbbing dick. I gently grip her chin between my thumb and index finger and angle her head to look up at me. The sight of her on her knees, looking up at me through her lust filled haze, steals my breath for a second.

Sensing she needs some encouragement, I say, "Open up those pretty lips for me, baby girl, and take my cock in your mouth."

She doesn't move, and I close my eyes, frustrated and angry at myself that maybe I've pushed things too far too soon, but when I feel her hot tongue flick over the head of my cock and she moans in appreciation, all thoughts leave my brain.

She repeats the movements and then takes as much of me as she can into her mouth and my cock thickens under her touch.

"Fucckkk," I hiss, leaning my forearm against the wall in front of me to steady myself. She starts slowly, and it's the biggest mixture of pleasure and torture.

I watch as she picks up speed, sucking my cock, then flicking her tongue over the end and I see stars.

"Yes, good girl, just like that." My hand comes to the back of her head. She gags, and I ease off a little. I gather her hair in my fist and pull her back. "Relax your throat, Mia cara. You can take all of me."

She does as she's told, and my cock slides in further when I feel her throat opening up and I nudge my hips forward slightly, encouraging her to continue.

"Now, suck."

She swirls her tongue over my shaft and it's nearly my undoing when I glance down and she looks up, triumph flickering through her eyes as she hollows her cheeks and takes me all the fucking, way.

"Fuck, baby." My breathing increases as the familiar tightening of my balls hits me, and I know I won't be long. "I'm about to come, Gabriella. If you don't want to swallow, stop now." I say hurriedly.

I prepare for her to pull away, but she doesn't stop. She quickens her pace, her hot tongue swirling around the head of my pulsing dick, catching my piercing, adding to my pleasure.

"Use your hand. Pump my cock." I plant my hand against the wall. "Fuck, baby, I'm going to co..." She takes me by surprise by cupping my balls, massaging them with the palm of her hand and I fucking go off. A roar rips from my chest as I spill my hot cum into her mouth, coating her tongue as she continues to suck me through my release. My body heaves as I fight to steady my breathing. I slide out of her mouth and take a step back, my breathing uneven and heavy.

"Open your mouth. Show me your tongue."

She parts her pink swollen lips and sticks out her tongue and there, coating it, is my cum, and my brain short circuits for a split second. The realization of what's just happened, what we just did, hits me and I know, I'll never be able to look at her as just my friend ever again.

"Good girl, now, swallow." She rolls her tongue back into her mouth and I watch her throat bob as she closes her eyes and swallows, then opens up her mouth, revealing her now clean tongue.

"Fuck," I groan. I pull her up to standing, maneuvering her so her back hits the wall and I crash my mouth down on hers, not caring that I can taste myself on her lips.

I don't know how I'm supposed to let her go when she decides she's done with this, whatever the hell this even is. I knew Gabriella would be a weakness for me. She has a gravity that I've never been able to fight against, and I know I am a fool for agreeing to this arrangement because if she asked for the world, I'd find a way to give it to her, no matter what the consequences were. She calms the storm inside me, and I don't know how I'm going to weather it alone again when I eventually lose her to someone else.

Chapter Twenty-Two

Gabriella

We sit in companionable silence in the car on the way to Brad's mom's house in Brooklyn. Last night was unexpected, and yet everything I didn't know I was craving. If that's how good sex is, and by sex, I mean the foreplay, because we haven't gone all the way yet, then I want more.

"You okay?" Brad asks, side eyeing me as he drives through the New York traffic.

"Uh huh."

We eventually pull up outside a brick townhouse with steps leading up to the front door. Balloons and a Happy Birthday banner hang on the door.

"Ready?" he asks, and I nod.

We exit the car, and Brad pops the trunk and lifts out the giant box wrapped in blue paper for his nephew. To my surprise, he takes my hand and leads me up the steps to the front door that he opens without knocking, allowing loud chatter and music to filter through the dark entryway.

Black and white tiles cover the floor, dark painted walls with picture frame after picture frame hang, making the space feel small yet warm and homely. The smell of Italian food wafts through the air, causing my stomach grumble.

Never letting go of my hand, Brad leads me to the back of the house, through a door where I'm met with women are huddled around a kitchen island, preparing food and chatting amongst themselves.

"...so I told her, if Ronnie is going to be out till all hours, she has the right to ask him, ya know?" a woman with long dark hair, wearing a black dress and big gold hoops yells above the chatter.

The room falls silent when they notice me and Brad and a woman screams, "Ahhhh, you made it." She runs over, and Brad releases my hand so he can wrap his arm around her.

"Hey, sis. Where's the little man?" She releases him and stands back to look me up and down as she smiles.

"Oh, he's outside playing. Who's your friend?" she asks with her thick New York accent.

"This is Gabriella," Brad says softly.

"Hi, I'm Alessia. It's nice to meet ya." I smile, expecting her to maybe shake my hand, but instead she hugs me, pressing a kiss on each cheek. "Hey, Ma, guess who brought a girlfriend?" she yells.

Girlfriend?

"What?" a woman yells from somewhere in the crowded kitchen."

"Marco brought a girlfriend." Alessia beams.

Marco?

I look to Brad in confusion, and he leans down and speaks quietly. "I'll explain later."

A woman comes up beside Alessia. She looks like an older version of her. She reaches for Brad, embracing his face with her hands. "My Marco. It's been too long."

"Hey Ma," I don't miss the way his spine stiffens when she holds him."

"Ma, this is my friend, Gabriella," he says, gesturing towards me.

"Gabriella, oh my god, she's gorgeous. Isn't she gorgeous?" his mom says, taking my face into her hands and kissing both my cheeks.

'It's lovely to meet you..."

"Bianca, my name's Bianca. Don't mind my son's manners. He forgets them from time to time," she teases, tapping Brad's chest with the back of her hand.

"Let's get you some food and drink. Follow me," Alessia says. We head down a set of stairs out to a patio where a large table filled with food and people sitting around under a parasol.

Alessia introduces us and my eyes immediately focus on the bouncy house at the bottom of the garden where children squeal and laugh. Brad's still clutching his nephew's gift, his jaw tight. I sense he's uncomfortable here, but knowing now isn't the time to push the subject, I slide my hand into his, caressing the back of it with my thumb to offer him some reassurance that I'm here. When he grips back, my heart flutters. The moment is broken when a small boy with dark hair comes barreling towards us. Brad bends down, so he's at eye level with him, sets the gift down on the grass and opens up his arms to catch his nephew. The little boy leaps and lands on Brad with such force, Brad falls back. His butt hits the ground, and the little boy giggles as Brad tickles him.

"Happy birthday, little man," His little face lights up when he tears the paper off the gift Brad handed him, revealing a Lego fighter jet.

"Thank you, thank you," the little boy squeals, jumping up and down in pure delight.

"You're welcome, bud. Hey, I want you to meet someone." Brad turns his body, still sitting on the ground, and points to me.

"This is my friend, Gabriella. Gabriella, this is Luca."

"Hey, Luca. Happy birthday. It's so nice to meet you. Are you having fun at your party?" I ask, looking into his big brown eyes that look just like Brad's. The genes are strong in this family. They all have the same eyes.

He nods his head quickly. "Yeah, my mommy got me a bouncy house and Legos, and I got a Lego cake. Want to see?"

"Sure do," I say excitedly.

"You're pretty."

I giggle and blush. "Thank you," I say, tucking a strand of hair that's fallen in front of my face.

Luca gets up, dragging the big box with him, and Brad stands up, brushing his jeans down as he looks up at me.

"Wait there," Luca yells as he walks toward the steps.

"We will, buddy," Brad calls back.

"You're very sweet with him." I hold a hand above my eyes to shield them from the bright afternoon sun. It feels like a million degrees in New York today and it's the perfect day for a garden party.

"Yeah, well, his dad isn't around, so I try and make up for that by being in his life as much as I can. He's a cute kid, so that makes it easy." And that right there has me falling for Brad just that little bit more. There's so much I am still yet to learn about him, and the more I uncover about him, the more I think I want him, and that thought makes the idea of stopping this thing between us cause a knot in my gut to form.

Brad has said he doesn't want to settle down, and that's what I want, or at least what I thought I wanted, but being with him has made me think about things differently and seeing him here with his family has just unlocked a new piece of the mysterious puzzle that makes up Brad, or rather Marco Russo.

Chapter Twenty-Three

Brad

I was right. Having Gabriella here has eased the stress I usually feel when I'm in this house. She is quickly becoming the person I look for in a crowded room, the one I want to reach out to and curl up with at the end of a long day, and the person I want to share my secrets with. Watching her with my family has my mind going into overdrive. Could I do the relationship thing? Could I give her everything she wants, needs, and deserves? Could I be the man worthy of calling her mine?

"…I told her, you go bending your back like that, Kayla, you got to stretch first. I mean, I know the girl can stretch. She's got three kids," my sister says, and I close my eyes and wince as she has no filter and says exactly what's on her mind.

Gabriella takes a napkin and brings it to her mouth, coughing, then falling into a fit of giggles.

"Well, you and Kayla are welcome in one of my Pilates classes anytime. I'll show her how to bend correctly," Gabriella offers, before taking a sip of her iced tea.

"Oh, I bet you could," my slimy uncle mutters from the end of the table and I give him a death glare. My uncle Lorenzo is my dad's brother, and we have never seen eye to eye since my dad and brother went down. He blames me, but what he doesn't know is, I blame myself. They needed to go down. They would have never gotten out of the life if they hadn't. Me? I was forced into a life of crime. It wasn't an option. Them going down gave me the opportunity to break free and do better, and many members of my family have never forgiven me for that. They see it as a betrayal.

My mom clears her throat and steeples her hands together. "So, Gabriella, when do you teach a class? Maybe me and Alessia could take a trip into the city and come by."

'Sure. I teach most days. Let me send you my studio details," Gabriella offers.

She picks up her phone, and she and my sister chatter amongst themselves. My mom glances over and gives me a small smile. I appreciate that she's welcoming Gabriella and making an effort.

My relationship with my mother is strained. I get her need to stay in contact with my brother while he's behind bars. He's her son, her blood, but my dad? I don't understand her loyalty to a man who beat her and cheated on her, a man who forced his sons into a life of violence and crime because he couldn't seem to do an honest day's work in his life.

My spiraling thoughts are interrupted when my sister whistles. "Gabriella Monroe, fancy name. Any relation to Marilyn?"

Gabriella lets out a nervous laugh and shakes her head. I watch as my mom straightens her back and looks over at Gabriella and her whole demeanor changes.

"So, Gabriella, where did you say you were from?"

"I've lived in New York the last twelve years, but I'm originally from a town near the Hamptons."

"And your parents? What do they do?"

I narrow my eyes at my mom. *Why is she asking these questions?*

Gabriella shrinks into herself at the mention of her parents. I know she hates talking about them.

"Uh, my mom stays at home and does lots of charity work, and my dad is, uh, works in the legal division."

"Really?" My mom's tone verges on sarcastic as she sips her wine and I don't like where this is going.

"What is he, like an attorney or something? That could come in handy in this family." She laughs, but there's an edge to it I don't like.

"He's a judge," she says quietly.

"Oooh, fancy," my mother drawls, and my uncle pushes back his chair and leaves the table. Everyone falls silent and eventually my mom gets up and follows my uncle into the house.

I give Gabriella a small smile. "Are you ready to go?" I ask and she nods. "I'm using the bathroom, then we'll leave. I get up, thankful when I hear my sister begin chatting to Gabriella and I take the steps two at a time to get inside the kitchen, where I find my uncle yelling in Italian, and my mom placing her hands on his chest to calm him.

I slide the door shut and storm over to them.

"Che cazzo era quello?" *What the fuck was that back there?* I yell.

My mother turns, her eyes filled with unshed tears as moves away from my uncle. He reaches into the pocket of his black suit pants, pulls out a packet of cigarettes and places one in his mouth and for a split second, I consider asking him for one.

"Just go, Marco," he breathes out, smoke from the now lit cigarette filling the space between us.

"I'm not going until you tell me what the hell that was," I say, stepping forward, ready to get physical if I have to; the old me getting ready to rear its ugly head.

My mom wipes her tears and sniffs.

"Marco, do—" I hold up my hand to stop her speaking, my stomach now in knots at the use of my real name. Suddenly, the room feels too small and the walls are creeping closer while that old feeling in my chest, which was an everyday feeling, seeps its way into my body.

I need to get out of this house.

"I'm leaving. I don't want you contacting me or speaking to Gabriella," I say sternly, heading to the door.

'You know who she is, right?" my uncle yells.

I turn on my heel to face him. My mother's hands cover her face, her body hunched over, crying.

"Who?" I ask

My uncle walks towards me, and I square my shoulders, ready to take him on. As a kid my dad and uncle would knock seven bells out of us if we ever stepped out of line, but now, I'm bigger and stronger than him, he doesn't have a hold over me any longer.

His lip quirks up into a snarl. "Your little girlfriend out there, her daddy, he's the prick that put your brother and dad behind bars."

Chapter Twenty-Four

Gabriella

We left the party in a rush. Brad seemed pretty tense and was silent the entire car ride back to his apartment. I have so many questions, but I'm too scared to ask. I know Brad has a past that he doesn't share. I've always found that part of him intriguing. How he can go from being stern and cold, and then soft and gentle and then back again has always made me wonder what led to him being this way.

We pull into the underground car park, and Brad's phone begins ringing. He exits the car and I've taken enough car rides with him now to know he will always expect me to wait so he can open my door. He gestures that he will be a moment and walks away. My phone begins vibrating in my purse, and I pull it out, my body tensing when I see Patrick's name flash across the screen for the third time today. I look over my shoulder and see Brad is deep in conversation, so I swipe the screen and bring it to my ear.

"Hello."

"Hey, Gabby, it's Patrick. I was about to send out a search party for you. You keep dodging my calls."

"I'm sorry. I've just been super busy, but what's up? Everything okay?"

"I wanted to arrange that date we keep saying we'll do. Are you free tonight?"

I take a second to think. Do I want to go on a date with Patrick? I glance over at Brad and instantly my heart races. He's the epitome of tall, dark, handsome, and a little dangerous. Then there's Patrick, who, to be fair to him, is really trying, and maybe I should give him a second chance. This situation with Brad was meant to boost my confidence and help me get out there, but that's all this. I can't get attached to Brad.

"Yeah, sure, sounds great," I say.

"Great, I'll pick you up at eight.

"Great, I'll see you later."

"Bye, Gabby." I end the call to find Brad is right behind me. I jump, nearly dropping my phone.

"Oh, my god," I shriek, my voice echoing around the underground car park.

Brad's eyes narrow and his jaw ticks. "Who was that?"

I think about lying, telling him it was Ali or Ria, but a really twisted part of me wants to see his reaction. "Patrick. He's taking me out for dinner tonight."

"How lovely," he says through gritted teeth as his jaw tightens.

I follow him into the elevator.

"I don't have my car here. Could you drop me back to my apartment, or I can take a cab?"

"I'll take you home. I have another call to make first." His responses are short and clipped.

We exit the elevator, and he lets us inside his apartment. I don't take more than three steps before he grips my hips, spinning me and pinning me to the wall. My purse and its contents clatter to the floor, and he's on me. His large hands slide into my hair and tug at the root, pulling a moan from my throat. His lips meet mine, and our tongues collide as the kiss becomes frantic. My fingers fist his shirt so vigorously that I'm close to tearing it from his skin.

This kiss feels different. It's as if he's claiming me, getting lost in me to quieten whatever noise is plaguing him, and I want to be that for him. He begins to slow the kiss, and I let him lead. I am his, and I'd let him have me in any way he wants or needs. That thought should scare me, make me run for the hills, but it doesn't, because it all feels different with him.

Our lips part, and he presses his forehead to mine, his erratic breathing matching my own. "I'm sorry. I shouldn't have done that," he rasps. "I just needed to…"

"What?"

"I just needed to get lost in you for a second," he admits.

I swallow hard, lost for words at his confession. He lifts his head. His whiskey eyes look more haunted than usual, and it pains me to see he's struggling with something. I want to take it all away for him.

"You can talk to me," I reassure. He closes his eyes.

"Look at me," I say, cupping his face. "Talk to me." His body softens, and he takes me by the hand and walks us over to his leather couch that wasn't here the last time I was here . I sit beside him, curling my legs underneath me. He never lets go of my hand, trailing his index finger over the back in intricate circles. I wait for him to begin, not wanting to force something he isn't ready to share.

"Going to my mom's house is always hard." His voice is so low I almost miss what he says.

"My full name is Marco Bradley Russo. Bradley is after my grandfather on my mom's side. Growing up, my dad was into some bad shit. He was an evil man. Beat my mom, beat us, ruled the house with an iron fist. Long story short, there was an incident. I was meant to be there with Matteo, but I didn't show up. Him and my dad went down for murder."

I try to hide my shock, but the gasp falls from my lips. I wrap my arm around his shoulder and lean my cheek against his head, letting him know I'm here.

"They went down for a long time. My mom sat me and my younger brother down and said we had two options: we end up like my dad and Matteo, or we join the military and build a new life. So that's what we did. I dropped the name Russo and went with Bradley, and eventually, I just became Brad. I just wanted to disconnect from that name, that life, that world. I struggled a lot, fighting for control. It's why I am the way I am. I have to be like this or I'll..."

He stops and I hold him tightly, my eyes welling with unshed tears. My heart is fit to burst, knowing he feels safe enough to open up to me. There is so much more to Brad than most realize.

"Thank you for sharing that with me," I say softly. "I can't imagine how hard that was growing up like that and going through all that."

He brushes his knuckles against my cheek, and my eyes flutter shut at the warmth of his touch.

"I have to go to LA tomorrow for a few days. Come with me." It's not a question, more of a plea, and I don't even have to think about my answer.

"Okay."

I sit across the table from Patrick in a swanky steak and cocktail bar in the middle of Times Square. It has white table cloths and little lamps on the tables and soft jazz music in the background, drowning out the conversations happening around us. We have an incredible view of the city, which has been a great distraction as he talks about his job and his plans to own a law firm one day. I admire a man with career goals and a life plan, but there is just something about him that doesn't get me going.

He's a nice enough guy, but I don't feel the spark. He doesn't give me butterflies when he smiles, he doesn't make me ache for him when we are apart, he doesn't have me hoping it's him every time my phone rings. No, Patrick doesn't do those things for me, but a man who will never fully be mine does and I need to get over that before my heart gets broken.

"Thank you for giving me another chance to take you out. I'm sorry If I was a bit of dick on our last date. Being around a woman as beautiful as you can get a guy all twisted up inside."

A blush flushes my cheeks. Okay, that was a little swoony.

"You're welcome. I've had a great time tonight," I lie. I've worn a black spaghetti strap dress I borrowed from Ali's closet. It's a little more revealing than I would usually go for, but in the spirit of trying new things and trying to break from my shell, I took a risk and Patrick's roaming eyes have made it very clear that the dress is a hit.

"I'd love to take you out again. What are you doing tomorrow?" Patrick asks as he signals the waiter for the check.

I'm going to LA with Brad. "I am going away with a couple of girlfriends."

"Nice, where are you going?" The waiter places the leather bill holder in front of Patrick, and he pulls out his wallet, slips his black Amex card inside it and hands it back to the waiter who leaves with it.

"LA, my friend has an audition with a new dance company, so we are going with her for support." The lie slips off my tongue so easily, but then again, I've been lying and people pleasing all my life. What's one more.

Patrick nods, placing his elbows on the table and resting his chin on his fists. "I like you, Gabby, and I want to see you again, so how about I whisk you away when you get back from your trip? I have a place in the Hamptons we can go for the weekend."

I blink rapidly, trying to think of an answer. I don't think I'm ready to go away with him. It feels too soon. I don't note how easily it was for me to say yes to going to LA with Brad. I don't have time to unpack that because Patrick is waiting for an answer from me and giving me puppy dog eyes.

Ugh. No, not the puppy dog eyes.

"Can I call you when I get back and we a make a plan then?"

"Sure, I look forward to your call."

To my surprise, Patrick shuffles in his seat and edges it towards mine. He reaches for my chair and tugs it towards his, and suddenly his mouth his on mine. I go with it. When his tongue pushes through my lips, I open, and instantly, a feeling of betrayal washes over me. I feel like I'm cheating on Brad. But we aren't anything. I'm not Brad's, and he isn't mine, and that idea hurts my heart. I break the kiss and pull away, clearing my throat.

I need to sort out my head and my heart and get them on the same frequency before someone gets hurt, because I think that someone is me.

Chapter Twenty-Five

Brad

We landed in LA earlier this afternoon, and I didn't realize how much I needed to get out of New York and clear my head until I felt the California sun on my skin. Maybe asking Gabriella to come with me wasn't my smartest idea, but having her near me brings me an inner peace I didn't know I was capable of reaching until we started hanging out more over the last few months.

I rented a place in the hills, a two bed, three bath white brick house with an infinity pool that overlooks the Hollywood Hills and lying out in the sun, soaking in the view, confirms that I miss living in a hot climate. New York is where my family is, and by family, I mean the ones I've chosen as my family, aside from my sister and nephew, but living in Miami after leaving the Marines confirms I need to be in a hot place.

I don't have any meetings until tomorrow, so the rest of today will be spent hanging out around the pool and ordering in. The sun is beginning to set, and an orange glow blankets the hills. I worry Gabriella is avoiding me. She said she had to teach a virtual Pilates class as she left for LA so last minute which I understood and I watched in awe from the living area out on the patio as she taught her class by the pool and contorted her body into all sorts of ways that had my dick pulsing and my heart racing.

We haven't had sex, yet I think not allowing it to go that far may be the only thing that will help me move on when this is all done with, but it's becoming harder with every passing day because she is all I see, and all I want but I know she's giving this Patrick prick a chance and that's a good thing. If I've helped her find the confidence to date, then I've achieved what we agreed to. I said I'd help her find herself, but then why do I have this painful weight that sits in my stomach, knowing I am helping her fall into the arms of another man and not into mine?

I give my head a shake and run a frustrated hand through my wet hair after my swim, looking up to see Gabriella appear, holding two glasses and wearing a tiny pair of denim shorts and a cropped black t-shirt, her toned legs flexing with every step she takes.

"Hey."

"Are you all done with your classes now?" I ask, holding a hand above my eyes to block out the sun.

"Sure am. One of the other instructors is going to cover my morning class tomorrow, so I'm free now till we go back." She places the two glasses on the table beside me, and I note their pink color and the cherries inside them.

"What are these?"

"Cherry Negroni. The perfect mix of bitter and sweet," she says with a little smirk.

"Just like us," I say flirtatiously.

"How poetic." She sits on the lounger beside me. "I saw there were cherries in the refrigerator, so I looked up a cocktail recipe. Don't worry, I've removed the stones so you can eat them."

I lift the tumbler to my lips, and I am hit with the sharp taste of the gin along with a floral tang. Two cherries float in my glass, and I take one out and bite it from the stem. It's cold, and the sweet juice fills my mouth, causing me to release a little moan. "Hmmm, tastes just like you too." Her mouth falls open, and I give her a wink.

She lies on her side to face me, and her eyes light up. Any worries I had earlier about things being weird between us leave me. I decide I am just going to enjoy this time with her and worry about everything else when we are back in New York.

"Do you have a party trick?" she asks, her voice full of excitement.

"No. What's one of those?" I ask, furrowing my brow.

"You must know. It's something you can do to entertain or a trick you can do." She sits up and sips the negroni.

"I can't say I've had the time to figure one out."

"Well, I was a bored only child, so I had to find ways to entertain myself. Plus, I had this really cool nanny from England, and she taught me how to play poker, solitaire, pairs, and snap. It's amazing what you can do with a pack of cards."

"I do like a card game. We used to play a lot when on tour." A memory of Harry losing to Jack at a game of poker that resulted in Harry setting fire to the cards comes to mind, and I laugh.

"Well, you'll have to play with me, because I am the queen of card games." Her tone is confident, and she straightens her spine as she smiles proudly.

"Okay, queen. Show us what you've got. I want to see one of your party tricks."

I wonder what the heck she's going to do, and then she pulls a cherry from her glass and pops it into her mouth. She holds the stem in her hand as she chews and then swallows the cherry.

She holds the stem out in front of me. "I can tie this in a knot with my tongue." She says it so innocently, and I sit up and place my feet on the patio tiles, giving her a challenging stare. "Prove it."

She matches my stare, sticks out her tongue, and places the cherry stem on it, rolling her tongue back into her mouth.

I watch as she works, but her focus never leaves mine. Her eyes flash with something that looks a lot like lust, and I fist the towel beneath me to prevent myself from reaching out and pulling her on top of me.

When she pokes her tongue out, my eyes drift down to where a perfectly knotted cherry stem sits on the end of her tongue and I nearly damn well lose it. I pluck the stem from her tongue, and a low growl erupts from my throat.

"Do you have any idea how fucking hot that is, baby girl? I can think of a few ways you can use that talented tongue of yours."

"Oh, yeah." She presses her mouth together and places her hands either side of her as she leans back.

"Take your clothes off," I demand, my tone firm, my body firing up.

"Why?" she asks innocently, cocking her head to the side.

"Because I'm about to perform my own party trick."

A sharp gasp escapes her, and she stills, eyes wide.

"Take the clothes off, Gabriella."

She looks around at the surrounding houses, the sun now setting so low that a little darkness has crept over the valley.

She reaches for the hem of her cropped shirt and pulls it up over her head in one swift movement, revealing a red string bikini, and fuck, red is her color. She stands and pops the button of her shorts, letting them fall to the ground, exposing a matching string bikini bottom that barely covers her pussy. I run my tongue over my top teeth and moan in appreciation. "You're fucking incredible."

I rise to my feet, towering over her, and she cranes her neck to meet my eyes.

"Where do you want me?" Her voice is far more confident than it was the first time we fooled around.

"I need to get you wet first." I pull her body towards mine, and before she can say anything, I wrap my arms around her thighs and throw her over my shoulder and stride toward the pool.

"Brad, oh my god, nooo," she squeals, but her words are cut off when I jump into the pool. Our bodies meet the water; it's cool and crisp and tingles against my burning skin.

I pull us both to the surface where she flicks her head back to move her soaked hair away from her face.

She coughs and falls into a fit of giggles, and I can't help but smile and laugh right along with her. She wraps her legs around my hips and her arms around my neck, and to my shock, plants a kiss on my lips. Tingles float up and down my spine with every stroke of her tongue. I move us till her back meets the tiled edge of the pool. A surge of desire works its way through my body. She's intoxicating, addictive, and I need her. I lift her out the water and settle her on the edge of the pool.

"What are you doing?" Her words are breathless.

"I'm about to show you all the tricks my tongue can perform."

I hoist myself out of the pool, water splashing onto the white tiles as I walk over to the little table and pick up my drink. I get back in the pool, keeping the glass above the water until I get back to her, and I maneuver her so I am standing in between her legs.

I take a sip and then wrap my large hand around her delicate throat and gently pull her closer to me, feeling her pulse stutter beneath my fingers. I move toward her, watching her pink lips part the closer I get. As soon as my nose brushes hers, I tilt my head, letting our mouths meet in a soft caress of lips. Then, slowly, I press deeper to her, this time with purpose. The drink lingers on my tongue as I let it spill slowly into hers, a warm rush shared between us. Her lips curve around mine, trying not to let a drop fall as a quiet moan vibrates against my mouth and I can't tell if it's me or her.

I pull back and watch her throat expand and flex beneath my inked fingers as she swallows down the last of the cocktail, wishing it was my cock in her mouth and my cum sliding down her throat.

Placing the glass beside her, I lean in, planting a kiss between her breasts, and work my way down her torso. She leans back, and I widen her legs.

I pluck the cherry from the glass and hold it to her mouth. "Suck it." Her mouth latches onto the cherry, and she closes her eyes and moans around it.

I dip the cherry back in the alcohol and repeat, my dick hardening.

I pop the cherry in my mouth, biting it from the stem and tossing it on the side, the sweetness filling my mouth only reminds me of how good Gabriella tastes.

I place open mouth kisses along her collarbone, and her head rolls in pleasure. Running my tongue between her breasts, I continue to just above her bikini bottoms and work my way back up her body, reaching my hands behind her back and tug at the tie of her bikini top and slide my hand to do the same to the one around her neck. I pull the red fabric away and if my dick wasn't already painfully hard before, it was now. Her perfect tits that are now just a shade lighter than the rest of her skin thanks to the California sun bounce free and with the sunset playing with her skin, making her glow like a goddess, the sight has my blood pounding in my ears.

I need her.

I watch as she casts an anxious look down her half exposed body and her teeth worry her bottom lip. My thumb tugs her lip free and I lift her head to face me.

"You have nothing to be shy about baby girl."

I press my forehead to hers, lightly brushing my lips with hers.

"I'm going to show you how badly I want you."

I press a chaste kiss to her lips and reach my fingers inside the glass tumbler, taking an ice cube and dragging it along her pouty lips before popping it into my mouth and hold it there.

She gasps when the ice meets her sun kissed skin and her hands find my hair and tug hard when I roll the ice over one nipple and then repeat on the other side. Her nipples pebble and I trail the ice in between her breasts till I reach the waist band of her bikini bottoms and then work my way back up her body, by the time I reach her throat the ice has almost completely melted. I plant my lips on hers and she sucks what's left of the ice from my tongue which has my dick straining painfully in my swim shorts.

My hands reach for the half-filled glass of Cherry negroni and I hand it to her. She furrows her brows and looks at me with confusion when I sink down lower in to the water.

"Pour that drink down your perfect tits and watch how I don't miss a drop." I plant a kiss in between her breasts. "And eyes on me at all times baby girl."

Mouth agape I give her just a second to do as she's told and fuck does she. She tilts her head back, exposing her neck and lifts the glass and begins tipping the red liquid over her chest, it trickles between her breasts. I brace my arms either side of her and flatten my tongue just above her belly button and lick a path up her torso, lapping up every single drop of the liquid trail she's left for me.

"More." I hum against her soft skin.

She moves the glass and lets the liquid run over her breast this time, her head still thrown back, her chest rises and falls, and she's gasping for breath.

"No, no baby girl, you're going to watch. Eyes on me."

She lifts her head, her blown pupils meeting mine.

My mouth covers her nipple and I nip and suck, dragging my tongue over her hardened nipple, the heady mix of the cherry, the bitterness of the gin and the warmth of the brandy explodes on my tongue as she continues to drip feed me the cocktail and I could do this all god damn night.

Her tiny whimpers turn into erratic pants of desperation as I lick a path back down and nuzzle my nose against the fabric of her bikini briefs.

"Touch me," she rasps and I almost miss it.

"Lie back. I'm going to fuck you with my tongue," I hum against her skin, and she does it without protest.

She sets down the now empty glass and makes a whimper when her back hits the tiles and goosebumps prickle all over her skin.

"Am I going to find you wet and ready for me, Gabriella?" My fingers work the ties of her bottoms, and I let the fabric fall away from her golden skin. I moan in appreciation, licking my lips at the sight of her glistening sex.

I swipe two fingers through her folds, and she whimpers when I push them inside her.

"Fuck, you are ready for me, baby girl." I work my fingers in and out of her slowly, enjoying her legs trembling with pleasure as I do. I lean down and swipe my tongue over her clit and her hands instantly fly to the back of my head.

"Keep your hands above your head," I order, and she pulls them back.

"Am I going to have to tie those hands, Mia cara?"

"No," she pants. She places her hands back above her head, and an idea flits through my mind.

I lift the other glass that is still full and lean over her body, placing the cold glass between her hands.

Our noses touching, our lips just a breath apart, I order, "You spill, I spank you." A sharp gasp escapes her.

"Keep those hands above your head and if you don't move them, I'll reward you, understand?"

I know I'm pushing the limits here, but my gut instinct tells me there is a little submissive inside Gabriella and I want to pull it out of her and give her everything she desires.

"Yes," she pants. "I understand."

I pepper kisses down her body and then bury my face in between her legs, inhaling her sugary scent and suck on her clit as I push my fingers back inside her. She's soaked, and it confirms that taking control turns her on.

I push my tongue inside of her and she tastes like fucking heaven. I don't relent, I spear my tongue in and out of her, the ice starts rattling against the glass as her body arches in pleasure.

I hum against her pussy and lightly flick my tongue over her swollen clit.

I rise up and insert one finger slowly, and she releases a moan that's a direct hit to my aching balls. Her legs fall open a little wider, as if inviting me, and I push a second finger inside her. The sound of her arousal fills the space between us, mixed with pretty moans of approval. The lights under the pool now illuminate the space as the sun has almost fully set, and watching Gabriella's body heave with arousal, coming apart under my touch next to the view of the hills and the sunset may be the most beautiful sight I'll ever witness in this lifetime.

I pump my fingers a little faster, and her walls tighten around me.

"Do you like that, greedy girl? Does your tight pussy like my fingers, or do you prefer my tongue?"

"Oh, my god, please..."

"Please, what... slow down?" I slow my pace and she growls in frustration.

"No, please, don't stop, just..."

"What, what do you want, baby girl?"

"I want you to..."

"What, Gabriella? Use that pretty mouth of yours and tell me what you want, and I'll give it to you."

The glass in her hand is close to spilling as she fights for control over her trembling body. "Make me come," she purrs.

I tap her ass. "Knees up."

She lifts her legs out of the water, the heels of her feet balancing on the edge of the pool.

I curl my fingers inside her, hitting her G-spot and her screams echo around us but neither of us seem to care.

"Oh God, it's too much. I can't..." I watch in awe as her fingers grip the glass with white knuckle force. I expect it to shatter the same way she is.

"Yes, you can. Just go with it, baby girl." I work my fingers in out quickly and her hot pussy grips me tightly, her arousal dripping down my hand, and I know she's right there. She just needs to let go.

"Come on, Gabriella, get outta that pretty head of yours and come for me. I've got you."

And that's all she needed, a little encouragement, a little reassurance. Her back bows off the tiled floor, her walls convulse around my fingers, and when I apply a little pressure to the bottom of her pelvis, her stomach muscles tighten beneath my splayed hands as she cries out, and then she squirts.

Holy shit.

"Fuck." I groan out, watching her in complete awe as her orgasm rolls through her body. I could come from just the sight of her.

When her body softens, and her legs go limp, I pull my fingers out and reach for the glass that's still clutched between her hands that's only spilled a little. I pull her up to sitting with my free hand, her heavy, sated eyes try to focus on mine.

"What just happened?" She's all flushed cheeks and blown pupils. Fucking perfection.

"You just squirted, Gabriella." I grin watching her mind absorb that information.

I hold the drink to her lips.

"Drink." She takes the glass and, to my surprise, downs it in one. The primal need for this woman takes over and I take the glass out of her hand and toss it to the side, hearing the glass shatter, but I don't give a shit. I kiss her with urgency. The mixture of her sweetness and the bitterness of the cocktail creates an explosive taste on my tongue.

"What the hell are you doing to me?" I growl against her lips.

"The same thing you're doing to me." She pants as she hooks her legs around my waist and pulls me closer, our wet bodies pressed together, and the need to be inside her intensifies, but I can't, I won't allow it. If I go there with her, I'm well and truly fucked in all senses. There would be no coming back from that, no recovering from the mark she will leave on me once I know what it feels like to be inside of her.

Chapter Twenty-Six

Gabriella

I can't describe the feeling that's pulsing through me right now. I am riding a high that's a mixture of alcohol, lust, and desire. He just made me come harder than I ever have. He made me squirt. I didn't think I was capable of that, especially out in the open, but I don't care. I want him in a way that I've never wanted anyone. Sensible Gabby would stop this; she'd end this and walk away with what was left of her dignity and pride intact. But sensible Gabby has left the building, fucked off back to New York and left me to make sense of this, and I can't. All I know is I want him, need him, and he's kissing me back like he feels the same way.

Our lips never part. Every time his tongue collides with mine, tingles spread throughout my body, driving my need for him forward.

Cold air hits my wet flesh as he walks up the steps and out of the pool and I break the kiss to look at him. His lust filled eyes darken, and I know we aren't done here; there's more in store. I bite down on my lower lip in anticipation.

We enter the large bathroom, walking past the white bath that sits in the middle of the room, and he opens the glass door of the double shower, turning the shower handle and pressing my bare back against the cold tile. The sound of running water clatters on the floor tiles as his hot mouth moves to my breast, sucking and swirling his tongue over my sensitive nipple, pulling a moan from me. I work my fingers into his hair as he repeats the movement on the other and sucks so hard it's to the point of pain, but I lean into it, craving more. I love it when he's a little rougher. It sparks something inside of me. When he takes control, I become putty in his hands. I'd let him do anything to me because I trust him. I have faith that he would never hurt me or push me too far. When he releases my nipple, I place my hands on his naked chest, pushing him back against the shower door, the water still running, steaming the glass.

I stare at his chest. The intricate artwork decorates his body like a story I could spend all day getting lost in. I want to ask him what they all mean, but right now, the need to have him inside me somehow takes over. I swipe my tongue over his nipple and a groan rumbles from his chest, making me grin. I do it again and again, and my own moan escapes me. A strong hand grips the back of my neck and moves me to look at him. He stares down at me with an intensity I've never seen before, and suddenly, I feel like the most powerful and desired woman in the world.

"I need that pretty mouth on my cock. Now." His voice is gravelly and low and it makes my clit throb.

He guides me down, his hand still on my neck. I sink to my knees, hooking my fingers into the waistband of his swim shorts, and pulling them down as I go.

His erect cock springs free, already leaking with pre cum and I hum in approval.

He releases my neck, and I waste no time, planting my hands on his thick thighs and taking him into my mouth. He hits the back of my throat, and I gag a little, remembering to relax the back of my throat like he showed me last time. I use my hand to hold the base and pull him out of my mouth just enough to be able to swirl my tongue like I'm tying the knot of a cherry stem over his pierced tip, earning a deep groan from him.

"Fuck, Mia cara. You keep doing that, and I'm going to shoot my load down your pretty little throat. Is that what you want?"

I nod.

"Good girl, that's it, take all of me."

His praise spurs me on and the need to circle my clit becomes too strong, so I reach between my legs to ease the ache, but he grips my hair, his cock popping out my mouth as I look up at him.

"Don't touch yourself. You only come if I say so."

And holy shit, his words have me on the verge of tears because my need to finish just hit an all-time high. I take him back into my mouth, working his shaft with my hand and cupping his balls and sucking and swirling my tongue and with every movement, my need to come becomes unbearable. I sense he's close when his cock twitches inside my mouth and I get ready take his cum.

But he pulls out of my mouth and drags me to my feet, not giving me a second to get my bearings before he spins me and presses my back to his chest.

"Hands on the wall and arch your back," he growls into my ear, and I do as I'm told.

Is this it? Is this the moment we take this to the next level, where we truly blur the lines of our friendship and connect in the most intimate way. When I feel his fingers push inside me, disappointment floods me, but it soon passes with every stroke of his fingers. My legs weaken, and my hands feel ready to slide down the shower wall as my orgasm builds to breaking point.

'Brad, please, I...' I say weakly, not able to finish my sentence, too lost in the building pressure working its way through my body like a tidal wave getting ready to crash against the shore.

"Fuck, your cunt is begging me to fuck you, isn't it? Look at you dripping all over my fingers."

My body quivers at his words, wound so tight I am ready to explode again and it would only take one rub of my clit with his expert fingers to make me shatter into tiny fragments. My fingernails scratch the tiles as my hands slide down while I try with all that I have to keep myself upright. One large hand covers both of mine, pinning me in place.

"Don't move." His breathing is ragged; it sounds like he's running. I turn my head to see as he works his cock in a vigorous motion himself.

"Touch your clit, now." I reach between my soaked thighs, bringing my fingers to my swollen clit and move my fingers in tight circles, and it's all I need.

"Do you want my cum baby girl. Did you want me to make you mine?"

"Yesss. I want it." I hiss out as the pressure between my legs builds, because all I want right now is to be his.

A deep groan comes from him, the sound pushing me over the edge, and I cry out as I glance over my shoulder and watch, open mouthed, as he releases onto my lower back, as if he is leaving his mark, claiming me as his. Hot ropes of cum decorate me and trickles between my ass cheeks and it's the hottest thing I have experienced.

He releases my hands and my body stumbles forward but he steadies me, clutching me by the waist, pulling me into his body, my sticky back to his bare chest and when his hand wraps around my neck, squeezing it and guiding me so I'm now faced so he can crash his lips down on mine I melt into him. He nuzzles his nose into my wet hair, and I close my eyes as he maneuvers us toward the running water.

I welcome the hot jets as it beats down on my damp skin and his mouth moves closer to my ear.

"I don't know how I'm going to let you go." It's barely a whisper and I almost miss it but I hear it, every word of it, and sadness washes over me as I realize, not only do I not want him to let me go, but I don't want to let go of him.

Chapter Twenty-Seven

Brad

My eyes are met with the California sunrise. We must have forgotten to close the drapes last night. After our shower, Gabriella and I collapsed into bed, and I slept better than I have in a while; I know it's down to having her beside me. I have grown far too comfortable having her around, and I'm starting to think I want things to be different with her. I don't think I can go back to just being her friend. The idea of her doing what we did last night with another man fills me with a rage that could cause me to do something that would land me behind bars right beside my dad and brother. I haven't thought about them since I found out Gabriella's dad was the judge involved in the case. I've spent most of my adult life blocking them out and what they did, what I did, or rather didn't do. So I'll block this out too. It doesn't change anything, they deserved to be where they are. Should I be there? Maybe, but I fought to get where I am today, to leave that life behind. A life that was controlled by threats, violence and drugs. Every day felt like living on borrowed time. It wasn't a matter of if we would get caught by the cops, it was just a matter of when.

I roll on my side and concern fills my chest when Gabriella's side of the bed is empty. I get up and go in search of her, forgoing my morning workout if I have to. I just need to find her. Relief floods me when I see her practicing Pilates out on the patio in front of the sunrise. I lean against the glass doors with my forearm and watch as she moves into a handstand and parts her legs, then places them down so her butt is in the air, the tightness of her yoga shorts showcases the curves of her ass and it awakens my dick. I tiptoe out and creep up behind her, wrapping my arms around her waist as she's bent over stretching. Her initial screams turn into girlish giggles as I place her down on her feet and turn her to face me.

"You scared me," she yells, tapping my chest playfully.

"Well, you scared me when I woke and you weren't there." My confession seems to startle us both and her eyes soften as her hands come up to cup my face.

"I'm sorry. I'd never leave without telling you. I just wanted to catch the sunrise and get my morning workout in." She releases my face and steps away and points to the view.

"That's the Hollywood sign just over there right? I've always wanted to see it up close."

"Let's go then," I say without giving it any more thought. "Let's hike up Mount Lee and go see the sign."

"Really, you aren't too busy? Don't you have meetings?" There's a hopeful tone to her voice.

"Not till this afternoon, but even if I was, I'd rearrange for you."

She chews on the inside of her cheek, stifling a grin. "You know, for someone who doesn't do the boyfriend thing, you sure are very swoony when you want to be."

"I know. I think I'm spending too much time with Jack. He's clearly rubbing off on me."

"Clearly, and we wouldn't want that now, would we?"

'No, we wouldn't, but focus on the 'when I want to be', baby girl. I don't act like this for just anyone." A beat passes between us, and I think about pulling her close and kissing her, telling her I want her, and that the idea of her being with someone else breaks me in two. But then I remember all the things she wants. The commitment to a life of 2.4 kids, the house, the happily ever after and I fear me and my fucked up past will seep out and ruin her. She deserves more.

To my surprise, Gabriella kept up with me throughout the hike. She wore a baseball cap and her hair in a braid and deep red shorts and crop set and I spent the entire hike up the hill staring at her ass with a stiff dick like a horny teenager.

"This view is insane," she says, looking out over LA, the breeze whipping around the loose strands that have fallen free from her braid.

"It sure is," I agree, my focus on her. We have to leave LA tomorrow, and I don't want to go back to reality and everything that awaits us in New York. I just want to stay with her in this bubble.

"We better head back. I have my meeting, and I've arranged something for you to do."

"Oh, my god, if it's a full body massage, I'll love you forever. My back is aching today," she says, placing her hands on her lower back.

"You'll have to wait and see," I say. My stomach does a weird, fluttery thing at her use of the word love.

"We need a photo before we go," she says, pulling her phone from the little bag strapped around her waist. She takes a selfie with the hills and the sign behind her.

"Come here," she calls, waving me over.

I'm shirtless and only in a pair of black running shorts, sweat coats my body from the LA heat and having a photo is the last thing I want, because photos capture moments we may forget; to keep as reminders, and if I don't get to keep Gabriella, I may have to try and forget her altogether, I don't need a physical reminder, because the memories of her, will be painful enough to live with.

She pouts and gives me those eyes I can't say no to.

"Fine," I grumble.

I stand beside her, and she looks at me deadpan.

"Please try and look like you wanna be here."

I chuckle and wrap my arms around her waist, and she snaps a photo.

"See, that wasn't so hard, was it?"

"No, it wasn't," I agree, my gaze locked on hers, and in a moment of madness, I lean down and kiss her like it's the most natural thing to do. The click of her camera sounds, and I realize she's taken another photo. I have become entirely too comfortable with kissing her like she's mine and it's going to hurt like a mother fucking baseball bat to the shin when it hits me that she isn't and never will be.

"Come on, old man, last one down the hill is cooking," she calls as she makes a start running. I give her a ten-second start before I set off behind her. She turns her head and lets out an excited scream when she sees I'm coming up behind her.

"Looks like you're making lunch, baby girl."

I run past her, scooping her up and flipping her over my shoulder with ease as if she weighs nothing, continuing our descent back to our rental with a lightness in my chest.

I spank her ass and she yelps. "And that's for calling me old."

Being around her feels easy, but fighting my feelings for her feels like the hardest battle of my life, and one I am slowly losing every day.

I pull up outside a large white building in the convertible Mercedes I hired while in LA. Gabriella spent the drive with her hands in the air, her hair whipping around her, singing along to some pop track I'd never heard. With every passing day, her confidence around me grows, and I love seeing her being herself and no longer hiding. So I hope my little surprise for her today helps with that even more.

"I will be a couple of hours. A woman named Paula is expecting you."

"If this is the part where you dropped me off at some weird sex dungeon, I'm gonna have to decline."

I throw my head back and laugh. "No, Gabriella, I am not dropping you off at a sex dungeon, but I love that's where your mind went."

She eyes me curiously. "Hmmm, okay." She presses a kiss to my cheek. "I can let myself out of the car," she whispers, taking her purse from the backseat before she climbs out.

I watch as she enters the building, my heart doing some strange fluttery shit when she turns to give me a wave. I put the car in drive and head to the construction site where the new potential club is being built, cranking the stereo and relaxing into my seat. If we go for this LA building, it would mean one of us potentially moving here for a short time or at the very least traveling back and forth for some time, which just feels like yet another roadblock on my path to wondering if Gabriella could be mine. I look at the time and realize it will almost be Luca's bedtime. I've never missed a FaceTime call, but he'll be in bed by the time my meeting has finished. I dial my sister's number and she answers on the second ring.

"Hey."

'Hey, sis, you good? How's Luca?"

"He's good. Just finishing up his dinner. You're calling early. Everything okay?" she asks, concern in her voice.

"Yeah, I'm fine. I'm going to miss Luca's bedtime. I'm just driving to my meeting."

"That's okay. You know you don't have to call every night? We understand you have a life."

I digest her words. Calling them every night has become part of my life, my routine since Luca was old enough to talk.

"Do you have anyone with you in LA? You didn't say yesterday."

I think about lying, but this is Alessia. I can tell her anything. "Gabriella is here with me. I just dropped her off at an appointment."

"Oooh," my sister coos down the phone, and I roll my eyes, getting ready for her comments. "So is it serious between you two?"

"There's nothing going on. We are just friends. All our friends are out of town. She was alone, so I invited her along."

"Hmmm, sure, because I too invite my friend, who I look at like a lovesick teen, along on trips."

"Excuse me?" I bark, her comment getting under my skin.

My sister's laughter filters through the phone. "Calm down, will you? Don't lie to me. I saw the way you looked at her, and I'm happy for you. I loved Gabby, and so did Luca." The news of my sister and nephew loving Gabriella makes my heart swell. They are two of the most important people in my life, and their approval means everything to me because whoever is a part of my life would be a part of theirs.

"It's erm, a long story and complicated," I mumble, hoping she'll let it go.

"Well, lucky for you, big bro, I have no life and I'm free as a bird, so start at the beginning and don't you dare leave out a thing."

Chapter Twenty-Eight

Gabriella

I walk through the revolving glass doors of what I assume is a hotel and to the reception desk, where a woman with dark hair in a sleek bun and a white blouse sits.

"Hi, my name's Gabriella. I am here to meet Paula?" I say it more as a question than a statement.

"Ah, yes, Paula is up on the top floor in the studio. Would you like me to show you the way?"

I shake my head. "No, that's okay. I can find it. Thank you."

I head back to the elevator and step inside, hitting the button for the top floor, wracking my brains as to what he could have booked me for.

I exit the elevator, and I'm immediately met with a sign that says 'studio' directing me to the left. I walk down the hall and push through double doors, stopping dead in my tracks when I take in the scene before me.

Lights, screens, a white backdrop, tables of makeup, rails of clothes lined up. This is a modeling studio?

"Hey, Gabriella, I'm Paula. It's great to meet you." A woman with thick black glasses, curly short blonde hair, who's maybe in her late forties at a guess, wearing a black jumpsuit, walks towards me holding a camera.

"Yeah, hi, my friend Brad said you were expecting me, but I don't know what for." A nervous laugh escapes me, and I begin pinging the elastic on my wrist.

"Why don't you head into the dressing room back there? There's something for you in there and then we can chat about how this afternoon will go. Sound okay?"

"Sure, thanks." The dressing room is filled with more rails of clothing, a counter with mirrors that line the wall surrounded by lights. There, on the counter in a crystal vase, are the most beautiful pink peonies I've ever seen. I inhale the scent and notice the card beside them with my name on it.

I open it with shaky fingers, still so unsure of why I'm here.

Gabriella,
I hope this experience helps you see what I see. A beautiful confident
woman, who is more than enough.
B x

"That's great, Gabby, just pop your hip a little for me... perfect." I do as Paula suggests, and the flashes go off. I've been at this for nearly an hour now. We've done several different looks and I feel like a million dollars after the hair and makeup artist were through with me. After each round, Paula shows me the unedited photos she's taken of me. I look carefree, the kind of girl you notice in a room, the one that's not overlooked or told she's too much, or not enough. No, the girl on the screen looks happy. She looks enough, and she is me.

"Now, there's no pressure, but we have some lingerie if you want to do any shoots with those. I hesitate for a second and then remember why I'm here: to see myself how he sees me.

"Let's do it."

"Gabriella, this is great. Have you considered modeling? If you haven't, you should." Her suggestion makes me blush.

"No, it's not something I've considered," I say shyly.

"Well, you should."

"I'd have to agree," a deep voice booms from the back of the room. I'd know that voice anywhere. Brad comes into view, and if a single look could undress you, then the way he's looking at me right now would have me naked in seconds.

"Okay, I think we are done here. Gabriella, you've been a dream. Seriously, if you want some modeling work, give me a call. I'll make a start editing these while you get sorted, . Everything you've worn today is yours."

"It's... it's mine?" I say in surprise.

"Sure is. You have your boyfriend here to thank for that." I don't correct her, and neither does Brad. She walks past him and taps his arm. "You're a lucky man. Look after her. She's a good one." Paula vanishes out of sight, leaving only me and Brad and a palpable tension that swirls between us.

"Oh, I know I am." His eyes darken as he scans my body. He takes a step towards me, and I swallow hard. "You look fucking incredible."

I pull my bottom lip between my teeth, and my cheeks warm.

"Thank you. This was amazing, and far too much. You didn't need to do this."

"It was nothing." He shrugs like it's no big deal.

"The thousand-dollar shoes I'm standing in would suggest it was something," I say, gesturing to the black heels with the YSL symbol in the heel.

"I just wanted you to feel good and feel seen." I almost melt on the spot.

"Well, mission accomplished." I press a kiss to his cheek, but as I pull back, he cups my face and brings his lips to mine. It's soft and tender and I fall into him, allowing him to take control. I could get lost in it, never coming up for air.

Our mouths part, and he tilts my face to look at him.

"I have something else for you." It's then I notice the red bag he's holding with words *Cartier* in gold across the center.

"Brad, you shouldn't have," I stammer.

"Open it."

I take the bag and set it down on the table beside me. Reaching inside, I pull out a small box. My heart hammers wildly as I open the oyster clasp and gasp in surprise when a beautiful gold signature bangle sits on a white silk pillow.

I remove it with a shaky hand as he takes the box from me. It's then I notice words engraved on the inside of the bangle.

More than enough

"Oh my god, Brad, this is stunning." I sniff. He lifts my wrist, the one I am forever pinging a band against when I am nervous or uncomfortable, and it's only now I wonder if he has noticed me doing it.

I hold out the bangle and he uses a tiny gold screwdriver to loosen the screw. When it opens, he hooks it around my wrist and fastens it together again. "Whenever you are doubting yourself, or on the days you don't feel good enough, or anxious, or you just need a reminder, I want you to look down at this and remember you are more than enough, just as you are."

I fight to keep the tears back that threatened to fall. This is the most thoughtful thing anyone has ever done for me.

"Thank you," is all I manage to say, my voice thick with emotion.

"I mean it. You don't need to change yourself to please others, Gabriella. You are perfect as you are."

He presses a light kiss to my forehead.

There are a thousand things I want to say but am unable to right now. But I hope he knows just how much this, what today has meant to me.

"And I'm taking you to dinner. Heels like that should be taken out."

"Just say where, and I'm all yours…"

Chapter Twenty-Nine

Gabriella

I definitely should have stopped drinking two drinks ago. Brad took me out for dinner as promised, and I ate the best steak I've ever tasted and drank pink champagne like it's water. I'm not drunk, but I'm nearly there. "Come on, have one with me," I plead, pulling a new bottle of pink champagne from the refrigerator and walking over to the white couch that faces the open doors that look over the valley and sit beside him. I'm going to miss watching the sunset and doing my morning workout on the patio.

Brad shakes his head and sips on the whiskey he's been nursing since we got back.

"Can I ask why? I don't think I've ever seen you drunk." It's a personal question; one I have no business asking. I go to apologize, but he offers me his reasons.

"When I was younger, I got caught up in some bad shit, and drinking and drugs were my go to way to cope with it all. When we lost Scotty on our last deployment, I could feel the temptation to go back to that life, so I like to keep in control. I just have a little, but never enough to lose control."

I reach for his hand and give it a reassuring squeeze. "That's incredibly admirable. Not many people possess that kind of strength."

I'm sure our conversation will end there, but he continues. "It's not easy, but joining the military gave me a focus. I joined with Scotty, and a year later, Noah, Jack, and Harry joined, and they all saved me in their own ways. The decision to join the Marines saved my life."

"You must really miss him," I say, referring to Scotty.

"Every day," he says under his breath, his voice cracking as he places a hand over his chest, over where I know a set of dog tags hang.

The need to comfort him becomes too strong. I place the bottle of champagne down on the table, crawl into his lap, straddle him and begin, stroking his jaw with the pads thumbs, loving the way his stubble feels under my touch.

I smooth my hands down his neck and onto his chest. He doesn't say anything, his eyes laser-focused on my hands as they undo the buttons one by one. I open the shirt, pushing it back, revealing his toned muscles, his tattoos and the dog tags.

I lift them and run my thumb over the cool metal, the embossed letters and numbers have a few scratches and dents over them.

"Are these Scotty's?" I ask softly.

"Yeah, his family gave them to me after the funeral. Said they wanted me to have them."

My heart aches at the sound of his tormented voice. I can't imagine losing Ali or Ria. It's something I'm not sure I'd ever recover from. He's been through so much, and underneath the harsh exterior is a man who cares deeply, and I feel honored to have been on the receiving end of it. Even if it's only for a little while.

I place the chain back down and trace my finger over the lines of his tattoos. "What made you get all your tattoos?" I slide my hand in his and interlock our fingers. "I really like these ones." I place a kiss to the back of the tattoos on his hand. I wouldn't have dreamed of being this brave a few months ago, but with him, I feel confident and free to be how I want to be.

"I got them to cover up the reminders of my past." My face falls at his admission.

"What do you mean?" Anxiety swirls in my stomach, wondering what he's done or what he's been through, that he felt the need to cover it up.

"I've done some bad things, Gabriella. Every time I looked at my hands, they were just reminders of the bad shit I've done, the people I've hurt and the people I couldn't save," he says quietly, his voice tight as he stares down at his hands.

"So, I covered them, and then it became an addiction; one that wasn't going to kill me, so I kept going. Everyone has a story, but…" He clears his throat, and I sense this is becoming too much, so I lean in and press a kiss to his chest to comfort him. His skin instantly pebbles under my touch, and I continue dusting him with kisses until I feel his body relax under my touch.

"Thank you for opening up to me," I say softly, between kisses.

"You're the only woman I could open up to like that, Mia cara." I raise my head to look at him. Those words mean everything. He's helped me in ways I can't explain, and if I can do that for him too, then why does this have to end when we go home?

"You help me forget all the bad in my life."

Oh, my heart.

"I want you," I whisper, my voice raspy and desperate, and I do one of the bravest things I've ever done, I crash my mouth down on his, and when his fingers weave into my hair and kisses me back with the same fervor, I rotate my hips over him, desperate for some friction. My hands work his buckle.

"I want you to have all of me," I confess through panted breaths and frantic kisses.

"We can't," he murmurs against my lips.

"We can. I need you." My breathing is hot and heavy as I reach inside his pants.

"Gabriella, stop." I stiffen and pull back, hurt by his words.

"I'm sorry." My words are barely a whisper.

Embarrassed at my boldness, I climb off his lap and hurry to the bedroom. God, I read that situation all wrong. Tears prick at my eyes, and I want to hide and cry over his rejection, but he's hot on my heels.

"Gabriella, wait."

"I'm sorry, I shouldn't have assumed. I just... Is it because you don't want me like that? Are we done with this now, or did I do something wrong? Did I..."

I don't get to finish my words. He clutches my waist, turning me to face the full length mirror opposite our bed. His wild eyes latch on to mine in the reflection. My racing heart is ready to break through my chest in anticipation for his words, his next move.

"Don't see you like that?" His words are laced in something I don't recognize and I try to step away but he holds me tightly, burying his face into the crook of my neck, nipping and sucking at my heated skin. My head rolls to the side, giving him more access.

"You, Gabriella, are all I fucking see."

He works the zipper on my red dress, and I hold my breath.

"... all I think about..."

The dress slides from my body and pools at my heeled feet, leaving me in nothing but a pair of black laced panties.

"... All I want."

I suck in a breath, closing my eyes, feeling a wave of dizziness wash over me.

"Open your eyes Mia cara. You are going to watch me…"

His large tattooed hand glides across my exposed torso, setting fire to my skin with each movement, and when he cups my breasts and rolls my nipples between the pads of his fingers, my head falls back into his chest.

"… I'm going to show you exactly what I see when I look at you."

He gently tugs on my nipples, and I gasp, pushing back my hips, searching for some friction.

"These tits, they were made to fit in my hands." He massages my breasts with the palms of his hands, and I lean in to his touch, needing more.

When he releases them, I whimper in disappointment, but I'm caught off guard when his hand moves to my throat and squeezes lightly.

"I'm going to make you come and you're going to watch and see what I see."

I swallow, and the feel of his digits around my throat sends a rush of heat to my core.

He brings two fingers to my mouth and pushes them inside without permission, and I welcome it.

"Suck."

I swirl my tongue, coating the pads of his fingers with my saliva. He pulls them out without warning and tightens the hold on my throat.

"Take off your panties."

I don't hesitate. I slide them over my hips and let them fall on top of my dress, and I can already feel how wet I am, how ready I am for him to take me; however he wants me.

His fingers swipe through my folds, smearing my arousal up over my swollen clit and my body jolts at the contact.

"So fucking wet already. Is your cunt begging for my cock, Gabriella, huh?"

I don't say anything. I slide my hands up to lace my fingers around the nape of his neck to steady myself.

"Is that what you want? Me, buried inside you." He circles my clit, over and over again, forcing my eyes shut and my bare ass to grind against him.

"Yes," I manage to choke out.

"Open your eyes," he growls.

"You are going to watch and see how pretty you are when you come."

I blink my eyes open, focusing on him in the mirror, his whiskey eyes now dark and hooded. I watch in fascination as his expert fingers work my clit and tremors rush through my body as my orgasm builds.

I bite down on my bottom lip to stifle another moan, his now growing erection presses into my ass and I circle my hips, encouraging him.

"You want my cock, Gabriella, then say it."

"I want..." He steals my words when he strums my clit faster.

"Say it," he hisses into my ear, his fingers flexing around my throat.

"I want your cock." I pant, my body beginning to convulse as the wave of my orgasm is about to reach its peak.

"Brad, please." His name falls from my lips like a prayer.

"Eyes on me." His words are rushed, his movements never relenting. I glance up, his fingers squeeze my throat a little tighter, our eyes lock, my body stiffens, and then he says.

"Gabriella, Come." And I fall apart. Warmth floods my body, my thighs clamp shut, trapping his hand between them, my world blurs, and all I feel is his hard body behind me as I go limp against him. His lips find mine, and he kisses me, breathing me in as I float back down to reality.

I'm startled when he pushes away, and I stumble. He swipes a hand through his hair in frustration, his chest heaving, matching the rhythm of mine, and I see the conflict in his eyes.

"You see, Gabriella, you are all I fucking want. I know how to take control of your body in the same way you do with my mind. But we can't go further than this." He gestures between us, and I feel anger bubbling inside me.

"Why? Tell me why?"

"Why? You want to know why?"

I nod, straightening my spine. He takes a step closer, cupping my face in his hands that tremble when his skin meets mine.

"Because, if we go there, if we connect in that way, if I feel what it's like to be inside of you, I'll never be able to let you go."

It feels too painful to swallow, his admission too much to process. He wants me.

"What if I don't want you to let me go?"

I barely finish my words before he crashes his lips down on mine, and our kiss turns frantic. He turns me and walks me back till my heels hit the bed frame, laying me down carefully as if I were made of glass.

He rips off his shirt and tugs off his pants and boxer briefs as I shuffle up the bed, my heels still on.

He crawls on top of me, covering his naked body with mine, and settles in between my legs. His mouth is back on me, and he kisses me with a want that is verging on feral.

I wrap my legs around his waist and move my hips, desperate for the friction. My swollen clit rubs against the slick head of his penis, and I whimper when he kisses the sensitive flesh of my neck.

"Yes," I hiss when his teeth graze me, the perfect mixture of pleasure and pain hitting me at once.

He pushes on the inside of my thigh to widen my hips and takes a moment to scan my body. "You look so beautiful, Mia Cara."

The use of that name has my eyes fluttering when I feel the head of his pierced cock pressed against my entrance. I prepare for him to push inside me, for us to break the final barrier that we have between us, but his head falls to my chest, and he lets out a frustrated moan.

"Fuck, I haven't got a condom."

That should be enough to slow this down. I never take a risk, but it doesn't. "I'm on the pill. We don't need one. I want this." He lifts his head and looks me dead in the eyes.

"Are you sure? I've never gone without one, so I'm…"

"I know," I say reassuringly. "I trust you."

He tells me he's dangerous and has a dark past, but why do I feel the safest when I'm in his arms?

"I'll go slow."

I widen my hips, inviting him in. His eyes never look away from me when he lines up his cock with my entrance and slowly sinks inside. We both moan in pleasure. A sharp sting hits me when he's fully seated, but the pain is fleeting, and it only takes a few seconds for me to grow accustomed to his size and the pressure his piercing creates. I suck in a breath when he begins moving.

"Are you okay?" he asks, concern in his voice.

"Yes." My voice is barely a whisper. "Don't stop." He swallows my moans and kisses me like the world will disappear. His tongue glides with mine; it's hot and wet, the sensation spreading warmth through my body tingling up and down my spine, making me feel a little dizzy. Needing to anchor myself for fear I will fall in some way, I grip the back of his neck and hook my leg over his waist, pulling him closer.

"More." I pant. "I need more."

He takes that as his cue to quicken his pace, sliding his hand into mine, lacing our fingers together, and pinning them above my head. I tilt my hips, and his piercing hits and ignites something inside of me. Every stroke alights my nerve endings, sending bolts of pleasure through my body, my orgasm now hovering near the surface.

"You feel so fucking perfect." He groans against the hot skin on my neck, sending goosebumps all over. My legs begin trembling, and I'm not ready for this to be over. I need more. I don't want him to treat me like I'm fragile. I want him to take me exactly how he wants me, so in a moment of recklessness, I utter words I may regret because I know they will never be true.

"Fuck me like you want me."

Chapter Thirty

Brad

Fuck me like you want me.

Words I hadn't realized I was so desperate to have fall from her lips until she said them. Want her? All I've done for months, probably since the moment I met her, is want her. With an action that steals her breath, I slide out of her, lean back onto my heels, grip her hips with force, and flip her on her front, dragging her to her knees before I slam back inside with a power that has the bed frame hitting the wall.

She screams in pleasure as I take control of her body. Winding a hand round her long hair, I tug, making her back arch as I drive into me. "Is this what you wanted?"

"Yessss." This is nothing like I've experienced or realized I was capable of feeling. It's as if I'm tuned into her body, knowing exactly what it craves and needs. Her hands fist the sheets, desperate for something to hold on to.

The sound of her arousal, our bodies coming together, and our breathless moans fill the room.

Her walls begin tightening, and I can feel she's close, and I am right there with her. Gabriella coming is one of the most addictive sights. Knowing she's seconds from shattering, I pull out and flip her back on her back and push back inside her, lifting her hips so I hit that sweet spot.

"I need you to come for me, baby girl. Right now." She falls apart, shudders wracking her body and I come right along with her, spilling inside her. My chest heaves as I watch her, as her neck arches, hands kneading her breasts, eyes closing as she surrenders to the pleasure I'm giving her.

"Look at me," I growl because it's a need. I need her to look at me. She does, her amber eyes laser focused on me as we crash back down to reality together. A feeling of contentment floods my body as it relaxes. I lean forward, covering her body with mine, and kiss her. Gabriella has me on a rush far more powerful than any drug or drink ever could, and I fear she's now become an addiction I'll need to feed and succumb to every day.

But she's not mine to keep, she never was. But with every passing day, she makes me believe I could maybe be the man who's worthy of keeping her. I slide out of her, pulling her close as I hold her so tightly, like she's about to be ripped away from me, because that's what it feels like, and it hurts. A mixture of emotions goes to battle in my mind as we lie there in a comfortable silence. It wasn't supposed to be like this. I was supposed to keep my soft spot for her under control and not let it grow. But it became bigger than me.

I wasn't supposed to fall for Gabriella Monroe, but I think that's what I've done and now I've got to work out how to tell her I want to keep her, and hope she'll want to keep me too.

Chapter Thirty-One

Gabriella

We've been back from LA for a few days now. I haven't been able to see Brad as I've been busy teaching classes, visiting my parents to make up for the missed dinners, and trying to dodge Patrick's calls, and if I'm being totally honest, I'm avoiding Brad.

LA changed everything, and now I'm more conflicted than ever. He is what I want. While I was trying to get to a place where I would be confident enough in my own skin to find a man to settle down with, I've ended up falling for someone I consider one of my best friends. My best friend who doesn't want the same future as me, who doesn't do relationships, or forever. But if there's one thing he's taught me, it's to be brave.

I need to stop stringing Patrick along, and then maybe it will free up the space to pluck up the courage to speak to Brad and tell him how I feel. If I looked back and was being truly honest with myself, it's always been there. This little spark that's been busy burning silently in the background, left unattended and ignored until it started to grow, and now it's become bigger than either of us to manage alone.

Yes, today is the day you are brave.

I pick up my phone and send a message to Patrick.

Gabriella

> Hey, I'm back from my trip. Are you free to meet for coffee this afternoon?

I place the phone down on the kitchen island and write a quick note for Ali. She lands this morning, and I've missed her so damn much. Ria got back from her Disney trip yesterday too. It's the longest I've gone without seeing either of them, and if it weren't for Brad and that complicated mess, I'd have felt so lost and alone. I pick up the stash of mail I've been saving for Ali and leave it beside the kettle, knowing she'll be wanting a cup of tea as soon as she gets in, and put the note on top.

My phone vibrates against the marble counter and Patrick's name flashes across the screen.

I open the message and I should be excited by his reply but I'm not, so I know what I'm about to do is for the best.

Patrick

> Sure am. I've missed your pretty face. I'll be at Joe's coffee shop by Central Park at 1 pm.

I sit across the table from Patrick. He's dressed in a navy polo and jeans, looking like the pretty preppy boy he is. I opted for a more casual look with leggings and a cropped t-shirt, and tennis shoes. I am past caring now or feeling like I need to make an effort for Patrick. After today, we will be nothing more than acquaintances that say hello if we see each other in passing.

As usual, I've listened, and he's talked, and I'm grateful that Joe's coffee shop is so busy because it's given many opportunities to zone out and people watch as Patrick droned on about his job.

".... does that work for you?" is all I catch.

"Sorry, what did you ask?" I ask, shaking my head.

"The Hamptons, this weekend? You and me?"

A sinking feeling in my stomach hits me. This is it, the moment I break this thing that isn't really a thing off. But he seems like a nice guy. I'm sure he will be cool about it.

I take a deep breath and offer a sympathetic smile.

"Patrick, you're a nice guy. I'm just not sure I'm looking for anything at the moment. I'd love to stay friends." *Lies, but I need to try and soften the blow.* "I hope you understand. It's not you, it's a me thing," I continue. *Yes, that's it. Blame yourself and people please, Gabby.*

A suffocating silence falls between and I watch his face morph like a Disney character from a gentle expression to narrowed eyes and a look of pure evil steaming off him. He cracks his neck and swallows hard. Panic simmers under my skin, and I'm relieved I did this in a public place where I feel somewhat safe.

"Yeah, the thing is, Gabby." My name leaves his mouth with venom. "That's not really going to work for me. I need you. I've got goals, and you're going to help me get there."

I furrow my brows, completely confused. He must read my expression because he continues, lowering his voice. "Your dad and your last name can open doors for me, especially in the legal and political sector. Your dad knows people, and I need his recommendations to get me ahead."

My voice gets lodged in my throat and I want to get up and run. "Patrick, I... I don't understand what I can do? I can talk to my dad, get him to write a letter or..."

He throws his head back and cackles. It's evil and calculated, and I fear he's been wearing a mask this entire time.

"Men like your dad don't just do favors for people, Gabby, just because you ask. Don't be so fucking naïve." I flinch at his words, but he continues, "Your dad is one of the most respected judges in New York City, his opinion, his words and his last name holds weight, so if I am with his daughter and he considers me to be the perfect potential son-in-law, I'll be able to walk into any law firm I want and land any role."

I blink, staring at him, trying to process what he's saying. This is not what I expected at all from him.

"I don't need you to be with me. I just need you to pretend. You know, attend functions with me, sing my praises to your parents, play the part."

I gulp. "And if I refuse? You can't make me date you, Patrick. What are you going to do?"

A cruel grin sweeps across his face. "I'm glad you asked." He lifts his phone from his pocket, taps on the screen, and slides it over to me. A video of a girl dancing on a stage in a black leotard and a red mask spins around a pole and works the stage, then moves into a crowd of men. The girl is me.

The blood drains from my body, and my vision blurs. "W-why are you showing me this? I don't know who this is." My voice cracks as I try my best at ignorance.

"Swipe right and keep going."

With a shaking hand, I swipe the screen, and there, in color, is a photo of me and Brad in the alley outside of the club the night he discovered my secret. We are in a conversation, and it looks intense. I swipe again, and it's Brad, cupping my face and kissing me. The next photo is of both our startled faces looking directly at the camera. I freeze. Tears prick at my eyes, and the background noise fades until all I can hear is the erratic beating of my heart.

There's no getting out of this, no denying, no running, no lying. It's all there, the part of my life I've left hidden, the part I've let myself have, so I could feel free has now been stolen from me and used against me so someone else can gain control of my life. I want the ground to open and take me.

Patrick's voice snaps me from my free fall into darkness. "I was there that night, that bachelor party, that was Henry's, and I must say you know how to work a pole. Who knew quiet little Gabriella Monroe was such a slut? Do you fuck the men too, or is that extra?"

Every word he spits feels like a slap to the face. It stings and now the tears begin rolling down my cheeks and fall to the table. I swipe them away, scared someone will see, and Patrick will spill my secrets.

"Imagine my shock when the girl in the mask was you. But really it was perfect. I have you right where I need you. So, if you refuse, which you'd be wise not to, I'll be sending these to Daddy. Imagine the scandal? I can see the headlines now: Judge Monroe's only daughter is a stripper."

Bile works its way up my throat. This can't be happening again. I've spent the last ten years making up for my mistakes, and now I am right back where I started. This would ruin my dad's life. My body doesn't feel like my own. The heaviness in my chest makes it hard to breathe.

I had Patrick all wrong. He's evil, selfish, conniving. How could he do this to someone? How could I have been so stupid to think no one would discover my secret? How naïve was I to think I could finally be free and live my life the way I wanted, be with who I wanted? *No*, I'm now back where I was ten years ago. Doing as I'm told and keeping quiet.

"Fine, but I'm not sleeping with you or touching you."

He barks out a laugh. "I don't want your pussy, sweetheart. I've got women for that. No, I just need your pretty face, you on my arm, and your last name in my back pocket." He swipes the phone and puts it back in his pocket. "So, this has been good. There's a dinner I need you to attend with me this weekend. I believe your parents are going, so get us on the list." He rises to his feet and walks away without another word, leaving me alone while my entire world crumbles around me, along with any chance of a forever with Brad.

Well done, Gabriella, you fucked up... again.

Chapter Thirty-Two

Brad

It's been nonstop since I got back from LA, and trying to schedule time to speak to Jack and Harry has been difficult.

It's been hard to focus when all I want to do is be with Gabriella. Without her knowledge, she has brought a calmness to my life. I've relaxed my routines without even realizing the very routines that keep my flashbacks and daily internal battles I go through at bay. With every day I spend with her, the need to have complete control and map out my day to the minute to ease my anxieties has faded. When I left the military, I began drinking a lot. It was the only thing that silenced my demons. I did the same thing with drugs in my teens to block all the shit that was going on at home.

When my drinking was impacting my daily routines, I replaced the drink with workouts, replaced drugs with cleaning, and the more I did it and the bad stuff didn't surface, the more it became my way of living and I feared if I didn't follow the same things each day, then my demons wouldn't stay buried. But Gabriella has shown me that maybe I can do life without restraints and strict rules for myself. I was meant to be helping her, but I think she's the one who's helped me the most.

I am more me when I am with her; the me I want to be, the version of myself I have been fighting to be. She said she wanted my help so she could find someone, but I don't want her to be with anyone else, and I need to tell her. I reply to a few emails, and my phone vibrates across my desk, an unknown number lighting up the screen.

I answer and regret seeps into my skin the minute I hear the words, "An inmate from Bedford Hills Correctional Facility is trying to call you. Please press one to accept or two to decline."

I always refuse these phone calls. I have no desire to see my dad or my brother, but something in my gut tells me I need to answer after my visit to my mom's house.

I press one, and a familiar voice filters through the phone. "Hello, son, long time no speak." His raspy voice, that's a mixture of old age and years of nicotine, makes my spine stiffen.

"What do you want?" I say in a clipped tone.

"Now, now, Marco, is that any way to speak to your dad? I want you to come and see me. We have things to discuss."

Anxiety creeps into my body, the same feeling that made my stomach bottom out when my dad told me he had a job for me or just before his fist would meet my face.

"I'm busy," I say flatly.

He laughs, and that the sound leaves the hairs on the back of my neck standing. "I think you'll make time. It's about your little girlfriend."

And those words are all I need to say.

"I'll be there later today."

I'm scanned, patted down, and searched, as if I were a criminal in order to get through to the visiting room. I'm shown to a booth; a hard plastic chair sits in front of a glass panel with a phone beside it. I sit. The white shirt I'm wearing feels like it's clinging to my body in ways that make me want to tear it from my burning skin. My knee bounces nervously, and I force it to stop when a buzzer rings out, alerting everyone that the prisoners are coming in.

I straighten my spine, my hands ball into fists, my fight or flight mode kicking in. I focus on a tiny drawing on the counter to keep my racing mind focused. It looks like a small child has drawn. It's a little flower with a sun beside it. This is no place for a child to be, and the thought sickens me.

I lift the phone receiver to my ear and just wait. I don't notice him arriving or taking a seat. It's the familiar rasp of his voice that has me lifting my head and staring back at a man who, unfortunately, looks like an older version of me. The version I would have morphed into if it hadn't been for the military saving me.

He's aged but he's still the good-looking fucker he's always been. Fine lines frame his whiskey colored eyes. His dark hair now graying at the sides and the rolled up sleeves of his orange jumpsuit showcase new ink he's gained since being inside. He's still muscular, no doubt in the prison gym on the daily, ready to fight anyone who dares cross him. I often wondered if he tried, he could have been a good man. He'd have treated my mom the way she should have been and not his punching bag. That maybe he'd have wanted his kids to grow up and go to college and get a decent job instead of following in his footsteps into a life of crime, drugs, violence, and lies.

My jaw's locked so tight I'm shocked I haven't cracked my back teeth. There's only ever been one person to make me feel like I'm two feet tall and worthless, and it's the man staring back at me with an impatient expression, who I have the misfortune of sharing his DNA.

I lift the black phone receiver to my ear and remain silent. The less I talk the less worked up I'll get.

"Hello, son, nice of you to make the effort to come and see your dad. You're looking well."

"What do you want? Why am I here?"

He leans back in his chair, balancing the receiver on his shoulder as he folds his arms. "Come on now, you haven't seen me in what, nearly eighteen years and you can't make time to have some small talk?"

'No," I say flatly.

He leans forward, taking the phone in his hands and balancing his elbow on the table. "A little birdie tells me you are dating the daughter of the motherfucker that put me and Matteo behind bars, and I need you to do something for me."

A surprised laugh escapes my lips, and I shake my head. "You are out of your mind. I don't owe you a damn thing. We're done here."

I go to place the receiver down, but his next words send a chill down my spine. "If you don't want her to get hurt, you'll do what I fucking say, Marco."

I clear my throat, a copper taste filling my mouth where I've bitten my tongue so hard to stifle the words I want to throw his way. "What do you want?" I grit out.

"Your brother is up for parole; he's kept his nose clean in here, and it looks good for him. I need you to work on her to have a word with Daddy to pull some strings and get me out."

I blink in confusion.

"Are you serious? You fucking killed a man, a cop, a father, a husband. You're exactly where you are meant to be."

"We're both killers, son. Don't act like you're above me."

I run my tongue over my top teeth in frustration. "If you are comparing my military career to your drug bust that went wrong, where you killed a man to save your own skin, then yeah, it's not the same."

"A spade is a spade; a killer is a killer. If that helps you sleep at night, son, you keep lying to yourself, but you are no better than me." His words cut me deep. I've been fighting my whole life to block him out, to try and be the furthest thing from him that I could be. My palms begin to sweat and I take a steady breath.

Do not bite back. Remain calm.

"I'm not asking her that," I say firmly.

His mouth turns into a snarl, and the look in his eyes makes my blood run cold. "I think you will. It would be a real shame if something were to happen to her. Your uncle tells me she's a pretty one, nice legs, great set of tits. I bet she sucks a cock like—"

I cut him off, slamming my hand against the glass of the booth. "You won't fucking touch her," I growl.

"Hey, let's keep things calm, gentlemen," a security guard aims toward us.

I run a frustrated hand through my hair, hanging my head and tugging at the roots.

"I'll play fair, give you some time to work on her, but the clock is ticking, Marco. Don't keep me waiting."

Chapter Thirty-Three

Gabriella

I leave the coffee shop in a daze. The anxiety is so strong it makes me feel unsteady on my feet. I'm not thinking clearly because I forget all about my car I parked at the studio. Instead, I flag down a cab and give the driver Brad's address. I punch in the security code and ride the elevator up to his floor, where I let myself in with the key he gave me.

I walk into the living area and see him on the couch. I want to fall into his arms, tell him everything and ask him for help, but when I'm met with a stoney-faced man who looks at me like I'm invisible, my body retreats, and I go into my safe mode. I shrink myself down.

I note the bottle of whiskey on the counter and the empty glass.

"Hey," I say quietly. "Are you okay?"

"Never better," he says flatly, his voice stern; a tone he reserves for others, but never me. He doesn't look at me, just stares at the floor, his shirt half unbuttoned and untucked from his suit pants.

"I can, um, leave if you want to be alone," I stammer.

He lifts his head slowly, and when our eyes lock, his face softens and I see him, my Brad. I drop my purse to the ground, rush over to the couch and settle beside him, wrapping my arms around him on instinct. He pulls me into his lap and clings to me just as tightly as I am to him.

Something feels off. I lean back, cradling his face in my hands and stroking my thumbs along his stubbled jawline, loving the way the roughness feels beneath my soft skin. He doesn't hesitate, he grips the back of my neck, crashing our mouths together in a frantic kiss, but there's an edge to it; it feels different. There's something very final about it, and with every stroke of his tongue, I feel him pull further away, and I am powerless to stop it.

He presses his forehead to mine, and we fight to bring our breathing back to an even pace.

"I think we need to talk," I breathe out.

"We do."

"I just saw Patrick," I say hesitantly.

"And what did he want?" he grits out.

I think about telling him the truth, but something stops me. "He wants to make things official."

Brad's nostrils flare, and his eyes squeeze shut as if he is having his own personal battle. He pulls away, and I watch as his jaw tenses.

"I think that's a good idea. This was the whole point, right? Help you feel comfortable finding someone. This thing we've been doing. It's gone too far. I think we need to go back as we were now we're home." He says it with a calmness that's borderline uneasy. I slide off his lap and wince when he gets up, grabbing the bottle of whiskey and the empty glass before he walks to the kitchen.

I think it would have hurt less if he'd slapped me. I came here, ready to open up to him, ask for his help, and he wants to toss me aside. I won't cry, I refuse. I was stupid to believe he would want more or to continue this. LA wasn't real, it was temporary. I was stupid to think that he would want more. I am the fool for falling for him. Stupid, young, naive Gabby. Of course, this is how it would end.

Life is returning to normal now. Everyone is returning from their trips, and now with Patrick's threats hanging over me. I need to focus on getting through that. I'll play the part of his girlfriend to hide my secrets and protect my family. I ruined their life once; I won't do it again, so maybe this is for the best.

I clear my throat, standing up and squaring my shoulders, doing my best to keep myself from falling apart. "Yeah, sure. I think I'm going to give things a go with Patrick. He really likes me and he's a nice guy, so..." My words trail off as I watch Brad's body stiffen and his fingers grip the edge of the counter.

"Good, I'm happy for you. He seems like a good guy." God, he has no idea.

"Yeah, yeah, he does," I lie. A silence so thick it could suffocate us both edges it's in and I want to scream, tell him the truth, but I know him. When he's made up his mind about something, it's a done deal. He never promised me anything other than what he has delivered on, so I need to go, walk away, and handle the mess I have now got myself in.

"I guess I'll go then," I say, my voice shaky, but I wait, pray, he will tell me not to go, beg me to stay, but the words never come.

"Yeah, I have work to do. I'll see you around." His voice is quiet and frosty, nothing like the warm and comforting tone I am used to. He doesn't look up, washing the single glass, avoiding my gaze. How did we go from all that we were in LA to this? I turn away and place my key on the countertop. I head for the door and run towards the elevator. Just as I hear the front door close, the sound of shattering echoes out, and I'm not sure if it's the glass he had in his hand or my own heart breaking.

Chapter Thirty-Four

Brad

It's been weeks since Gabriella walked out of my apartment, taking a piece of me with her. The urge to fall back into my old coping habits becomes stronger every day. I spend my nights tossing and turning, battling with myself, but I know keeping her at a distance, making my family believe she means nothing to me is the only way to keep her safe. It's maddening when, in reality, she is everything. I wake up groggy, skipping workouts, and I bring work home when I can instead of working from the club. With Harry still in London and Jack on his honeymoon, it's been easy enough to fly under the radar, but tonight we have a busy night at the club, and I have to be there.

The club is packed, the music so loud it vibrates beneath my feet. The smell of high end liquor never normally bothers me, but tonight it pulls old cravings to the surface, making my hands twitch and my body feel on edge. There are only two things that could calm these feelings: giving in and drinking past my usual one, or her, and I can't have either.

I spotted Ali in here earlier with Cassidy, and that just sent warning signals. I've had a quiet eye on her all evening, something is off. Harry said Ali left without saying bye and has been avoiding his calls. I've dodged the girls' apartment because until I have a grip on my emotions, I can't set eyes on Gabriella. I feel like a shitty friend to Harry because I haven't tried to speak to Ali for him so I make it my mission to speak to her tonight, calmly, and try and get to the bottom of what's going on. But when I see the face of a man I sure as fuck know isn't Harry, all over Ali, I'm rounding the bar and ripping the fucker off her.

"Ali," I call. She turns and her face falls. "I need to speak to you."

"I'm a bit busy right now," she says, holding a hand in the air that's linked with the drunk bastard.

"That's exactly what we need to talk about," I yell, directing my focus to the guy. "I'm gonna need you to fuck off," I say through gritted teeth.

The guy scoffs, "Excuse me, she's mine tonight."

"I don't think so." I take Ali by the hand and drag her toward my office, leaving the drunk stranger standing alone, utterly dumbfounded.

"Get off me," she shouts, trying to free herself from my grip. I open the office door and pull her in, slamming it behind me.

"What the fuck are you doing?" I bark, my voice bouncing off the walls.

"Excuse me. What the hell was that?" she bites back, stepping into my personal space.

"I wasn't about to let that guy fuck you in a back alley."

She grins, her eyes heavy and drunk. "Oh really, did you want the job instead?" she slurs, moving closer, pressing herself against my chest. My body stiffens. What is she doing? This isn't her.

"What the fuck?" I say, eyes widening.

"Come on, let's have some fun. God knows, you need it. You are wound so fucking tight most of the time." She reaches for the button on my pants, and I grab her wrists, stopping her.

"Ali, I am not going to fuck you, nor will I ever, and I'm not going to let you go with anyone else either. Not on my watch." My heart's hammering. *How could she do this to Harry?*

"Since when did you become my keeper and have a right to tell me what to do?" she spits.

"Since you started fucking around with my friend, that's when. What the hell, Ali?" I growl, letting go of her wrists, and she stumbles back on her heels.

"Well, for your information, we're done. Over. No more fucking around, so I can fuck around with whoever I want."

"Does he know that?" I question.

"Who?" she says, wrinkling my nose.

"Harry. Does Harry know you're done? Because from what I heard, you have been avoiding him."

She folds her arms across her chest and sneers, not answering me.

"Yeah, I didn't think so. What the hell is going on with you? You've been in here most nights with Cassidy and that other girl. They're bad news, Ali. Why the hell are you hanging out with the—"

"Hey, don't you judge them? You have no idea who they are or what they've been through, so don't you dare comment on how they behave or what they do. You have no idea." And there it is. She's going through something, and she doesn't know how to manage it. I recognize it, the destructive behavior, the empty look in the eyes.

"Are you talking about them or yourself there?"

"I'd like to leave, please."

"Not with him you aren't." My tone is stern.

"I'm going back to my friends, if you must know. I also need to pee. Do you wish to escort me there too?" Her words are laced with sarcasm.

"You need to talk to him. He doesn't deserve your silence, Ali," I say, trying to soften my tone.

"Don't lecture me about what he deserves. Most of us don't deserve the hand we are dealt." Her comment hits me square in the chest, because, she's right. We aren't.

She brushes past me, but I catch her arm. "If you need to talk, I'm here. I'm your friend Ali, not your enemy."

She shrugs me off, reaches for the door, and slips out of my office.

I fall back into my chair, rubbing my hand over my stubble in frustration. What the fuck was that? Sure, Ali is wild but she'd never act like that with me. There was something haunting about her eyes. I've seen that look before, staring back at me in my own reflection, I know what it's like to carry secrets, regrets and fight daily to not allow them to swallow you whole. Worried for her safety, I leave my office and go in search of Ali.

"Kate," I yell, leaning over the bar. She walks over holding a bottle of vodka in each hand.

"What's up?"

"Have you seen Ali?"

She shakes her head, and I flatten my mouth in annoyance.

"Sorry, it's been packed in here. I haven't seen her for a while. Maybe she left?"

I give her a nod of agreement, and she walks back to her station.

I ball my hands into fists and exhale in annoyance. Where the fuck is she? I head up to the VIP floor to check up there, and when I reach the top of the staircase and see Patrick with his tongue down some girl's throat, who isn't Gabriella's, which, truth be told, I am grateful for, I see red. I don't think; I don't let myself count to ten and think of a logical way to handle this. No, I go into bulldozer Brad mode and stride over to his table and tower over them. They part and he looks up at me, his expression dropping when he sees it's me.

He whispers in the girl's ear, and she giggles, stands, and walks towards the bar. The prick turns to face me, leaning back in his booth with a smug smile creeping across his face.

"Bradley, good to see you again."

I've never wanted to punch someone more than him.

"What the fuck are you doing?" I grit out, my anger building.

"Trying to get laid, and I must say you're cramping my style."

I slam my palms down on the table. "You're meant to be with Gabriella, you prick." The words taste like poison on my tongue, and a pain rips through me.

He's with Gabriella, and he's treating her like this.

He rises to his feet and steps out, away from the table. "My relationship with Gabriella is none of your damn business."

"It is when you are in my club disrespecting her. She doesn't deserve that."

He squares up to me. "Gabriella is not your concern. Let me worry about what she does and doesn't deserve." His tone makes me uneasy.

I look him up and down, my lip turning up in disgust. "I don't understand what she sees in you, why she picked you."

His eyes flash with recognition, and he laughs. "You want her, don't you?" I say nothing, I just try and stare the prick down. "She picked me because she chose the better man. A man whose arm she can be on and be proud.

I step in closer, almost nose to nose, my anger about to reach its peak. "If you want to keep that arm, I suggest you leave my fucking club right now."

He lets out a huff, turns on his heel, and signals for the woman to follow him, which she does. I can hear my heart beating in my ears and the shirt I'm wearing feels as if it's constricting my breathing.

Fuck!

I make my way through the staff entrance behind the bar. The volume at which the blood is pumping round my body has my vision blurring, and I sit at the top of the staircase that leads to our stockroom. The faint thumping of the music is the only thing, along with my heavy breathing, that can be heard in the vacant stairwell. I slam my fist against the wall, wincing in pain, but in a twisted way, I welcome the throbbing pain.

The shrill ring of my phone startles me, and with a slight tremor to my hand, I pull it out of my pocket and sigh in relief when I see Ali's number. I swipe and bring it to my ear, expecting her to apologize and ask for a ride home, but when her horrified voice screams my blood runs cold.

"Ali are you—" There's panic in my voice.

"Help, help, please. It's Cassidy. She's, she's dying."

"What the fuck? Where are you?" I'm up on my feet and running back inside.

"The VIP booth at the back. Hurry," she pleads, sobbing hysterically.

I race back to the VIP area where I see Ali in a booth, a limp body laid across .

She sags in relief when she sees me. I look down at Cassidy. She's pale, unmoving. I press to fingers to her pulse point and freeze when I don't feel one.

"I don't think she's breathing. Please help her," Ali begs, panic laced in her voice.

I lift Cassidy, cradling her in my arms, her body like a rag doll as I run to the back exit, and through the fire doors into the back alley where I lay her on the ground. I press my ear to her chest, but I hear nothing. "Call 911," I bark, feeling Ali behind me.

I check Cassidy's airways are clear and cover my mouth with hers, not thinking about contamination or going to get the first aid kit, or to wait for paramedics. No, I've done CPR before, and lost someone because I waited too long to begin, and I refuse to lose someone else. I blow into her mouth, her chest rising and then I start compressions

Her lifeless body as it lies on the damp concrete of a New York alley as I try to revive her. The smell of urine and trash fills the air and bile rises into my nose, the urge to vomit is strong. With every pump, visions of Cassidy and then Scotty flit between each other. I shake my head to remind myself she isn't Scotty. It's not Scotty beneath my hands, my best friend, bleeding out, the life slowly draining from his body.

I give another rescue breath and yell, "Ali, call 911, now."

I check her pulse again and nothing. I will her to breathe as I continue CPR. "Come on, come on, sweetheart. You're not dying on me today," I pant.

Ali sinks to the floor beside me. "Cassidy, wake up... breathe," she wails, taking her limp hand into hers.

I don't know how much time passes, but suddenly, Cassidy takes in a sharp breath, and I sag in relief. I collapse against the wall, bracing my head in my hands, my breathing ragged as Cassidy coughs and groans.

"Help's coming, Cass. You're gonna be okay," Ali soothes. Blue flashing lights appear down the alley, and suddenly realization hits me. I saved her life, but still, that guilt I can never let go creeps its way back in. I may have saved Cassidy but I couldn't save one of my best friends.

"I need to go with her," Ali says.

"No, no, you're not. I need to take you home."

"But—"

"Don't fight me. Ali," I say sternly.

"Okay." She nods. "But I need to call Brooke."

"I'm sorry," Ali whispers.

"What did you take?" I ask, staring straight ahead, taking a drag of my cigarette.

"N-Nothing," she stammers.

"Don't lie to me," I hiss, tossing the cigarette. I turn to face her and give her a challenging stare.

"I didn't take anything." - I shake my head, hurt and disappointed that she would lie to me. But I know anger isn't the way here, not with her. She's clearly in pain, and me coming down on her won't help.

"Look me in the eye and tell me you didn't take anything," I say, my tone a little softer this time. She reluctantly lifts her head, but she wilts under my glare. A mixture of anger and sympathy swirls in my stomach when I look at her.

"Look at you. Your pupils are dilated. I know what drugs do to a person, trust me. So don't bullshit me, Ali." My tone is thick with emotion. I just want to help her.

She doesn't answer. She doesn't say anything, because what could she say, other than the truth, and I sense she's not ready to tell me. But I know. She can't deny it.

Tears fall down her cheeks, and she wipes them away, black smudges under her dilated eyes. "I'm so sorry. I'm so fucking sorry. I've ruined everything. It's all my fault," she sobs, her body heaving. I wrap my arms around her, pulling her into my chest as I try my best to soothe her, because no matter what, we're close and someone I'm sure is the love of my friend's life.

"I need him, Brad. I need him so fucking much. He's the only one who made it better, but I'll ruin him, like everything else I touch. I need to stay away from him, but it's killing me."

Her words hit me like a dagger to the heart, because I'm doing the same thing. I'm staying away from Gabriella for the same reason, because I believe I'll ruin her life if she has me in it. And just like Ali needs Harry, I need Gabriella, and it's so painful to admit.

Chapter Thirty-Five

Gabriella

I stare blankly at my soup bowl, stirring the spoon till the croutons disappear. Days have turned to weeks, and weeks have turned to nearly two months since I've seen him. I've overworked myself to the point of exhaustion, teaching extra Pilates classes and taking on more accountancy work just to keep my body and mind busy. I need to quit the club, too terrified to continue working there for fear of someone else exposing my secret, but I haven't been able to face them. I've made excuses as to why I can't work, but tonight is the night I go and tell them I quit and collect my stuff. I haven't gone to heel class; I've avoided Luna's texts. Ali hasn't been herself since she got back from her trip, and I'm getting concerned. Ria has been super sick since she got back from honeymoon. She's almost three months pregnant now, so I don't want to add my problems to the mix.

"Are you not enjoying your soup, Gabriella?" My father's voice has my stirring come to an abrupt halt, and I lift my head to look at him.

"No, it's fine, I'm just a little tired," I say, lifting the spoon to my mouth as I fight back against the dry heaving my body wants to do.

"Are you having too much salt in your diet? You are looking a little puffy," my mother says in between mouthfuls.

Leave it to my mother to find a way to make me feel even worse than I already do.

"No, I have just been busy working."

"Well, I hope you aren't coming down with anything. We have the Miller's dinner this weekend. You're bringing Patrick, yes?" my mother asks.

"Yes, he'll be there." And the urge to dry heave is back. Patrick has thankfully kept his distance and only bothered me once to attend a dinner with some work friends last week. But I know this dinner is a huge part of why he's forcing me to play the part of his girlfriend. Some very influential people will be attending. Political, celebrities, business owners, and we will be sitting with the CEO of the biggest law firm in Manhattan, and I know Patrick wants an interview. So, I'll have to work my charm on my dad and get him to recommend Patrick.

"Good," my father says before patting the corner of his mouth with his napkin. "I have a tennis match in fifteen, so if you'll both excuse me." He stands, placing a swift kiss to my mom's cheek and then doing the same to me, before walking away from the dining table of the country club, leaving just my mom and me.

"I thought we could get our hair and make-up done together before dinner. It's so lovely you will be joining us this year, now you have a date."

Yes, so lovely, because, God forbid, I could turn up to one of these functions without being a man's arm candy. Mom.

"Yes, sounds great," I say, trying to muster up as much enthusiasm as I can.

"Lovely. I'll call Claudia at the salon and get us booked in."

My mom's hand covers mine, and I flinch at the contact. My mom never shows me any kind of affection, so it concerns me.

"We are so happy to see you with Patrick. His mom tells me he's always speaking about you. I just wanted you to know your father and I approve. Don't let this one go."

On the one hand, I want to scream, tell her what Patrick is really like, but then there's the other side that feels elated at having got the approval I have craved since I was a teen, and then the reality hits me like a brick to the head. This is going to crush my parents when this ends with Patrick, and I'll be blamed, and then I'll be back at square one. Tears threaten, and I need to make an excuse to leave before my mom notices.

"Mom, I'm so sorry, I forgot. I have a meeting with a client. Let me know about the salon appointment."

I enter the apartment, and it's eerily quiet. I head for Ali's room, dropping my purse on the small entry table beside our front door, and kick off my heels. Her room is dark, the drapes pulled, and the room is cluttered with clothes but I see her blonde hair peeking out from under her comforter.

I kneel beside her, brushing the hair that covers her face away. She stirs, and when she moves, I notice how pale she looks. This is the third day she's been in bed, and it's so unlike her.

"Ali, are you okay?" I whisper.

"Yeah," she groans, but she doesn't sound like herself.

"Shall I call Ria? Get her to come over? I'm worried about you."

"No, I'm just sick."

"Shall I call a doctor?"

"No, just, just lay with me," she asks and my heart sinks. She's hurting. I glance over to the nightstand and see the familiar orange pot of sleeping tablets she takes when her nightmares get too much and her past keeps her awake at night. A knot of worry forms in my belly, and I don't want to leave. Ali only takes them when her nightmares are bad.

I climb in bed beside her, not caring I'm still in my itchy skirt and blouse. I wrap my arm around her waist. She feels frail, tiny, and alarm bells start ringing. I need to keep an eye on her. I decide I'll give her a couple more days to work through what she's dealing with, and then I'm calling Ria, and we'll try and get through to her. Sometimes we need to work through things alone and sometimes when we've fallen too far, we need people to help lift us and carry us when we don't have the strength anymore.

That thought makes me think of Brad. I wonder how he's doing. If he misses me as much as I miss him. Does he spend his days buried in work to pass the time like I do? Does he wish we could get a second chance, a redo? Does he have regrets like I do, because, while I was asking him to help get me to a place where I could find someone who made me feel wanted, loved, secure and desired, I didn't notice that I had already found that in him, and now I fear it's too late and I've ruined everything.

Chapter Thirty-Six

Gabriella

"What do you mean, you quit?" Chloe, the stage manager, barks. "You are one of our main girls, Gabriella, and you've left us high and dry recently."

"I know. I know. I'm so sorry. I just have some personal stuff going on, and I can't commit anymore. I'm here to hand back my things and clear out my locker."

"Could you at least work tonight as your final shift. Luna is out as she's on vacation, and I need another dancer."

I want to say no, should say no, but I find myself agreeing, and maybe it's the closure I need. A farewell to the part of my life that's now died. Something that brought me so much joy has now flipped my world upside down and been used against me.

"Sure, I'll work tonight."

My final shift was bittersweet. I'll miss the feeling of being on stage gave me, the bright lights and the way my adrenaline spiked and pumped round my body. How free I felt. The only other thing that has given me that feeling is Brad, and now I've lost him too. Thinking about him makes my skin feel too tight for my body, and makes it hard to breathe. I hang up my leotard and mask for a final time and wave goodbye to the girls before I head out to the parking lot, heaviness weighing on my chest as I walk away from one of the places that helped me find a part of myself that I spent years trying to suppress.

I am just a step away from my car when a large hooded figure steps in front of me, startling me. On instinct, I grip the strap of my tote tightly, and try to stand tall, fearing he wants my purse.

"You were great tonight," he drawls, taking a drag of his cigarette. "I can see why they like you." The hairs on the back of my neck stand on end. Why do I feel like I've heard this voice before?

I don't say anything as I try to step around him, but he steps in front of me. My internal alarm bells start going off. We get the odd guy hanging around outside, but usually security is out here moving them on. I glance over my shoulder, but I can't see anyone. I step backward and he turns his face just enough for me to notice he has a tattoo of a scorpion below his left eye and it unnerves me.

He leans in closer, his body mere inches from mine, and I swallow down the scream I want to let out.

"You're prettier than I thought." There's a slight slur to his voice that tells me he's intoxicated, and this may give me the upper hand here if he were to try anything, as he may be unsteady on his feet.

"I need you to get out of my way, please," I say as confidently as I can.

He chuckles, but it's deep, calculated, and makes me uneasy.

"Sure thing, sweetheart. I'll be seeing you around." He steps aside and I listen to his boots crunch against the gravel and when I think he's far enough away I quick step to my car, jumping inside and locking the doors.

My trembling hands turn on the car, and my heart sinks when the warning symbol for a flat tire flashes on my dashboard. Panic floods me, and my whole body trembles. I fish out my phone and dial the only number I know I can. The one person who knows my secret and, even though we aren't talking, I pray he answers.

It only takes two rings for him to answer, and as soon as his rough voice sounds down the phone, I choke out a sob. "Brad, I—"

'Where are you?"

"Diamonds. Can you come and get me?"

Without hesitation, he says, "I'm on my way."

Brad arrives in record time. He took one look at my car and told me two of my tires had been slashed. He barely said another word to me, just called a pick-up service who took my car to a local garage.

The silence in his car now is suffocating. There's so much I want to say, want to ask, but I'm too scared. My head and heart are stuck in two different places. Stuck between ruining mine and my family's life, again, if I don't do as Patrick says, and hurting myself and maybe

Brad in the process, because the fact he can't even look at me tells me he is struggling with something just as much as me.

He pulls up outside my apartment building and puts the car in park, never releasing his firm grip on the steering wheel as he looks out the windscreen, avoiding eye contact with me.

"Thank you for rescuing me," I say quietly, twisting the bangle on my wrist that hasn't been removed since he put it there.

"You're welcome."

"Why did you come and rescue me?" I ask, not sure if I really want to know the answer. I didn't tell him about the man in the parking lot. I didn't see the need to worry him. He turns to face me, and it's then I see the pain in his eyes. They look hollow and empty, all the light in them gone. He looks like a man haunted, and I want to take away whatever is causing him this pain.

"You called, so I came."

I tilt my head, willing him to elaborate. He lets out an exasperated breath and runs his hand along his jaw. "Gabriella, it doesn't matter who you're with, if we haven't spoken in months, years, or if you hate me. I will always answer your call."

I chew on the inside of my cheek, praying I don't break down.

"If you call, then I run to you. It's as simple as that." He turns back to look out the windscreen, and I scoop up my bags, needing to break free from this car. It's too much, my emotions, my guilt, my pain.

"Goodbye," I manage to say before closing the car door and walking towards my apartment, feeling his eyes on me with every step I take and it takes what little strength I have left not to turn around and beg him to take me home with him while I tell him everything.

Chapter Thirty-Seven

Gabriella

"... do you agree?" The stylist's words startle me as I had zoned out while she was doing my hair.

"I'm sorry. Could you repeat the question?"

"I suggested we leave your hair down. It's so beautiful, it feels a shame to hide it all in an updo."

I nod. "Sure, whatever you think is best."

My mom is in the chair beside me, her hair in rollers, having her makeup done. Mine has been done—minimal, just the way my mother likes it.

"Oh, please put it up. It will get in her way," my mother chimes in.

My mouth flattens and I want to scream that it's my hair. But, of course, I don't. The stylist matches my expression in the mirror.

"How about we go half and half?" she says quietly, pulling back pieces and creating a style that I really like. I glance over at my mother, who gives me the nod of approval, so I signal for the stylist to continue.

I didn't like leaving Ali earlier. She still hasn't got out of bed and it's been five days now. She's not been in work all week and that's so unlike her. We have Brad's birthday this weekend and Ria called earlier, asking if Ali was well enough to go. I'm torn between wanting to go and not. I want to see him, yet I don't.

I reach for my phone and send a text to Ali and then Ria.

Gabriella
> Hey, babe, are you feeling okay? I'm going to try and leave this event early and come home. xx

Gabriella
> Hey, Ri, I hope that little bump has eased up and stopped making you feel so sick. I'm worried about Ali, and I'm at this stupid dinner with my parents. Could you check in on her? xx

My message to Ali still hasn't been seen, but I breathe a sigh of relief when Ria texts back.

Ria
> Hey, sure thing. I'll stop by later and bring her some soup, so don't worry, I got her G enjoy your night, and no, baby Lawson will not let me eat anything except graham crackers and apples. xx

"Okay, all done," the stylist chimes. I look into the mirror as she holds a smaller one so I can see the back of my hair, she's twisted pieces and curled them and they hang down my back like a vine of wild ivy.

"I love it, thank you."

"You're welcome. You have the most amazing hair, and your makeup turned out flawless. Your date is a lucky guy. Did he get you that bracelet? Those things are pricey. You're a lucky girl."

Her words leave me with a pit in my stomach as I twist the bracelet Brad gave me. "It was a gift from a friend," I say.

"I need better friends," she jokes. "Come on, let's get you into your dress."

We ride the limo to the MET. Patrick and my dad are in a black tux, my mother wears a silver gown with a high neck, and I'm in a strapless black satin gown. Patrick has spent the entire ride ignoring me and sucking up to my dad and my dad annoyingly has been eating up his crap.

I want to be anywhere but here. Ria called before and said Ali ate the soup and seemed to be doing a little better. Maybe it was the flu, and I've been worrying over nothing.

Our limo stops, the door opens, my dad and Patrick get out first, and I follow after my mother, taking Patrick's waiting meaty hand that makes me shudder every time I touch it. These events always blow my mind. We are here to raise money and awareness and resources for local charities, yet hundreds of thousands have gone in to hosting it when it could have gone straight to the charities. It's just another opportunity for the rich to flaunt their wealth and status, and my mother lives for these things.

We are offered glasses of Champagne as we enter the main hall, and Patrick wastes no time inserting himself right up my dad's ass crack. We make small talk and are introduced to some of my dad's friends and colleagues and I do my part; I slip on my mask and play the dutiful daughter and girlfriend.

"Oh, what a beautiful couple," a tall woman with old money blonde hair who's clearly a fan of the filler swoons.

Patrick wraps an arm around my waist and pulls me into him. I smile through gritted teeth.

"She's a keeper. Imagine how good looking our children will be." My jaw nearly hits the floor.

My mom's smile is so wide she looks ready to explode. "I didn't know things were getting this serious between you two." She fans her face with her clutch.

It's news to be too, Mom.

"I think your daughter could be the one, if you get my drift." I turn my head and see Patrick wink at my mom, and she holds her hand to her chest, clutching her necklace.

Is he joking? No, this is going too far.

"Patrick, can I steal you for a moment?" I say, tugging his hand.

"Aah, young love," someone calls from behind, but I'm too busy seeing red and storming to a quieter corner to have it out with Patrick.

I glance around, making sure no one is in earshot. "What the heck are you doing, implying marriage, babies? I didn't agree to that. I got you here. You can butter up my dad's friends and then we can call it quits."

His jaw ticks and I get the sense he didn't appreciate my tone.

"I think you are forgetting who has the power here, Gabby. If you want to dissolve this agreement, sure, we can do that. One email to your daddy and this will all be over for you." I gulp, shrinking under his gaze. "So this," he gestures between us, "will go as far as I say it does, got it?"

I blink back tears that threaten to fall. I'm trapped with no out. I can't have my world crumble again, so I nod in agreement.

"Good girl." Pressing a kiss to my forehead, he walks off without me, and I shudder at the words he used. They feel wrong coming from him. I don't want his praise. I want him to leave me alone.

Chapter Thirty-Eight

Brad

She's here. Gabriella is at this event, standing just a foot away from me. She looks absolutely stunning in a satin gown that hugs her body, and her hair is twisted back from her face. She's perfect. It feels unnatural to not go straight to her. To take her in my arms and hold her, especially when I can see she's hurting. She's been crying, her cheeks are flushed, her eyes watery and even though I've been in pain since she left, the pain of seeing her like this is far worse. When her name flashed across my screen last week after nearly two months of silence, I held out hope this would be the moment we came back together. But when I saw her, I just couldn't do it to her. I can't put her at risk. No matter how much I miss her and want her.

"Hi," I manage to choke out; my voice has a morning gruffness to it despite it being the evening. Probably due to the excessive smoking and the extra whiskey I've been consuming in her absence.

"Hi," she says, her voice quivering as if she's surprised to see me too. "What are you doing here?"

"I got invited by a couple of potential investors."

"Are you with anyone?" Her eyes widen once the words leave her lips and a dick part of me is pleased that she's bothered by the idea.

"Are you here with Patrick?" His name tastes like acid on my tongue.

She nods. "And my parents."

"How cozy," I say bitterly.

"Brad, I..." She goes to speak, but I'm not in a place to hear it. I don't want her apologies or to hear how happy Patrick makes her. I hold up a hand to silence her.

"Gabby, it's fine." She flinches as if I've struck her, and I realize my error. I called her Gabby, like everyone else, and I feel like a dick.

"I better get back to them. They'll wonder where I am," she says, flicking her hair over her shoulder, exposing her collarbone, and all I want to do is pull her into me, sink my teeth into her skin, leave my mark and make her mine. But she doesn't want me. She chose him.

Her amber eyes, which once reminded me of a lioness, now look hollow and lost. I brush the back of my knuckles against her cheek, and she surprises me by leaning into my touch.

"Gabriella," a stern voice calls from behind me. She jumps and steps aside as her face falls in shock.

"Dad."

Oh fuck.

"Patrick has been looking for you. What are you doing?"

She pastes a smile on her face and points to the painting of The Ballet class by Edgar Degas mounted in pride of place on the wall.

"I just came to look at the painting. You remember, you got me a print when we came here that one time."

"Yes, I remember." His eyes bounce between me and Gabriella as if he were trying to make sense of what was going on.

"Well, I was in here and I bumped into my friend. This is Brad Russo." She gestures to me. "He's in business with Ria's husband, Jack. Remember me telling you about him?"

"Ah, yes, Brad. I've heard a lot about you." He reaches out his hand for me to shake, and I do so, his touch firmer than needed.

"It's a pleasure to meet you, Mr. Monroe. Your daughter speaks highly of you."

"I'm sure she does." His tone is clipped, and yeah, this guy fucking hates me.

"Gabriella, come on, your mother will worry, and we need to find our seats."

Mr. Monroe gives me a terse nod, and Gabriella dutifully follows him, leaving me standing alone with an unsettled feeling in my stomach. Something is wrong, but I just can't work out what.

Dinner was good; palatable and full of business talk. Each table had a representative from a local charity and ours was from a local support group for teens to get them off the streets and into sports. It's something I can get behind and want to support. I wish there had been something like that when I was growing up, maybe it would have saved me sooner. Maybe it would have saved my brother.

I took the guy's card and said I would chat with Jack and Harry and be in touch about a donation. In an evil twist of fate, my table was not far from Gabriella's, and so I had a front row seat to her and Patrick. I watched every time she pulled away when he touched her, the moments in between conversations where she would stare blankly into her wine glass, and the fake smile she painted on every time she was spoken to. I need to get her alone again and talk to her. Above anything, she's my friend, and I need to make sure she's okay.

I watch on as she gets up from the table alone, and I see that as my window. I'm about ten steps behind. I'm certain she will head for the ladies' bathroom, but when she darts down a corridor away from the event, I follow. I speed up, taking her by the arm and pulling her into a corner. She squeals in surprise as I press her to the wall and cover her body with mine, trapping her so she can't flee.

"Tell me what's going on," I demand.

I watch her throat bob as she swallows. "I don't know what you are talking about."

"Patrick. Something is off. What is going on? Why are you with him?"

"B... because I like him and—"

"Bullshit," I hiss. "I know you're lying."

"How?" Her body softens a little under my firm grip.

"Because when you were with me, you never flinched when I touched you." I smooth my hands over the natural curve of her body as if proving my point. "You didn't recoil when my lips brushed yours." I rub my thumb along her bottom lip, pulling a whimper from her throat that awakens something in me that's been dead since she walked out on me. "Because, when you were with me, you had a light in your eyes that's now gone out. That's how I know something is wrong, Gabriella."

She closes her eyes, and a single tear rolls down her cheek, and I brush it away with the pad of my thumb.

"Tell me what's wrong, and I can help you," I beg, bringing her face just inches from mine, fighting the urge to kiss her.

"I need to get back to my table."

"Mia cara, please, tell me," I whisper, my tone desperate.

She shakes her head. "Whatever we had, it's over. You need to let me go. I'm with Patrick now."

"If I mean nothing, if we meant nothing, why are you still wearing my bracelet?" It gives me hope that maybe we can claw our way back to each other, but I need to understand what's going on with her.

"I was yours, and you pushed me away too. I'm with Patrick now. You need to accept that and let me go." She sniffs, and I'm struggling to believe her words and internally kicking myself because she's right. I pushed her away.

"You may have only been all mine for a moment, and maybe you'll be his forever, and I'll have to find a way to accept that, but I won't ever be able to fully let you go. Not when you found a way into my dark heart and left your mark."

I lean in to brush my lips with hers, but she pulls away, tears now falling freely. "I'm sorry," she says, a slight crack in her voice. I release her and she walks away from me again.

And I let her, again.

Chapter Thirty-Nine

Gabriella

It's Brad's birthday, and I don't want to be here. It's been weeks since I saw him at the MET, and every day without him becomes more painful than the last. But if I hadn't come tonight, it would have raised questions, which would have meant more lies, and I am already struggling to carry the many I already have. I couldn't face another. Ali came here with but she's barely said a word, but she assures me she's just recovering from the flu.

Patrick has been blowing up my phone all day, and I've ignored every call. I told him I had plans this weekend. He only seems to want me when he needs me. Needs me to be his arm candy or go on a lunch date with my parents. We bumped into Harry last night, and I could see he wasn't convinced by my display when I introduced Patrick as my boyfriend. That term and Patrick shouldn't be used in the same sentence, but what can I do? I've been doing everything he's asked and yet he still hasn't ended my suffering.

I may look confident on the outside, but on the inside, I'm in so much pain it's hard to function, and that pain only increases when I see Brad leaning against the bar dress in a black dress shirt, the top two buttons open, the sleeves rolled up to the elbow showing the tattoos that I could draw from memory, and black pants. His facial hair is a little longer since I saw him last, and my body is finding it hard to adjust to feelings of craving him, with the need to run from him. Our eyes hold each other in a way our bodies can't. It's only when Ria calls my name that I am snapped from my trance.

"Ahh, Ri, look at you."

She rubs her growing belly. "I know. This baby is not shy. She's already letting the world know she's on her way."

"She?" I say excitedly.

Jack chuckles. "We don't know if it's a she, but we have a feeling it is."

"You are both destined to be girl parents, I can see it." I beam with pride watching them just be in love. Simple, uncomplicated love, and I wonder if that's something I'll ever experience.

I make my way over to Brad, leaving everyone to chatter amongst themselves, knowing it will be best to rip the band aid off and say hi, rather than spend the rest of the evening avoiding him. With every step I take, his eyes travel up from my feet, up my body to my face.

"Gabriella," he greets, his voice as smooth as the whiskey he's drinking.

"Happy thirty-fifth birthday," I say, my voice sounding light and sugary as I lean in and hug him. I can do this. I can act like everything's fine. I've been doing it my whole life. I can act like he means nothing more than a friend to me. I can pretend I haven't fallen for him and that it doesn't physically pain me to be here in front of him. Yeah, I can do it.

Lies.

I think it will be a quick embrace, but when his hand finds the base of my spine and pulls me closer, his hot breath in my ear, I know I'm screwed.

"You look beautiful." I freeze, waiting for him to release me, but he doesn't. It's only when Harley shouts my name that I break the embrace and stand awkwardly. I hold a finger up to let her know I'll be a second.

"I'm sorry, I didn't bring a gift with me. I wasn't sure if you would want me here, so..." My words trail off, and I chew on the inside of my mouth in anticipation of what he will say, and when he speaks, my heart flutters.

"You being here is the only gift I wanted." He twirls the glass of amber liquid in his hand before drinking the rest and placing the glass on the bar.

"I better go see what Harley wanted," I say, gesturing over my shoulder. I don't wait for a reply. I turn and leave, feeling his gaze burning into my back as I head back to the group around the table and pray with every step that I can keep it all together and bury my feelings for the evening.

There's something off. A thickness in the atmosphere that I can't quite put my finger on. I've managed to avoid chatting to Brad as much as possible. When the waitress brought over an ice bucket of champagne and sparklers to the table and spent far longer than needed with her hand on his arm, it stirred up a level of jealousy I didn't know I was capable of. I wanted to tear her hand off and tell her he was mine. But he isn't, and I only have myself and my stupidity to blame.

"Ooh, who's the hot blonde at one o'clock?" Kate slurs, sipping on her mojito. I turn to see where she's facing, and my blood runs cold when I see Patrick dressed in navy pants and a white polo shirt, looking around. He stops and grins when he spots me.

What the hell is he doing here?

I leap up out of my seat and storm over to him.

"Ah, there you are," he says.

"What are you doing here? It's my friend's birthday," I hiss, glancing over my shoulder to see my friends are open mouthed.

"I've come to see my girlfriend since she's been ignoring my calls all day. You do remember you have a boyfriend, right, Gabby?"

"How could I forget?" My tone is laced with sarcasm.

He leans in, wrapping an arm around my back. To spectators, it would look like he's embracing me, ready to kiss me, but his voice is full of venom and sends chills down my spine as he grips my wrist with a bruising force that makes me let out a little whimper of pain. "I'd watch your fucking tone with me. When I call, I expect you to answer. Got it?" I nod, and he plants a kiss on my lips that makes me want to hurl.

"You're hurting me," I say weakly. He releases my wrist and I bring it to my chest to massage where he held it.

"Now, take my hand and show me off like a proud girlfriend or I'll be telling all your friends over there what you really get up to in your free time."

He has me over a barrel and there's nothing I can do but obey him. My shaky hand reaches out for his and I fix my smile as we walk over, hand in hand, to the booth.

"Everyone, this is my boyfriend, Patrick. Patrick, this is Kate, Harley, Mason, and Brad. It's his birthday." I point to Brad, and the look on his face crushes me.

Patrick greets everyone with a hug or a handshake and when he reaches out to Brad's, Brad ignores it.

"We've met," Brad says flatly.

"Yes, you're right we have. Sorry, you just have one of those faces that's easy to forget."

Brad scoffs and his eyebrows raise, and I want the ground to swallow me up.

"Why don't we get a drink?" I suggest, trying to break the tension.

"Good idea. I take a scotch on the rocks," Patrick says, taking a seat next to Harley.

"You're not going to get the drinks?" Brad asks, his tone annoyed.

"Gabby's a big girl. She likes her independence, don't you, honey?" I fight back the shudder that wants to roll through me at the use of the word honey. I don't want him to give me a pet name.

I clamp a hand round Brad's arm, stopping him from causing a scene.

"Yes, does anyone else want a drink?" No one answers me. Patrick already is commanding the attention of everyone, and I turn and head to the bar, with Brad hot on my heels.

"Why do you let him treat you like that?" he spits.

"Just drop it," I say through gritted teeth, taking a spot at the bar, waiting for a waitress.

"You know he's cheating on you, right? I caught him with another girl in my club." His words should hurt, cut me in two, but they don't. I don't care what Patrick does. All it does is make me angry that Patrick can get away with doing what he wants, and I'm expected to go along with his games.

"You deserve better," Brad says, pressing his front to my back and I could so easily melt into him and beg him to save me, but I deserve this. I've fucked up, and this is my punishment.

"Brad, with all the respect in the world, my relationship isn't any of your business."

I stare straight ahead, and I feel his hand come to my waist and circle my stomach with his fingers, sending zaps of pleasure right to my center.

"Whether you like it or not, Gabriella, you are my business and will always be my business. I can't stand by and let some piece of shit treat you like that."

I tap my foot impatiently, trying to block out his words.

"Follow me," Brad mutters.

I gasp when his teeth nip my ear.

He moves away, and I turn around. Everyone is still talking, so no one is paying attention to us. I slip away from the bar and blindly follow Brad into a corridor where the faint sound of the music can be heard.

"Look, I don't know what you want me to—"

My words are cut off when he pins me to the wall, covering my body with his.

"Tell me I mean nothing to you, that what we had meant nothing, and that Patrick is the one and I'll back off."

I gulp, my head feeling light and dizzy. "I…"

"Tell me. Tell me he's the one that can give you everything you want."

"Brad, I…"

"Tell me." His tone is firm as he pushes his thigh between my legs. I fist his shirt in frustration. I want, need him. It's been months since I felt his hands on me properly, his lips on mine, and I feel like I've been holding on for dear life, trying to get through each day, carrying the weight of my secrets and longing for him.

"I didn't think so," he murmurs. Pulling back, he looks me up and down, a pained expression on his face, and then he walks back toward the club. I sink to the floor and cradle my legs, balancing on my heels in a vain attempt to make myself feel as small as I feel.

Congratulations, Gabriella, your life is a fucking mess, and it's all your own doing.

Chapter Forty

Brad

I slam the glass down on my kitchen island so firmly I'm shocked it doesn't shatter. It's my third one, and I have no intentions of stopping. Thirty-five, and I still don't know when to stop. But I need it. I need something to mask this pain I've felt since she left. Since I pushed her away. I still don't know how I'm supposed to get my dad out of prison. I've not heard a thing from him since I saw him and that puts me on edge. He won't go quietly. It's only a matter of time till he's calling again. I just need to think of a way that doesn't involve Gabriella. I lift the whiskey bottle to pour my next drink when a knock sounds at the door. I look at the clock; it's nearly 2 am. I make my way to the door, opening it half expecting someone related to my dad to come barging in, but when I see Gabriella standing in my doorway, a flicker of fire in her eyes and it takes me a second to question if she's really here.

"You're right." I back up, letting her in. "I don't want him."

I clear my throat, my heart hammering wildly. I go to speak, but she continues.

"When I'm with him, all I think of is you. Is that what you want to hear?" She jabs her index finger into my chest angrily. "My biggest mistake was picking him. Is that what you want to hear, Brad?" She's yelling now, and I've never seen her this angry.

"But you pushed me away. You told me to be with him." My nostrils flare. She's right, and it's a decision I have regretted every day.

"I know," I whisper.

Her eyes swirl with a mixture of hate and desire, and I want to take her in my arms and never let go. She might be someone else's, but right now, I don't care.

"What do you want, Gabriella?"

Indecision flickers across her face.

"What do you want, Gabriella?" I repeat, closing what little space there was between us.

"You," she says breathlessly, and that one word is all it takes for our restraint to snap. I'm on her. I lift her, and her legs wrap around my waist and our mouths crash together in a bruising kiss.

"Fuck, I've missed you," I moan against her lips.

"Me too," she gasps between kisses. "I want you to be rough with me."

"Oh, I plan to be. My bedroom. Now." I put her down, and take her by the hand, dragging her towards my bedroom, the blood pumping around my body at an alarming rate in anticipation of what I plan to do to her.

"Strip, leave the heels on," I command, and she does. I watch in fascination as she tugs at the side zipper on her dress and lets it fall to the ground and it's then I realize she has no bra on. Her heated gaze meets mine, and I point to her panties.

"Lose the lace." She pulls them down and steps out, standing there like a goddess, naked in her heels that drive me wild. I slowly unbutton my shirt as I circle her, watching as her chest rises and falls in anticipation of my next move. I toss the shirt, foregoing my usual routine. No, tonight all the rules have gone out the window. I come up behind her and press my mouth to her shoulder, smoothing my hand down her stomach till it reaches her clit and I circle it with the pads of my fingers. Her head falls back against my chest, and just when I feel her breathing rate pick up, I stop.

"Hands on the edge on the bed and bend over. I'm going to drive you wild, baby girl." I nip her ear, and she whimpers. She does as I ask her, ass in the air, round and perky and I grind my teeth, fighting the urge to take her now, the way I want her. But no, I want to have some fun first.

I stand behind her, stroking the palm of my hand over her ass cheek before I give her a light slap on her ass. She jolts forward, letting out a moan of pleasure.

"Is that too much?"

"No, it's not enough."

"Does my naughty girl like it when I spank her?"

'Yes."

"If I touch your pussy, will I find it dripping for me?"

She doesn't say anything. I stroke my fingers over her ass crack and she whimpers. I continue until my fingers find her soaked pussy and I push two fingers inside her.

"Oh god," she cries out again as I tease her, pumping slowly."

"So, fucking wet."

I get on my knees, my eyes now level with her entrance. I watch as my fingers push in and out, her arousal coating my fingers. I quicken the pace, the sound of her arousal echoing around my bedroom. I spank her lightly and her walls clamp around my fingers.

I let out a low chuckle. 'Dirty girl, you like it when my fingers pump your tight cunt and I spank you? Is that it? Is that what you like?" Her legs begin to tremble, and she buries her face into the comforter.

"Please," she begs.

"Please, what? Stop?"

"No, no," she says desperately.

"Please, more?" I say, teasing her, pushing my fingers all the way in, curling and hitting that sweet spot.

"Yes, more, please, more," she begs, fisting the sheets. Her ass backs up, grinding down on the palm of my hand, and the sight makes me feral.

"I love it when you beg," I growl.

I pull my fingers out, cup the globes of her ass cheeks and bury my face into her soaked pussy and she lets out a strangled moan that has my dick throbbing, desperate to be inside her. I push my tongue inside and reach my hand in between her legs and rub her clit.

"Yes, yes."

I smile against her pussy, knowing I've got her right where I want her.

Her legs quiver, and I tap her ass once again before I rise to my feet pulling her up. Her body falls into my chest, and I wrap my hand around her slender neck, running my tongue up the sleek arch of her neck.

"I want you on your knees, baby girl. You're going to suck my cock, and then I'm going to fuck you until you forget his name."

I undo my belt as she sinks to her knees. I back up, removing my suit pants and then take a seat on the chair opposite her.

"Crawl to me."

I wait for her to tense up, falter, retreat to shy and nervous Gabriella, but to my surprise, she doesn't. She outstretches her toned arms, her back arched as she moves like a feline, as if she were moving to a sultry beat, and watching her takes me back to watching her perform for me at the club. My body heats, coiling so tight I grip the arms of the chair to stop myself from reaching out and rushing this. When she reaches me and glides her smooth hands up my thighs and pushes them apart, I'm fucking gone.

"Is this what you want, Brad? Me, at your mercy?" I could come right now just from the sound of her voice.

"Fuck," I groan out.

I don't know where this version of Gabriella has come from. Maybe it's been there all along, buried and weighted beneath her need to please others.

She reaches for the hem of my briefs and pulls them down and my erect dick springs free.

She wastes no time taking my cock into her mouth, sucking and swirling her tongue as she cups my balls and I nearly go off. My nostrils flare, a deep rumble comes from my chest, and I fist her hair, holding her firmly as her head bobs up and down.

"Fuck, you look so beautiful on your knees, taking my cock. She flicks her tongue over my piercing, making us both moan.

My balls tighten and I pull her back. She looks up at me with watery eyes, a flash of disappointment in them.

"Oh, we aren't done, Gabriella."

I lead her to the edge of the bed and sink to my knees in front of her, pushing her thighs apart. Her glistening pussy comes in to view and I run my tongue along my bottom lip.

"Watch my fingers." My tone is stern. We both gasp when my tattooed fingers disappear inside her and I pump slowly, hitting that sweet spot every time. "Look how wet you are for me."

She whimpers and it's almost a pained cry as she fists the sheets beneath her.

"Leg up," I demand, tapping her right leg and she hooks it over my shoulder, still wearing her heels that drive me wild and widens her hips, giving me a better angle. I help her with my free hand, pinning her thigh to the mattress. She's so flexible it's easy to maneuver just the way I need her.

"Oh, my god, it's too much. I can't." She whimpers.

"Do you want me to stop, baby girl?" I tease.

She shakes her head, and I know she's so close to coming.

Her head falls back, her pussy juices now running down my wrist and into the palm of my hand.

Her walls tighten and when she's once again on the edge I pull out, slapping her pussy and she gasps, which is followed by growls of frustration.

"Are you fucking kidding me, Brad? I was just about to come." I've never heard her speak that way and it turns me on more. I grin, gripping her chin with my hand that's covered in her arousal.

"You'll come when I fucking say you can. I'm just giving you a taste of your own medicine, baby girl"

She looks at me, confusion fills her eyes.

"I'm driving you wild, the way you've driven me since the day you walked into my life. Now on the bed on your knees."

She freezes for just a second and then she does it. I settle on the bed behind her. I wrap her ponytail around my hand and line up the head of my cock that's leaking with pre cum with her entrance. I push inside, sinking my cock into her hot, wet cunt, and it feels like heaven.

She circles her hips and it steals my breath away when she says, "Fuck me like you want me."

Chapter Forty-One

Gabriella

I wake with a heaviness in my chest, guilt the emotion I'm feeling. I don't owe Patrick anything. We aren't really together, so why do I feel like I cheated? Brad's arm lays heavy across my body and I slide out gently, so as not to disturb him. I pick up my discarded undies and dress and slip them on, feeling dirty and cheap, because even though I didn't technically do anything wrong, that's not how the rest would view it. To the outsider, I cheated on my boyfriend last night.

Well done, Gabby. Another fuck up to add to your mounting list.

But it felt good. So good, to be in arms again and hand my body over to him, because I trust him with it. I need to figure this out. Maybe come to another arrangement with Patrick that will have him backing off. I slip on my heels and search for my phone when Brad stirs, sitting upright, his sleepy eyes trying to focus on me.

"Are you leaving?" The morning gruffness in his voice almost has me climbing back into bed with him.

"Yeah, I need to check on Ali. She was sick last night, and I need some time to..." My words trail off.

"To what?" he questions, pushing his fingers through his hair. He throws the covers back, rolling out of bed and picking up his briefs off the floor and slips them on. He steps towards me, every muscle in his body ripples when he walks, and he's not making my choice to leave any easier.

"Don't tell me you are running back to him." His tone is annoyed.

"Brad, I, it's complicated. I need to—" He cuts me off.

"Are you fucking serious? You're going to go back to that piece of shit? How can you be that naïve, Gabriella. He's controlling you. What does he have hanging over your head? Why do you let him treat you like that?"

My hackles rise because he's hit a nerve. "Don't judge me. You don't know anything about my relationships, and besides, you pushed me away. You were the one who said we were done." My voice is a lot louder than I intended.

"I did that to keep you safe."

I furrow my brow. "Safe? Safe from what?"

"From me, Gabriella, and trust me, the less you know, the better."

"Oh, so I'm supposed to tell you things, but you can keep secrets? Is that how this works, Marco?"

He sneers at the use of his real name and I regret it the moment it leaves my mouth. 'I'm sorry, I—"

"I think you need to leave. Shut the door on your way out."

The cab ride back felt long and lonely. I replayed my conversation over and over with Brad and decide I need to sort my life out. I'll call Patrick later and ask him to meet for dinner, find an agreement that works for us both and pray I can appeal to his kind side that has to be buried deep inside him. I reach our floor and the faint sounds of an argument can be heard in the hallway.

Convinced it's one of our neighbors, I turn my key in the lock, but the yelling gets louder as I step inside. I make my way to Ali's room, where I can hear the voices.

"Al, you in here—" I enter her room and stop, my eyes widen as I look between Ali and a half-dressed Harry.

"What's going on, are you two…"

Ali closes her eyes, and Harry hangs his head and stares at the floor, looking utterly defeated. Something is wrong. I can feel it in my bones.

"Can someone explain, please?" I plead.

Harry hands me a folded piece of paper. "Don't leave her on her own," he says firmly before he grabs his clothes and heads for the door. Before he disappears from view, he says, "I mean it. I'm not giving up on you."

His footsteps fade away, and the door slams.

A sickening silence falls between me and Ali as my shaky hands unfold the paper and I read the opening lines.

Dear Miss Hart...

My blood runs cold, and my hand flies up to cover my mouth. Ali chokes on a sob.

"Ali, I..." I gasp, looking up from the paper and watch my beautiful, strong friend, who has been through so much in her twenty-nine years, crumble in front of me. Guilt and disgust at myself hits me like a slap to the face. How did I not see? How could I be so blind to her pain? I knew something was wrong, and I ignored it. I should have been here. Instead, I was selfish and went to Brad, instead of being where I should have been.

"They want to let him out Gabs, they are going to let him out," She sobs, her legs giving way and I reach her just before she hits the ground, the letter falling from my fingers as I hold my broken friend up.

"I've got you, it's okay, I've got you," I repeat, holding her and pulling her in towards my chest as we sit in the middle of her room.

I reach for Ali's phone that lies on the floor and dial, bringing the phone to my ear, relief flooding me when she answers.

"Hey, Ri, it's me. Ali needs us."

Chapter Forty-Two

Brad

I sit at my desk in my office, sipping on my coffee, and going through our accounts. The past month was our biggest loss. Someone is stealing money, and I need to find out who. I've been in a shitty mood since Gabriella left. I don't know where we go from here. I was kind of an ass to her. But last night, it was everything. Sex has never felt like that with anyone but her. But it's not just about the sex. I just want to be around her.

My phone buzzes on the table and Harry's name flashes on the screen.

Harry

Where are you?

I text back.

> Brad
>
> At the club, waiting on a delivery. Is everything okay?

I put my phone back down as Jack walks through my office door.

"Morning," he says, a little groggy.

"You look worse than me. Rough night with the girls?"

"No, they stayed at my parents because we were out with you. No, Ria tossed and turned all night and then was up early, throwing her guts up. Morning sickness is a bitch." He flops onto the coach.

"Sounds it," I say in agreement.

"I feel bad. Like it's my fault."

"Kind of is. You did knock her up," I tease.

The door to my office hits the wall.

"Harry?" Jack says. Harry's eyes zone in on mine and he charges at me, like a bull to a red flag. He grabs me by the collar.

"What the fuck?" I roar as I try to move away, but he shoves me back with such force, I groan in pain as my spine hits the wall.

"You knew. You fucking knew, and you didn't tell me," he yells. Balling his hands into fists, he goes to swing. I get ready to block, but Jack covers Harry's fist with his hand.

"Harry, stop!" Jack yells, trying to pull him off me, but he can't. The adrenaline pumping through him right now has taken over.

"No, he knew, he knew, and he didn't tell me. If you had told me I could have stopped her, if I hadn't got there—"

"Stopped what? Harry, you are talking in riddles. Back away and talk to us," Jack begs.

I'm now nose to nose with Harry, his breathing ragged, eyes wild, his body vibrating with rage. It breaks me to see my friend in so much pain and it hurts even more to know he thinks I'm the reason for it.

"Harry, I don't know what you are talking about. She only told me that—" He doesn't let me finish. His large frame collapses into me and it takes all the strength I have to hold him upright and keep him together as he splinters. The usual confident life and soul of any party is now a broken heap on the office floor, and as I listen to every gut churning detail, all I can do is blame myself. I should have noticed, seen she was struggling, pushed her for more answers.

But I didn't and when the mention of Gabriella's name and a therapy group they all met at when they were teens breaks through the haze of guilt, I feel numb, and all I want to do is run to Gabriella and try to save her, because everything in my core tells me something is wrong.

Chapter Forty-Three

Gabriella

It's been a long night and an exhausting day. I haven't even got dressed. Ria stayed with us and helped clean up Ali's room. Ali protested, but we called a doctor out to the apartment and they checked her over and suggested rest and some therapy will help her heal. When she told us what's been going on, what led to last night's events, it broke a piece of me that I don't think will ever heal.

I should have been here. I should have known she was suffering. It was clear, the signs were there, and I was too wrapped up in my own lies and my messed up situation with Brad to notice. I should have gone home with her last night.

She sleeps peacefully on the couch as I clear up the dishes. Every time I glance over to check on her, I have to fight back sobs. She's more like my sister than my friend. She saved me, took me in when I was a lonely teenager trying to find her place in the world. Just like Ria, they never judged me, loved me unconditionally and the thought of her not being here is too much to comprehend. They are the sisters I never had but longed for and if I lose either of them I don't think I'd ever recover.

This was the wake up call I needed. I need to make better choices. Stop being selfish and focus on who and what matters. Luna has tried calling me all day and so has Patrick, but I can't speak to either of them.

My focus needs to be on Ali. I text the studio and canceled my classes for the week so I could be here to watch her. I don't want to leave her on her own. A soft knock sounds from the front door. Half expecting it to be Ria and Jack, I open the door and my body stiffens when Brad fills the doorway, his forearm leaning against the wooden doorframe. He lifts his head to look at me and he looks as broken as me. He looks like he hasn't slept, his eyes bloodshot and there's a faint hint of stale whiskey on his breath, which makes me worry. He's dressed in a black tee, jeans and military style boots, but something about him isn't as put together as he usually is.

"Can I come in?" His voice is low and deflated and my natural instinct is to throw my arms around him and comfort him, knowing what he's also been through after Ali explained everything.

I gesture for him to come inside, and I close the door quietly. He follows me towards the kitchen and hovers behind me as I pull two mugs from the cupboard.

"Coffee?" I ask, assuming the answer already.

"Please." He speaks softly, not sounding himself at all and it hurts my heart. The sound of water trickles through the machine in to the waiting cup and the scent of strong coffee fills the air.

"How's Ali?" he asks.

"Hurting, but she's strong. She'll get through this." I glance over my shoulder and watch as he looks over at her sleeping soundly on the couch.

I turn and take his hand, giving it a squeeze. "I heard what you did for Cassidy, that's must have been awful. I'm sorry."

He clears his throat and sniffs, as if he were fighting back tears. "Yeah well, anyone would have done it in that situation. I'm no hero."

"I think you are, not everyone would have or could have." He shrugs his shoulders as if it were no big deal.

"How are you doing?" I ask, concern in my tone. I worry it's stirred things up from his military days. I don't know the ins and outs, but I know he was there when Scotty died, so Cassidy flat lining on him must have affected him somehow.

We just stand in silence. The coffee machine beeps, and I turn around to place the second cup under.

"We need to talk," he says firmly and the hair on the back of my back stand on end.

"I know something happened to you when you were a teen, and I need to know what."

I grip hold of the counter to steady myself and close my eyes. My heart beats so loud it muffles his voice.

"Gabriella," he says loudly and I spin to face him, worried he will wake Ali.

"Brad, please not now," I beg.

"No, right now is when we are doing this, Gabriella." He cups my face, and I can feel the tremors going through his body.

"It was a long time ago. It doesn't matter. Please don't ask me to relive it."

"Why won't you tell me?' he asks, hurt filled in his voice.

"Probably the same reason why you won't tell me why you pushed me away. Some things are just better left buried." I say.

He shakes his head, releasing the hold he has on me.

"This is messed up." He mutters under his breath. He's right, it is.

"Are we going to talk about the other night?" he asks, closing the space between us.

I lower my voice. "That night was a mistake. I shouldn't have come over. It was a moment of weakness."

"Bullshit," he spits.

"I think we need some space." I say, not meaning a single word of it because all I want to do is to be with him. But I need to sort this situation with Patrick before I can think of pursuing anything with Brad. It's not fair to him to have him believing my relationship with Patrick is real and string him along. I need to be here with Ali. She's going to need me over the next couple of months while she prepares for the parole hearing. I fear I've let her down too much already.

"Why, tell me why?" He brings my face just inches from his and it would be so easy to press my lips to his and just get lost in him.

"Because Ali needs me, I need to be here for her and I'm... I'm with Patrick."

"But what do you want, Gabriella? What does your heart and mind crave? Because, I could easily tell you what mine does."

I shake my head and step out of his hold.

"What you want matters." He reaches for me again and I hold up my hands in defeat. No, if he says it's me I'll crack. I'll break and I'm not sure I'll be able to piece myself back together.

What I want doesn't matter, it's never mattered, and I was naïve and silly to believe it did. I should have stayed in my lane, in the background like I always have, and no one would have got hurt.

He steps closer and we both startle when we hear Ali stir. I turn and begin making her a cup of tea and he walks over to her on the couch. My hands tremble as they carry the mugs over to them.

I make my excuses to go get changed and head for my bedroom, stifling down the sobs that want to tumble out of me.

I close the door, run to my bathroom, turning on the shower and fall back on the hard tiled floor and cover my mouth with my hand and let my tears fall. It's all one giant mess and I don't know where to begin with the clean-up. Either way, there's a risk. I risk losing my family and ruining their lives, and my own, or I risk hurting the only man who has made me feel seen, who wanted me for me and not a version of myself that I put out there. The one man who made me feel like I was more than enough.

Chapter Forty-Four

Gabriella

It's been nearly two weeks since Ali's incident and every day she gets a little better. We rotate being with her. When I'm working, Ria comes over, Jack and Brad pop in most days too and Harry has spent every night on the couch. Ali eventually told us everything about what's been going on the past few months and with the parole hearing looming she needs all the support in the world.

Brad and I have had a few awkward exchanges as we pass each other in the apartment and Patrick thankfully hasn't bothered me, which is a relief and also worrying. I sit the opposite end of the couch to Ali, we are wrapped up on blankets in our yoga pants and sweatshirts and eat Thai green curry watching Sex and The City.

It feels like forever since we have just hung out together like this; we would always do this before life got complicated and men came into our lives. I'm not stupid enough to believe we will live together forever, but I'll miss these days when they are gone.

"I think I am probably the Samantha of the group," Ali says with a mouthful of curry. I snort a laugh.

"Yeah, with some Carrie thrown in," I suggest.

"Yeah, and Ria is for sure Charlotte, hiding in the pantry to get a break from the kids." We both laugh and it's light and airy and it's the most I've seen her smile in months.

"Oh great, does that make me the workaholic with the cheating husband," I deadpan.

She flattens her mouth and snorts. "Speaking of husbands. How's things with Patrick? You haven't said much about him."

I go to speak, but my phone buzzes.

Brad

> I MISS YOU

"I don't know. I think it's going okay. He's busy with work, so we haven't seen each other much," I lie.

My phone buzzes again.

Brad

> I NEED YOU

Worry stirs in my belly. Something is wrong.

Another message pings and it's a photo, one from my photo shoot I did in LA and my heart sinks. I look happy. I remember how good I felt that day, what Brad did for me, the bangle, the confidence he helped me re-claim. The night we shared together. It all comes back and now every part of my body aches in that way it does when you get sick, when the flu takes over and ravages your body. But this isn't the flu, no this is pain; this is longing, this is wanting, needing and missing someone you know you can't have.

"Who's that?" Ali asks, making me jump.

"Oh, erm Patrick," I answer vaguely, placing it face down on the couch and tucking back into my food.

"What did he want?" she asks, in between bites.

"He just wanted to invite me over, but I'll see him another time."

"Go, go see him."

I turn my focus away from the television to face her. "No, no, we are having a girls' night. I'll see him another night. I'm not leaving you," I say firmly.

"Gabs, I'll be fine. I have to be alone at some point. Please, go see him. You haven't seen him in ages."

I stare at her, conflicted. I want to go. Something feels wrong, but I don't want to leave Ali alone.

"Please, if I need you, I will call you. I swear." I eye her suspiciously. "Scout's honor," she mocks, putting her fingers to the side of her head to salute me, and I chuckle.

"Are you sure?" I ask.

"Yes, go, please. I will be fine here with my Thai food and Sarah Jessica Parker."

I place my empty bowl on the table. "Promise me you will call. I won't stay out. I'll be a few hours and I'll be back."

"I'll be fine. Take as long as you want," she says, waving her hand.

Chapter Forty Five

Brad

I stare at the wall, swigging whiskey straight from the bottle now. I've gone past using the glass that's beside me on the floor. I don't know when I last slept. Maybe three days. Every time I close my eyes, I see Scotty lying on the floor. Every time I look down at my hands, I see his blood trickling between my fingers. I've scrubbed my hands so many times to get rid of it that I've made them raw. There's a heaviness in my chest that only she made feel lighter. Everything that's happened the past few months has fucked me up and I can feel myself slipping.

I play the voicemail from Dad over and over.

"Marco, I need an answer. Tick tock, if you don't find a way, then I will."

To further prolong my torture, I open up the file of photos the photographer sent me from Gabriella's photoshoot. I swipe right, one photo after the other. Each one more beautiful than the last.

Her wide smile, her dazzling eyes, her sexy poses feel like repeated punches to the gut. I throw my phone aside and drag a hand over my face.

I'm drowning here. I don't know which way to turn other than hoping I'll find it at the bottom of a bottle. I ball my hand into a fist, pissed at myself for letting someone have control over my emotions. This is why I don't feel, don't let people in, keep to my routines. I was stupid enough to believe I could control how I felt about her, I had control over everything else but not her, not the way I feel about her, and now she's with someone who doesn't see her worth and there's not a thing I can do about it. I've never felt so weak in my life.

In a moment of desperation, I text her earlier to tell I missed her, that I needed her. There's a pain in my heart that only she can heal but I don't know how much longer I can be around her and watch her be with someone else. I should have told her sooner how I felt about her, then maybe I wouldn't have to miss her. I thought I could handle just having pieces of her, but it seems I need all of her.

I pick up the glass and launch it, watching it hit the wall and shatter to the ground the same way my heart is right now. I take another swig of whiskey and my ears prick up when I hear her familiar voice. "Brad, are you here?"

She comes round the corner and her face falls when she looks down at me.

"Your door was open. Are you okay?" There's concern in her voice as she scans the mess that is my apartment.

"Never better, baby girl," I slur, waving the bottle of whiskey before I take another sip, gasping when the burn hits the back of my throat.

"How much have you drank?"

"Your guess is as good as mine. I lost count after glass number eight or was it ten?!" I snort and take another sip. She snatches the bottle from my grip and I growl. "What the fuck?"

"You've had enough," she says sternly.

"You don't get to decide that. I'll decide when I've had enough." I try to snatch the bottle back, but my back hits the cupboard door.

"You've proven my point; you can barely sit up. What have you done to yourself? This isn't you." There's an edge of sadness and concern in her tone, and I scoff.

"Don't act like you care, Gabriella,"

"I do care." She looks wounded and it turns my stomach knowing I am the cause. I'm being an ass. I reached out and she came. I should be pulling her in and yet I'm here pushing her away.

"I don't know what's happening to me. I had everything under control and then..."

"And then what?' she asks softly, placing her hands on my thighs and scooting in between my legs.

"Then you happened." I want to reach out and hold her. "You spun into my world and made feel again," I say, hitting my chest with my fist.

"You brought something inside of me back to life and now you're gone, and you took it with you."

She cups my face, the soft pad of her thumb brushes over my cheek. "Oh, baby, what have you done to yourself?" she whispers, and her words feel like a sharp dagger to the heart.

I squeeze my eyes shut and move my head, so her hand falls away. "Don't, don't call me that."

"What?"

"Baby. That's what you should be calling him, right? He's yours."

She chokes out a sob and her tears free fall down her cheeks. "I'm sorry."

Watching her fall apart begins to break down my walls. I can't have her believing this is all her doing.

"It's my fault. I pushed you into his arms. I let you walk away without a fight because I thought you deserved better than what I could give you. I was just trying to keep you safe."

"Safe from what?" Her brows furrow.

"Me and everything my fucked up life could do to you."

"I've messed up too. It's not all on you and I'm trying to fix it." She hangs her head in shame.

"Let me help you." I reach out and wipe her tears away.

She shakes her head. "You can't. I've got to do this on my own."

"What happened to you when you were younger? Please let me in and tell me because the things I'm imagining are keeping me awake at night."

She covers her face with her hands, and I reach for her wrists and pull them apart.

"I'd never judge you. I just need to know. Please. It's eating me up inside."

I release her wrists, and she sucks in a deep breath.

"It was my fault. I put myself in a situation I know I shouldn't have been in and I'm now living with the consequences of it."

"Just tell me, please," I beg, needing to understand what she's been through.

She adjusts her position, getting into a more comfortable one. I trail my gaze down her body where I see her twisting the bangle I gave her and I brace myself for whatever words she's getting ready to utter about her past. "When I was fifteen, I snuck out and went to a party I wasn't supposed to be at. It was the first time I tasted alcohol. I got drunk, passed out, and a guy I had been texting filmed us having sex."

My blood runs cold.

"I didn't have any memory of it. I only found out when he sent the video to my dad, threatening to leak it if my dad didn't pay him a ton of money."

"What the fuck?" I hiss.

"My dad paid him and secured the copies of the videos and destroyed them. My parents moved us to New York. We never talked about it, but they never looked at me the same, especially my dad. It could have ruined his career. They put me in a therapy group and that's where I met Ali and Ria. I always felt like a fraud at that group, like I didn't have a right to be there."

"What, why?"

"Because I wasn't assaulted. What happened to me was my own doing."

I blink rapidly. *Is she fucking serious?*

"Gabriella, what happened to you, that... that was rape."

She shakes her head. "No, no, don't say that. I put myself in that situation. I knew I shouldn't have been there. I liked him."

"Did you consent or have memory of consenting?" She shakes her head and I grind my teeth. "That's rape, Gabriella. He took advantage of you and then used it against you." A burn in my chest has me rubbing it with my palm. "He should have gone down for what he did. Your dad should have..." My words are cut short when sobs wrack her body and I reach out and hold her and having her in my arms sobers me. "I'm so sorry, baby. I'm sorry that happened to you. But it wasn't your fault. You are not the villain in this story. He is. Your parents are. They should have protected you, not blamed you."

I hold her till she stops crying, until her small frame molds into mine and I press a kiss into her silk hair. "It wasn't your fault."

She pulls back, wiping her tears and lets out a long breath.

"I'm sorry."

"Sorry? For what?" I ask in confusion.

"For breaking down like that. I thought I'd dealt with it all, but maybe I haven't. It just got brushed under the carpet when it happened. Other than therapy, I never talked about it with my parents. I just spent my days trying to make it up to them, for ruining their life, moving, risking my dad's job."

"Is this why you're with Patrick? To please your parents? To make up for shit that wasn't your fault?"

"It's complicated." She sniffs.

"Help me understand how."

Silence falls between us, and I watch as she twiddles the bracelet once again.

"Do you love him?" I ask, not really wanting the answer.

She just shakes her head and relief floods my body.

"Then leave him." I know I'm not thinking clearly. I know my dad's threats are looming over my head still, but right now, all I see is her, and I need her. It's selfish and reckless, but I don't care.

"Be with me. I've never wanted anyone the way I want you." My voice cracks and suddenly it feels hard to breathe.

"It's not as simple as that." She says it so quietly I almost miss it.

"What hold does he have over you? Has he hurt you too?"

She doesn't say anything, and that makes my mind spiral. Has he touched her, forced her to do something? Hit her?

The black hole that's been threatening to drag me in reappears in my mind and images from my past flash through my mind. My dad's fists connecting with my jaw when I fucked up, my uncle's kicks to the kidneys as I lay on the ground curled in a ball. Scotty on the desert ground, bleeding out, his thick dark blood coating my hands as I try desperately to bring him back to life, Cassidy lifeless on the ground as I pump her chest, Ali's accident, Harry breaking down in my arms. The thought of some piece of shit taking advantage of Gabriella and then the image of Patrick holding Gabriella down and hurting her all becomes too much. My chest feels incapable of expanding and I fist the fabric of my suit pants and reach out for her hand. "I can't... I can't..."

"Hey, hey look at me." Gabriella's voice sounds far away, but logically I know she's there and I fight to stay present.

Her small hand presses against my chest, covering my heart. It hammers against her palm and her warm hand cradles my face.

I try desperately to suck in greedy breaths, but it doesn't feel enough. My vision blurs, my mouth goes dry, and I feel like I can't steal enough air to breathe.

"Focus on my voice and feel my hand. Focus on those two things."

"I... I can't..." I try to say, but the words won't come.

"Ssssshhhh, it's okay," she soothes. "Breathe in and out. Look at me and just be with me. It's just you and me. Be with me in this moment." Her firm hand presses firmer over my chest and her voice feels like it's closer. "I'll chase away your demons, even its just for a little while."

My breathing begins to slow. I focus on her voice and cover my hand with hers, lacing our fingers as my chest rises and falls beneath our connected hands.

She presses her forehead to mine and whispers, "Just tell me what you need, and I'll give it to you."

I swallow down the lump in my throat.

"You. I just need you. I need you to help me breathe again."

I close my eyes, preparing for her rejection but her soft lips dust mine and she climbs into my lap and straddles me.

I weave my fingers into her hair and pull her closer, I kiss her like she's my oxygen supply, the only thing keeping me alive, because that's exactly how it feels and that scares me, I can't put that pressure on her. I need to save myself. I can't rely on her to do it. Sometimes things have to fall apart in order to be rebuilt, stronger and better than before. I need to give her some space, to figure out what she wants and who she wants. I can't force it. It has to come from her.

"You've always had me, I just, I need…"

"Time," I say finishing her sentence. She nods.

"Just give me something Gabriella please, give me hope that one day I'll win you back, that there's still a piece of your heart that belongs to me because all of mine belongs to you."

Her words are soft, but I hear them. "Brad, I need you to know. Everything I'm doing, it's so I can come back to you. Just hold me like I'm still yours for tonight, please."

Chapter Forty Six

Gabriella

After checking in with Ali and when I knew she was safe at Harry's apartment with him for the night, I slept over at Brad's, and by slept I mean I helped him to bed and spent the night laid in his arms, replaying last night over, my confession, his words as I watched him, making sure he didn't choke on his own vomit, or have another panic attack. It broke me in two to see him that way. The always strong and guarded man was a heap of broken pieces on the floor, and I helped break him. My head and my heart are in two different places. I want to be with Brad, but I'm terrified of the repercussions of that. I'm usually the fixer and these days, all I seem to do is break everything. After cleaning up the mess and broken glass in his kitchen, I snuck out while he slept peacefully and took a cab to see the only person I feel can help me right now, the only person I can think of that is strong enough to shoulder this burden with me.

I tap the door three times with my knuckles and it's only a brief moment before he answers and I instantly sag in relief. My bottom lip trembles and I'm not sure I can hold myself up any longer.

"Gabby?" Jack's calm voice is my breaking point. I step forward, stumbling, and he catches me.

Sobs wrack my body and he holds me tightly, the way I'd imagine a big brother would. I never had, always wanted one. I've always envied Ria's relationship with Noah. I always wondered what it would be like to have a sibling, a teammate in life. Someone you could get up to mischief with, hide from mom and dad and play tricks. Comfort each other when you are sad and make you laugh when you haven't smiled in days. I may not have a brother, but I do have this.

"Hey, you're okay, I've got you," he soothes, stroking my hair as I cry into his chest.

"I... I've messed up and I don't know what to do," I choke out, my voice not sounding like my own.

"It's okay, whatever it is, we'll figure it out. Come on." He releases the hold he has of me and guides me into the apartment.

"Ria is taking Lexi to school and then heading to the salon. She won't be back for a while."

"It's actually you I wanted to see." I sniff.

I choke out a laugh and point to his gray tee that now has a wet patch on the chest.

He looks down and shakes his head. "I'm used to it. If it's not tears on my shirt is snot or vomit."

I feel myself begin to relax already. Jack has a way about him that makes you feel secure. He's the most levelheaded and calm person I've ever known. If anyone knows what to do, it's him.

"I've got Elle home. Let me put on a movie for her and I'll make us some coffee." I follow him toward their open plan living space. The entire back wall is glass looking out over New York. It's a breathtaking view.

"Elle, look who's here," Jack calls as he makes his way over to the area where Elle is playing with a bunch of dolls.

She looks up and her big blue eyes just like Ria's sparkle when she sees me as I give her a wave.

"I'm going to talk to auntie Gabby in the kitchen. Can you be a good girl and watch Minnie Mouse?"

She jumps up and toddles over to the couch, clutching her big Minnie Mouse stuffie and gets comfy.

"Okay, Daddy," she says in her cute toddler voice that makes me melt.

I take a seat at the kitchen island and scroll my phone: a text from Ali, nothing from Brad, and my stomach knots every time I think of him and the memory of last night.

Jack settles in the seat next to me, placing a steaming mug of coffee in front of me. I cradle it, not caring that the ceramic is burning my hands, I feel too numb to feel it.

"I need you to keep an eye on Brad, he's going through something and I can't be the one to help him."

"Okay." Jack says, his tone mixed with confusion. "Can I ask why?"

"Because I'm the one who helped cause it." I don't look at him, I just focus on the hot steam that rises form my cup that wafts in my face.

"Has something happened between you two?" he asks softly.

"Please don't ask me that." My words barely a whisper. He doesn't press me further and I'm grateful.

"What do you need me to do?" He asks. I think about telling him everything but decide its safer to only tell him what he needs to know.

"He's drinking a lot, he's struggling. I think the thing with Cassidy and Ali has stirred things up for him and I…" I stop myself from going anything further.

"I'll make it worse being round him, so I need you to check on him, help him. He's hurting and he needs help and I need someone to help him until I am able to." I express to him, my words coming out far shakier than I intend.

"Are you in trouble Gabby? Do you need help?"

Yes, yes, I do, I am being blackmailed by a man who's controlling me and threatening to implode my entire world and everything I have been trying to hide and make up for years, I internally scream but instead I lie. I'm getting good at that.

"No, it's just complicated and Harry has a lot going on with Ali and helping her, Ria is pregnant, Noah is god knows where and I know you have stuff going but I just need someone to help him." My rambles turn into soft cries and Jack wraps an arm around me.

"I'm sorry." I choke out.

"Don't be, I'm glad you felt you could come to me." Jack says reassuringly.

"Leave Brad to me, he will be okay, he's strong and resilient, but we all need a little help to get ourselves out of the darkness."

"Thank you." I sniff.

"You know you can tell me anything, right?" I nod. He's giving me the dad look, and I'd laugh if it weren't for the seriousness of the situation. I'm lucky to have someone who cares, who's in my corner, but it's still not enough to expose my secrets. No, this is a battle I have to fight alone, I just had to make sure Brad didn't fight his solo because he's spent his whole life fighting, it's time someone fought for him, and that's what I'm going to do, I'm going to fix this mess, and hope he'll forgive me when I've done it.

Chapter Forty Seven

Brad

I'm woken from my slumber to the sound of someone beating down my door. I lift my head, squinting at my beside clock: 11.38 am.

Shit!

I clutch my head; a wave of dizziness and nausea hits me as I bring myself to a seating position. Blurred memories of last night fight their way to the forefront of my mind. Gabriella, whiskey, tears, flashbacks. I pray it's all a bad dream, but when I swallow and the taste of stale whiskey hits, I know it's all true.

The banging gets louder, and I throw back the sheets. I'm still in last night's suit pants and nothing else. I make my way to the front door.

"What the fuuu…" I stop when Jack, holding Elle in his arms is the only thing I see.

"Language," Jack scolds.

"What are you doing here?"

"Well good morning to you too, sunshine," Jack says sarcastically. He pushes past me, not waiting for an invite.

"Look as lovely as it is to see you both, I'm kind of busy. I've got things to do."

"By things to do you mean drowning yourself in whiskey and avoiding your responsibilities?" Jack eyes me as he balances Elle on the edge of my kitchen counter and hands her a snack out of what can only be described as a carryon bag.

"You are not changing her diaper on there," I say in a panic, remembering the horror of diaper-gate last year.

"Calm down, she's in big girl pants. We are using the potty, aren't we, sweetie?" he says, stroking her hair out of her face. Elle nods, biting down on her cookie. "Coffee," I ask, needing to distract myself.

"Please."

"Does Elle want some juice?" I ask Jack, but I look at Elle. When she turns her head and her angelic face smiles it calms me in a way I've not experienced. Had she not been here, I'd have slung Jack out, yelled and banged around, and blocked out the world. But she doesn't deserve to see that.

I make our coffees, black for me, creamer for Jack, and pull one of my nephew's plastic cups I keep here for when he visits and fill it with apple juice.

"So..." Jack begins, clearing his throat. "Gabby came to see me." My spine stiffens. "I don't need to know. I'm not here to judge and I'm all ears if you wanna talk, but she's worried about you, and so am I."

I pass him the drinks, and lean back against the counter, resting the coffee mug against my bare stomach, not giving a damn that it's scolding hot.

"I'm fine. She didn't need to worry you." I shrug.

He eyes me like I'm full of shit.

"Look, I'm just going through some stuff. I don't want to talk about it and I may have had a drink or two but it ends today."

"Really?" Jack questions.

"It was just a little relapse. It's been a lot lately and..." I stop, my emotions getting caught in my throat.

"I'm fine, but I do appreciate you coming over."

There's a knock at my door.

"Am I running an open house today," I mutter, heading for the door, opening it with force and my tenses when I see Harry standing there.

He looks up at me, and I brace myself for his anger, his hurt, his pain. But instead he steps towards me, wrapping his arms around me. "I'm sorry." His broken words hit me in the chest.

"You don't have anything to be sorry about, I—" He cuts me off pulling back, his face looking war torn and broken.

"Yeah, I fucking do. I took my anger and my fear out on you. I was wrong. But I want to thank you. She told me what you did for her. How you took care of her after what happened to Cassidy. I'm glad she had you. I'm glad I have you." His nostrils flare and he clears his throat.

All I manage is a nod of acknowledgment. We've been through so much together, too much to have anything break us, and though I didn't need his apology, it means everything that he gave me one anyway.

"So, you look like shit. What's eating your ass?" he teases, fist pumping me in the chest and I let out a sigh of relief. We are back to us.

"Fancy breakfast? I have a house full."

Chapter Forty Eight

Gabriella

Life has returned to some sort of normality. After Ali's court case, Brad flew out to LA to sign off on the new club they are opening and stayed out there. It's been over a month, and as much as I have missed him, it was the space we both desperately needed. It's given me time to think, to rebuild myself. Brad's words hit hard. What happened to me wasn't my fault. I was taken advantage of and while I'm not quite ready to confront my parents about it, that revelation has helped heal a part of me that I didn't know needed healing, and I have him to thank for that.

I've only had to see Patrick twice in the last month. He has his interview next week and after a conversation with my dad, it sounds like he will land his dream role and then we can end this entire mess.

I whirl the blender, and the sound fills the kitchen. I've been for my morning run and I feel ready for the day. Tonight, the magazine Ali works for is having a campaign launch party.

Butterflies flutter in my belly when I think of Brad and if he will be there tonight. Harry mentioned he was coming back to the city sometime this week. Not only do I want to see him for my own selfish reasons, I need to talk to him about their accounts.

The guys noticed money has been missing, and I've been going through their paperwork and accounts. I need access to some more information before I can piece it all together, and Harry said Brad was also looking into it.

I turn off the blender, twisting the jug out and turn around to pour it out when Ali stands across the island eating the fruit out of the container I've used to make my smoothie.

I scream. "Jesus, Ali, you scared me."

She chuckles. "Sorry, your blender woke us. We really need to get you a quieter one."

I quirk an eyebrow. "Oh, I'm sorry. I didn't think you would be able to hear it over all the noise you guys have been making this morning." My tone is sarcastic.

She grins and pops a strawberry into her mouth. "Oh, you heard that," she smirks.

"The whole building heard it," I deadpan.

I continue pouring my smoothie into my glass, stick a straw in and stir.

"Look, I'm so happy for you both, really I am, but could you maybe stay at his tonight or a hotel? I'll pay."

"Sure." Her tone is confused. I worry I've offended her, so I continue.

"I just can't listen to another night of you making that noise when he's doing god knows what to you."

She scrunches up her nose. "What noise?"

"You know, the noise." I eye her.

"No, you're going to have to help me out here, little G," she says, folding her arms.

"It's a kind of wooooo noise and then a little aaahhhh at the end, but your voice goes really deep, like it's verging on painful."

"Oh." She grins. "That noise."

"Yeah, that noise."

"By the way, I totally knew what noise you meant. I just wanted to hear you make it." She chuckles, popping another piece of fruit into her mouth. I roll my eyes and take a sip of my smoothie.

"But I do love it when he does that," she says, wiggling her eyebrows.

"The whole building knows you love it," I say, slamming my glass down on the counter.

"The whole building knows you love what?." Harry says, sleepily running a hand through his hair and coming up behind Ali and wraps his arms around her waist, kissing her cheek and a pang of jealously hits me, not of them, but of what they have.

"That thing you do when I make that noise."

"Oh, you mean when I put my finger in your—"

"Harry! Please," I yell, far louder than needed. "I don't need the details. Hearing it is bad enough."

Ali flattens her mouth and tries to stifle a laugh and Harry grins. "Sounds like you need a finger up..."

I stick my fingers in my ears and begin yelling, "La la la. I can't hear you." I pull my fingers out my ears and they are both staring at me like I am some sort of wild animal.

"Yes, well thank you both for scarring me for life," I tease. "I'm going to get on with my day."

"Are you bringing Patrick tonight?" Ali asks.

"Ummm, no, I think he's busy," I lie. I haven't even asked, because why would I? This whole fake boyfriend thing is exhausting, but I need him to secure his job and then I can cut ties.

Ali just nods, accepting my lie.

"Oh, can you swing by the club today. We have the files ready that you requested." Harry asks, taking some fruit and eating it.

"Yeah, sure," I say.

Harry begins nuzzling Ali's neck and she giggles. I'm so happy for them and though I tease them, I'm so pleased they found their way to each other.

"I'll leave you both to it," I say, scooping up my smoothie and head to my bedroom, a mixture of anxiety and excitement brewing inside me, hoping today is the day I see Brad.

My phone rings out and I have to move the pile of dresses I laid out to try on for tonight's party. I find it and groan when I see Patrick's name. I swipe the screen and bring it to my ear.

"Yes," I say. We don't even greet each other now.

"I need you to be at a dinner tonight." His tone is demanding.

"I can't. I have an event to go to."

"Well cancel. This is with my parents. They want you to come to dinner."

I roll my eyes in frustration. "I'm sorry. Can you make it another time? It's a big deal for Ali. I can't miss it. Look, tell your parents I'm sorry, and I'll see if I can get my parents to do one of their dinner parties and invite your parents.

"Okay, deal."

He hangs up, and I toss the phone on the bed. I don't think I've met a bigger prick in my life. I can't wait to get shot of him. I've been so close to coming clean to my parents. I mean I haven't worked at the club in months, but every time I picture their disapproving looks, I think better of it.

I flop back on my bed, stare up at the ceiling, and mentally prepare myself for tonight to see him. My heart races, hands tingling at the thought of being able to see him, touch him, feel his presence. I've missed it all. I scan my room and the red dress from LA hangs over my door I had a bold idea I could wear it tonight. I know Brad loves it, but I think I need something more low key. I don't want to draw attention and cause any chaos tonight.

Chapter Forty Nine

Brad

I landed back in New York last night after over a month in LA, and it's exactly what I needed. I flew in so I could be here for Ali's campaign party. I know this is a big deal for her and after everything she's been through, I want to show up for her.

I needed to escape the city and my troubles. I've been my version of sober for over two months, and though I'll never fully be able to let go of my habits because they keep me in check, I'm not as regimented, and it was Gabriella who showed me that life doesn't have to be kept to a schedule. That sometimes just being in the moment and letting life flow is okay.

Now I'm back, I know I need to face my dad. I lied before I left and sent a letter saying I was close to sorting it, and he should hear from a lawyer soon to buy me some time. I needed to make sure he wouldn't bother Gabriella in my absence. But now I'm back, and feeling stronger, I'm ready to deal with things and then find out where Gabriella's head is at.

Harry texted to say Gabriella was going to stop by and pick up the files and I've anticipated her visit all morning. I clear my last email and my office door creeps open. Expecting it to be Gabriella, I rise and head for the door, but I'm shocked to find Cassidy there, dressed in a figure hugging blue dress. Her brown hair is shorter than when I last saw her; she looks well.

"Hi," I say, furrowing my brow, surprised she's here.

"Hey. I heard through Ali that you were back home, and I wanted to see you."

"Come in."

I sit on the edge of my desk and she fiddles with the strap of her purse.

"I wanted to thank you for saving my life." She looks me straight in the eye as she says it.

"You're welcome. Anyone would have done the same in that situation."

She shakes her head. "No, you're wrong. It was heroic and part of my program is to thank the people who saved me, make amends."

"You're in a program?"

"Yep, sixty-three days sober, go me."

I give her a smile because that is something to be proud of. "Congratulations, Cassidy that's really great."

She takes a step forward, her eyes roaming up and down my body as she does. "I'd like to make it up to you, you know, for putting you through that." She closes the space between us, running her index finger down my chest. I stiffen at her touch.

"And how exactly are you going to do that, Cassidy?" My tone is clipped.

"Are you going to Ali's magazine party tonight?"

"Yes."

"Maybe we could go together and have our own after party," she says in a flirtatious tone, dragging her index finger down my chest. Her fingers attempting to unhook the buttons.

I need to shoot this down right fucking now.

She leans in so close our lips almost touch. I pull away to find Gabriella standing there, eyes wide, looking between me and Cassidy.

"I, um, can come back." She turns to leave, but I brush Cassidy aside and head for the door.

"No, Cassidy was just leaving." I glare at Cassidy, and I don't like the expression on her face. Grinning, she walks past me and Gabriella, her hips swaying, running her index along my chest as she does.

"See you tonight." Her voice is as smooth as velvet. I don't say anything. I get up and close the door behind her, and an awkward silence falls between us. This isn't how I wanted our reunion to be.

"I'm sorry if I interrupted. I just stopped by to pick up the files." She looks around my office and spots a pile of brown files on the cabinet behind my desk. "Is that them?"

"Yes, but, Gabriella, that wasn't what it looked like," I say.

"Brad, you don't have to explain yourself to me. You don't owe me anything." There's an edge to her voice, and I don't like it. In fact, it pisses me off. I shove my hands in my pocket to keep them busy because the need to pull her to me is becoming too hard to bear.

"I assume you will be there tonight," I say.

"I will."

"And Patrick will be there?"

"He might be," she says like a petulant child. O*h, she's pissed.*

"I better get to work on these," she says, holding up the files as she brushes past me, but I catch her arm and stop her. My nose nuzzles her hair, her cherry scent I've missed so much invades my nose and it feels familiar, safe, and comforting.

"That wasn't what it looked like," I repeat.

"It's none of my business." She shrugs me off and walks out of my office without a backward glance.

Well, that wasn't how things were supposed to go.

The magazine party is bustling. Crowds of people, celebrities and socialites flood the building. My eyes dart around the room, waiting for Gabriella to arrive.

"Are you sure you don't need a chair?" Jack asks Ria, and she rolls her eyes.

"No, just like the other three times you asked me. I appreciate the concern, but if I need a seat, I'll tell you."

Ria is now very pregnant, and I too have been wondering how she balances on those heels with that bump.

"I just want to make sure you're okay, sweetheart," Jack says softly.

I feel a hand on my shoulder and turn to see Cassidy. She's wearing bright red lipstick and a short silver dress that barely covers her ass.

"Hey, handsome. Fancy seeing you here," she purrs.

"Well, seeing as I saw you earlier, and I confirmed I was attending. It shouldn't be that much of a shock to you."

I take a sip of my cola, still very much on the sober train, so I'm shocked when I see her holding a glass of wine. "I thought you were sober." I eye the glass and notice it's nearly gone.

"Pills, sweetie, not the Lord's juice." She throws back the wine and I roll my eyes. If she is going to hang around me all night, this evening is going to be long.

"Aren't you going to introduce me to your friends?"

"Hey, I'm Cassidy." She introduces herself and they all look at me with recognition in their eyes. Yes, this is the Cassidy, the Cassidy who overdosed in our club and I had to perform CPR on yes, that Cassidy.

"It's nice to meet you, Cassidy" Ria says warmly. Thank god for her and her sweet nature because I am ready to drag Cassidy out of here and throw her in a cab.

"Where's Ali?" Cassidy asks.

"She's backstage getting ready," Harry answers.

"Oooh, are you the boyfriend?" Her eyes roam up and down Harry's body, her tongue peeking out her mouth and running along her bottom lip.

"Lucky, Ali." Harry gives her a disapproving look and then his eyes widen at something over my shoulder.

"Holy shit, is that Gabby?" I turn to look, and fuck, it is.

My jaw almost hits the floor. She's wearing her YSL heels, the strapless red dress she wore when we were in LA, and her hair is out in full, the curls bouncing as she walks. I grin to myself, imaging peeling her out of that dress later tonight the way I did before, her heels wrapped around my head as I devour her, but my grin soon fades when I see that two steps behind her is that prick she calls a boyfriend.

They reach us and Gabriella stands beside me, Patrick to her side, his arm wrapping around her. She glances at me as if awaiting my reaction. I stand there, unmoving and but then Cassidy's arm comes up around my waist and Gabriella's eyes flicker to where her hand rests.

She then leans into Patrick's touch, which ignites a fire inside me and I'm ready to fly for the guy, but instead, I pull Cassidy into my side. Yes, it's a dick move, but it was that or punch Patrick.

Oh, it's going to be a fun evening.

Chapter Fifty

Gabriella

Cassidy James, is he serious? Of all the women he could get involved with, he chooses her? Do I have a right to be pissed, no. But am I? Hell yeah. Here was me thinking we could rekindle something once I shake Patrick. I was going to tell him everything, how my relationship with Patrick is fake, but if he is entertaining her, then I'm not sure how we can ever find a way back together. I know I am being unfair here, but there's nothing going on between me and Patrick, absolutely zilch. I wouldn't piss on the man if he were on fire, but I get that Brad doesn't know that.

Ugh, this is a fucking mess.

Patrick took me by surprise when I pulled up in my cab and he was standing outside waiting, declaring he was attending as my date. I didn't have it in me to argue, and knowing Brad would be here with Cassidy, I thought, why not, let's add to the chaos.

"Hey, are we excited for the show?" Ali sing songs, standing next to Harry. She's dressed in a white robe and her hair in rollers.

"So excited," Kate squeals. "How's my sister doing back there? Is she doing as she's told?"

Ali laughs. "Kennedy's doing great. She's a natural assistant."

Kate smiles proudly, clearly happy with Ali's reply. Kate's little sister has started interning at the magazine, and Ali has taken her under her wing.

"I shouldn't be out here, but I wanted to come see you all before the show started. Thank you for being here. I reserved you all seats in the front row."

"We wouldn't miss it," I say, giving her a wink.

"Okay, I've got to go. But when you hear the song "Queen of the Night" I'll be walking."

'I'm just going to wish her luck." Harry says with a wink, and follows Ali.

"Yeah, we all know what that's code for." Jack jokes.

"Could you get me a drink?" I say sweetly to Patrick.

He huffs but does as I ask and heads over to the bar. Seriously, who raised this man and taught him how to treat women?

"I'm going to visit the ladies," Cassidy says, pressing a kiss to Brad's cheek and waltzing off. I have to physically bite my tongue.

Jack and Ria are busy with their conversation so don't notice when Brad leans in, placing his hand on my lower back, my skin instantly tingles under his touch.

"You look incredible."

I inhale sharply. "Thank you." Did I wear this dress on purpose, knowing he'd be here and it's his favorite color? Yes, I did. I'm done with hiding, being the shrinking violet. I'm going to finally do what I want, and that begins with Patrick. After tonight I have to end this thing with him. He keeps moving the goalposts, has me over a barrel, and I can't live like it anymore.

"I need to talk to you," Brad whispers into my hair, his hot breath in my ear making crave it elsewhere on my body.

"I don't think your girlfriend would like that." The words taste sour in my mouth.

He spits out a sarcastic laugh. "She's not my girlfriend, Gabriella, and that's a little rich coming from you when you're the one parading around your boyfriend."

I get ready to bark back a reply but Patrick comes up beside me, handing me a glass of I don't know what. I don't even care at this point, and I toss it down my throat, wincing when the taste of bourbon hits my tongue.

I give him a what the fuck look and he shrugs his shoulder.

"Ladies and gentlemen, please take your seats in the main room. The fashion show will begin in twenty minutes." The announcement floods the speakers, and everyone begins making their way through the archway to the large room where a catwalk takes center stage and chairs line either side.

It looks incredible, and I can't wait to watch Ali walk. I know this is a big deal for her, and I couldn't be prouder of her. We find our seats in the front row. Patrick sits on one side and Brad on the other. *Dear God, this won't be awkward at all.*

"Hey, is that Beckett Taylor?" Jack asks, pointing to a man dressed in black with an earpiece, talking to a group of men dressed similarly.

"Yeah, looks like him," Brad confirms.

"Who's Beckett?" Ria asks.

"We served with him. He left not long after us, set up a security firm. We use him for stuff at the club, but he has some big clients now. Celebrities, people like that, I heard his company is doing the security for the current Miss New York Darling. I think she's here tonight," Jack explains.

"Oh, yeah, she is the pageant queen," Ria says, and Jack nods in confirmation.

"Beckett is hot." Kate swoons.

Harry returns, sitting two seats down from me, a wicked grin on his face.

"Where the hell have you been?" Jack asks.

"Just giving Ali a good luck kiss."

"We can see that. You have her lip gloss all over your face," Ria says and reaches to wipe his face the way a mother would with her small child.

Harry chuckles. "Who said it was her lip gloss?"

Everyone groans in disgust.

I busy myself reading the magazine that was left on our seats. Patrick gets up without a word and walks off; I really couldn't care where he's off too. Hopefully, in a cab home.

"Well, things look like they are going really well between you and Patrick." I slam the magazine closed and slap it down on my lap.

"Excuse me?"

"I'm just commenting on what I see," Brad smirks and I want to swipe it off his rugged face.

"Well, you can keep your observations to yourself." I lean over and point at the empty chair.

"Where's your date? Instead of commenting on mine, why don't you go and find her? Maybe she got lost."

He leans in closer. "You are so wrong about all of this, it's almost funny."

"Well, I'm glad I'm providing some entertainment. Cassidy doesn't strike me as someone who can hold a conversation for very long." There's venom in my voice and I know I sound like a bitch, but I can't help it.

"Oof, jealously looks hot on you." His voice sends a shiver up my spine.

"I'm not jealous. Don't flatter yourself," I protest.

"I'd lose the attitude, baby girl, before I make it drip out of you." His words have my clit throbbing and I cross my legs to suppress the ache. It's been so long since he touched me. He smirks when he notices.

Dammit.

Before I can say another word, a waitress walks down our row, handing us glasses of champagne. I take one and drink the entire thing, welcoming the cold fizz into my dry mouth.

Brad hands me his glass. "Please, take mine too. I'll look forward to carrying you to bed later." He winks, his lip quirks up, and I toy with the idea of kissing him or slapping him. Both sound good right about now.

It's a stupid move, but clearly, I'm not myself tonight, so I take the drink and down it in one. I give him a sarcastic smile and hand him back the empty glass.

He leans into my ear. "Excuse yourself in one minute and meet me near the bathrooms." I don't get to respond. He's up and out of his seat, disappearing into the crowd. I internally count to thirty and decide to go find him.

"I'm just going to use the ladies before it starts," I say to our friends. I leave my purse on my seat and push through the crowd. I follow the signs for the bathroom, and I find Brad leaning against the wall near reception. I reach him and he immediately takes me by the hand, dragging me down a corridor and through a door that says, 'staff only'.

"Where are we going?" I pant, trying to keep up with him.

He looks over his shoulder, opening a door and looking inside. He pulls me in, and we are in a storage closet.

"What are you do—" He swallows my words when his mouth comes down on mine. My back hits the wall and I whimper.

But I don't fight it. He steals my breath and I willingly let him. I melt into him and kiss him back with as much passion as he kisses me. Our hot breaths collide, and he kisses me with a primal need. This, this is passion. It's raw and reckless, but that's how he makes me feel. Reckless in the most delicious way. Being with him is addictive and though it may be wrong to the outside world, it feels so right. He lifts me and I wrap my legs around his waist; my dress rides up over my hips then he's placing me down, my skin hits the cold metal of the table.

"I fucking missed you," he murmurs against my lips.

His confession only makes me need him more, because I've missed him too. He slides a hand up my thigh, is fingers stroking the hem of my dress.

"We shouldn't be doing this," I murmur.

"Well, then we've got a problem, baby girl, because I can't stop doing this."

"Brad... I..." I struggle to find the words.

"End it with him Gabriella." He says as sucks on the sensitive flesh of my neck where my pulse thumps erratically.

" I..." my words are cut short when his hands glide down my waist and he tugs me closer.

"Brad, please I'm handling it, I...."

He pulls me up to standing, gripping my chin.

"I'm a patient man Gabriella, but even I have my limits. Loose him."

My chest heaves against his as he looks down at me, with a wildness in his eyes, a possessiveness I've not seen before. I should give him a straight answer. End this game of push and pull that we've been playing for what feels like months, maybe years now. But for just a moment I want to be selfish and take what I want from him and give him what he needs.

I will tell him. But not now.

"And what if I don't?' I challenge him.

He lets out a frustrated laugh. "Do you really expect me to believe that he's the one you want, Mia cara?"

I lick my lips and do my best to steady my breathing.

He dusts the backs of his knuckles down my cheek and my eyes flutter shut.

"I know what you want, what you need, does he...?"

My body trembles in anticipation of his next move. The faint sound of the MC announcing the start of the show can be heard.

In a moment of bravery or utter stupidity I goad him.

"Then prove it."

Like a predator catching his prey, he spins me. My hands plant the cool metal table

As he pushes up my dress over my hips and palms the globes of my ass. He drops to his knees, dragging my soaked underwear with him. "Part your legs," he commands, and I do. "These fucking heels drive me wild." He glides his hands from my ankles up my legs to my inner thigh, his touch leaving my skin tingling. He groans when he reaches my pussy and strokes through my folds. "Fucking soaked, aren't you, baby? Does he get you this wet?"

"No, just you," I breathe out.

I shake my head, the feeling too intense as he teases two finger inside me. He rises to his feet, his fingers still buried inside of me and pumps his fingers, slowly. The angle at which I stand has him hitting my G-spot instantly and my head rolls back in pleasure.

"Is this all for me, Mia Cara?" My walls begin trembling at the use of that name. He pulls his fingers out and I wince at the loss. I glance over my shoulder to watch as he pushes his fingers into his mouth and sucks.

"Mmmhm, so fucking sweet." He pushes his fingers back inside me again and I whimper just as he removes and forces his fingers into my mouth and I welcome them.

"Taste that. Taste what my touch does to you. Does he do that to you?"

It tastes sweet, and I'm so turned on my hips grind into his erect cock that tents his pants. I'm desperate for some friction.

He wraps a hand around my throat and squeezes, biting the shell of my ear and I cry out.

"Please," I whimper, my tone desperate. I love that he takes control, and I am willing hand my body over to him every time, but damn, he knows how to push me to the brink, slowly and almost painfully.

"Please what? What do you want, Gabriella?"

Applause and the vibrations of music can be heard through the wall, letting us know the runway show has started.

His fingers move to my clit and begins with slow circles with the pad of his finger, the pressure of my impending orgasm builds and I reach behind for him, and my nails dig into his wrist.

"Make me come. I need you to make me come," I beg, any dignity I had now long gone. I'd do anything he asked, and maybe that makes me a fool, or maybe this is what it feels like to be in love with someone.

Cupping my chin, he twists my head to face him, our lips just a breath apart.

"You are going to have to do better than that. I'm not letting you come until you are fucking begging." His tone is full of authority and I'm done for.

"Please. Fuck me, fuck me like I'm yours, only yours." I shudder, desperate for some type of release.

"You need to be quiet, or someone will come in here." I nod. He presses my stomach flat against the table and angles my ass up and my fingertips grip the edges of the table, my heartbeat so loud it thumps in my ears. I hear the familiar sound of a belt buckle and a zipper and then his hands are back on my hips and there's no waiting, there's no time. He slams into me and I moan but he covers my mouth, pushing two fingers into my parted lips and I bare down, sinking my teeth into his hot skin as he drives into me, every stroke hitting just where I need it to.

"I'm gonna fucking enjoy watching you sit next to that prissy boyfriend of yours, knowing your cunt is dripping with my cum. Does he know what a filthy girl you are, Gabriella? Huh? Or is that just for me?"

I moan around his fingers, at his words, feeling the wave of my impending orgasm that's building, one I fear will pull me into the depths of euphoria and I'll not want to come back from. The way he controls every part of my body and truthfully, my mind has me falling over the edge and when he spanks my ass, my muscles pull tight.

"Now you can come," he growls into my ear.

My legs quiver, knees buckle, and a scream works its way up my throat. His hand clamps tighter over my mouth, muffling my cries of pleasure. I feel the telling jerk that he's right there with me.

My head falls forward as he pulls his hand away from my mouth, and I gasp for air. The heat of his body moves away from mine and I anticipate feeling the evidence of what we've just done between my thighs, but he sinks to the floor, palming the globes of my bare ass and begins lapping up everything with his tongue. I pant as he cleans me up and I am close to coming again when he flattens his tongue and flicks over my clit. I want to beg for more, but I slump in frustration against the table when he drags my underwear up and pulls down my dress.

"We need to go."

I must look a mess, but there's no time. The song *Queen of the Night by Whitney Houston* is being played by the band, and I know we have minutes till Ali is walking the runway.

I turn, pulling down my dress. "But... I..." I try to speak but he swipes his thumb over the corner of mouth, removing my smudged lipstick. He takes me by the hand, exiting the room and he drags me through the crowds of staff and backstage workers, pushing through the door and we run into the main room.

Lights flash on the stage and the room's thankfully dark aside from the stage that's lit up in a lavender color. Girls descend the stage wearing the new season collection and I can't take my eyes off them as Brad pulls me towards our seats.

Our friends eye us curiously. I glance over to my right and Cassidy is looking at me like she wants to scratch my eyes out.

The MC announces Ali and her face flashes across the tv screens. The lights change and the music tempo ramps up and we all cheer. She steals my breath away.

When she reaches us, we are all up and out of our seats. Tears of pride prick my eyes. When she notices, she blows us all kisses and gives Harry a wink, and I think he was ready to climb on the stage and drag her backstage. I dab at my eyes as a familiar hand slips into mine. Brad's thumb rubs circles over my thumb and in that moment, I'm so grateful for the gesture. It's only small, but it means so much. He notices the little things, the moments when I need a little comfort, the moments when I feel nervous and need reassurance. He sees me and I need him to know that I see him too. I'm done with this bull crap.

The house lights go up and we release our hands. It's only then that I realize Patrick's seat remains empty. I mean, I am grateful, but what the heck? Where did he go? I pull my phone and scoff in disbelief when I see his message.

Patrick

> Got a better offer so I bailed. My parents are expecting you Saturday at noon.

I turn and bump into Cassidy.

"I saw you." Her tone is dark and venomous.

"Saw what?"

"You and Brad go into that closet."

My spine stiffens and I square my shoulders. "I don't know what you're talking about," I say confidently.

"I know what I saw. You want him." There's a slight slur to her voice and her pupils are dilated. From what I've heard about Cassidy James, she's unstable and an addict whose behavior is unpredictable.

"Are you high? I think you were hallucinating."

"You don't want to fuck with me, little girl." She presses her body into mine, trying to intimidate me.

"Gabs, everything okay?" Ali calls.

"Yeah, all good," I call back, my eyes contacting never breaking with Cassidy's.

"Do your friends know that you're fucking around behind your boyfriend's back, you slut?"

Her words would have hurt a few months ago. I'd have believed every word she spat out, but I'm done with being bullied.

"You don't know anything, and you don't know me. You are just a jealous pill-head who is chasing a man who doesn't want you. Take the hint Cassidy, desperation isn't a good look on you."

"You bitch." Cassidy slaps me across the face. I don't anticipate it, so I go flying, but strong hands catch me.

"Hell no," I hear Ali yell.

"Retract the claws Ali Cat," Harry shouts as I try to regain my focus and look up to see Brad was the one who caught my fall.

Ali is nose to nose with Cassidy and signals for security to remove her. Tears threaten and my cheek is burning.

"Are you okay? What was that?" Ali asks, worry etched all over her face.

"I, I don't know, I think she's been drinking, and I couldn't understand what she was saying. I'm sorry, I don't mean to ruin your night, I'm so sorry, I..." My words trail off.

"Hey, you didn't ruin anything," Ali reassures me.

"Would you be mad if I went home?" I say, a slight tremble to in my voice. I need to get out of here.

"Of course not, but I don't want you going alone."

"I'll take her," Brad offers.

We say our goodbyes and Brad drives us back to my apartment. The journey back silent as I replay the whole evening in my head. This all needs to stop. Now.

We enter the apartment, and I toss my purse and kick off my heels, heading for the refrigerator and take a swig of last night's rose right from the bottle. I carry it away with me and head to my bedroom, taking another swig, and Brad follows.

"We need to talk."

"Not now Brad. I'm tired and my cheek is throbbing." I press the cold bottle against my cheek and close my eyes as the sting subsides.

"No, we are doing this now."

I roll my eyes in frustration and take another swig of the wine.

"And you're going to be sober for it." He reaches for the bottle, and like a petulant child, I hold it out to my side. He groans in frustration. "Fine, have it your way, but we are talking. Why the fuck are you still with that prick?" he barks.

"Why are you with crackhead Cassidy?" I bite back.

"I'm not," he says sternly.

"Well, you might want to tell her that because you both looked very cozy today in your office."

He folds his arm across his broad chest and grins.

"Jealous, are we? Careful baby girl this fiery side of you is doing things to me."

"No, I'm not. You're a free man, do what you want. As a matter of fact, please, leave, go find her, and fuck her into next week." I take another swig, my anger reaching a boiling point. Why am I so mad, I have no right to be. These are the consequences of my actions and my decisions. I'm blaming him, but the only person I should be angry at is myself.

He takes a step closer, and I take a step back.

"Is that what you want, Gabriella? For me to go to her and fuck her."

I swallow down the bile that works its way up my throat. The idea of him being with Cassidy is making me feel physically sick.

"I don't really care." Lies, complete lies.

He takes another step closer and as I take one back, my back hits the wall and I gasp. He lets out an amused scoff as he leans a forearm above my head, boxing me in, and suddenly it feels hard to take a breath. He trails an index finger from my throat, down my chest, along my exposed skin, leaving a burning heat as he moves down my body.

"So, you'd be okay with me bending her over, burying my cock into her tight cunt, and fucking her?"

"I..." I try to speak. My chest is rising and falling so rapidly I've forgotten how to breathe. A deep burning jealousy now taking over. "Sure," I say as steadily as I can. "Then I'll give Patrick a ca..."

I don't finish my sentence. His hand wraps around my throat and I drop the bottle of rosé, letting it shatter onto my hardwood flooring. "Like fuck you will," he growls before his lips come crashing down on mine.

I fold and let him devour me. I don't want to play this game anymore. I want him, and only him.

His grip on my throat tightens a little, just enough to earn a deep moan from me. He releases me and lifts me by the waist, his shoes crunching against the broken glass as he carries me to the bed and tosses me onto it. I'm up on my knees, crawling to the edge and as he begins unbuttoning his shirt, I get to work on his buckle, needing to taste him.

But he stops me, gripping my chin with his thumb and forefinger, pulling my gaze to focus on his. Heat blazes in his eyes and it sends a thrill through my body. He brushes the pad of his thumb over my mouth, no doubt smudging what's left of my red lipstick.

He pushes his thumb into my mouth, and I instantly suck. He groans in pleasure and then pulls his thumb out of my mouth. I waste no time pulling his pants and briefs down his thick thighs and take him into my mouth.

I've never felt like this; the need for him so intense it makes me feel dizzy.

I swirl my tongue over his wet tip, flicking my tongue over his piercing, and then take him all the way in until his cock hits the back of my throat.

"Fuck, baby, yes, suck my cock." He gathers my hair into his hand as my head bobs up and down his hard length.

The need for some friction becomes too much and I reach a hand between my legs and begin rubbing circles over my clit as I continue to suck his cock. He pulls back, his chest heaving, breathing ragged as he looks down at me on my knees for him, a wild look in his whiskey eyes.

And to my shock, he pulls up his pants.

"What are you doing?" I pant.

"I'm not doing this with you, I... I can't." He runs a frustrated hand through his hair.

"Can't do what?" I feel my heart fracturing, sending an unbearable pain through my chest.

"Cassidy, because of her.? I'm sorry, I..." I stutter.

"What?" he hisses. "No, it's got nothing to do with her, she means nothing to me, Gabriella. I can't do this because I can't do this," he gestures between us, "and then watch as you go running back to him. It's fucking tearing me up inside. The thought of you being with him, him touching you, him..." His voice shakes on the last word as his face contorts in pain and a lead weight of guilt lands in my stomach.

"What?" My words are barely a whisper as I step closer and press my hands against his chest. His nostrils flare as he squeezes his eyes shut.

"Treat you like you're nothing. There's something going on and you won't tell me and I need to know."

"Why?" I fist the lapels of his shirt. A lone tear rolls down my cheek as I silently beg for him to the say the words I'm desperate to hear.

"Because I want to fix it for you."

I shake my head. "Why?" I choke on a sob.

He rests his chin on my head as I let my silent tears fall. Is this it? Is the moment I tell him how badly I've messed up and the web of lies I've got myself caught up in. "Why?" I repeat. Waiting for his answer, but it doesn't come.

I take a step back and look into his eyes, which looked hollow and pained. I hate myself for causing this, but I can't keep a lid on my emotions; it all comes bubbling to the surface. "You can't fix this for me," I yell, making him flinch.

"Yes, I can," he says reassuringly.

I shake my head rapidly.

"No, no you can't. This is all my fault, my doing. It's me who has to fix it, not you, and I'm sorry if that hurts but you just have to trust me that I know what I'm doing and—" I'm rambling, the words falling out of my mouth like it's confession time.

"Gabriella, please, let me—"

"No, you don't get it, this is my fault, I messed up, again, and now this is my punishment, I don't deserve your kindness. I don't even deserve you, but I do deserve your hatred, so just leave, please, I'll fix this, but you need to go if you can't stand to be around me."

"Tell me what's going on."

"I can't."

"Why."

"Because... Because I can't."

"Gabriella, please, there isn't a thing you could say that would change how I feel about you."

I close my eyes, squeeze them shut and pray that when I open them he will disappear and this conversation no longer exists. I want to believe them, but if I say it all out loud, the gravity of what I've done will become too much and he will never look at me in the same way.

"Why?" It's a stupid question but it's all I can manage.

"Because I'm fucking in love with you, Gabriella," he bellows and a silence so deafening you could hear a pin dropping falls between us.

I feel like I've had the wind knocked out of me. I reach for the bed frame and sit on the edge of the mattress. "You love me?" I repeat in utter shock.

He falls to his knees in front of me and cups my face. "Yes, I'm in love with you. I've loved you for years, but knew I couldn't give you everything you wanted, everything you deserve. But if you want to get married? I'll marry you tonight, you want kids? I'll give you three. You want the suburban life in the country, let's move." He takes my hand and places it over where his heart beats. "Because this, this right here, you made it beat again. You made me see color again, made me breathe again. I'll give you the world, Gabriella, if you just let me. So, please, don't be with him. Be with me."

My forehead falls to his as I take a second to register his words. He loves me, wants to give me the world, and I want to let him. I'm done with this, I don't care about the repercussions. I'm done with it all.

"Say something, please." His voice is pained.

I take a deep breath and a leap of faith that whatever happens after this, he'll have my back.

"I love you too." I throw my arms around him and press my lips to his. He rises, never letting me go, and places me on the bed, covering my body with his. He tugs at the zipper on my dress and slides it down my body, peppering kisses over my bare breasts and down my body, every one striking my body like a match, setting me on fire.

The need for him to take me, to claim me, to truly make me his is so strong. I slide my panties off as he tears at his shirt and briefly gets off the bed to remove the rest of his clothes and then his body his back, hovering over mine. I hook a leg around his waist, as he sucks on my neck in that sensitive spot.

He slides deep inside of me and with every thrust he becomes harder and thicker. He angles my hips allowing him to take me deeper, so deep that we now feel a part of one another. It's a heady mix of something I can't decipher. It's passionate yet rough, and at the same time, I have never felt more connected to him or felt this level of passion.

Our eyes meet, and it all feels too much. I want to cry, scream out in pleasure, declare my love for him over and over again.

"You are so fucking beautiful, Gabriella." He rolls his hips, hitting that spot that has my back arching off the mattress. "... and so fucking mine."

"Yes," I breathe out as the wave of pleasure works its way through my body. "I'm yours," I pant and then I detonate. He swallows my cries as he finds his own release, a deep growl erupting from his chest as he spills inside of me which prolongs my pleasure.

I tighten my grip around his waist with my leg, not wanting him to slide out of me just yet. Not wanting this moment where only he and I exist to end, where I have to face the reality of my choices and finally come clean. No, I want to cling to this moment, where everything feels perfect, where only our love and us matter; the last moment of calm before everything could come crashing down around us.

Chapter Fifty-One

Brad

I stare down at Gabriella, who's cradled in my arms, and I watch her as she sleeps. I could stay like this forever. I meant every word I said to her. Whatever she wants, it's hers. I know there is a lot to figure out, to talk about, but the only thing that matters, the only thing that is important, is that we feel the same way about each other.

She stirs in my arms, rubs her eyes and looks up at me, a sleepy smile sweeping over her face as warmth fills my chest. I want to spend every morning waking up with this woman and have her look at me like that.

"Good morning, Gabriella."

"Good morning." she repeats with a yawn. "So, what's the plan for today?"

"Dumping your jackass of a boyfriend should be number one on the list," I say dryly.

She bursts into a fit of laughter and I stare at her deadpan. She sits up, wrapping the bedsheet around her body and faces me, leaning in to press a kiss to my mouth and I instantly soften.

"I will, but I fear he won't go without a fight." Her voice has a hint of worry to it. I take her hand, interlocking our fingers.

"I won't let him hurt you." She nods.

"It's just..." She stops mid-sentence.

"Gabriella, no more secrets, okay? I've got you. Tell me."

She inhales deeply and lets out a slow breath. "Okay, but hear me out fully, okay? Before you go and kill him."

"I'm not making any promises," I confirm, folding my arms across my chest.

"Brad."

"Fine, I won't kill him... yet."

She rolls her eyes.

"So Patrick found out that I was working at the club. When I tried to break things off with him when we got back from LA, he showed me a bunch of videos and photos of me dancing and you and me in the alley the night you found out."

Nausea hits me. I'm terrified of what she's going to say next. "He said if I didn't stay with him, then he would send the files to my dad and I..." Her voice cracks and on instinct, I and pull her into my chest. "I'm going to fucking kill him."

"No, please..." she wails into my neck.

"Ssssh. It's okay." I hold her as she lets it all go. A deep throb in my chest begins to burn, knowing she's been keeping this secret all these months; handling it all without anyone knowing.

"He wanted my dad to put in a good word for him at this law firm and said that if I played the part of his girlfriend, it would look good for him. My name has meaning and all this crap. I tried to break it off, but he kept threatening to send the files to my dad and after what I did when I was a teen I couldn't do that again. I couldn't have them look at me like—"

I cut her off, moving her to face me.

"That wasn't your fault. Some asshole took advantage of you. That isn't on you. Your parents should have protected you, not made you feel like it was your fault, and this isn't your fault either. You are a grown woman. You can do what you want with your life. You should have told me."

She sniff. "I wanted to, but when I came to your apartment, you told me that I should be with Patrick, and we should end things."

Guilt hits me and I feel like the biggest piece of shit. I pushed her into Patrick's arms without realizing it. "Baby, I'm so sorry, I had my reasons for doing that. I was trying to keep you safe."

"From what?" she asks, searching my face for the answer.

"From me," I say quietly.

"You are the person I feel the safest with. How could I be anything but safe when I'm with you? I trust you with my life."

And that declaration right there means just as much to me as those three words she uttered last night. She trusts me with her, with her life, and I'm going to make sure I am worthy of words.

"I'd never let anything happen to you," I confirm, lifting her into my lap.

"I know you wouldn't." She reassures, lifting our hands where they are still linked and she kisses the back of my hand.

"I love you." I say, the words falling so easily, and it feels like the most natural thing to say. I've never told anyone I love them. I wasn't sure what it meant, or how it should feel. But with her, I know I do. I feel lighter when I'm with her, it feels easier to breathe. Everything feels easier and when I'm not with her, there feels like a piece of me that's missing and she's the only one who could fill it.

Her amber eyes light up and I could spend my day getting lost in them.

"I love you too."

"Leave Patrick to me, okay?"

She nods and I breathe a sigh of relief as I silently plot how I am going to ruin Patrick's life.

Chapter Fifty Two

Gabriella

We've had a slow morning, which included sex in the bed, some fooling around in the shower, and I now need to fully sanitize the kitchen counter after Brad had me for breakfast. I feel lighter this morning. I hadn't realized how the weight of my lies and secrets were impacting me. Opening up to Brad felt so freeing. I know things could still get worse, but it's a risk I'm willing to take. He makes me happy; he makes me feel everything I've been searching for and now I've finally found it. I'm not letting him go.

I take a sip of my coffee and highlight another transaction off the accounts sheet that is laid across my lap. I've been working through their accounts for the past couple of weeks, and I've had a hunch where the missing money has been going, or rather who the culprit is, but this final file confirms it.

I toss the file into Brad's lap. "I've solved it. I know who's taking your money at the club." I smile proudly.

"Who?"

"It's Amy," I say confidently.

"Amy?" His brows furrow and he picks up the file, scanning the pages. "Our barmaid Amy."

"Uh huh."

"She worked her last shift last week." I say, furrowing my brows at her.

"I checked her log in, and the money always seems to go missing the days she works."

"On the last page, did you know Kate's log in was used to access your payroll system several times over the last year and Amy's pay was adjusted?"

"Kate would never," Brad says sternly.

"No, I know she wouldn't, but I bet Amy would. The dates match when both Amy and Kate were on shift."

Brad shakes his head in disbelief, and I take another sip of my coffee.

"So between her moving money to pay herself a bigger salary, your output vs input it's about 10k difference, my hunch is she's not putting through the orders and pocketing the cash when working the bar."

"Fuck," Brad growls.

"But why?" he huffs in frustration.

"I don't know, but something's off. She's been doing this long enough that it wouldn't get noticed until now. She's kind of a smart girl," I say, somewhat impressed.

"So, looks like I'm adding Amy to my shit list for today."

I chuckle. "I'd report her to the police. What she's done is a crime."

He tosses the files onto the coffee table.

And leans his head back against the edge of the couch.

"Shit, what a mess."

"Yep," I say, popping the p.

He smooths a hand up my bare thigh and under my oversized t-shirt. "Thank you for doing this. You're a very smart woman."

I bring my hand to my chin as if I were framing my face. "Why, thank you. One of my many talents."

His hooded eyes darken and he runs his tongue along his bottom lip. I know that look, and it sends a rush of heat to my core.

"Oh, yeah," he says, plucking my mug out of my hand and placing it on the coffee table. "Why don't you show me some of your other talents?"

He steals my breath when he reaches over and lifts me into his lap, my bare ass now straddling his thick thighs, his erection wedged between my cheeks and I rotate my hips, earning a deep groan from him.

His hands smooth over my bare skin and squeeze my cheeks.

"Naughty girl, no undies." He spanks my ass, and I gasp, sending a surge of desire through me.

I trail my index finger slowly down his six pack, tracing the outlines of his artwork. "I love these." I bite down on my lower lip as my fingers brush over his Adonis belt.

"Do you?"

"Yeah, I call them fuck me lines," I joke.

He lets out a laugh, weaves his fingers into my hair, and pulls me down my mouth is just inches from his, his grip almost painful but I welcome the sting.

"Well, what are you waiting for, baby girl? Ride me." He releases me and I rise just enough for him to pull down his briefs. My hand grips the back of his neck to anchor myself as I sink down on him, and we both let out a moan as he fills me to the hilt.

We've never done it like this. He's so big it takes me a minute to adjust and for the burn to ease, but when it does, holy shit.

I rotate my hips slowly and already I feel the pressure building. He grips my hips and growls, "Bounce on my cock, Gabriella."

I move, up and down, and dear God, it's like nothing I've felt before. My head rolls back in pleasure as one of his hands pushes my t-shirt up, exposing my breasts. He clamps his mouth around one and sucks, forcing me to let out a cry of pleasure. When he bites my nipple, I nearly catapult off him.

"Fuck, yes," I hiss, picking up my pace. There's no finesse, no easing into it. It's rough and fast, but there's always passion. No matter how he takes me, there's something palpable between us and it's how I know he's it for me. All I've ever wanted.

My walls tighten around him. He releases my nipple from his mouth and his thumb finds my clit. With just a few perfectly timed flicks, I go off, and he's right there with me. My chest heaves, his arms wrap around my body, and he holds me tightly as my body convulses, fracturing me and then putting me back together in a way that only he can. Our moans echo around my apartment and just as I begin to float down to reality, my world moves in slow motion when my apartment door opens. My eyes widen and I freeze when my gaze meets two sets of eyes.

"Ali?"

"Gabby!" Her tone is just as shocked as mine.

"You're meant to be at Harry's," I stammer.

"And you're meant to be with Patrick."

Chapter Fifty Three

Brad

"*And you're meant to be with Patrick.*"

Those words have the blood draining from my body.

"Well, well, well, what's going on here then?" Harry's gleeful voice booms behind me.

"Oh, my god," Gabriella shrieks and reaches for the blanket on the back of the couch and covers herself.

"What are you doing?" Ali's shocked voice rings.

I turn my head and the grin that's already smeared across Harry's face makes me want to crumble in shame. Not for me, but for Gabriella.

"Hey," I say casually, as if I don't still have my dick inside of her.

Just when I didn't think it could get any worse, Ria and Jack appear, one holding a box *Dunkin' Donuts* and the other holding a tray of coffees.

"Oh, my.." Ria shrieks. "Are you two…"

"Yep, yeah they are," Harry confirms, and his grin is now so wide it makes me want to punch him for enjoying our torment so much.

"Oh God, I feel like I've just walked in on my baby sister and my best friend going at it," Jack says, the color draining from his face.

"Well, now you know how Noah felt when he walked in on you bending Ria over the kitchen island that one time," Harry snorts, enjoying every second of this carry on.

"That was Noah's damn fault. He should have knocked," Jack barks.

"What was my fault?" Noah's voice rings out and it's then I wish the ground would swallow us both up and end our misery.

Gabriella whimpers, curling into me and letting her head fall on my chest.

"Hey." Noah chuckles looking at me and Gabriella.

All I can do is put a thumbs up.

"Yeah, sure, add more people to this. When the fuck did you get here?" I say rubbing my temple, feeling a headache coming on.

"I flew in this morning. I tried to get back for Ali's show but my flight got delayed. So, what's going on here then?" Noah's grin now matches Harry's, and I officially hate him too.

"Brad and Gabby are fucking," Harry explains.

"Cool," Noah says casually.

"No, no that's not what we were doing." Gabriella's head springs up and I don't know how she thinks we are getting out of this one, but I'm willing to go with it.

"We just walked in on you riding him like he was your own personal show pony," Ali deadpans and Gabriella's cheeks heat.

"And is he still inside of you?" Ali questions.

Gabriella lifts slightly and slides off me which doesn't help my situation at all. I yank up my briefs and adjust myself as best I can and then stand up.

"No, I was just helping Gabriella look for the missing money." I point to the files on the coffee table.

Ali folds her arms across her chest, giving me a challenging stare. "Really? Well, you aren't going to find the missing money in her pussy are you, Bradley?"

Gabriella whimpers and covers her face with her hands and sinks down into the couch.

Everyone lets out a little laugh and Harry holds his hand up to high five Ali. "Good one, babe." She claps her hand with his.

"I preferred it when you two hated each other," I say, narrowing my eyes at them both.

"Well… who wants donuts?" Ria says, trying to change the subject.

"Me," Jack says, following her to the kitchen island where they begin whispering to one another.

I turn my focus back to Ali, Harry, and Noah who are all smirking.

"I knew you'd be pierced." Ali teases. I look down and there, pressed against my white Calvin Kleins, in all its glory, is my erect, pierced dick.

Harry covers Ali's eyes with his hand and I reach for a cushion to cover myself.

"Why are you all here anyway? I didn't get the memo that we were due a fucking family reunion," I grit out.

"We all wanted to check Gabriella was okay, but I can see she's more than okay." Ali giggles.

Gabriella pops up like a meerkat, wrapping the blanket around her. "I'm just off to, um, wash the shame away." She rushes past everyone, and when I hear her door slam, I flinch and close my eyes. When I open them, five pairs of eyes are on me, and I think about running and locking myself away too.

Jack clears his throat and my focus moves to him. "Well, start talking. What the heck is going on with you two?"

Oh shit, well, there's no getting out of this...

"...and so that brings us to you guys walking in ..." I finish the entire tale but Harry interrupts before I can finish my sentence. Ria and Ali went to check on Gabriella before I started relaying the entire soap opera that is my love life. Noah leans against the kitchen island next to me and Jack and Harry sit across.

"And you had your dick buried in Gabby, just so we are clear on that."

I give him a death stare. He's too far away for me to do anything, so Jack kindly taps the back of his head.

"Ouch," he yelps.

Noah laughs and shakes his head. "I miss you fuckers. Never a dull moment."

"Yes, you caught us. But it's more than that, I..." My words get lodged in my throat. This is the most vulnerable I've ever been with them. I don't do feelings. I'm a listener, not a talker.

"You love her." Jack says it like a statement, not a question.

I run a hand down my face in exasperation.

"Yeah, yeah, I'm in love with her." I await a teasing comment from Harry, but it doesn't come. Instead, they all give me a prideful look, and my throat feels thick with emotion.

I'm in love with Gabriella Monroe and I don't care who knows it.

"So that relapse you had, that was to do with this?" Jack asks. I nod, still ashamed I let myself fall so far off the wagon.

"You could have told us," Harry says, his features softening and even though we all banter, I know these guys would quite literally go to war for me.

"You all had shit going on. I thought I had a handle on it, but it turns out love really does do a number on you."

"Sure does," Harry and Jack say in unison. I glance over at Noah, who stares at a blank spot on the counter, deep in thought. When he catches me looking at him, he looks like a child that's been caught eating candy when he shouldn't.

"So, what are we going to do about this prick, Patrick?" Noah asks.

"He's first on my hit list," Grinding my teeth in anger at the mention of his name and everything he's done to her.

"Well, we've got your back, whatever you need," Jack says and Harry and Noah nod.

Chapter Fifty Four

Gabriella

Shame, embarrassment, regret, all feelings I am very well acquainted with, but nothing could compare to how I feel knowing our friends walked in on us and now think I am some cheating skank.

I've been sitting in the bathtub, hearing whispers from the kitchen, as I'm sure Brad relays all the sordid details of our affair.

Well, Gabriella, this may be your best fuck up yet. Take a bow girl.

I sink under the water and hold my breath. Enjoying the silence and the feeling of being weightless for just a second. I rise to the surface, smoothing my hands over my face and hair and scream in fright when two figures stand beside the bathtub.

I move into a seating position, water splashing over the sides onto the tiled floor.

"What the hell?" I yell.

Ali and Ria look at me, confused.

"What are you doing?" Ria asks.

"Washing away my sins." I sigh, laying back in the tub.

"In your t-shirt," Ali says, pointing at me.

"Yes, it's tainted now. So let me drown in peace, please," I mumble.

Ria snorts. "Come on, stop being so dramatic. It can't be that bad."

"No, it's worse than you think," I confirm.

"Well, the dildo of consequences never arrives lubricated Gabriella," Ali says, folding her arms.

Both Ria and I turn to look at her as if she has two heads.

'Huh?" Ria says. "Do you hear yourself before you say the words, or do you just say it?"

"I just say it," Ali says, shrugging her shoulders.

Ria pats her on the back. "Thought so, but it's why we love you."

Ali beams with pride.

"I don't get it," I say.

"I mean, the consequence of our actions are never going to be easy to accept. But whatever it is, it's going to be okay. We can help."

I huff in frustration. "I don't know. My sins are pretty bad."

"Well, move over. If you have sins to cleanse, I sure as hell have more," Ali says, kicking off her shoes and standing in the tub and lowering herself, fully clothed in her sweatpants and sweatshirt she was wearing.

I burst into laughter as the water splashes over the side.

"Make room for my pregnant ass," Ria says, taking off her jumper, so she's left in a stretchy back dress that showcases her perfect bump.

I move to the middle of the tub and sling my legs over the side so they hang over the edge, knowing Ria will need the width of the tub. The water rises when she gets in and more water splashes over the side and we fall into a fit of giggles. The three of us look ridiculous, sat fully dressed in the bathtub.

A moment of silence falls between us all. I know they are waiting for me to spill, but where to begin.

As if they can read my thoughts, each of them takes a hand and squeezes it.

Ali is the first to speak. "Why don't you start at the beginning, little G."

"Yes, and don't leave anything out..." Ria says, wrapping an arm around my shoulder.

I take in a deep breath and exhale.

"Girls, I really messed up...'

I'm not sure how long we've been sat in the bathtub, but Ria has topped up the hot water twice to keep us warm. I told them everything. Every sordid detail, every secret I have been keeping for months.

"So yeah, that's everything." I say, flicking the water, waiting for one of them to speak.

"That's... a lot," Ali says. I nod.

"And you quit working at Diamonds?" Ria asks.

"Yeah, I wasn't stripping. Can I stress that again."

"Babe, we couldn't care if you did. We'd be there with a wad of dollar bills cheering you on," Ali says, and Ria nods in agreement.

I sniff. I really do have the best friends. They don't judge, they just listen. Every girl needs friends like that.

"Gabs, you could have come to us," Ria says softly.

"I know but you had just got married and found out about the baby. I didn't want to ruin any of that, and Ali," I say, turning to face her.

"You had the court case and everything you were going through. I just figured I could handle it all. I didn't want to burden anyone with it." I hang my head in shame, my nose burning with the threat of tears.

"You are not a burden," Ali says.

"No, never," Ria echoes.

"Can we make a promise: to never, ever think we are a burden to each other again? I don't care if I'm in labor, if you need me, you call me, got it, both of you," Ria says firmly.

"Agreed, anytime, it doesn't matter," Ali says.

"Agreed." I sniff.

"I told Brad everything," I say quietly, flicking the water with my index finger and thumb.

"Everything?" Ria asks, surprise in her tone. "The stuff with your parents, what happened to you?"

I nod.

"What did he say?" she continues.

"He was, understanding, compassionate. Told me it wasn't my fault."

"Because it wasn't," Ria confirms.

"No, it wasn't," Ali echoes.

"I think I see that now." I exhale.

"So," Ali says, bumping her shoulder with mine.

"Do you love him?"

I can't help the grin that sweeps across my face and the heat in my cheeks.

"Yeah, yeah I do." And I have never been surer of anything in my life.

Both Ria and Ali let out girly squeals and we all burst into laughter.

"I'm so happy for you Gabs." Ria says, tucking my now drying hair behind my hair in that affectionate way a mother does. Ria has such a nurturing way about her and I am so lucky to have her in my life.

"Me too, little G," Ali says, wrapping her arms around me. "But I had a feeling."

"A feeling about what?" I ask, narrowing my eyes at her.

"That you and Brad would get together, I think he's always secretly loved you. It was just a matter of time till you both found your way to each other."

I don't say anything, I just digest her words and realize that maybe she's right. Maybe Brad and I were always going to be. It just took us a while to realize it.

"I think we should get out of this tub my fingers look like prunes," Ali says, holding up her hands, now white and wrinkly.

"Same, I must resemble a killer whale in this tub," Ria jokes, rubbing her hand over her belly.

I snort a laugh and then we all fall into a fit of laughter. Tears of contentment roll down my cheeks.

"I love you both."

"We love you," they say in unison just as a knock at the door echoes and the door creaks open.

There stand the guys, who assemble into the small bathroom one after the other.

"What are you doing?" Harry asks in confusion.

"What girls do best. Crying it out in the bathtub and putting the world to rights," Ali answers.

Jack shakes his head and laughs.

"Girls are weird," Harry mumbles.

"Come on, help your pregnant wife out the tub." Ria waves her arms in the air and we all chuckle as Jack lifts Ria and water splashes everywhere.

My eye catches Brad, who's leaning against the doorframe, now wearing a pair of sweatpants. He gives a wink and first the first time in a long time, I finally feel like everything might be okay and work out after all. I just need to deal with Patrick.

Chapter Fifty Five

Gabriella

"You better put me down." I giggle as Brad nuzzles into my neck, breathless from where he just fucked me in the shower—my new favorite way to start the day.

"No," he teases, grazing his teeth along my sensitive skin, stirring something up inside of me that will be hard to suppress if he keeps it up.

"I have classes to teach." He lifts his head and runs his tongue along his bottom lip.

"Cancel them."

I shake my head and laugh. "I can't, plus I need to swing by my apartment. I'm running out of underwear."

"I'm good with you not wearing any."

"I bet." My smile is so wide I can feel it reaching my eyes. I love this playful side of him, and I'd love nothing more than to stay in this bubble, just me and him.

He presses a tender kiss to my lips, then brushes his nose with mine.

"I don't want to go but, I really need to." I huff, not wanting to end our morning.

He lets out a disgruntled groan. "Fine, just make sure you bring enough stuff for the next month back from your apartment."

I lift my head, my body stiffening. "A month?" I question.

He shrugs. "Yeah, bring it all if you want."

My mouth feels dry as I swallow, trying to understand what he's saying.

"Are... are you asking me to move in?" I ask hesitantly, scared I'm wrong and I've now made it weird.

He grins in that way that has me willing to give this man just about anything he wanted

"I don't know. Do you want to move in?" There's a hint of a teasing tone and it creates little flutters in the pit of my stomach.

"I, um, well, I mean, yeah, sure, but you know it's quite soon and you might regret it, and then what if you get sick of me because I can be messy and you are like super clean and—" He cuts off my rambling with a rough kiss that has me whimpering.

My fingers push into his hair as he thrusts his tongue into my mouth, and I welcome it. It's as if he's kissing away my fears.

He breaks the kiss, leaning his forehead against mine.

"We can live here, live at your apartment, live between the two or buy somewhere new. I just want to be with you, Gabriella, in any way you want to be. If it's too soon I get it, but, I want this. I want you. I know we have a lot of shit to figure out, but we can do it together."

My limbs feel light, my body weightless as his words sink in. He wants me, he wants this, every day.

"Okay. Yes, let's do it. Let's figure it out together." I beam, dusting my lips over his and kiss him fiercely holding on to him so tightly, like it's the last time I ever will.

Chapter Fifty Six

Brad

It's been nearly a week since everyone found out about me and Gabriella. She spent the weekend at my place, and it was the first time in months I slept well and felt content. We worked out together, ate together, watched her show that she loves to watch, and if this is what love feels like, sign me up forever. I don't want to go another day without her. But first, there are some loose ends we need to tie up before we can truly move on from all the crap we have been through.

We are in a New York diner across the street from a restaurant that Patrick and some blonde entered an hour ago. I told Gabriella I would deal with him and I meant him. I want to kill him with my bare hands. Tear him apart limb from limb, but I know that won't help Gabriella; or me.

I sip on my bitter black coffee, wincing when the taste hits my tongue. "God, this coffee takes like shit."

"I like it," Harry says, shoveling a forkful of pancakes into his mouth.

"It's two in the afternoon, why are you eating pancakes?" Jack asks. Harry was the only one who ordered food.

"This place does the best all day pancake breakfast. Want some?" He holds out a fork of fluffy pancakes with syrup that drips onto the table.

I chuckle to myself, looking at Jack's wrinkled nose.

"No, and chew your food before speaking," Jack scolds.

"Sorry, Daddy."

"I really have missed you fuckers," Noah says, looking round the table. We've missed him. It's always felt like there are missing pieces since we lost Scotty and Noah decided to stay in the military.

"Any chance you are going to stay this time?" Jack asks his now brother-in-law, which is weird as hell to think.

"I'm considering it," Noah says, spinning his now empty mug in his hands.

"Well, we want you to stay, and you know Ria and the girls do. It means a lot that you are coming to the lake with us this weekend," Jack says.

"When are you leaving?" Harry asks, finishing his pancakes and dabbing his mouth with a napkin.

"Once we deal with that asshole," Jack says, pointing out across the bustling street, where Patrick stands, kissing a blonde.

"Fucker," I hiss, standing up.

"Give it a second." Noah says, gesturing me to sit down.

We watch on as Patrick waves down a yellow cab, puts the blonde in the back and waits until it drives away.

I ball my hands into fists looking at him, internally thinking of all the ways I could make him hurt for hurting Gabriella.

He turns to head down the street.

"Let's go," I say. Harry throws down some twenty-dollar bills to pay and we all leave. We cross the street and stay about five steps behind Patrick. I speed up when I see he's close to where I know there's an alley. I clamp a hand on his shoulder, my grip firm, and his body stiffens, but he doesn't stop walking.

"I think you and I need a little chat," I hiss into his ear.

He tries to shrug me off, but I don't release my grip.

"Fuck off, or I'll call the police," he mutters back.

"You're not going to want to do that," Noah says calmly, taking his other arm and directing us down an alley.

Harry and Jack aren't far behind us. Noah throws Patrick up against the wall and I'm on him.

My hand wraps around his throat, his meaty little hands cover mine as he fights to release my hand.

"What the fuck is your problem?" he tries to yell, but I silence him by tightening my grip. His face turns bright red, his eyes bulging. I clench my jaw so tightly I almost crack a tooth. I could do it right now, right here. End his pathetic life for what he's done to Gabriella, for what he's put her through.

He tries to fight against me, but I'm too strong for him.

"Brad, ease up a little," Jack says calmly, forever the sensible one in the group.

I release Patrick and he slumps to the ground, clutching his neck, taking in sharp, greedy gasps of air.

I snarl, feeling nothing for this man other than pure hatred.

"What is this about?" He wheezes, trying to get up on his knees.

"Gabriella," I say sternly.

"That slut. What's she done now?"

I see red. I don't wait, I just react. I kick him, ramming the cap of my boot into his rib cage so forcefully I'm sure I've broken his rib.

"What the fuck did you just call her?" I yell.

"I..." Patrick tries to speak, but I kick him again. He curls into the fetal position, and I go to strike him again, but Harry pulls me back.

"Okay, we aren't here to kill him," Harry says. My nostrils flare, my chest heaving. All I see is a red mist and if they weren't here to pull me back, I think I would kill him.

I crouch down over him. "Does it make you feel like a man? Hurting women, trying to control them?"

He whimpers and spits out a mouthful of blood. "I, I will have you locked up for this."

I lean in closer. "See, I don't think you will, Pat, because if you do, I'll make sure everyone knows what you did. How you manipulated her, hurt her, for your own personal gain, I don't think Judge Monroe would be happy to hear what you have been up to."

"He wouldn't be happy to know his daughter is a slut, a stripper." His words are like another red flag to a bull. I ball my fist and punch him in the face. Pain radiates up my hand as I shake it out.

"Ughhh, you..." Patrick whimpers, blood now streaming from his nose."

"You won't say shit, you hear me?" I spit.

"I have evidence," Patrick argues as he wipes his nose with the back of his hand while he pushes himself up to a sitting position.

"Oh, you mean on this?" I turn to see Noah holding Patrick's phone. He tosses it to the ground, smashing his boot on the screen until there are nothing but fragments of the device scattered across the ground.

"That's my phone," Patrick roars.

I stand up and lift Patrick by the collar, slamming him against the brick wall. He whimpers.

"Now, this will be the only warning you get. Got it? If I have to find you again, I'll kill you with my bare hands and then dispose of your body so that no one will find you.

Patrick gulps, his body begins trembling and the twisted and dark side of me reels in the sight. Knowing he's as scared as Gabriella has likely been all this time.

"You will never, ever speak to Gabriella again. You won't look at her, you won't contact her, you won't touch her, and you won't breathe a word of this to anyone, or I will kill you."

I move closer, so close I feel his quivering breath against my face.

"Got it?" I say through gritted teeth.

He nods.

I release him, and he falls to the ground. I give one final kick and he lets out a yelp. I walk off and all I can hear is one kick after the other as Patrick makes a bone chilling cry. I don't know who's doing it. I don't care. All I care is that they had my back, they have Gabriella's back and Patrick won't ever hurt her again.

The final thing on my to do list: find Amy and get some answers.

Chapter Fifty Seven

Gabriella

"Great job, ladies. I know that was a tough one, but you'll be thanking me in the summer." The class erupts into laughter. I roll up the last of the mats and stack them in the rack at the back of the room before I shut off the lights and sling my gym bag over my shoulder.

I walk past the reception desk and give Mike a wave.

"Night, Mike," I say cheerfully.

"Do you want me to walk you to your car?" he asks.

"No, I'm good."

I push through the glass doors, out into the parking lot. The New York evening air has a slight chill now we are in fall and the breeze whips through my ponytail. I'm thankful I am wearing yoga pants, but regret my choice of a yoga bra instead of a long sleeve.

I cross my arms, rubbing my palms up and down my arms to warm myself up. I walk across the empty parking lot, dimly lit only by the sign of the studio that is on the building. I reach inside my bag for my key and when I look up I notice a car with a figure in the front seat.

The hairs on the back of my neck stand on end and my heart rate picks up. That sense women have when something isn't quite right. Yeah, that's what I am having right now. I quicken my steps to my car, tapping the key fob with a shaky hand, and jump inside, relief flooding my body when my car starts instantly. I pull out the parking lot onto the main street.

I check my rearview mirror and the car comes into view.

Shit!

I need to stay calm and try to lose him. I turn right, knowing I need to carry on and the car follows. I turn the next left, knowing to will take me back to where I just came from, and the car does the same.

He's following you Gabby. You need to call someone.

I take another turn and sure enough, the other car does the same. We stop at a red light and I squint to focus on the driver. He has a black hood pulled up and I can just about make out a tattoo on his hand that holds the top of the steering wheel. The light changes green and I floor it, breaking the speed limit, but he is right on my tail. I clutch the steering wheel with white knuckle force.

I take a sharp left and a car beeps its horn as I cut across them, but my only goal is to lose this driver. We approach another set of lights, and I press my foot to the floor, making it across just as it turns red, leaving my follower stuck.

I sag in relief, knowing I am close to my apartment. I park up outside, taking my phone out of my bag and clutch the bag in my hand. I look around cautiously, but there's nothing. No sign of the car.

Thank God.

I dial Brad's number, but it rings and rings as I approach the door to my apartment building. I punch in my code and the door opens. I step inside and something feels off. I live on the third floor, and I begin to take the steps one at a time. I reach the top of the staircase on the first floor and I see something move out the corner of my eye. I lean over the stairwell and a dark figure moves up the stairs.

I clutch the phone and my keys, my limbs trembling, and take the stairs two at a time.

Just one flight to go, Gabby. It could be nothing.

I sprint up the stairs, the adrenaline pumping through my body. I just need to get inside. I pump my arms as I run as if my life depends on it towards my door, my trembling hand trying to get the key in the door. I look down the corridor to see the dark figure running towards me.

I manage to twist the key in the lock, and I fall through the door panting in fear, my keys and phone slide across the hardwood floor, as my body heaves with fear. I scramble to my feet and shove the door closed, but it meets resistance, and I let out a scream as I am pushed backward and land on the ground. I try to stand but the figure stands over me. He steps over me as I scramble backward, trying to reach for my phone.

"Help," I screech at the top of my lungs.

He takes two slow steps towards me. I think about running to my bedroom, running to Ali's bedroom, and locking the door, but wherever I run, I'm trapped.

"Hello, Gabriella," his deep voice rasps and it sounds familiar.

"Who... who are you?"

He removes his hood and his eyes meet mine. He looks like Brad, sounds like Brad, but it isn't him. I gasp when a familiar scorpion tattoo on his cheek comes in to view. It's the guy from the parking lot at the club and my blood runs cold and my limbs begin to tremble, an unsettling thought settles in my stomach. He must have known where I lived.

He steps closer and I whimper in fear. Bile works its way up my throat as different scenarios flit through my mind with all the possibilities of what he could do to me.

My phone ringing startles us both, and when I see Brad's name flash across the screen, I dive for it landing on my stomach. My fingertips brush across the screen just enough for me to answer the call before a heavy weight comes down on top of me and I let out a blood curdling scream.

"Help. Help."

I wriggle and writhe beneath him, trying to free myself, but he's too strong.

"Feisty little bitch, aren't you? You like it rough, huh?"

He moves, and it allows me to pull my arms free and roll onto my back. I keep my arms tight to my chest and kick my legs.

Fight, Gabby, come on.

I hear a faint roar from my phone and I know it's Brad. My heart cracks and I begin to sob. "Please, please, don't hurt me," I beg, my body trembling with fear.

The man gives me a smirk that has me dry heaving. I know what's coming.

"You'll like it, pretty girl, don't you worry." He reaches for the button on his pants, and it gives me just enough room to kick him in between the legs. He folds over in agony, and I roll away, swiping the phone before running toward the bathroom.

I bring the phone to my ear and scream.

"Gabriella?" Brad's voice calls out. I almost buckle with relief that he's still there.

"There's someone in my apartment. Help me, please," I wail as I try to close the bathroom door, but a strong hand clamps around the door and I drop the phone.

I reach for anything I can find and begin throwing them at him. Everything hits him, but he doesn't flinch.

"You are going to fucking pay for that, bitch," he growls, reaching for me. I throw my hands up to shield myself, my chest burning, my body no longer feeling like it belongs to me. I shove him, but he shoves me harder. I lose my balance and tumble backward into the tub and my entire world goes dark...

Chapter Fifty Eight

Brad

I am putting out fires all over the place today and it feels good to finally tie up all these loose ends so Gabriella and I can get on with our lives. Patrick has been dealt with, I'm visiting her parents with her this weekend to tell them about us and I've called Amy in to the club to have a chat.

I lied and said she needed to fill out some forms to officially terminate her employment. Little does she know, I'm on to her and know what she's been doing. My usual go to in situations like this would be my one glass of whiskey, but I settle for coffee, knowing I need to be level headed for this. Since Gabriella and I admitted our love for each other, my need for control has lessened. I've learned that the world doesn't fall apart if I miss a workout, if I have two whiskeys instead of one I haven't fallen off the sobriety wagon that I never needed to be on. No, she has taught me that the world doesn't end if I don't follow the same steps each day. She healed a part of me I thought would be forever broken, and for that, I owe her everything.

A soft knock sounds at my office door.

"Come in." I call out.

Amy, sweet, quiet, mousey Amy, stands in my office doorway, dressed in light jeans and a white cardigan. Her glasses perched at the end of her nose and her straight brown hair meets her shoulders.

"Hello," she says so quietly I almost miss it.

"Please sit." I gesture to the seat on the opposite side of my desk.

She sits down, her eyes darting round the room nervously.

A thick silence falls between us as I stare blankly at her.

"You... you needed me to file some paperwork?"

"No." I open the drawer on my desk, pulling out the file, which includes every transaction of Amy's deceit. I slam it down on the desk and she flinches. "I want you to tell me why you have been stealing our money."

She looks down at her lap, avoiding my gaze.

"Amy," I say sternly. "You can tell me or the police. Your choice."

'No, please, don't call the police. I will pay you back. I..." Her lip trembles and she cradles her face in her hands and sobs.

I have no patience for this. "Start talking, now."

She sniffs, wiping her nose with the back of her hand. "I used to do some volunteer work at a local shelter, for people who were transitioning from prison to real life again. One of the organizers handed out a flyer, pen pals for prisoners. So, I got talking to a few guys on there, and I got paired with Matteo, and we fell in love over letters."

The hairs on the back of my neck stand on end.

"Matteo?"

"Yes," she says quietly, avoiding my gaze.

"As in Matteo Russo, my brother?"

She nods and I slam my hand on the desk in frustration and she flinches.

"Keep talking Amy," I yell.

"He told me his story, and my heart broke for him."

"Yes, my heart bleeds for my brother, who helped murder an innocent man." My tone is dripping in sarcasm.

"It wasn't like that. If you had…" I slam my hand down on the desk.

"I'd watch what you say Amy, I appreciate you have been told his version of events, but my brother is a dangerous man, I can dial that phone and have you removed from here in cuffs and you can end up where Matteo was." She shrinks under the weight of my stare, and I nod for her to continue.

"He was asking me for money which I've been sending to him for a while and then when he got approved for a parole hearing, he knew we needed money so we could move away, start a new life. When he found out I worked here, he said I should take what was his."

"What was his? Is he fucking serious? I worked for this. I built this business from the ground up. Me and my friends. Matteo had fuck all to do with it," I growl, running a hand through my hair, my chest burning with anger.

"I know it was wrong." She sobs. "I will get the money back. We are leaving tomorrow. I'll get the money back, just please, please, don't call the police."

I brace my hands against the desk just as my phone begins to buzz. Gabriella's name flashes across the screen and I go to answer, but I need to wrap this up.

"No, you aren't leaving. You are going to go to Matteo and tell him I want every single cent back or I will be calling the police. Got it?"

My phone dances across my desk, Gabriella's name flashes up on the screen, but I need Amy gone before I answer.

Amy stands, doesn't give me a second glance as she leaves my office without another word. I sag into my leather office chair. The phone stops ringing and I stand, pacing the room.

"Fuck," I breathe out, digging my heels into the floor and hit the files on my desk with my hand. They scatter across the desk and floor. I lean my head forward, cradling my head in my hands.

Things in my life are good, and then this. I have so many questions, ones only my brother can answer.

I'm up and out of my seat, swiping my keys and rushing out my office to head out to my car.

I dial Gabriella's number; it rings and rings and just when I fear it will go to voice mail someone answers and my blood runs cold when I hear her screaming.

"Help. There's someone in my apartment." Her terrified voice has my blood running cold.

"Gabriella," I yell, but she doesn't reply.

The phone connects to the car as I drive and panic claws at my throat when I hear his voice.

"Feisty little bitch, aren't you? You like it rough, huh?"

A guttural roar erupts from my chest as I punch the steering wheel. Horns blast as I swerve to miss a car.

He's got her. He's got Gabriella.

Pressing my foot to the floor, my only focus is getting to her.

I think my body shuts down, goes into autopilot because the next thing I know, I am walking into Gabriella's apartment, where I find her slumped on the floor in her entryway. My legs give way. I fall to the ground and scramble over to her, my heartbeat ringing in my ears.

No, please, please let her be okay.

But I never make it to her. A pain ricochets through my temple and something warm and wet trickles down my face as a voice I haven't heard in years seeps into my brain.

"Hello, little brother. It's been a while."

Chapter Fifty Nine

Gabriella

Everything aches, every part of me feels heavy. I blink, fighting to focus. I see two figures. One in a chair slumped over, another stood beside him.

"Nice of you to wake up. We have company."

Brad, it's Brad's voice. He's here. I push up on shaky arms and fall against the couch, my body too weak to hold me up.

The throbbing in the back of my head is so bad I clutch the back of it. When I touch something warm and wet I gasp. Bringing my hand to my face, I see the dark red blood covering my fingers.

I'm dragged to my feet, but I stumble and reach for something to steady myself.

"Easy, easy. This won't be fun if you can't hold yourself up." I look up. It's funny how eyes that look the same evoke a different reaction. When Brad looks at me, I feel safe, but these eyes show me nothing but evil.

"Let her go." I turn my head to find Brad in the chair. He lifts his head, blood stains the side of his face, and I gasp.

"Oh my god, Brad." I take a step towards him, but when cool metal is pressed to my temple and I hear a click, I freeze.

"Take another fucking step, and I'll blow your pretty little brains out. Got it?" I scrunch my eyes close, swallowing down a whimper as I nod.

"Good girl."

"Matteo, this has nothing to do with her. Please, let her go and we can talk."

"Oh, she has everything to do with this." He grips my arm tighter. "Does she know?"

Brad doesn't say anything.

"Does she know that her daddy…" His tone is mocking when he says the word daddy. "Is the reason me and dad went to prison, huh? Does she know he is the fucker who sent Dad down for life and me for twenty-five years?"

"I, I uh can talk to my dad, make him…" I offer, trying to make this right.

Matteo laughs manically. "You had your chance." He points the gun at Brad. "You were meant to fix it, get our dad out with me, but typical Marco didn't follow through. So now, I'm going to fix things." He presses the barrel of the gun back against my temple and brushes his nose against my neck. I shudder in disgust. "But maybe I should have a little fun first and make you watch, little brother."

Brad growls, fighting against the restraints that have his hands pinned behind him. "Don't you fucking touch her," he roars.

Matteo runs his hot tongue up my neck and onto my cheek, and I recoil. His stale bourbon breath wafts in my face and I fight to keep down the vomit that's working its way up my throat.

"Mmmmh." He hums in pleasure. "I bet she tastes so fucking sweet. Am I right, little brother?"

Brad stops moving, he's as still as a stone statue, his gaze laser focused on his brother. "If you touch her, I will skin you alive and then feed it to you."

Matteo throws his head back and laughs. "He's always been all talk and no action. Is he the same in the bedroom, Gabriella? I bet you're desperate for a real man to fuck you, huh?"

I shake my head. "Please, just leave. I won't say anything to anyone, just let us go."

"Just let us go," he mocks. "Nah, I think I'll just end this now."

He presses the barrel of the gun so deep into my temple I let out a pained cry. "Say goodbye to your little girlfriend."

There's a click and I brace myself. I look at Brad. As I want him to be the last thing I see, I can't watch him break. I close my eyes and mouth, "I love you."

Something shoves me hard. I keep my eyes closed as my body goes limp and the sound of a gunshot rings out.

"Matteo, no…"

Chapter Sixty

Brad

If I have any hope of getting me and Gabriella out of this alive, I need to remain calm.

I wiggle my hands, stretching my arms as far as I can to create a little slack in the rope that binds me. I hook my finger in the loop of the knot. The burn in my arms is almost unbearable as I try to work myself free, but it doesn't compare to the searing pain in my chest when I look at Gabriella's terrified face. I caused this. She's in this position because of me.

I feel rope loosen, but I keep a tight grip of it, not wanting him to know I'm free.

I swallow the hard lump in my throat, "If you touch her I will skin you alive and then feed it to you."

I mean it, I will have no problem ending him. If he touches her, harms her, my life would be over anyway.

"Say goodbye to your little girlfriend," Matteo sneers.

I look at Gabriella, her eyes squeezed tightly shut as she mouths "I love you," and it's as if everything happens in slow motion and the only thought is to save her.

Matteo's shocked face looks at me and then the gun as I lunge at him.

"Matteo, no," I yell, my voice no longer sounding like my own. I reach for Gabriella and shove her sideways. She slumps to the ground with a thud as I reach for Matteo's hand that wields the gun. A shot fires and the sound of glass shattering rings out behind me. I tackle Matteo to the ground, taking his hand and smashing it repeatedly against the floor until he releases the weapon and I swipe the out of his reach.

We both fight for control, years of pent-up anger, hatred, and frustration released with our fists. Blow after blow, I never relent and he does the same. There's pain coming from all angles as he pummels my face and body. I have no idea how long we go at it, but eventually his body sags and he holds his hands up in surrender.

"You-You win little brother," he says between gasping breaths.

"You, are, dead to me," I hiss. I glance over at Gabriella who's awake, dragging her body across the room to where I see a phone. I pray she's calling the police, anyone for help.

Not wanting Matteo to see I keep his focus on me.

"You, are going right back to prison where you belong, you hear me?" He laughs. "You belong there with me, brother. You just got lucky."

"I wasn't there. I didn't kill a man, or try and cover it up."

"No, but you should have been." He chokes. "You should have been there. If you had maybe Dad wouldn't have killed that officer. Maybe I wouldn't have ended up in prison right alongside him. You should have been there." For a split second, an overwhelming feeling of guilt sucker punches me in the gut, the blow more painful than any of the ones Matteo has just given me.

I should have been there.

"I'm-I'm sorry," I stutter.

"Sorry doesn't erase the last eighteen years, Marco. Do you know what they do to people in prison? Do you?" The pain is clear in his voice.

I dread to think what my brother has been through, but I haven't had it easy either.

"I don't claim to, Matteo, but it's been no picnic for me either."

He rolls onto his side, spitting blood onto the floor as he brings himself to a sitting position. "Yeah, it looks like you've had a really hard life with your hot girlfriend and your clubs and all your money. My heart fucking bleeds for you, Marco."

Anger vibrates through my body. "You have no fucking idea what I've been through. The pieces I had to pick up and put back together when you and Dad went down. What I went through in Afghanistan. Don't play the victim with me. You made a choice, and you paid the consequences."

I bend over, clutching my chest, the pain of my memories almost too much to bear.

"Brad," Gabriella cries out. "The police are on their way."

Matteo tries to stand and head for the door and anger lights up my body, no, he's not walking away from this.

"No, you, you are going back to prison you piece of shit." I stand up, the heaviness still in my chest but I need to keep him here.

I muster all the strength I have and charge towards him, knocking him back down to the ground. We roll and tumble once again. His arm reaches out and Gabriella lets out a scream. "Brad, the gun." It takes me a few seconds to register her words and focus.

Matteo points the gun at me and my reflexes kick in. I move my head to the side, covering the gun with my hand. He fights back as we wrestle for control. A shot fires and a burning pain lands in the center of my stomach.

The gun clatters to the ground and Gabriella wails, but she sounds so far away. I press to my shirt, wondering why I feel so strange and I'm met with a thick, warm liquid. My wide eyes look into Matteo's. The color drains from his face.

"You," is all I manage before my vision darkens around the edges and I slump forward, my head hitting the hardwood floor.

Gabriella's face comes into view and she repeats the same words over and over. "Help is coming. You're going to be okay. Stay with me."

I fight to stay awake, to focus on the woman hovering above me. The only woman I have ever and will ever love. I lift my arm, using the last of my strength to stroke her cheek. My blooded hand leaves a smear.

"I love you."

"I love you too," she sobs. "You're going to be okay. They're on their way."

A coldness sweeps over my body, then visions of Gabriella jumping in our pool in LA, her dancing around my kitchen island, us tangled together within the white sheets of my bed, her amber eyes and her smile, that lit up my whole world, become the only thing I see as my last thought is, I hope she knows she was always more than enough.

And it's then it hits me what's happening.

"You're going to be my seven minutes."

Chapter Sixty One

Gabriella

I love you.
Stay with me.
You're going to be my seven minutes.
Gabriella, Gabby, Gabby...

My eyes ping open.

"You're okay. It was just a dream." I look over to Ria sits beside the bed I'm in, holding my hand. Beside her is Jack and I glance around the white room and see Harry and Ali, the other side and Noah.

"Brad, he, he..." I choke out, fighting for my next breath.

Ali's soothing hand sweeps across my forehead. "He's in surgery. They're fixing him, okay?"

"What do you mean?"

"They took him for surgery. He lost a lot of blood, but the doctors are hopeful. We are just waiting for news," Ali says calmly, but when

I look into her broken eyes, I close my own and let the tears tumble down my cheeks.

"I thought he..." I break into uncontrollable sobs. My hand covers my mouth to smother my cries. Ali climbs into the bed beside me and cradles me in her arms, rocking me as if I were a small child.

"He's strong, Gabs," Noah says, clearing his throat. "I know he'll be in there fighting to get back to you." His words bring me a small sense of comfort, but it doesn't take away the gaping hole inside of me that only seeing Brad can fill.

"We called your parents. We thought they should know. They will be here soon. They were out of town, otherwise they would have been here sooner." Ria says, stroking the back of my hand. I nod in understanding, wanting to see them for the first time in a long time.

"How long has he been in there." I sniff.

"About an hour." Jack says quietly, not sounding like the strong, confident man he usually is.

"Why don't I remember getting here?" I ask.

"You were in a bad way when we got to you. They had to, erm, sedate you," Harry says, his voice cracking.

"When you got to me?" I look round at my friends confused.

"Yeah, when Brad knew you were in trouble, he called us, we had already arrived at the lake house so it took us a little time to get back, when we got there you... he..." Jack tries to finish his sentence but his words falter. Ria takes his hand and leans into his chest.

"You were trying to save him. Jack had to lift you off his body so we..." Harry gestures to Noah, "could work on him until the ambulance came."

The room falls silent and an uncertain feeling blankets the room. No one knows if he's going to wake up, make it out of surgery, and even if he does, will he ever be the same after today's events? The idea of losing the man I love in one way or another makes my heart splinter just a little more. The door to my room flies open and Mom rushes in.

"Gabriella," she wails, throwing her body over mine as she begins sobbing.

I wrap an arm around her, realizing that this is the first time since I was a child that she's held me or shown any real emotion. It feels nice.

"We'll give you some time," Ali says.

My friends leave the room, and my dad, who I hadn't noticed until now, closes the door behind them.

"Oh darling, what happened? I called Patrick, but his mother answered and said he had been attacked too and was in the hospital. Is it the same man? Your father called the police department and—"

"Mom, stop," I interrupt. "I'm not with Patrick, Mom. Never was."

My mom's horrified face turns to me and the usual guilt I would feel at disappointing my parents isn't there. This is it, the moment I come clean, stand my ground. No place like a hospital than to rip off the band aid.

"Sit down, we need to talk."

The saying, she was too stunned to speak really does apply here. My mother stares blankly at the white wall after I tell her every detail. The black mailing, the club, my relationship with Brad, all of it. My dad stares at his lap, and I've spent the last four and a half minutes counting the seconds on the clock that's hung on the wall, as it goes round and round.

Not able to take the painful silence a minute longer, I speak up. "Please say something, anything. I'd rather you yell than be silent."

My father clears his throat. "I don't know what you want us to say, Gabriella."

His words feel like a slap to the face.

"Oh, I don't know, Dad. How about, we love you? We're glad you didn't die. I'm sorry we've made you feel this way. We should have protected you better. We should have made you feel like you could come to us for anything and that we wouldn't judge. How's that for starters?"

"Gabriella, please, we need..."

"What, Mom, you need what?"

"Time. That is a lot to process."

"Yeah, no shit."

"Gabriella, watch..." my dad scolds, but I'm done. I am so over the way they made me feel. I let it all out.

"My tone, my words? Is that what you were going to say? I am done pleasing you. If you can't accept me for who I am, and what I do and who I love, then I don't want to be in your lives. I have never ever felt enough, and I've finally found people, friends, a man who makes me feel like I'm enough, and there is nothing you could say to change how I feel."

I sag in relief, waiting for the guilt to hit me, or the bundle of nerves to knot in my stomach after displeasing my parents, but it doesn't come. Instead, it feels like a burden I have spent my life carrying has just been lifted from my shoulders and I can finally breathe.

The door creaks open and Ali peeks her head inside. "I'm sorry to interrupt but, Gabby, it's Brad..."

Chapter Sixty Two

Brad

I always wondered what it felt like when you were dying. After I watched the life leave Scotty's body, I wondered what he felt, what he saw, what he experienced, and, well, now I know. Maybe it isn't the same for everyone, but for me, all I saw was her.

But someone, maybe Scotty himself, was watching over me when I flat-lined twice. Once in Gabriella's apartment and the second time on the operating table. When I came round, the nurse asked who Gabriella was because I asked for her when I was drifting in and out of consciousness.

"Your vitals look good. You're a lucky man. Your friends helped save your life," the nurse says as she hangs up the bag of fluid on the stand beside my bed. The clear liquid feels like ice water as it enters my vein through the back of my hand. I'm hooked up to an IV for liquids, and I'm told I had a transfusion after I bled out on the table when they removed my gall bladder.

"Yeah, I am feeling damn lucky," I rasp, my throat feeling dry and sore from the tubes.

"Your sister, Alessia, keeps calling the ward. I've told her you're out of surgery and she's on her way but, there's someone else here to see you. Can I let them in?"

I nod.

She leaves the room, and it's only a few moments until Gabriella stands in the doorway. A white hospital gown drowns her tiny frame, her hair a wavy mess, hanging over one shoulder, and a bandage wrapped around her head like a band.

She worries her bottom lip with her teeth, and I smile.

"Hey, baby girl." Her hands cover her face as she lets out a cry and then runs towards me, throwing her body over mine. I wince from the pain, but I don't care. I hold on to her like it will be the last time and inhale the last remnants of her cherry scent.

"You have no idea how good it is to hear you say that," she says, her face nuzzling into my neck.

"I think I do because it feels just as good to say it," I croak out.

She lifts her head to look at me, her amber eyes look dim and hollow, but when I smile, I see a flicker of the light that once shone in them. "I thought you'd left me forever."

"No chance. I'm never leaving you, okay?" She nods before she presses her lips to mine; her touch brings a little part of me back to life.

"I'm sorry. I should have called the cops first. You shouldn't have been there. Then maybe you wouldn't have…"

"Hey, listen to me. You call, I come running. It's as simple as that."

She climbs on the bed, curling her body into mine and we don't say anything, no words are needed. The bleeping of my machine letting me know my heart is still beating is the only noise in the room, reminding me that I am here, that I get a second chance. I'm not wasting another day restricting myself, obsessing over the what if's, punishing myself for the things I didn't do or could have done differently.

"Knock, knock." My eyes open and watch as our friends fill my hospital room. One by one they enter, giving me sympathetic smiles and unshed tears.

The doctor told me I was lucky to be alive. If it hadn't been for Jack, Harry and Noah, and their medical knowledge, I'd have bled out on that apartment floor. They each bump my fist, my body too weak for much else.

"How are you feeling?" Noah asks. "A few pounds lighter thanks to my gall bladder being ripped out," I joke.

Ria and Ali look between them and take Gabriella by the hand. "Why don't we go get some snacks and coffees?" Ria suggests.

Gabriella looks at me with fear in her eyes and I stroke her cheek. "I'll be fine. Bring me back a strong coffee, yeah?"

She presses a kiss to my cheek and leaves with Ali and Ria, their arms around her, holding her together.

The door closes and the four of us look between us. How do I put into words how grateful I am for them?

I look at them all and Jack clears his throat. "You're welcome."

I choke out a laugh. "I didn't say anything."

"I know, but we know, and you're welcome. Semper Fidelis, remember?"

My tongue feels thick and heavy with emotion, and I bite it to prevent the cry that wants to escape. There are not many people who get to say they have people in their lives who would go to battle for them, defend them, fight for them and save them, no questions asked, but that's what these men do for me and I for them. It's a bond you can't explain, it's just silently there, no matter what we have going on in our lives. If one of us needs the other, we drop and run and I count myself as being one of the luckiest mother fuckers on the planet to have these guys in my corner, along with the women in their lives and the one girl that made me want to start living again.

"Good, because I have another thing I need you to help me with…"

Chapter Sixty Three

Gabriella

It's been a few days since Brad was released from the hospital. His brother was arrested without bail and awaiting trial. Between me, his sister, and our friends, we have all rallied round to help since he came home. I've not left his side and don't intend to. It took nearly losing him to realize that life is short. I deserve to be happy and my parents have stepped up in a way I have been longing for since I was a kid.

My dad contacted Patrick's boss. He lost his job at the law firm and apparently will be moving back in with his parents. It will take a while to repair my relationship with my parents, but it's a start.

"Oh, and this will help you poop," I say, pointing to the murky-looking smoothie. Brad chokes on the coffee and then groans in pain clutching the dressing on his side.

"I'm sorry, I'm sorry," I say, taking the coffee cup from his hands and placing it on the tray I've brought him.

"I'm fine, Gabriella. I just thought it would be awhile before we killed the romance with that kind of talk."

"I know, but I was reading up on gallbladder surgery and the body can still fully function without it? It's like the only organ you can live without, but it takes a while to adjust and so you need to be careful what you eat because no one wants to not be able to poop. Once, when I was on vacation, I didn't poop for like four days and my nanny had to…" I look up to find Brad smirking with amusement. "And I'm rambling and over sharing again."

"You are, but it's one of the reasons I love you." My heart somersaults.

"Yeah, what else do you love?"

"Hmmm, your eyes, how passionate you get when you watch that episode of Friends, even though you've watched it a thousand times."

"But they weren't on a proper break, no one said 'let's see other people,' I mock, using my fingers to make air quotations. "I don't get how he didn't get that."

Brad snorts.

"I love how accepting you are, how big your heart is and how you always put other people before yourself, even when you shouldn't."

I feel my cheeks heat. No one has ever said such complimentary things. I grew up never feeling enough, and here he is telling me every single thing he loves about me.

"You're making me blush. Those meds are making you soft." I wink.

"No, dying on that table and thinking I'd never spend another day with you did that, Gabriella."

I still as his words settle between us. There could have been a very different outcome, and I'd be sitting here, clutching his t-shirt and using it to wipe away my tears, instead of wearing it while I start my day with him.

"Close your eyes," he whispers.

I eye him curiously before doing so.

The mattress dips.

"Hold out your hand."

I open my hand, palm facing upwards and feel something small and hard placed in it.

"Open your eyes."

I look down to see a small red box.

He reaches for my free hand, and I inhale sharply.

"You deserve all the grand gestures money can buy, and when I am back on my feet, I will do this right, but I've waited a lifetime to find someone that quietens the storm inside of me and that someone is you. When my life quite literally flashed before my eyes, all I saw was you.

I don't want to let another day go by without you by my side, so…" He opens the box to reveal a stunning round solitaire diamond on a gold band, and I think I stop breathing. "Gabriella Diana Monroe, Mia cara, mi vuoi sposare?" *Will you marry me?*

I don't need a second to think about my answer. I've never been surer of anything in my life.

"Yes, I'll marry you." He slides the ring onto my finger and I climb into his lap as gently as I can, wrapping my arms around him. He kisses me the same way he did the first time, with a want and a desire that makes me feel like the only woman in the world.

"And you don't need to do it again. This was perfect. I don't need a grand gesture or an elaborate proposal. I just need you." I brush his dark hair, that's a little overgrown, away from his forehead.

He brushes his lips against mine and I melt into his touch.

"I love you, and I'm going to spend the rest of my life, every day that I am graced with, showing you just how much."

Epilogue

Brad

Three years later

"*Happy birthday to Mia, happy birthday to you.*" Gabriella and I lean I either side of our daughter and help her blow out the candle on her first birthday cake.

Our friends clap and cheer and it all clearly feels too much for my sweet angel. Her bottom lip trembles and her big eyes, just like her mom's, look up at me. On instinct, I scoop her up out of her highchair and cradle her in my arms as she nuzzles into my chest.

"Aww, I love that she's a daddy's girl," Ali swoons. "Men with babies, instant turn on."

Gabriella laughs and presses a kiss to my cheek as she rubs a comforting hand on Mia's back.

"Tell me about it. Why do you think I'm ready for baby number five?" Ria says as Jack wraps an arm around her waist and whispers something in her ear that makes her laugh.

"We could try making baby number three, Ali Cat," Harry suggests, waggling his eyebrows.

Ali points over to where their twin boys are running round with plastic swords, chasing Jack and Ria's younger girls out on our lawn.

We moved to the lake when Mia was six months old. Gabriella was missing the girls, and we agreed city life was no longer for us now that we had a young family.

"Have you met your boys?" Ali snaps.

"They are just spirited." Harry shrugs.

There's a crash, and one of the girls begins crying. Jack wastes no time in marching over and Harry face palms himself.

"Yeah, you best go see which one of the Lawson girls your spirited boys impaled with a plastic sword?" Ali says, pointing over to where Jack is now holding a crying child.

Ali turns back to face us. "Yeah, maybe I take back what I said."

"No way. A man with a baby is sexy as hell. I'm ready for him to impregnate me again." Gabriella winks in my direction and the sound of metal clattering against fine china startles us all.

"Gabriella, please, you have guests," her mother chides, clutching her pearl necklace.

"Sorry, Mom," Gabriella says, rolling her eyes. It took some months, but Gabriella repaired her broken relationship with her parents, and they have become doting grandparents.

Her mother places her plate on the table and holds out her arms. "Now Bradley, hand me that baby. Her papa wants to tell her all about his recent golf score."

I hand Mia to her grandmother. "Perfect, she was due a nap," I tease, and Catherine looks at me deadpan as Gabriella flicks me with the back of her hand.

"Play nice," Gabriella whisper shouts, and I give my best toothy smile as Catherine wanders off with Mia in tow. My relationship with Gabriella's father is a little strained, but I keep the peace for her and Mia's sake. I'll never understand a man who prioritized his reputation and career over his daughter's wellbeing, and now I have a daughter of my own, that realization is even more unfathomable to me. But Gabriella wants him, them, in her life and I'll support whatever she wants.

Our guests chatter amongst themselves and I smile as I watch my nephew play a game of cards with Lexi. My mom and sister sit out on the deck sharing a bottle of wine and a warm feeling spreads through my chest when I watch Gabriella's mom sit down beside my mom and holds out an empty glass for her to fill.

Three years ago, I never thought we'd be here. In a place where we would not only have both our families but also our friends all under one roof.

Gabriella begins clearing dishes, and I step up behind her, placing my hands on her hips, grazing my teeth over the shell of her ear. Her body shudders in that way I know she's longing for me just as much as I am her.

"Follow me," I whisper.

She gives the room a quick scan, seeing that our guests are occupied, then takes my open hand. I drag her through our open plan kitchen, scoop her up and throw her over my shoulder, taking the back staircase that leads up to our bedroom. I close the door, then toss her onto the bed. She bounces, the light pink dress she's wearing rides up and I tear off my shirt before I'm over her, peppering kisses down her neck.

"What are you doing?" Her words are a breathless whisper.

"Making a baby," I say between kisses.

"Oh, my god." She giggles. "You can't be serious right now."

"Oh, I'm serious. No time like the present." I moan against her silk skin, sinking my teeth in, just enough to leave my mark, pulling a moan from her.

"Ssssh, Mia cara, you don't want your mom hearing." She clamps a hand over her mouth as I take a moment to look into her eyes. "One whole year," I say proudly.

"The best year," she says, and I nod in agreement.

I was half a man before Gabriella spun into my world, showing me there was more to life than routine and control. She was a force too strong even for me to fight and I am thankful it was the one battle I lost. She's given me a second chance at a life I didn't think I deserved, a home that's full of love, a beautiful daughter who's the best parts of both of us, and with all that, she's given me a life full of color.

Epilogue

Gabriella

Two years later

The breeze from the lake whips in my hair as I raise my arms and stretch, inhaling deeply as I look out at the view from our porch. It's my favorite spot to do my morning Pilates, something that has really helped me in the post-partum phase and transitioning from one to two kids.

Two in two years was demanding on me both physically and mentally, but Brad was there for me, every step as we muddled our way through. Mia is almost three and Scott, who we named in Scotty's memory, is almost two. I know how special he was to not just Brad, but all the guys, and so having his name live on in some way meant a lot to all of us.

I roll up my mat, ready to go inside to prepare breakfast, but the door slides open and two pairs of feet and four paws scurry out the house.

Mia and Scott toddle past me out onto the lawn as they chase after our new retriever puppy.

"Harry's a dead man," is all I hear from the house. I chuckle to myself, keeping my eyes on the kids as they run around with Doodles. Mia chose the name. We put up a fence to stop the kids running into the lake but I am always on high alert when they are outside in case they opened the gate. I watch as Mia's long dark hair, that's just like mine, trails behind her as she chases after the puppy. Scott tumbles to the ground and Doodles licks his face, causing cute giggles to float through the air.

Brad steps outside in a pair of black sweatpants and yellow washing up gloves. He glances out to see the kids and then his focus is on me. His face is red, the frown line in his forehead, that's become more prominent since Scott was born, now clearly visible as he points at the puppy.

"Do you know what Doodles did?" he says through gritted teeth.

"No, what did Doodles do?" "He took a shit on the rug, so we need to throw that out, then he chewed your new tennis shoes. Oh, and he chewed the head off Mia's doll, so I've been consoling her for the past twenty minutes. The dog is a menace."

I cover my mouth with my hands, trying to hide my humor at the situation.

"And why is Harry a dead man?"

"Because he suggested we get the damn dog. He took Mia to see the puppies when they looked after them last month and then she came home with her own puppy dog eyes saying *'pweese, Daddy, can we get a doodle dog?'*"

"Oh, yeah, she did say *pweese*."

Brad nods. "And you know I'm weak when she says pweese. So, Doodles got a new home. I just hope Harry's new puppy Dennis shits in his shoe and he steps in it."

I walk over to him and wrap my arms around his neck. "Why don't you chill on the porch and watch the kids, and I'll clear up Doodles' mess."

He shakes his head. "Oh, I'm not clearing it up. I'm marching over to Harry's and dragging his ass over here and he can scrub the dog shit out of my rug." I fall into fits of laughter, my forehead falling against his chest.

"I am glad you find this entertaining."

"It's kind of funny," I say, squinting my eyes and pressing my thumb and forefinger together leaving a tiny space. "Just a little funny."

He pinches the bridge of his nose, and I fight to keep down the laughter that wants to rip out of me. He has let go of most of his OCD habits, but cleaning, isn't one of them. He needs order and cleanliness and who am I to argue? My house is always spotless.

"You go get Harry. I'll feed the kids."

He presses a kiss to my forehead. "Deal."

"What. A. Day," I say as I flop down on the mattress and Brad does the same.

"I'm fucked," he announces. "I love them, but those Walker boys…"

"I know," I say in agreement.

"Poor Aubrey. I hope Jack and Ria got the paint out of her hair," I say reliving the moment Aubrey walked outside her hair dripping in blue paint from our craft cupboard while Blake and Brayden followed her, their tiny hands covered in said blue paint, but they of course denied it was them.

Our weekends, and truly most days, are spent going between our three houses. We nag at Noah and his family to move to the lake, and I think we are close to breaking them down.

I still teach Pilates virtually and now specialize in postpartum. I love it. I do a workshop every so often in the city, but for the most part, I do it remotely and work around Brad. Thanks to the now five clubs they have, he's able to spend more time at home with us and has people doing the day to day running. I'm thinking about opening up a dance studio nearby, but that's something for the future when Mia and Scott are older.

If someone had told me five years ago, I would be married and living the domestic lake house life with Brad Russo, I'd have thought they were crazy. This was everything he swore he never wanted, and yet, I've never seen him happier.

He tugs me closer, his eyes searching my face as if he's seeing me for the first time. That's the thing about Brad. Every time he looks at me, kisses me, he looks at me as if it were the first time and the last.

He stares at me so intently. I feel it stir in my core. "What?" I smirk.

"What? Can't a man just look at his wife?"

"Of course he can, and I hope he's going to do a lot more than that." I wink.

A low growl erupts from his chest as he flips us. I straddle his lap and lift my night dress above my head, dropping it beside me. His dick stirs to life beneath me, and I rotate my hips.

"I'm one lucky man."

Being desired by him, wanted by him, loved by him. It ended up being everything I was searching for, and he stayed true to his word. Not a day has passed that I have doubted him. Since the day he asked me to marry him, he has spent every day showing me, proving to me that I am more than enough.

Thank you

Thank you for reading Brad and Gabriella's Story. I would be grateful if you could leave a review. https://mybook.to/desiredbyyou

"If everything we have been through lead to this, I'd fight in every war just to get to her."
Noah and Tori's story is up next! (date to TBC)
Pre order here https://mybook.to/savedbyyou

Acknowledgements

Thank you to...

I have so many people to thank, people who made this story possible, but firstly I want to thank you, the reader for reading and loving this series.

Meghan – (Meghan Hollie Author) My spiral sister, thank you for all your help and support. I truly could not do this without you. The voice notes, the tears, the laughs and late night plotting sessions. I am so lucky to have you in my life.

Tash- I could not do this without you. You support me, keep me organized, run my street team and cheering me on every step of the way. Thank you for everything you do for me.

My amazing BETA readers, Emma, Lynsey, Kayleigh and Clare. Thank you for being on this wild ride with me and supporting me and loving my characters.

My Street team. Than you for all your support and our wild chats. You girls keep me going and I adore you all.

A huge thank you to the team of people who have helped me. Ellie at LovenotesPR, my editor Sarah, My proof reader Jo, I couldn't have done this without you.

A big shout out to my agent Katie Monson, thank you for believing in me, I cant wait to see what the future holds.

To my family, my mum, Jason, my brothers, their partners, my dad, my nan, my cousin, my best friends (you all know who you are) Thank you for always supporting me in whatever I do.

To the rare group chat girlies/authors. Thank you for all the laughs and your support. To best friends (you know who you are) and my baby K, thank you for all your support and encouragement.

And finally, Thank you to my husband and children.

To my three beautiful children, my little tribe. I did this for you, to show you can achieve anything you set your mind too and give you a mummy you can be proud of. I love you all to the moon and back, to the moon and back.

Rich- Thank you for supporting me, for believing in me and encouraging me to pursue something I have dreamed of for so long. I would have given up months ago had you not talked sense into me and told me to keep going. Thank you for never giving up on me, I love you, always and forever.

About the author

Natasha is a military wife, mother of three children and a Labrador, living in the South west of England. You will find her either juggling, work, mum life or tapping away at her laptop creating characters and worlds for you to fall in love with and get lost in.

Follow Author NL Amore on Instagram, Tik Tok and Facebook

Printed in Dunstable, United Kingdom